THE FAMILY WAY

The Family Way

A NOVEL

Christopher DiRaddo

ESPLANADE BOOKS

THE FICTION IMPRINT AT VÉHICULE PRESS

ESPLANADE BOOKS IS THE FICTION IMPRINT AT VÉHICULE PRESS

Published with the generous assistance of the Canada Council for the
Arts, the Canada Book Fund of the Department of Canadian Heritage,
and the Société de développement des entreprises culturelles
du Québec (SODEC).

Canada Council   Conseil des arts
for the Arts   du Canada

Esplanade Books editor: Dimitri Nasrallah
Editorial assistance: Willow Little
Cover design: David Drummond
Typeset in Minion by Simon Garamond
Printed by Marquis Printing Inc.

Dépôt légal, Library and Archives Canada and
Bibliothèque nationale du Québec, second quarter 2021
Copyright © Christopher DiRaddo 2021

LIBRARY AND ARCHIVES CANADA CATALOGUING IN PUBLICATION

Title: The family way : a novel / Christopher DiRaddo.
Names: DiRaddo, Christopher, 1974- author.
Identifiers: Canadiana (print) 20210119489 | Canadiana (EBOOK)
20210119519 | ISBN 9781550655650
(softcover) | ISBN 9781550655711 (EPUB)
Classification: LCC PS8607.I7 F35 2021

Published by Véhicule Press, Montréal, Québec, Canada

Distribution in Canada by LitDistCo
www.litdistco.ca

Distribution in the US by Independent Publishers Group
www.ipgbook.com

Printed in Canada.

For Millie, Theo and Greg

"You become responsible, forever,
for what you have tamed."

–Antoine de Saint-Exupéry

ONE

Little Bird

1

I OPENED THE FRONT door to our building and started the climb. I began the ritual, the call up the stairs. It's the sound of a dog barking—a hound dog. Some kind of *rawr rawr rawr* noise. Sometimes—whenever I felt wacky or tired—I'd elongate the sounds. Add a couple of *barrools* if I heard Michael bark back. I don't remember how this started, this way to tell each other that we're home, but we'd been doing it for months. Ever since Michael and I first moved into the place.

The door to our home was unlocked. I entered and one of the cats came running. Funny how they never react to my bark, I thought as I grazed Malone's head. Am I doing it that badly? Sutherland remained unimpressed on a chair nearby, looking at me with two suspicious eyes.

"You're not scared of me either, are you?"

"What's that?" Michael called out from one of the rooms.

"Nothing," I shouted back. "Just talking to the cat."

I took off my coat and shoes and dropped my satchel on the floor next to Michael's gym bag. I found him in our home office, in jeans and a plain T-shirt, sitting at his desk and sketching in an old notebook. The room smelled faintly of pot.

"Hey, buddy," Michael mumbled as I entered, his focus lost in the lines of his drawing.

"Hi, buddy," I replied. Over his shoulder, I snooped the nascent outline of what appeared to be a boat. "Whatcha doing? Sketching?" My questions turned into a yawn as I crossed my arms and rested my body against the wall, by the window, the familiar hum and smell of the room sedating me with its comforts. I shook my head to wake up.

"Here, sit," Michael said, and jumped up from his seat. He led me down to the chair with his hands and began to knead my shoulders from behind. "I just felt inspired. It was a good day. I got a job painting an office in Mile-Ex—it's huge, going to be at least two weeks' work."

I looked over my left shoulder to Michael's broad, busy hand—cracked and dry, his fingers as solid as carpenter nails. "Your hands aren't dirty," I said, but then closed my eyes and collapsed under the force of his grip. "God, that feels good…"

"We only discussed colours today." Michael dug in harder. "Jesus, you're tight," he said, and with a gentle tug, pulled the back of the chair from his desk and swivelled me towards him. He planted a hungry kiss on my mouth.

"What are you doing?"

"Having my way with you." Michael moved down my neck, his lips pressing into its scattering of short hairs. "I just got back from the gym. Nothing like showering in a room full of men to get you thinking about sex. I swear, I flunked high school the year I discovered boys."

"I have to get ready."

"I'm not stopping you."

I looked at the clock on the wall, a lime-green monstrosity that Michael had shipped last month, along with a few other items, from his parents' home in Moncton. It was late, but there was time for a quick romp if I wanted. So I relented. I closed my eyes and surrendered to Michael's touch. But as soon I did, the thoughts were there. Everything I had to remember.

"Before I forget, your mom texted me. She wants you to call her."

Michael stopped, but only for a second. "Here I am, getting all hot and you have to bring up my mother?"

"There's a seat sale and she wants to book her flight. She wants to know when to come."

"… Aren't you supposed to tell me?" he said, now behind my left ear.

"I don't know. You said she wanted to come in July? Any time in July is fine… Well, except that first weekend— and then at the end of the month, that's no good either."

"Couldn't you have told her that?"

I sighed. "You've got to call your mother, Michael."

He stopped again, short. "Ok, ok, I will. Now, can you please stop?"

I sat back and did what I was told. Michael pulled at my tie, loosening the knot and tugging the length from my neck. His fingers slid down the front of my shirt, popping open the buttons along the way. Soon, his thin arms were behind me untucking my shirt. He dragged me with it up and out of the chair, and led me out of the office and into the cats milling

13

about the hallway. The two beasts scattered as we stomped towards the bedroom. I pulled off his shirt, and we collapsed onto the bed.

Michael smells like the gym, I thought, as I kissed him. It wasn't the smell of sweat, but of shower gel—the kind Michael insisted on buying. Some generic brand that's brown and has a masculine-sounding name, like "Corduroy." I had a flash of him in the shower at the gym, the diluting lather running down his naked legs and on to the blue-grey tile. I saw the foam and water disappear into the drain and thought maybe, instead, I should get Michael soap. Real soap. Like a bar of it. Sometimes you want the feel of a full bar of soap. And despite its attempts to sound butch, all shower gel ends up smelling like perfume anyway. Like Michael did now.

"Let the train go," Michael said. "Don't worry, there'll be another."

I closed my eyes and tried to empty my mind, but instead thought about Michael's drawing. What was he working on? I hadn't seen him sketch in his notebook for years, ever since we'd started dating. And then there were the emails waiting in my inbox. My boss was supposed to send me notes on the documents I had to prepare for Monday's press event. Maybe I should write to remind her before heading out? I also had no idea what to wear to dinner. Should I dress up? What does one wear on such an occasion? And I'd have to shower too. All of this before Michael and I had to leave in less than an hour.

"Sorry buddy," I said, placing my hand on his bare shoulder. "It's not going to happen."

Michael stopped and smiled. "That's okay," he said, a bit

out of breath, and flipped over to lie on his back at the bottom of the bed. "We can't always be in sync."

"There's just too many things to do before we head out."

"About that…" Michael rolled over onto his side and placed his hand atop my belly. Mine was much rounder than his. "Is it okay if I don't come?"

"What? Why?"

"Well, Gus is on his way back from San Francisco." He moved up to play with the dark hairs on my chest. "He's asked if I could pick him up at the airport, and I want to hear about his trip. Plus… I think you should go by yourself. You know what they're going to ask."

"So? It doesn't mean you shouldn't be there. Wendy and Eve would want you there."

"But it doesn't involve me—I mean it *does*, but this is your decision and I don't want to influence you one way or the other." Michael gasped and a sudden smile grabbed hold of his face. "Another grey hair!" he almost whispered.

I opened my mouth to say something, but Michael continued. "Listen, there'll be a lot for you to talk about and I know I'm going to say the wrong thing and ruin everything. Just tell them something came up. Or tell them the truth, I don't care. You can tell me all about it tomorrow."

"That might not be why they're in town," I said, sitting up. "It could be something else."

"Please," Michael said, shifting over. "I'm not the only one trying to get you to give up your sperm."

The stupid comment made me smile. "Fine, fine. Have fun with Gus."

"You're not mad, are you?"

I looked at Michael's bright young face, the same goofy mug that never ceased to make mine curl up in a smile. He was right. Even though he and I had been together for over three years, my friendship with Wendy and Eve went back almost two decades. The seeds of what we were about to do were planted long before Michael showed up. "No, I'm not mad," I said. "But I'd like you to see them while they're here. Tomorrow night, maybe? We could have them over for dinner."

"Deal!"

I got up off the bed and reached for my towel behind the door. "One thing, though. If you do go out tonight, can you please try to…" I was interrupted by a strange, guttural noise coming from the kitchen. "What the hell is that?"

Michael turned his good ear towards the hallway. "Oh, the cat's throwing up." He swung his feet onto the floor. "Go on," he said, standing up. "Take your shower. I'll handle this."

An hour later, I ran out the door and headed to the Metro. I took the subway to Beaudry station, arriving ten minutes late to meet Wendy and Eve.

I darted into the restaurant and made my way through a large group waiting at the front for a table. The place was packed and warm with the din of cutlery and conversation. I looked for my friends and spotted them at the back, near the open kitchen, where a swell of steam rose from rumbling pots.

"Sorry I'm late," I said, walking up to their table.

Wendy and Eve cried out and rose to greet me, all smiles and big eyes and open arms as we hugged across the white tablecloth. "It's so good to see you," Wendy said, pulling away.

"Don't you look sharp!"

"This? This is all Michael," I said, gesturing to the dark T-shirt and cream-coloured blazer he had picked for me to wear. I noticed that my friends, too, had dressed up: Wendy in a gleaming white blouse and Eve a grey button-down and dark blue vest. "You both look great," I said. We sat down together, Wendy and Eve on the same side of the table like managers conducting a job interview. I apologized again for being late.

"Stop, don't worry about it," Eve said, and patted the half-empty bottle between them. "We got familiar with the Valpolicella. Where's Michael?"

"He sends his regrets," I said, pulling my chair closer. "He had to help out a friend last minute. He's sorry he couldn't come. We were hoping you might be free for dinner tomorrow. You could see our new place."

"We can't tomorrow," Wendy said, disappointed. "We're seeing Eve's folks."

I knew what Wendy was thinking. She would much rather have a night out with the boys than spend her Saturday evening with Eve's parents. But since their move to Toronto a few years ago, Wendy had learned to accept that any visit to Montreal meant at least one dinner at her in-laws.

"Well, next time," I said, wishing that I'd pushed Michael to come.

"Here, let's get you some wine." Eve reached over to fill my glass. "Cheers!" she said, and we all toasted.

I swallowed a big gulp of red and realized I was nervous. I'd need to slow down if I didn't want to be drunk by the end of the night. I placed the glass back down on the table.

In my face, I felt the heat from the open kitchen and the glare of the incandescent lighting above. I reached for a napkin on the table and dabbed at my brow.

"So, how is the new home?" Wendy asked. "You settled yet?"

"Almost," I said, now playing with the clasp of the watch on my arm. "It's been... about six months since we moved in? We've painted all the rooms and found a place for most things, but Michael just shipped a few boxes from his parents' home. A lot of tchotchkes from his childhood, all of which hold plenty of nostalgia but nothing we have a place for."

"No place for nostalgia?" Wendy said, raising her glass to her lips. "That's not the Paul I know."

I smiled. "I told him we could put them all on a shelf, but only if he builds one."

"You're lucky your partner is a handyman," Wendy said, casting a side-eye at her wife. "Some butch you are, you can't even change a wall sconce."

Eve smiled at the gentle ribbing. "No, my love, I pay people to fix things now."

Wendy turned to me. "Do you remember that *shithole* we used to live in on Logan? You could've placed a marble on the kitchen floor and it would've rolled down the hall all the way to the living room."

"I liked that place," I said, irked Wendy had called it a shithole. "We had some great times there. But it's true, we did have mice in the winter and the water pressure was horrible and the landlord wouldn't fix a thing."

"You have Michael for that now," Eve said.

"It must be exciting," Wendy said. "Your first home."

18

"Well, Michael and I did live together for two years before the move."

"No, you know what I mean," she said. "You two spent all that time cramped in a small space. And Michael moved in with *you*, which meant it was all of *your* stuff in the apartment—*your* decor, *your* childhood knick-knacks on the shelf. Now you're starting on the same foot. And you own it! Of course, he's going to want to personalize your home."

"I didn't say he couldn't. I let him choose the paint colours."

Eve smiled. "Must be nice," she said, teasing her partner. "I think I was allowed to choose the bath curtains."

Wendy chuckled. "You do all your decorating at the office," she said, referring to Eve's occupation as a set designer. "I didn't want you to bring your work home." With that, Wendy downed the rest of the wine in her glass, surprising us all. "God, why am I so nervous?" she said. "Listen Paul, I'm sorry that Michael isn't here. We'd hoped to see you both tonight but, well, you know we wanted to ask you something and I can't wait any longer. Eve and I are ready to start our family, and we want to know if you would be our donor."

My friends' faces exploded in wide, round excitement. All I could do was smile and blush and look at the tablecloth. "Wow, really? I wondered if that's what it was."

"Did you?"

"Well, of course," I said. "I mean, I was already best man at your wedding. What else could you want to ask me?"

Eve elbowed Wendy. "See? I told you he knew."

"We talked about it once," I said. "In the hypothetical. But that was *years* ago, and I wasn't sure you were serious. I was never a hundred percent sure you wanted kids."

"We've always wanted children," Wendy said, indicating she'd like a refill by pushing the stem towards her wife. "We just wanted to be settled first. As you remember, our first few years together were all about partying."

Eve filled up Wendy's glass before her own. "And then we went travelling and lived in Vancouver for a year."

"And then I went back to school and we moved to Toronto and bought the house."

"We were waiting for the right time, but there never was one."

"It's 2011," Wendy said. "I'm going to be thirty-six this year, and so if I'm going to do it—now's the time."

So that's it, I thought. Wendy will carry the baby.

"And no offence, Paul. You're not getting any younger either."

"Forty!" Wendy said, and grabbed my hand across the table.

"Not yet!" I pulled away in jest. "Still thirty-nine for a few months, anyway."

"But if we want your swimmers, we're going to have to act soon."

"A man gets less fertile in his forties," Eve said. "And his sperm quality decreases."

I attempted a joke. "Well, I haven't had any complaints."

My friends humoured me with a laugh as our waiter walked up to take our order. Caught unawares, the three of us scrambled for the pile of thin menus on the table. "We're going to need a few more minutes," Eve said, and he left. As soon as he was gone, we dropped our menus and reached again for the wine.

"At some point I thought you weren't going to ask," I said, taking another large sip. "That maybe you'd decided to go the anonymous route."

Wendy shook her head. "We've always wanted it to be you, Paul."

"Well," Eve started, looking at Wendy, "there was a time when we were going back and forth about it. Trying to figure out what would be best for the child. A part of us wondered, since Wendy would be carrying, if we should have a Chinese donor. Would it be easier for our child if they looked more like me? Would it be easier for my parents? But in the end we decided we wanted someone we had a special history with. Someone our child would get to know and who would play an important role in their life."

"You've got fantastic genes, Paul," Wendy said. "You're smart and handsome and funny. You'd be a great influence. You're already such an important part of our lives, and now we'd be making it official. Becoming a family. We've been friends for so long."

That much was true. Wendy was one of my oldest friends. We'd met sixteen years earlier, back in 1995, while working for Montreal's Gay Pride. I was in charge of communications and she parade security. One lazy afternoon, while I sent out press release after press release at the tired, old fax machine, Wendy sat with me and bleached my hair. We talked about love and sex and music and our childhoods. Soon after, we were going out to bars and talking on the phone every other night. And then, a few years later, when it came time for me to find a new place to live, Wendy suggested we move in together; so we did, taking over the lease of her friend's rickety two-bedroom apartment in the Village. And then, a year after that, she met Eve at our friend Charles's Christmas party and invited her to move in with us. The three of us had remained close ever since.

"I know it's a lot to take in," Eve said. "But what do you think?'

What did I think?

I'd been mulling over that question for the past week at home, at the office, on my morning runs, once Wendy and Eve had told me they had something important to ask me. And now, here, drinking wine in this bright, warm room with all of its noise and life and my dear friends sitting across from me, it felt like everything in our lives had led to this moment. Sure, there was much to discuss, but I knew that nothing would change my answer. "You don't have to convince me," I said. "I'd be honoured."

Wendy yelped and the whole restaurant turned. "Oh, I'm so fucking happy!" she said, jumping up to grab me as I, too, stood up. "Eve says I'm going to have to stop swearing once the baby gets here."

Eve hugged me. "I'm going to make her put a loonie in a jar every time she does."

"You'll have the kid's education paid for in no time," I said, as we all sat down.

"Oh, Paul," Wendy said, almost breathless. "Thank you. I don't know what we would've done had you said no."

"But we want you to be sure," Eve added. "We want you to take your time and think about it. To make sure this is something you can do."

"I know."

"I mean, have you ever wanted children of your own?"

"No. I've never had any desire for kids. You know that."

"Still. When you see the child," Wendy said, "you might feel different. Do you think you'll be able to handle it? To be in our child's life, but not the father?"

"We won't be using terms like dad or father to describe your relationship," Eve said.

"You'd be her cool Uncle Paul," interrupted Wendy, "who helped her two moms start a family and who lives in Montreal."

"You can have as much, or as little, involvement as you like," Eve continued. "But it's important for us to know where you're coming from. If you were to tell us that you wanted to have a child one day, then maybe this wouldn't be a good idea."

"And Michael?" Wendy asked. "How does he feel?"

"Well, we talked about it," I said. "When I thought you might ask."

"And?"

"And, he's happy for me—for us—whatever we decide."

"Does he want kids?"

"God no, are you crazy? Michael's too much of a kid himself."

"We know a couple in Toronto," Eve said, "who were going to use a friend. But the guy's partner had a change of heart. All of a sudden he wanted the four of them to co-parent and raise the child together. It wasn't what our friends wanted and, thankfully, it came out before they started trying. But then, of course, they had to find a new donor and things weren't the same with their friend. We'd want to avoid that."

23

I reached for the glass of water on the table and took a sip. "Well, all I can say is that neither Michael nor I want to have children. It's nothing we've talked about in the three years we've been together. As for how I'm going to feel in the future, I can't say—but I'd be surprised to find myself wanting custody, if that's what you're worried about."

"You'd have to sign away your paternity," said Wendy, almost apologizing. "You wouldn't be on the birth certificate, and we'd have to write up an agreement. Not sure what kind yet, we'd have to find a lawyer or a notary. But it would be to protect the child. God, I hate talking about all this legal stuff." Wendy made a swiping motion with her hand. "We can save that for another time. We just want to be upfront and honest with you about what we're looking for. You understand, don't you?"

I looked at my friends—so nervous, so excited, so eager to be mothers. It felt weird to think that they needed something, anything, from me to make that happen. But whatever it took, I knew that I would help. "Of course, I understand," I said. "And yes, I would love to do this. Seriously, this is wonderful. I'm thrilled you asked."

"That's great, Paul," Eve said, all smiles. "Thank you."

Wendy grabbed my hand from across the table and mouthed *I fucking love you.*

"I fucking love you too," I said.

Eve picked up her glass and made another toast. "To the future."

"To the future," Wendy and I repeated. The three of us clinked glasses.

2

THE NEXT MORNING, like clockwork, Malone came into our room at around seven. He jumped onto the bed, and with his little chirrups announced it was time for the two of us to wake up. Michael and I did what we always do: separate and make room for the cat to curl up between us. We collapsed into half-sleep as he gnawed on one of his nipples, his purrs a white noise machine keeping us under.

I dozed for another twenty minutes before pulling myself out of bed. I got up and changed into my running gear in the near darkness of our bedroom, then went out into the bright kitchen to make a pot of coffee. I don't drink coffee, but I do like the smell of it. It was a weekend tradition for me to get up on Saturday mornings and start the coffee machine for Michael before going out to grab the newspaper. I wrote him a short note on a Post-it and left it on the kitchen island: "Gone for a run. Back soon!"

Outside, it was April and most of the snow had melted. My shoes kicked up pebbles as I ran across the neighbourhood. Yellowed patches of grass were turning green and some of the trees had started to bud. There were not too many people out at this time, but I did pass a few neighbours on my jog to Jarry Park—men and women in sweats and sunglasses walking their dogs and their cell phones, teenagers with backpacks heading out for the day.

Michael and I lived in Villeray, in the central north part of Montreal. I hadn't thought to look here when we first started our search for a bigger apartment. Originally, I had figured we would move to another rental in the Village; but one afternoon, as I ogled the real estate listings (which Michael called my porn), I came across a property on Saint Denis Street. It was a five-room apartment on the top floor of a brick-faced triplex, with large windows, high ceilings and two balconies. Saint Denis Street is a six-lane thoroughfare that connects the north and south ends of the island, so I was less interested in the location, thinking the rush of cars and street noise would be too much, but whoever had taken the listing's pictures knew how to play to its strengths. There was so much light and space in each room. I could easily see Michael and me and our two cats living there.

Owning a home had long been a dream of mine. As a kid, I'd play in the model kitchens and bathrooms when we'd visit the big box hardware stores. And I'd draw make-believe houses in pencil crayon at night in front of the TV (always a three-storey mansion), imagining the rooms on the different floors and what the gardens looked like. When I got older, in my early twenties, I daydreamed about my first apartment. Most young gay men fantasize about the sex they'll have once they leave home. I did that too, but I also fantasized about where it would happen. Growing up, far away from the city centre, in the west-end suburb of Pointe-Claire, had me longing for a queer life downtown. And I often imagined what that domestic life would look like: stark white walls, queen-size mattress, dark grey sectional, ten-speed bike against the wall by the kitchen, a table for two.

After meeting with my bank, I discovered that I qualified for a mid-range mortgage and could afford the purchase price. Sure, a second income would've been helpful in finding us a nicer place. Work for Michael was erratic, and he had no savings to draw from, but I understood that. Michael had cashed in whatever he had left when he packed up his life and moved here from New Brunswick. However, there would be other ways he could contribute.

I hadn't heard him return home the night before, but I did feel him getting into bed with me—the shifting of weight on the mattress, the pressure of him pulling me in from behind. I couldn't wait to tell him my news. *We might have a kid! A pint-sized version of Wendy and me! How fun is that?* I knew of only one other couple who'd done this. A former colleague who, with her partner, went the anonymous route. Looking at the pictures on her desk, you'd never think they created their family any differently. But so much planning went into their kid's conception. I mean, with us, none of this happens by accident.

Wendy, Eve and I had spent the remainder of the previous night discussing plans. We finished off a second bottle of wine, Wendy lamenting how she would have to quit booze altogether and the both of them asking if I too would cut back. I also had questions for them: How would we do it? When would we start? What would they need from me? We agreed to keep everything private for now and tell close friends only. Parents too, although I didn't plan on telling my dad and his wife yet. Honestly, I wasn't sure how he would react. I wasn't even sure my dad would have an opinion, but Debbie might.

Generally, I didn't have a problem with my dad's wife, but she could be nosy at times. Once, after I told my dad that Michael and I had rescued a cat from a barn outside the city, she called me up to tell me she thought it was a bad idea, and that Malone would bring all these "barnyard diseases" into our home that would either kill or harm Sutherland (she even mailed me an article about it that she had clipped from a magazine). I thought it was ridiculous, but I shrugged it off the way I did many things Debbie said. Her behaviour never bothered my dad though. More than anything, I was relieved that he had found happiness after my mom's death, even if it did mean moving across the country to Kelowna to start a new life.

My mother, when she was alive, was much more easygoing. How would she have handled this news? I wondered. How would she have dealt with the things I did with my life? My mom died long ago, when I was twenty-one. She never learned that I was gay. She didn't get to see the man I would become, nor did she get to meet Michael or Wendy or Eve or Danny or Charles or Alan, or any of the other people who have played an important role in my life.

At least I had Kate to confide in. I would have to tell my sister about this, and soon. She'd be hurt if I waited too long. But I wasn't sure how to share this news. I had no idea how she would react. What would it be like for her to hear that I might have a child? To know that the only grandchild our dad would ever get would be from me?

28

After my run, I stopped by the dépanneur to pick up the weekend newspaper and grabbed a bar of soap for Michael. I made no dog barks as I climbed our stairs—it really was an after-work thing. I opened the door to our place and was greeted by the rich smell of coffee. Michael was still in bed, both cats curled up like croissants on the comforter.

"Morning, buddy. You awake?"

"Kinda. Did you go for a run?"

"I did."

"That's my man," Michael said, peeking out from the covers. "How was last night?"

"Well, they asked."

"And?"

"I said yes. Wendy will carry the baby. You were missed."

"Congratulations! That's wonderful! Did they understand me not being there?"

"Yes. Unfortunately, they can't see us tonight. They're having dinner with Eve's parents."

"I'm sorry, buddy… How do you feel?"

"I feel… great. Don't know what to expect, but I'm honoured they asked."

"Well, of course they asked." Michael sat up, all smiles and groggy eyes. "You're Paul. Who wouldn't want Paul genes?"

I sat down on the bed and took off my runners. "They wanted to make sure that you and I don't want children of our own. Don't want us changing our minds at the last minute. I think the Toronto lesbians are putting ideas in their heads."

"They're just being prudent. You should draw up some papers."

"We will."

"To protect you, as much as them."

"Whatever. They have nothing to worry about."

"I know…"

Michael began to pet Malone at his side, the cat offering up his belly. "I wonder if it'll be a boy or a girl."

"Who knows. And these days who cares, right? Anatomy's not gender."

"That's true… Still, you must be wondering."

Michael was right; I had been. "I hope it's a girl," I found myself saying. "Wouldn't that be cool? When she's fifteen, she could visit on her own, or come with us on holiday. I could take her to see plays and we could talk about who she has a crush on."

"Well, I'm happy for you." Michael was deep into kitty belly now, Malone's paws reaching out in all directions. "They couldn't have picked a nicer guy—your genes, your intellect, your soul. You're the perfect donor."

"You sure you don't mind me doing this?"

"Of course not. We've talked about it. As long as it doesn't affect our lives too much, and we don't have to give up all our vacation time to go visit. But like I said, it's your decision. I wouldn't do it, but that's more about my own crazy genes. The family line stops with me."

Michael's comment made me wonder if he had called his mother back. I doubted it, but then stopped myself from reminding him. I didn't want to be a nag.

"I think I'm going to bring Malone to the vet today," he went on, caressing the little guy's tummy. "See if they can take him for a check-up. There was more puke when I got home last night."

"Hairballs?"

"I don't know. I want to make sure he's okay."

"Don't you need an appointment?"

"I'm sure it's fine."

"But you don't want to go all that way for nothing. Why don't you call first?" I grabbed my towel from the back of the door and walked over to the window to open the curtains. "Fuck," I said, stepping on a cat toy. "Can you please not bring home any more cat toys? I'm going to break my neck one day."

"You're no fun. What are the boys supposed to do all day?"

I let in the daylight, then left the room to take my shower. Standing in the tub, I noticed a single screw on the ledge next to the shampoo. It was a flat Phillips head, three inches in length.

Michael walked into the bathroom and closed the door behind him. He peed into the toilet.

"Were you doing renovations?"

"No, why?"

"What's this screw doing here?"

"I reinforced the cabinet yesterday. It was loose."

I had found a smaller screw on the kitchen island the day before while chopping vegetables, and there were four or five of them on the bureau in the hall. It was like Michael was shedding. "Shouldn't it be in the wall?"

"It's an extra."

"Does it need to be here?"

"No."

"Then why didn't you put it away?"

"To annoy you, I suppose," he said, and laughed. Michael flushed the toilet and the water in the shower started to run hot. "Oh, sorry," he called out, sincere, remembering too late as I stepped out of the way. "So, did you discuss what you'd be called?" Michael asked.

"Uncle Paul, probably. Not Dad, that's for sure."

"But everyone will know you're the father."

"Yes, but I won't be *the father.*"

"That's weird."

"Is it?"

"What's the big deal? Why not call you the dad?"

The water returned to its normal temperature and I stepped back in. "Because I'm not the dad. And it's what Wendy and Eve want. There's so much that comes with that term. I don't need to claim any ownership of their kid. I won't be this child's parent. All I'm doing is jerking off into a cup."

"It's more than that. You'll be in the kid's life!"

"I'll be the donor. The uncle. The *spunkle*, as we were joking last night."

"Don't ever say spunkle again," Michael said, serious.

I laughed. "Look, it's fine. The child will have whatever relationship it wants to have with me. It might not want one, you know."

Michael opened the shower curtain and got in the tub. "That'll never happen."

I moved aside and let Michael into the rush of water. I watched him from behind, that same familiar body, like mine, but only in that I knew it so well. Michael is eleven years younger than me, in his late twenties. It was in moments like this that I saw our age difference. Sure, I had been jogging for the past few months and seen a subtle change in my body. I had lost a few pounds around the middle and chiselled out parts of my figure that I thought had been buried forever. But everything hung effortlessly on Michael—from the strong lines of his neck and shoulders, down to the soft curve of his bottom. God I love that ass, I thought as I lathered up, and felt a sudden rush of desire. But then I stopped myself and let the feeling dissipate. I needed to get out and start the day.

"I picked us up some soap," I said, placing the bar back on the ledge.

"Thanks," Michael said, changing positions with me so I could rinse. "But I prefer the body wash."

"How was your night with Gus?"

"His flight was delayed an hour and it took him forever to get his bags. We went straight to the bar for drinks. It was dead, but George was working. We bought shots and caught up."

"You didn't drink and drive, did you?"

"Relax, I only had three drinks. And I was there for a while, you know."

We finished washing, got out of the shower and got dressed.

"So, I'm going to have to get tested," I said, pulling on a T-shirt.

"Of course."

"And you should too."

"I figured."

"And we're going to have to be closed."

"I'm not seeing anyone," Michael said. "Not sleeping with anyone else."

"I know. I mean, we've never discussed it. But you know. If you were, you'd have to stop. At least while we try this."

"I know."

Once I had dressed, I switched off the coffee maker and made Michael and me breakfast. After we ate and cleaned up, I helped him corral Malone into the cat carrier, which proved difficult. He didn't want to go and made drawn-out groaning noises that caused Sutherland to run and hide.

"You're such a baby," I said to Sutherland, as he watched from under the couch.

With Michael gone, I put on a load of laundry. The hamper was filled with his work clothes—paint-stained T-shirts and ratty jeans—so I separated out my own dress shirts and slacks and put them on delicate. I went into the office and powered up my computer. The email from my boss had come in overnight, so I had what I needed to work on the documents for Monday.

I tinkered with the texts for about an hour and then, almost absentmindedly, I opened up my web browser and populated it with two windows: one with a popular porn blog, and the other a gay chat site. I surfed through the profiles I found on the latter; shots of men's faces, chests and other body parts. The site granted access to one hundred people if you weren't a member, but that was more than enough for my purposes. I just wanted to look. Michael, however, did have a profile on the site. He used his for work, for networking, for making new friends and contacts. It was how he got the job painting the office in Mile-Ex. Normally, what would happen is he'd be chatting up a guy online and the person would ask him what he did for a living. Michael would then tell him and suddenly the man would be more interested in his professional services than his body (or maybe it was both). I often wondered how many people hired Michael because they found him attractive, perhaps harbouring handyman fantasies. Whatever the case, it didn't bother me that he flirted to get the job. It showed entrepreneurialism, and I didn't mind Michael using his youth or good looks to get ahead.

But I wasn't sure why I kept visiting the site. Curiosity, I suppose. Boredom. I wasn't interested in chatting with any of these men, let alone hooking up with them. Mostly, if I came across a handsome face I'd click on it and see what the bio said. Sometimes I'd think, this is the guy I'd write to if I were single. And on rare occasions, if he was hot, I'd save the picture to a folder on my computer.

It didn't take long for me to come across Michael's profile. His image showed up on the second page, a small stamp-sized square on the bottom right-hand side of my screen. I clicked on it and his profile opened in a new window: *Partnered*, it said. *28 years old. Looking to chat only. 420 friendly. Handyman and Cat Butler. Hit me up if you need help with your home.* He looked adorable in the photo, silly, a crooked smile on his smooth face and a mess of dark brown hair under the same black trucker's cap he had on the night I met him.

Scrolling along, I came across Michael's friend Gus. At first, I didn't recognize him with his shirt off. Gus wasn't my type, but in his profile pic I could see what others saw in him. He looked lean, yet muscular, with strong arms and visible abs. His head was shaved and he was showing off the garish tattoo on his left pec: a black circus bear balancing on a red-

35

and-white striped ball. Gus was in a bar, from what I could tell, and slick with sweat, which made the hairs on his chest look dark. His profile was succinct and to the point: *31-year-old sex-positive events producer looking for fun. No femme-o-phobes or racists. Come to my next party: Unicorn Blowjob May 5th at the Royal Phoenix.*

"Hello?"

The voice came from outside the door to my apartment. I jumped up from where I sat and closed the lid on my laptop. "Hello?" I called out, heading into the hallway. "Danny? Is that you?"

"Yes, it's me," Danny called. "Sorry, your door downstairs was wide open so I thought I'd come up."

I unlocked the door and let my friend in. "I'll have to get Michael to look at that," I said, and kissed him hello on both cheeks. "Sometimes it doesn't catch—the joys of home ownership. Come in, come in."

I closed the door and led Danny towards the kitchen. He admired the artwork we had hung in the hallway. "The place is coming along nicely."

"Slowly, but surely," I said. "So, to what do I owe this honour? I thought you had a date last night. Shouldn't you be in bed with someone's ear in your mouth right now?"

"It wasn't a date," Danny said, placing a plastic bag on the kitchen island. "I was supposed to meet Andre for a drink, but really to return his things. God, *Andre*—you've pretty much determined your child's sexual orientation when you decide to name him *Andre*. Anyway, I was going to give him one more chance. See if his attitude had changed and, if not, give him his things back. I mean, I hadn't heard from him in three weeks and he left all this junk at my place." Danny pulled out pieces of clothing from the bag. "Who does that? Stops seeing someone and leaves all their shit at the other person's apartment? Look at this! There's a pair of Diesel jeans here—I can't even fit into these jeans! And three dress shirts. And look, this old Ramones tee. He didn't even know who the Ramones were—just picked it up at a thrift store. I have to stop dating twenty-four-year-olds. Twenty-four! That's not an age, it's a case of beer!"

"So, he didn't show?"

"No, he didn't show!" Danny stuffed the clothes back into the bag. "I don't know what's wrong with this generation. We live in a day of smart phones and text messages. God knows he was on that thing every moment we were together. He could have called me or texted if he wasn't able to make it, but I bet you he went to another bar and is in another twenty-four-year-old's bed right now. There they are, naked, in each other's arms after a night of marathon sex. I waited for him at the bar for an hour! It's disrespectful. I mean, he seemed interested in me enough as it was to begin with. *He cruised me!* These kids have got to learn this is no way to treat another human being." Danny took a deep breath. "But I'm not going to let it ruin my Saturday. I was on my way to drop his clothes off at the church and thought I'd swing by and pay you for Provincetown." He took out a cheque and handed it over.

"You sure you're okay?" I asked, folding the cheque and putting it in my pocket. "You sound stressed. Want some coffee? Tea? Chamomile, perhaps?"

"Sure, why not. I've nowhere to be." Danny sat down on

a stool and moved the bag of clothes onto the floor by his feet. "Hey, why don't we go out tonight? Drinks? Strippers? God, I just need to be around men my own age."

"I can't," I said. "I have a press kit to finish for Monday."

"They work you too hard."

"Well, I'm hoping for a raise," I said. "My mortgage payments are way more than rent used to be, and with Provincetown coming up I need as much money in the bank as possible."

Danny sighed. "I understand," he said, collapsing onto the counter. "I don't mean to be a bad influence. I'm just so fucking frustrated. And horny! Have you been outside? It's spring out there! It's like I'm rediscovering my penis."

Danny's comment made me laugh as I took out two teabags from the kitchen pantry. It was odd to think that we had once dated—if you could call it that. Danny and I had seen each other for three short weeks more than a decade ago. He must have been not much older than this Andre fellow at the time, and only a year out of the closet. Back then, Danny needed a good friend more than a lover. And I wasn't in such a great headspace either, Alan having died the year before. Danny's presence was a godsend that winter; he was warm and alive and made me laugh in a way that I hadn't in a long time.

"You know," he continued, "you're lucky that you and Michael found each other and don't have to swim in the crazy that I do."

"What are you talking about?" I said, filling up the kettle and turning on the stove. "Being in a relationship has its own amount of crazy. Don't get me wrong, I love Michael, but sometimes I feel jealous of all of your sexual freedom. Meeting all those men. All that strange new sex."

"What men? What strange sex?"

"You know what I mean. Going out. Flirting with strangers."

"Have you hit your head?" Danny asked, straightening himself on the stool. "I think you forget what it's like out there. You know, I went out with Charles last week. Two girls, out on the town. Trying to get Andre out of my mind, but secretly hoping to run into him. We went to Sky, and all of a sudden I'm dancing next to this tall hunk. I can't tell if he's into me or not, but he's got this huge smile and keeps looking in my direction. Anyway, he goes into the bathroom and I decide to follow. Perhaps to say hi and ask him his name. And as he's at the urinal, I'm waiting in line for my turn. And you know how Sky has those mirrored walls on one side of the bathroom? Well, I catch a glimpse of myself, with him right in front of me, and I realize how fucking big I am. Jesus, Paul, why didn't you tell me?"

"What are you talking about? You look great."

"Remember when we first met, how thin I was? I went through an old photo album the other night, pictures of us from back in the day. We were so young, remember? Fresh and new. I'm a stale loaf of bread now."

"Stop it. You were too thin back then. The meat looks good on you."

"I feel like an elephant."

"Come on, how much do you weigh?"

Danny told me his weight. "Do you know how much that boy must have been? "One-hundred-and-fifty pounds. One-fifty! That's not a weight, it's a price!"

39

"Jesus, Danny, you weigh less than I do."

"But you have a thicker frame. And you're taller! I wasn't always like this. It's like you wake up one morning and all of a sudden you realize: I'm a bear. It just happens. You don't plan it. Now it all makes sense. Once you reach your mid-thirties, one of two things happen. You either become a gym bunny and spend all your time working out, or you turn into a bear."

"I jog, but I'm big. What does that make me? Some kind of bunny/bear hybrid?"

"You've always been a bear, Paul," Danny said, with reverence. "A stocky bear. An Italian bear—an *orso*," he added with gusto. "I mean look at your chest and legs. And you've got that beard and all that body hair. Me? It's all flab around the middle and I'm as hairy as a shark."

"Why don't you come running with me? You'll lose a few pounds and start feeling better. If you start now, you can run the half-marathon with me in the fall."

"You're going to run the half-marathon?"

"Why do you think I've been training these last eight months? You could do it with me—well, not the whole half-marathon, but there's a 5K. We can set you up with a training schedule over the next few months to meet the goal."

"You're my hero—the half-marathon, buying this place, angling for a raise. You're really checking things off your bucket list, aren't you?"

The kettle started to whistle and I filled up the teapot. "Running is hard at first, but once you get used to it, it feels amazing."

"No, no. It's not for me. But I do have to do something. Maybe I'll go back to the gym. But I don't understand, I never needed to go to the gym before. Perhaps it was all that self-hate that kept me so thin in my twenties. That's the problem. I like myself too much now."

That got me to chuckle. "So, who cares if you've gained weight? Embrace your thickness. Stop trying to keep up with the Andres of the world. I guarantee you they're not any happier."

"Maybe," he said, not entirely convinced. "You know," he went on, as I opened the cupboard to take out two mugs. "I had the most remarkable dream the other night. I flirted with some cute boy. He liked me and I liked him, and we were at a party. He was about to leave, but I convinced him to stay. We kept looking for each other but getting sidetracked. Nothing much happened in the dream, but I remember having goosebumps when he put his arm around me. Actual goosebumps in a dream! I can't remember the last time someone gave me those in real life. I don't know, maybe I need to flip my mattress or something. Have Michael over to help me redesign my apartment. If I want to attract people into my bed I'm going to have to rethink my sexual *feng shui*. God, just once I'd like to have a lover who is around longer than the milk I buy."

"Cut out the dairy," I said. "That'll help in many ways."

Danny was about to say something, then stopped. "Wait, where did you get this?" he asked, looking at one of the two mugs I had taken out for tea. It was a cheap ceramic mug that had a super campy image on it—an illustration of Lady Diana and Freddie Mercury over a rippling Union Jack with the words "My Queen!" spelled out across it in bold black lettering.

"Great, isn't it? My sister got it for me about ten years ago for Christmas. Picked it up at a second-hand store in Ottawa."

"How have I not seen this before? I just *love* your sister."

"And she loves you."

"Oh please, no one loves me."

"I love you."

"Yes, but you don't love me with your mouth."

I laughed again. "All right, all right," I said, getting ready to share my news. "No more pity party. It's my turn to tell you something…"

3

I OPENED THE DOOR to the Stud. The place was half-full of men, many of whom, like me, had come straight from work, with blazers and shoulder bags wrapped around their bodies. I walked over to the counter and ordered a bottle of sparkling water. The bartender who passed it to me and rang in my order wasn't someone I recognized. He was new—bearded, early twenties, wearing ripped jeans and a leather vest. His chunky torso and furry arms were awash in colourful tattoos. I noticed several letters adorning his hairy knuckles as he handed over my change. They spelled "Bear" on one hand, "Life" on the other.

The bar smelled like urinal cakes and bleach, like the cleaning crew had just left. Too cool out to open the front patio windows, the room was stuffy and warm with electric heating, male voices and the colour red. It all made me want to have a beer, but I had decided I wouldn't. I had learned, from the pamphlets Wendy and Eve had left, of the negative effects alcohol had on sperm count and quality, lowering testosterone and affecting motility. If that was the case, I had no problem drinking less in the coming months. If anything, the one habit I had trouble adopting was the wearing of boxer shorts. My preference was for briefs, but apparently they too were a problem as they raised testicle temperature by keeping them too close to the body. To improve the quality of my sperm, I was encouraged to let my boys dangle. It was distracting.

I grabbed my water and took a seat at a table near the tinted windows. I checked the time on my watch: 6:40 p.m. I was early. There was a flyer on the table for a party on Saturday called Rump. The brooding man on the flyer had a chiselled body. Not my type, but I wouldn't have said no. Especially this week, with the city thawing and all this talk of healthy sperm production. It had been a while. I knew it was normal for a couple's sex life to slow down after being together for a couple of years, but the days of raucous sex between Michael and me seemed far away. We still had sex— maybe two or three times a month—but when we did it was quick and predictable, not the frenetic possession it had been in the first year of our coupling.

At the other end of the bar sat a handsome man alone, texting. Curious, I opened the app on my phone to see if I could locate his profile. I found it on the first page: *Brian, 27. Bottom. Hairy. Musician and grad student looking for friend-ship, NSA and dates. More LTR oriented, but open to options when the mood strikes. En français aussi.*

I'm always surprised about the personal things you can learn about strangers online. What would Alan have made of this technology? I wondered. He was such a Luddite. Even his watch—the one I wear now—was analogue. Would he have found this method of communication cold? Or would he have loved it? If he were alive today, would I be texting him now, asking him to join me? He had lived just a few blocks from here. God, how I'd love to see him again. I remembered his number. What if I texted something to that number? No, that wouldn't work—Alan's number was a landline and none of us had cell phones back then. So who owns that number now? I wondered. Who lives in his old apartment?

There was some commotion at the bar. A drunk young man in a Lady Gaga T-shirt had ordered a beer and was trying to pay for it with a paper receipt. *That's not money,* the bartender said in French, as the kid tried to concentrate on the slivers of paper in his wallet. He finally found a green twenty and paid for his drink. The bartender gave him his change along with a cup of water, but the boy left the cup on the counter and went into the other room.

His drunkenness reminded me of meeting Danny. It had been many years ago. I was walking home from Charles's holiday party one December night when I came across a well-dressed man around my age stumbling up and down the cold streets of the Village without a coat. I didn't know him, but I recognized him from the bars and marches, his thick black hair frozen in clumps on his forehead. I stopped and asked him if he was all right. He was drunk and slurring, couldn't look me straight in the eye. I had trouble understanding him, but soon made out that he had been bar-hopping and had forgotten where he had left his coat. In his frozen hands he clutched a coat-check ticket, a generic yellow tag that offered no clue to its origin. I asked him if he could remember his address and he told it to me. I hailed him a cab and helped him into the car, negotiating with the driver a fee to bring him to his door.

Danny wouldn't remember this bit of kindness, wouldn't recognize that it was me who had helped him when we would meet again, a year later, at a networking cocktail for gay and lesbian business professionals. I saw Danny at the far end of the bar and walked up to introduce myself. He gave me his card, a laminated rectangle that revealed he worked in fundraising and development at the McCord Museum. After a few minutes of small talk about their current show, I told him that we had met before. Danny turned pale as I recounted the story and pulled me aside to thank me, expressing both gratitude and humiliation. "I had no idea how I got home that night," he had said. "Thank you." I told him it was no big deal and shared with him one of my own embarrassing tales (I drunkenly fell down a flight of stairs at an AIDS fundraiser—not once, but twice). We both laughed hard and spent the rest of the night sharing stories of youthful indiscretions (we had plenty). When the event ended an hour later, I invited him home with me.

It surprises me to think we've had sex. It may have been more than a decade ago, but I once touched and kissed Danny with the same passion and desire that I've felt for the other men I've been with. We did things together that make me squirm to think about today, but only because I think of him now as a brother, as family. At the beginning, I'd go over to his place after work for dinner and a make-out session on his couch. An avid music collector, Danny had crates of vinyl he would take out to play while we got acquainted. It was early December then, and his apartment was so cold that my boots were still frozen when I'd put them back on, hours later, to go home. And in the mornings, if I'd stayed over, I'd struggle to leave his warm comforter for the kitchen where he'd made us breakfast. Danny loved to cook. One night, as Christmas approached, he put on an old Dean Martin album and attempted to make a puttanesca sauce. The pasta dish came out way too salty and we had to order in a pizza. Afterwards, he gave me a blowjob on his living room floor, the Christmas lights flashing, and I came in his mouth.

I winced, sitting there at the table, thinking about that. I've never been one to sleep with my friends. The exception, of course, being Alan. Alan and I had continued to sleep together, on and off, for a few years after we broke up. I'm not sure how much of it was sex and how much of it was cuddling that turned into sex, but as with Danny, that too feels like a lifetime ago. It was a different era when Alan and I dated— the fashion, the hairstyles, the politics. Alan was thirty-two when I met him in 1994, and I was twenty-two. We dated for only one year, but in that brief time so much happened. Alan taught me all about sex and queer history and culture. He got me involved in community radio and AIDS activism. He took me to my first protest. And he brought me to Provincetown and New York for the first time. Alan was the smartest, most compassionate man I have ever met, and he died at thirty-eight. I'm older than him now, which feels impossible. But unlike me, Alan would never get to turn forty.

I finished my Perrier and chucked the glass bottle into the recycling bin behind the bar. I thought I'd check on the drunk kid in the Lady Gaga T-shirt and make sure he was all right. I grabbed my bag and headed around the corner to the dance floor where two men were dancing despite the early hour. This was the same spot I had met Michael one January night.

He was dancing by himself in front of the DJ booth, and I couldn't stop watching. He moved with such rhythm and joy, like he was the only person in the room. Michael wore a black trucker's cap that night, and he played with it as he danced—tugging and pulling it around, spinning in place.

"You must've worked up a thirst," I had said that night, once Michael left the dance floor. "Can I buy you a drink?"

He froze for a moment, caught off guard. "Sure," he smiled. "I don't think they have what I want, but I'll take a beer."

"What do you want?" I asked.

"I could *really* go for a piña colada right about now," he teased. "But I don't think they make tiki drinks."

I smiled along with his joke. All this bar was known for were kegs of beer and video lottery machines. "Yes, I hear there's a pineapple shortage in the Village," I said. "Tragic really. I guess, tonight, a beer will have to do."

Michael laughed at my dumb joke.

Eleven years. We figured out the math right away. Well, I did. Michael didn't care about age, but I needed to know the difference. I was thirty-six and he was twenty-five. That meant when I came out at twenty-two, Michael was only eleven. Normally, I didn't go for younger guys. Alan had made me realize that I preferred older men. But when I spoke to Michael that night, I felt no age difference. Michael spoke with informed confidence on topics like city planning and the environment, and he knew about things that I didn't, like cars and baseball and overseas manufacturing. He also looked older than the other twenty-somethings in the room, and he dressed less deliberately too, like he had left home wearing whatever was clean. This made sense when I later

48

learned that he made his living as a handyman and that most of his clothes were either tattered or stained.

"Where did you grow up?" I asked. "You're not like the guys I usually meet here."

Michael smiled. "Oh, is this a place to meet guys?"

I smiled back. "You know what I mean."

"I'm from Moncton," he said. "I moved here a few months ago. On my birthday."

"Why'd you choose Montreal?"

"Why? What do you mean why?" He was being playful. "Why do *you* live here?"

"I guess because I grew up here. That, and I love the city."

"What's not to love? Seriously, this place is incredible. Numerous gay bars and people who genuinely like themselves. But honestly, any place is better than Moncton. I mean, have you been?" I shook my head, no. "Such a dead-end town. It tries hard to be Halifax or Toronto, but it's too small and depressing. The downtown is tiny, the buildings are falling apart. Everyone stays put because that's what's expected of them. No one is interested in learning about what life might be like outside the city. I mean, I'd have killed myself if I had to stay there any longer. I couldn't be like my brother—living at home, having my mom cook and clean for me while working the same dead-end job for my dad."

"What's he do?"

"My dad? He's a mechanic. Owns a garage off the Trans-Canada Highway. My brother works there with him—well, all my brothers did at one time. Me too, for a while."

"How many brothers do you have?"

"Three," he said. "One's dead now. Died of a drug overdose when I was a teenager."

"Oh, I'm sorry," I said.

"Don't be," he said, flippant for the first and only time that night. "He was a jerk to me. They all were. How about you? What's your family like?"

"Much smaller. I have one sister, Kate. My dad is retired and lives in Kelowna with his new wife—I say new, but they've been married for eight years. My mother died when I was twenty-one. An accident."

"I'm sorry to hear. What happened?"

"She was a flight attendant," I said. "One morning, on a layover in Chicago, she was on her way to take the train back to the airport when a heavy branch broke off from a tree she was passing under. She died instantly."

Michael looked horrified. "I'm so sorry."

Even after many years, it felt impossible telling this story. "Thanks. I spent my whole youth afraid to lose her in a plane crash, only to have her taken from me in this random way. I mean, how do you protect yourself against something like that?"

Michael seemed at a loss for what to say, and I felt it too. It was too soon for us to probe such depths. Even though I was curious to learn more about his family life, his brothers, his past, there would hopefully be time for that. Right now, all I wanted to do was flirt, to revel in these first moments of getting drunk on each other's smiles and brushing arms as our elbows kept our beers company at the bar. As we spoke, I noticed that Michael had to stay on my right and would reposition himself every time I moved. "What? Sorry," he ultimately said, "I don't hear too well out of that ear." Then Michael told me about the car accident that happened when he was five—how an airbag had exploded near his head, which resulted in some hearing loss in his right ear. "Not enough to warrant a hearing aid, but some days I wonder if my parents should've got me one."

"Want to go some place quieter?"

We walked the seven blocks to my home and I gave him a quick tour of my apartment. Michael spent time examining the art on my walls and showed me a few of his sketches in a notebook he kept in his backpack. He put on my slippers and drank juice from the carton in my fridge. He cuddled with my cat—only Sutherland at this time—as we got acquainted on the sofa. Once we started to kiss, Michael wasted no time pulling off my clothes. "What are we listening to?" he asked, tossing my shirt in the corner.

"You've never heard of Bronski Beat?"

"Should I have?"

Maybe this wasn't a good idea, I thought. He's too young. But then that thought disappeared as we continued to kiss and the CD came to an end. In the following silence, I became too preoccupied to put on more music. All I wanted to hear was his breath, the sound of his skin upon mine. I was surprised at myself, at how Michael's young body filled me with such desire; and I was thrown by his hunger for me too. Michael was voracious in his pleasure, but also loving and tender. He held my face as we kissed and he focused on my eyes as we fucked. "I love that you have brown eyes," he said to me afterwards, as he rolled himself a joint at the foot of my bed.

"Why?" I asked, noticing that his were green.

"Because I feel like I can trust them."

After his smoke we went at it again, and by the time we were done and the sky was getting light, Michael's body no longer felt like a stranger's. He stayed over. He didn't ask if he could, nor did I offer. We just fell asleep in the positions we'd collapsed in. At some point I got us under the covers and I spooned him, softly strumming the few hairs on his chest like the strings of a guitar. And when I awoke, I loved how he looked wrapped in my sheets. How, when he got up, his strong body would crack like the floors of a cottage, like a roof under the weight of falling snow. It was too soon, but I knew that I wanted Michael to live nowhere else but here, his head nuzzled deep into my chest.

There was no sign of the guy in the Lady Gaga T-shirt so I left the dance floor and headed back to the bar. On my way, I ran into Michael.

"Hello, buddy!"

"Hi, buddy."

"Sorry, I'm late."

I glanced at my watch. "You're not late. The clinic isn't even open yet... Want a drink?"

"I got it," he said. "You want anything?"

I shook my head.

The new bartender was gone and in his place was a familiar one. "Hey, Dad," Michael said to George.

"Hey, kid," George said, and gave Michael a kiss on the cheek. George nodded at me. "Paul. What can I get you boys?" I shook my head; Michael ordered a beer.

"Why do you call him that?" I asked, once George had walked away.

"Look at him. Doesn't he look like he could be my dad?"

In his late fifties, George was a legend. He had bartended at all of the city's most renowned gay bars over the years— Garage, K.O.X., and Sécurité Maximum—and throughout remained in incredible shape, dazzling the generations of men who waited to order their drinks from him. On this night, he looked as attractive as ever, a solid chest of grey the focal point of any man who approached the bar.

"You know," Michael said, "if you're looking for something to get me for my birthday this year, it would be a Paul and George sandwich."

"What?" I teased. "No Ringo or John?"

Michael laughed. "You and your jokes. Don't be silly."

I laughed too. "Come on, wouldn't that be weird?" I asked. "Both your dads?"

"You're not my dad, you're my man."

We sat down at a nearby table, and I asked Michael about his day. He pulled out his wallet and thrust a wad of twenties at me. "Here, this is for Provincetown," he said. "And I'm buying us dinner tonight. Nowhere too fancy. I didn't have time to go home and change." I shoved the money into my front pocket, not counting it, relieved to have more for the bank.

As Michael pulled back his head to take a swig from his beer, I noticed a thin gold chain around his neck. "Where'd you get this?" I asked, and reached to examine it.

Michael grabbed at it too, pulling it further out on top of his shirt. "It was in the box of stuff I shipped from my folks. I got it for my confirmation as a kid. I took the cross off. I like the way it looks without it."

Suddenly, from behind, a gate was pulled to the side

and another section of the bar opened up. This room was better lit and there was a table and a set of chairs off to the side. Immediately, Michael and I stood up and headed over. I wasn't sure if anyone else was here for an STI test, but I wanted us to be the first. "Bonjour," I said to the nurse.

"Bonjour."

The two of us sat down. The nurse was an older man with a dyed black beard and horn-rimmed glasses. He was francophone, so we spoke to him in French. *Are you together?* he asked. "Oui." *Do you want to do the tests at the same time?* "Oui." *These tests remain anonymous,* he said, *but we keep track of the information so we can communicate the results to you.* He asked us questions about our sexual history. *How long have you been together?* "Un peu plus de trois ans." *Are you monogamous?* "Oui." *Do you practise safe sex?* "Oui." *Oral sex?* "Oui." *Anal sex?* "Oui." *Always with a condom?* "Toujours." *Do you take drugs?* "Non." *Just pot,* Michael added. He continued down the list of personal history questions until the nurse took out the vials for blood samples and put on his rubber gloves.

I was the first, an old pro by now. I unbuttoned the cuff on my right arm and rolled up my sleeve. The lighting was bright in this section of the bar, so the nurse had no trouble finding my vein. I looked away from the vial and concentrated on the walls of the room. Seeing the space like this reminded me of high school drama class—the sets, the props, the dark paint. When it was Michael's turn, I could see him sweat and turn red and look away as the needle slid in. Then he laid his head down on the table and passed out for a moment.

"Est-ce que ça va?" the nurse asked. After a beat, Michael

raised his head and the colour returned to his face. A cotton swab went over the puncture hole and the nurse asked Michael to press his finger at the site to stop the blood. He gave us both a card and asked us to call back in four days.

4

THE NEXT MORNING, I got up early. I had set my alarm for five, but awoke minutes before it went off. Careful not to rouse Michael, I slipped out of the sheets and put on my bathrobe. We had gone off to bed holding hands—like otters, Michael had said—but at some point separated, and I woke up in the middle of the night freezing cold with the covers off. Michael was often too hot to touch when he slept, and sometimes I had to stuff a pillow between us or sleep on top of the blankets if I got too warm. I often wondered what went on in there. Why all that churning inside that restless young body?

At this hour, our home was cold and dark. I crept into the kitchen and fixed myself a bowl of cereal and boiled water for tea. I took my breakfast into the living room where I settled on the couch with a blanket. I turned on the TV, making sure the volume was low, and flipped to the station playing the wedding.

I had set my PVR to record the entire thing—the pre-show, the arrival at the church, the ceremony—but I wanted to catch some of Prince William and Catherine Middleton's wedding live. I have this fond memory, from when I was a kid, of getting up at the crack of dawn with my mother and sister to watch Prince Charles marry Lady Di. Our mom was obsessed with Princess Diana, as well as the Queen and the rest of the Royals. I'd often find her reading unauthorized biographies about the family or collecting commemorative dishes for her curio cabinet. And every year, when we were little, she'd make us gather to listen to the Queen's Christmas Day broadcast. When I reached my teens, I asked her what it was about the Royal Family she liked so much. She told me she had been fascinated by monarchs and kingdoms ever since she was a young girl; there was something about tradition and ceremony and history that enchanted her, and as a result she had developed a keen reverence, as well as great pity, for modern nobility.

When Princess Diana died years later, I finally understood. I was surprised to find my sister and me devastated, ripped out of the late-night movie we were watching when the news broke. Diana's violent end brought us back to the death of our mother four years earlier. It was odd, watching the funeral a week later, seeing the sad faces of her two children and knowing what they were going through. Soon after, Kate and I found ourselves sharing random news about the Royal Family on our phone calls. It started out simple enough, a way to remember our mother. But then Kate began reading mom's dusty old biographies and I started purchasing copies of *Hello* and *Majesty*.

Sutherland showed up in the living room, sitting tall and staring at me and my breakfast. "Hey, buddy. Feel like joining me?" I asked, and moved over to make room for him on the blanket. Sutherland jumped up and curled into a ball next to me, and together we sat and watched as motorcades of black cars pulled up to Westminster Abbey and the aristocracy emerged to the clamouring sounds of church bells and cheers from the public. Everyone looked well-dressed, graceful, perfect. If my mom were alive, she would have loved it: the fairy tale, a dream for her children.

Soon, the commentator announced the arrival of the Duke of York and I watched as a Rolls-Royce pulled up and out came Prince Andrew in full naval regalia followed by his two daughters. "Oh my stars," I said, my mouth filled with cereal. "Sutherland, will you look at that?" Princess Eugenie and Princess Beatrice had emerged from the back of the car holding on to their headwear—Eugenie with a small blue heart-shaped hat, and Beatrice wearing some godawful beige contraption that looked like an upended toilet seat.

My cell phone rang, loud and vicious at this time in the morning. "Hello?"

"Are you watching this?" It was my sister, Kate.

"I wondered if you were up."

"I've been up since four-thirty. I couldn't sleep."

"I just started. What the hell is on Beatrice's head?"

"It's called a fascinator. Princess Kate wears them all the time. But poor Beatrice. Someone should have told her that her headpiece looks like an alien vagina."

"Kate!"

"Well it does. Have you seen William yet?

"No, not yet."

"He looks so handsome. He's wearing the Irish Guards uniform—you know, the red tunic, but with an Order of the Garter sash. Very striking. His mom would've been proud.

I can't wait to see the dress, but I think I'm going to have to head out. Busy day. Anyway, I'm calling to see if we're still on for tonight."

"Yes. At seven? Where you staying?"

"The Queen Elizabeth."

"Of course you are."

"But we can meet anywhere."

"How about the hotel bar?" I suggested. "Seems like the perfect place for today."

Kate agreed. We said our goodbyes and I hung up.

I continued to watch for another few minutes before I left Sutherland on the couch to go for a run in the morning dew. Returning home, I took a hot shower and assembled my look for the day from the clean clothes hanging on the drying rack in our living room. It would be a busy day for me, too. The agency I worked for repped a new line of household cleaning products, and we had an important client presentation scheduled for that afternoon.

This job was very different from my previous ones. I had spent much of my twenties and early thirties working for non-profits, promoting their activities and social programs. But then, a number of years ago, I got fed up with all the bureaucracy and infighting and made the leap to the corporate sector. I was surprised at how much easier working in media relations was at a marketing agency. Somehow, I had fewer egos to deal with and my boss left me alone to complete my tasks. The money was good too.

Kate also worked for a big company. She was a senior brand manager for a popular Canadian clothing line and lived in Ottawa with her husband, Christian. When she first moved there ten years ago, when Christian landed a plum job with the federal government, I thought she'd be bored. At the time, Kate's work experience had consisted of stints as a bartender and a keyboardist in a horror-themed ska band called The Bloody Skanks. But then she found this job that allowed her to combine her university degree with her love of fashion and travel. I thought back to when we were both in our twenties: me with my activism, her with her music. We were such different people now.

The day was long and hard, but not without its accomplishments. After wrapping up the client presentation, I ran across town to meet Kate for drinks at Les Voyageurs, the bar lounge in the Queen Elizabeth Hotel. The place was thick with money—plush carpets, dark drapes and large leather club chairs. Kate was at a table when I arrived, dressed for work: black pantsuit and expensive shoes with her long straight brown hair worn down past her shoulders. She was drinking whisky, neat. "Order whatever you want," she said, after we had hugged hello. "I'm expensing this."

Sitting down, I ordered a Perrier from our waiter.

"Perrier? Why Perrier?"

I shrugged. "Don't feel like drinking. Did you catch any more of the ceremony?"

"A little," she said, sipping her drink. "The dress was *gorgeous*. Did you see the sleeves? The perfect combination of tradition and modernity—much like Grace Kelly's wedding dress but with a distinct McQueen flair. She's stunning. I'm going to watch it all from the start as soon as I get home."

"How were your meetings?"

"Fine. Mostly ins-and-outs with partners." Kate looked

at what remained of her drink, twisting her lips. "But actually, Paul, I'm not here just for work."

"No?"

"No… Remember the last time I came to town?" she said. "About a month ago? You couldn't make it. Something about a friend's birthday? Well, I ended up going out with Karen for dinner that night, and she took me dancing—I hadn't been out dancing in years. We went to this party her friend was throwing at Le Passeport. We had a great time. There were a bunch of people from the old days too—Joyce and Melissa, and a few I remembered from my days in the band. Anyway, as I was about to leave this guy came up to me and asked for my number."

"Really?" I said, nodding my thanks to the waiter who had delivered my drink.

"He was super charming. I couldn't remember the last time a guy hit on me in a bar," she continued. "I tried to be funny, brush off his flirtatious comments with a joke, but he wouldn't let up. He was sweet and handsome and…"

I choked on my first sip. "Kate?"

"I gave him my number. I couldn't believe it, but I did. I smiled and didn't say much and then left. We've been chatting ever since."

"Oh my god."

"His name's Ben. He's thirty-five. Works as a financial advisor for TD Bank, but he's got this other side too. He's a writer. He hasn't published anything yet, but he's working on his first novel—a mystery. He also works with wood and makes small pieces of furniture in his spare time. You wouldn't think he was a banker either. He's got a shaved head and all of these tattoos on his back and arms he has to hide when he goes to work."

"Kate, are you telling me you're here to visit him?"

"I arrived yesterday. We spent the evening together, and then this morning. He called in sick and we watched part of the wedding together. I ended up cancelling my first meeting too. I couldn't pull myself away. Do you remember the last time you couldn't get out of bed?"

I sat there with my mouth open, part shocked and part horrified. My sister was having an affair! "I don't know, Kate," I said. "I mean, yes, I do remember that feeling. Although it's been a while for me too."

"Has it been two years?"

"Two years?"

"Yes, two years." She finished off the whisky in her glass. "Two years of no sex. At first I thought it was because of all the doctors' appointments and medical procedures. We really had taken all the fun and romance out of trying to make a baby. Sex became a chore. But then, once we realized it wasn't going to happen, we never started up again. And it's not because I didn't want to—I did! I wanted to be touched and held and feel like a person again, but Chris never wanted it. There was always an excuse. And then I stopped asking. At night we would sit at home and watch cooking shows. Or I would work late. And I forgot what it was like to have a sex life."

Kate caught the eye of our waiter and ordered another whisky. I decided I needed a stiff drink too and ordered one with her. "So, you've slept with him?"

Kate's head rolled back along with her eyes. "Yes, oh god, yes. And it was good! So good, Paul. I had forgotten what it was like—when you first meet someone and can't keep your hands off of them? That all-encompassing, earth-shattering, physical connection? I got here yesterday evening and that's all we did. I don't think I've ever met anyone who's been my match, sexually. You know me. I've been around the block. I was in a band. God, I was a lesbian for six months in the nineties. But a part of me seemed to disappear with Chris. We may have started out as two young punks hooking up at shows, but somehow we got caught up in the whole marriage/ suburban life thing. And then, when the kid thing didn't happen, we didn't know what to do next... I'm forty-one, Paul. I'm still young. But I keep asking myself: What do I want the rest of my life to look like? And I don't know the answer."

Our drinks came and we both took quick sips. "Jesus," I said, the whisky burning a hole through the surprise I felt. "What about Christian? Does he know?"

"Of course Chris doesn't know!"

"Are you going to tell him?"

"Are you nuts? He'd flip."

"But, I mean, can't you talk to him about how you're feeling?"

Kate sighed and shook her head. "I've tried to talk to him about it. Tried to get him to come to couples' counselling, but he won't. He doesn't think we have a problem. He's happy to sit in front of the TV all night, downing beer after beer and falling asleep in his chair. These days he feels more like a roommate than a husband."

This made me sad to hear. I liked Christian. I liked him better than any of Kate's previous boyfriends. The first time we met, he was so nervous about making a good impression that he brought me flowers and sweated through his dress shirt at the dinner table. I had been surprised, though, that my sister ended up with a guy like him. Christian may have been smart and attractive, but he was dull. Not the type she usually went for. When he proposed and Kate accepted, we were all taken aback. I never thought Kate wanted to get married, but she quickly took to being a bride-to-be and then a wife. I had forgotten how much of a wild and free spirit she once was, and now this free spirit was awake and at the table.

"Listen, I don't know how long this thing is going to last," she said. "It could be weeks, could be just this once. But I have to allow myself to do this. I have to allow myself to have this experience and listen to my body and do what's right for *me*. It might not win me any medals—with Chris or Dad or Debbie, or with you—but I have no choice. I have to be true to who I am, Paul, even if other people are hurt by it. I hope you can understand that."

Of course I understood that. How could I not? It may have been a long time ago, but I once had felt that way too—in the small bedroom of the suburban home we grew up in, sitting with the all-consuming urge to kiss boys instead of girls. Kate was the first person I had come out to, and once I did she was my fierce champion. Kate had my back before anyone else, defending me when my dad was unsure how to feel and speaking up at extended family gatherings if someone made a disparaging remark about gays. Hell, she even bought me my first issue of *Numbers* magazine when I was too afraid to walk into the adult bookstore to get it myself. How could I fault her for listening to desire?

"I do understand," I said. "Completely. I just don't want you to get hurt."

"I don't plan on getting hurt," she said, serious. "But if I do, at least I will have felt *something*. I have forgotten what it's like to feel. It's like I'd been erased. But now, after all this time, I can feel my outline coming back." Looking determined, she put her glass down. "Listen, I know we said we'd go for dinner, but I leave early tomorrow morning and I want to see Ben again."

"You're an animal," I said, trying to add levity.

"You have no idea." Kate smiled. "He's insatiable. He's thirty-five. I hardly remember what it's like to be thirty-five. I used to tease you about Michael being young, but now I understand. Michael's what, twenty-eight now? You have all these years of great sex ahead of you."

I didn't say anything. Maybe on another night I'd talk with my sister about our sex life, but not tonight. "Listen Kate," I said. "I also have something to tell you. Something good."

"Well," she said, eager. "What is it?"

I told my sister about my dinner with Wendy and Eve, and what they had asked of me. I said it as fast as I could, checking her face for signs of sadness or disappointment. All I could see, though, was polite surprise and a bit of reserved joy. "That's great, Paul!" she said, once I was done. "How do you feel? You must be excited."

"I am. Really, really happy."

"What's your relationship going to be like? Are you going to be the dad?"

"Well no, not the dad. The uncle. Or maybe the *spunkle*,

as we were joking." Kate didn't laugh, so I felt stupid telling the joke again. "But the child will know where they come from. Who I am. Who you are."

That got her excited. "Does this mean I get to be an aunt?"

"Yes, of course. And they want Dad and Debbie to be grandparents too. I just won't be *the dad.*"

I could see a puzzled frown form on her forehead; I kept talking. "Really, it's all such new and uncharted territory. There are still things for us to work out, but Wendy and Eve want us to be involved. Kate, I didn't think I'd ever get to do this."

"Did you tell Dad or Debbie?"

"No. Not yet," I said. "I had to tell you first. But honestly, I don't want Debbie in my ear right now. I don't want anyone saying anything to get me to change my mind."

"I don't know how Patrick and Sue do it," Kate said, referring to our stepbrother and stepsister, who also lived in Kelowna, blocks from where our dad lived with their mother. "They seem so well adjusted."

"Or so we think." Kate and I had met Debbie's kids only once; at her wedding to our father. They were ten years younger than us (with the same number of years between them). Sometimes, when I thought of Patrick and Sue, I'd imagine them as alternate-universe versions of Kate and me: conservative and churchgoing, each married to their high school sweethearts and not doing anything to disappoint their families. "Have you spoken to them recently?"

"Who?"

"Dad and Debbie."

66

"A few days ago," Kate said. "I'm heading to Vancouver next month for work and going to make a quick stop in Kelowna to see them on the way home… When do you start?"

"If all goes well, soon. June, I think."

I looked again at my sister, searching for any cracks in her armour that might show how she truly felt. "You sure you're okay with all this?" I asked.

"Of course I'm okay. How could I not be?"

"I don't know, I thought this might be tough."

"Listen, just because I can't have kids doesn't mean you shouldn't." Kate finished off her second whisky. "Listen, let's get another round to celebrate," she said, lifting her glass. "Then I've got a date to get to."

After we were done, I said goodnight to Kate and headed home. I texted and called Michael several times to tell him I was on my way, but there was no answer. Why did he insist on keeping his phone on silent?

It's moments like this—when I can't reach Michael, or haven't heard from him in a while—that the worst flashes through my head. I know it's unlikely, but sometimes I think that maybe he's hurt, or been in an accident or got arrested for smoking pot. It was bad when we first met and he was still skateboarding. My imagination would go to a dark place where I would see Michael's limp body being surrounded by strangers—passersby in the street who had seen what had happened and would stay with Michael until the ambulance came.

It was like that when my mom was alive too. I hated her job. I hated knowing that she spent her days trapped in a metal fuselage travelling 35,000 feet above the ground at top speed. Sometimes, I'd get these unwelcome thoughts of the plane crashing. A scenario would find its way to weasel into my brain and show me images of the aircraft losing control and my mother having to take her jump seat, spending the last few moments of her life in fear and thinking about me and my sister. I don't know where these images came from, but they'd present themselves without warning and refuse to go away.

For a while I tried to negotiate with them, force myself to finish my homework or clean the house from top to bottom in exchange for her safe arrival. Then I'd wait for the call from her to come in, telling me that she had arrived at her destination. It wasn't much different than the calls she asked me to make when I was young and would head off to play at a friend's house. "Call me when you get there," she'd say as I ran out the door. It was a simple ask, one I wished Michael understood. I always checked in with my mother. I never saw her concern as an intrusion. It was just a way to show her love—like telling me to drive safe every time I borrowed the car. After she was gone, I found that I missed those requests the most. There was no one to worry about me in the same way any more.

By the time I got home, though, my worry had turned to annoyance. I could see from the street that the lights were on. I walked in to find Gus over and the two of them on the couch drinking beer, painting their nails and watching TV on mute with music playing.

"Hi, buddy!" Michael shouted.

"Is your phone dead? I've been trying to call you."

"Oh, sorry. I probably left it in the kitchen."

"Hi, Gus," I said.

"Hi, Paul." Gus sat on the floor, painting his left thumb-nail a bright red. The two were watching the recording of the wedding.

"Did you see Beatrice's crazy hat?" Michael asked. "It's hideous."

"They all look like they got birds stuck in their hair," Gus added.

"But the cars are *gorgeous*," Michael went on. "All these custom-built Bentleys. Now that's money!" Michael drained his beer. I looked at my watch. It was 8:30 p.m. How long would his friend be over? "Gus, do you want another beer?" Michael asked, and got up to head to the kitchen. "Babe? Want anything?"

I hadn't eaten, but it was too late now. Perhaps I'd have a piece of toast. "No, thanks." Michael kissed me and left the room. I sat down with Gus and reached for the remote. "Mind if I turn this up?" I asked, adding volume. Gus reached over to turn the music off.

"I have your money, Paul," Gus said, reaching into his pocket and pulling out a wad of cash. Gus, too, would be coming with us to Provincetown. I liked Gus enough to invite him, but I had invited him more for Michael's sake. Gus was three years older than Michael, but had only come out six years earlier. However, he was making up for it, transforming himself from a video game–playing recluse living in his parents' basement to a free-loving party promoter. I figured, with Gus there, the two boys could bounce off each other's energy while the elders played house.

"Thanks," I said, pocketing the money.

Michael walked back into the room and handed over the beer to his friend. He checked the screen of his phone, now in his hand, and saw all the messages from me. "Sorry babe... My mom called too."

Michael called in to his voicemail, Gus and I watching the ceremony. "Holy shit," Michael said, putting down the phone. "My mom left my dad."

5

I WAS IN THE KITCHEN, washing dishes, when I heard the barks come up the stairs. I barked back and Malone went running to the front. The door to our home squeaked open and closed.

"Hi, buddy!" Michael shouted from down the hall.

"Hi, buddy," I hollered back.

It was a hot and muggy June day, and Michael had returned home from his new job, working the afternoon shift at a nearby coffee shop called Café Minnelli. The place was run by two gay men in their early thirties who had painted the walls black and white and hung framed pictures of Liza Minnelli everywhere. Michael had got the job by becoming a regular and making the owners laugh. His role was to fix things, clean dishes, work the cash register and, at times, make coffee. It wasn't full-time, and he was often on call, but it was perfect for him; it provided a base from which to work and a promise of a couple hundred bucks a week if he was lucky.

"It's so hot in here," he said, walking into the kitchen with Malone propped on his left shoulder. Michael kissed me hello and steadied the cat. Malone looked uncertain about the situation, his paws hooked around Michael's neck.

"Who's my little buddy?" Michael said, petting under his chin. "Who's a happy cat?"

"I'm not sure he likes that," I said, my hands in the sink.

"He's purring, isn't he?"

Michael gave the cat a big kiss on his forehead and placed him down on the floor. He opened the screen door to the balcony and dragged the running fan I had directed on me towards the outside. "You should point it away from you," he said. "To pull the hot air out of the room." Michael turned towards the refrigerator. "I'm famished," he said, opening the door. "Is there anything in here?"

I had just cleaned out the fridge. "There's an apple in the top drawer if you're hungry."

Michael grimaced and closed the door behind him.

"How much time do you need to get ready?" I asked.

Michael grabbed a sailor's cap from his back pocket and pulled it on his head. "I'm ready now."

"You're not wearing that out, are you?"

"Oh yes I am," Michael beamed. "Wore it at work all day too."

I shook my head and smiled. "I hope you got good tips. Some mail came for you," I said, and gestured towards the kitchen island. Michael picked up the letter. It was from the federal government. "You going to open it?"

Michael dropped the letter like it was diseased. "Nope. Not now and not before a joint, that's for sure."

"Ok, but do you mind finishing up here first?" It had been hot the last few days and neither of us had felt like doing dishes. I had made headway with the pile, but there were about a dozen left. "I have to change."

Michael rolled up his sleeves and reached for the sponge. "Been doing them all day, what's a few more?"

I headed off to the bedroom to find something clean and cool to wear. Sutherland was on the bed and watched as I changed into a pair of jean shorts, which still felt strange to pull up over boxers. I took off my T-shirt and began rummaging through my dresser drawer, looking for a tank top. I found one buried at the bottom—navy blue and not too tight—but before I had a chance to put it on, I heard a sharp ring and the word "Fuck" being spat out from the kitchen.

I ran back to where I had left Michael, the tank top in my hand. "What? What's wrong?"

The blood had drained from Michael's face. "I broke your mug," he said, standing over the sink. I looked into the silver basin. The "My Queen" coffee mug my sister had given me lay in chunks at the bottom. "I'm so, so sorry. It slipped out of my hands."

I felt a sudden rush of anger staring at the fragments. The mug had broken into five jagged pieces. I picked them up, one by one, out of the sink and placed them on the counter. Then I counted to three… I wanted to get mad at Michael, at his carelessness; but as I looked at him in his sailor hat, a terrible expression of guilt and sadness visible on his long pale face, my anger began to dissipate. "It's okay," I said, breathing through my words, not believing them yet. "It's just a thing… Did you hurt yourself?"

"No." Michael pulled off his hat. His face was slick with sweat.

"Don't worry about it," I said, suddenly over it. "It was an accident. It's not like you did this on purpose, Michael."

The words came back to me. "It's just a thing."

He examined the pieces. "I can try and fix it."

"No, it's all right." I made him put them down. We were going to be late. "Listen, if I wanted to keep the mug forever, I would have stored it away and never used it. But no, I wanted to use it, and I did—often." I could tell he wasn't convinced. "It's fine, Michael. Really. Now go smoke your joint so we can get out of here."

Michael walked out of the kitchen towards the office, and I stayed behind to finish the dishes and rinse out the sink. What to do with the pieces? Throw them out? I decided to leave them on the counter for now and feed the cats instead. They came running as soon as they heard the electric can opener.

Michael soon emerged from the office and closed the door behind him. He was quiet but wearing his sailor cap again. "Ready?" I asked, and he nodded.

We left and headed down to Michael's car, parked in front of our building. "Someone needs a wash," I said, before we got in.

"Have you seen the road work happening in the city? I'm constantly driving through dust clouds." Michael turned on the ignition and pulled out of his parking spot into traffic. I watched and waited for him to reach over and pull on his seatbelt, which he only did after driving a block.

Michael's car was a 1986 white BMW 325i that he nicknamed Baby. He had bought it used, with help from his father, back in Moncton when he was twenty-one, and proceeded to add 80,000 kilometres to it before packing up his life and driving it to Montreal. Michael's love of cars was one of the

74

first things I had learned about him the night we met. I knew nothing about cars, nor did I have any interest in them, but still, on our second date, I surprised Michael with tickets to the Auto Show. It was fun to watch him freak out as we walked into Palais des Congrès, losing his mind on the new models on display. "That's what you get, growing up around 'grease monkeys," he said.

I didn't get to meet Baby right away. Michael kept her off the road in the winter, in a heated parking garage, and only brought her out once the salt was off the road and the potholes were filled. She was a battered old car, with frayed seats and stickers of nineties alternative rock bands pockmarking her dash, but Michael drove her like she was an extension of his body, popping the clutch, making U-turns, burning through yellows, passing slow drivers. There was a handle above me on the passenger side that he called my "Oh shit! handle," as I would often instinctively reach for it whenever he merged into traffic or made a sharp turn. Somehow, though, I never felt unsafe when he drove. Michael had such faith in his car, and that faith had been earned; she had got him through rough times. He would never take her off the road, and he intended to be buried in that car.

Heading down Saint Denis Street, we arrived at a light and stopped. There was a young man with a squeegee approaching cars and asking for money. Michael reached for his wallet and handed over some loose change before the light turned green.

"That was sweet of you," I said.

"Don't," he snapped. Although it warmed my heart every time Michael showed compassion to someone less fortunate, my loving pride always made him uncomfortable. "Do you mind if I borrow a few bucks for gas?"

I took a look at the fuel gauge, the needle dipping below E. "Sure," I said. "Maybe get her a wash too?"

As we neared our destination, Michael pulled into the service station off Ontario Street to gas up. I took a few minutes, while I waited, to open my phone and check the apps. We were in the Village now and there was a whole new roster of faces looking to connect, Danny and Charles among them.

"Thanks," Michael said, getting back into the car once he was done and returning my credit card. "I'll pay you back."

We pulled up to the automatic carwash. Michael keyed in the number to the machine and the door's jaw opened—the roar and whir of the contraption coming to life. We rolled up the windows and Michael manoeuvred Baby inside. He pulled the parking brake. There was a deep thud and with it the sound of equipment locking into position. I looked up from my phone to watch the spray of foamy soap: red, yellow and green; the gusts of water blasting away the suds like rain, causing a river to cascade down the wind-shield around and above us. "It's like being in a washing machine," Michael said.

Music played on the radio—fun, muffled pop. I soon felt queasy, the smell of the stale air in the car making my stomach churn. "Can you get carbon monoxide poisoning in here?" I asked.

"What?" he asked over the clamour of music and machine, his good ear now turned towards me. I repeated myself. "Sure, I suppose it's possible," he answered. "If you stay in here too long."

I went back to my phone and checked my text messages.

There was one from Michael's mother from earlier in the day. "I forgot to tell you, your mom texted me."

"She texted me too. I called her on my break."

"How is she?"

"Fine. She's at my aunt's place in Saint John now. It'd be great if she could find a place there to live or move in with her sister's family—if they'd invite her, that is. She's looking forward to her visit. Wanted to know if we needed anything."

"She asked me the same. I told her just to bring herself. I was thinking though, we should get an air mattress."

"No, my mom will be fine on the couch," Michael said.

"Or maybe the two of you could share our bed and I could take the couch."

"Please, Paul, no. I'm not sleeping in the same bed as my mother. She'll be fine on the couch."

"I just thought she'd be more comfortable."

"She's only coming for five days and we have this nice new couch that she can sleep on. I fell asleep on it the other day, and I was fine."

"If you say so."

There was a loud beep and a change in the light, signalling us to move to the next position. Michael took off the parking brake and we moved forward to another noise that demanded we stop again. The car dried as a funnelling heat blew onto the hood, roof and windshield, sending water droplets out in all directions. The door to the exit unlocked and rose, and we pulled out onto the open street.

Charles and Danny were at the bar when we arrived, sitting on stools at a tall table by the window. "You're wearing it!" Charles cried out when he saw Michael in the sailor's cap.

Michael kissed our friends on both cheeks. "Of course I'm wearing it," he said. "I love it! Been wearing it all week."

"Is that one of the ones I think it is?" I asked, pulling up a stool. One Halloween, Charles had dressed himself, Alan and me up as three sailors for a party in the Village.

"Yep," he said. "That hat's seen some crazy things in its day." Charles's attention was diverted by an incoming text. "But I've started to downsize," he said, grabbing his phone to type up a response. "I've way too much stuff now."

Charles's closet was a treasure trove of costumes, accessories and props, all collected over decades working wardrobe at Black Theatre Workshop and the clubs along Sainte Catherine Street East. Now in his mid-fifties, he didn't take them out as often, but we knew they were there. We had worn them ourselves over the years—at parties, Pride, public demonstrations, or at one of his infamous *souper des femmes* where a dozen of us would dress in drag and drink our dinner. It was Alan who had introduced us. The two of them were old friends and exes. I don't think Charles liked me at the beginning; he was protective of his friend and thought I might be trouble. But that concern, of course, was unfounded. I feel fortunate we've remained close over the years.

"Well, feel free to pass along anything else you think I might like," Michael said, adjusting his hat. "I grew up with older brothers, so I'm used to hand-me-downs."

I noticed that Danny wore Andre's T-shirt, the same one he had said he was going to donate to the church. "Speaking of hand-me-downs, I didn't realize you were such a Ramones fan."

Danny huffed. "More of a fan of stealing my ex-boyfriend's shirts."

"I don't think you can call Andre an ex-boyfriend," I teased. "Are you wearing it in case you run into him?"

"Oh, I couldn't care less," Danny said, flicking his wrist as if shooing away an invisible annoyance. "It's a shame to let such a great T-shirt go to waste, so I kept it when I donated his other stuff."

"Before I forget," Charles interrupted, reaching for the knapsack at his feet. "Here." He pulled out a complete DVD set of *The Mary Tyler Moore Show* and handed it over the table to Michael.

"Yay!" Michael eagerly took the box and looked it over. "Thank you! I'm sorry, I meant to return the last one you lent me."

"Exposing him to the classics?" Danny asked. "What was on last week's syllabus?"

Charles almost sang the title. "*Mahogany*."

"Loved it," Michael said.

"I so wanted to be Diana Ross when I first saw it as a kid in Baltimore," Charles said. "Did you know she designed the costumes for the film too?"

Michael was impressed. "Really?"

"I can see that," Danny said. "You're kind of like her character. Industrious and talented, escaping the gritty streets of America for the faux-European ateliers of Montreal. All that's missing is a handsome Billy Dee Williams to walk you home."

"Well, he did get in her way," Michael said. He turned and

asked if he could borrow a few bucks for drinks. I opened my wallet and gave him a twenty. "What can I get you?" he asked, and I requested a bottle of sparkling water. Michael went off to the bar, where George greeted him with a broad smile.

"Still not drinking?" Danny asked. "How in the hell are we going to celebrate?"

"Celebrate what?" I asked.

"There are *so many* things to celebrate," Danny said. "Summer's here, dad shorts are back, Beyoncé's new album, your upcoming birthday. So glisten…"

"I'm glistening."

"What's the plan for your fortieth?"

"What do you mean, *What's the plan*? We're going to Provincetown."

"That's at the end of August. *Besides* that. What do you want to do on the day of?"

It was the middle of June and we were still seven weeks from my birthday. "I don't know. I haven't thought about it much. I'll probably host a small dinner."

Danny was disappointed. "That's it?"

"I'll have it catered. Ten people max."

"I'd like to see the guest list before I confirm."

"You're not going to hook up at my birthday party," I said to Danny. "You already know everyone I know. It'll be the four of us. My sister probably. And I'll invite Wendy and Eve, although I don't think they'll come. We don't know how long this baby-making is going to take, so they're saving all their vacation days for insemination—"

"Me too," Danny interjected.

"—but who knows, maybe Wendy's cycle will sync up

80

and it'll end up being a birthday conception. Or, maybe it'll work on the first go and she'll be pregnant by then."

It had been ten weeks since my dinner with Wendy and Eve, and we were finally ready to start trying. In that time, I had done all they had asked of me. I had switched to boxers and ate pumpkin seeds. I drank litres of water and avoided soy and alcohol. I took daily vitamins and stuffed my diet with folate, fibre-rich carbs and antioxidants. I took an STI test and even went to a private clinic to have my sperm checked. The results arrived three weeks later. When I opened the envelope, I tried to glean information from the numbers. My sperm got a grade of 43.8. Was that good? The only thing I was able to tell from the two pages of columns was that the colour was "off-white" and the viscosity was "normal." Wendy reassured me, though, that everything was where it needed to be and that we were ready for the first attempt.

"So, that's this weekend?" Charles asked.

"Tomorrow," I said. "Wendy and Eve are driving up in the morning, but we're not telling too many people so please keep it to yourself for now."

There was another notification burst on Charles's phone. "Honey," he said, reading it, "I am the soul of discretion."

Of that, I had no doubt. Charles could always be trusted with a secret, and he was often cagey or quiet about his own personal affairs. I rarely knew who was on the other side of the texts and messages that competed for his attention every time we got together. Charles rarely introduced us to the men he dated. He talked about them, sure, but they might as well have been characters in a favourite new book he was reading. After a while, it was hard to tell the difference between a Scott or a Russell or a Trevor he had met online. The one thing they all had in common, we knew without asking, was that they were young.

"Hot date tonight?" I asked.

Charles smiled as he put his phone down next to his pint. "Kevin. He's an actor I met on set." For the last five years, Charles had worked as a costume designer for film and television, and he was currently working on a 1980s-era crime drama being shot by a French-Canadian filmmaker whose last release had won a slew of awards. "It's amazing how much time there is to kill between scenes. He was bored and lonely, so he found me on the apps and *voilà*."

"Sounds promising," I said, looking over my shoulder to see what was keeping Michael. He was still at the bar, with both of our drinks in front of him, now talking to someone I didn't recognize. This man was older than me, with a shaved head and a trim grey beard; there were smiles on both of their faces.

"Well, Kevin plays the gay son of a judge taking bribes from the mafia," Charles said. "Let's just say it doesn't end well for him."

Michael and the man turned their heads and looked in my direction. It was then that Michael pointed at me; I smiled and nodded, then looked back towards my friends.

"What I don't get is how these young men just throw themselves at you," Danny said to Charles, exasperated. "I mean, where do you meet them?"

"Mostly on the apps," Charles said, glancing again at his phone. "I swear, apps and antiretrovirals saved my sex life."

Danny shook his head. "No, the apps don't work for me.

I'm this close to deleting my profile. Everyone I chat with turns out to be a flake. No one wants to meet in person."

"How old is Kevin?" I asked.

Charles picked up his phone to respond to another message. "Twenty-two."

Danny furrowed his brow. "I don't know what it is you see in these *kids* you date," he said, annoyed. "Beyond the glow of youth, that is. I mean, what do you even talk about?"

"Lots of things," Charles said, amused by Danny's frustration. "These guys are much smarter than you give them credit for. You were in your twenties once, were *you* an idiot?"

That got me to laugh.

"I was not," Danny responded. "I may not have been *out* at twenty-two, but I was bright-eyed and accomplished. I was the editor of my university's student newspaper and graduated with honours in art history."

"And Kevin's been acting for a decade," Charles said. "And he came out at thirteen! His generation is more mature than we ever were at that age."

"Well, I don't know if I'd go that far," I said.

"Still," said Danny, pleading his case, "wouldn't you rather be with someone your own age?

"I'm not attracted to people my own age."

"Oh, come on," I said.

"But I'm not." Charles was unapologetic.

"Tell us," Danny said. "Who was the last older guy you slept with?"

"I don't know. It must've been that guy from Toronto last Pride. He was thirty-four."

"Thirty-four!"

"It was fun, he was nice. But it was just the one time." Another text came in that caught Charles's attention. "I don't know. Men in their early twenties are perfect, flawless. They have all this energy and none of the baggage older gay men have. They taste different too, like butter or cotton candy."

"The last guy I was with tasted like burnt haggis," Danny said.

"And they seem genuinely interested in me too, so what does it matter?"

"But it's not always going to be this way!" Danny argued, more frazzled than usual. "Aren't you worried about ending up alone?"

"Should I be? Honestly, I get more satisfaction from work."

"Success is nothing without someone you love to share it with," Danny said, quoting *Mahogany*. "You may be fit now, but in ten years you'll be sixty-five," Danny said. "And Kevin will be in his early thirties and still have his whole sexual life ahead of him. Do you expect him to stay home at night and take care of *pampa*?"

"*Pampa*?" I said.

"I don't expect anything from anyone," Charles answered.

"Who cares if there's an age difference," I said to Danny, "as long as they like each other. There's an age gap between Michael and me, you know that. You're just sore because some twink ghosted on you and you're starting to feel your age. Andre was not that much older than Kevin, if I remember."

Danny finished off his beer. "Well, he was a mistake. I'm never dating someone that young again. All I'm saying,

Charles, is yes you're having fun now, but what about when you're older? Do you expect to be inviting boys over at three in the morning to sit on your face? Or would you rather relax on the couch and watch a movie with someone you can grow old with?"

"These are my options?"

I had to laugh. "What's with you tonight, Danny?"

"I don't know," he said. "I'm frustrated with places like this—with the apps! I never meet anyone any more. Why can't it be like the old days, you know? You're going to think I'm joking, but I'd seriously consider an arranged marriage if the opportunity presented itself. Unfortunately, I don't have the dowry."

"Why don't you try one of those queer sports leagues?" I said. "Remember how many teams we saw march at Pride last year? You also said you wanted to get in shape. You'd be killing two birds with one stone."

"I never got that metaphor," Danny said. "So bloody violent."

Michael returned to our table with the drinks. "Finally!" I said, feigning impatience. "And who was that?"

"Some guy." Michael grinned. "Pascal." Michael held up his gold chain. "He said he liked my jewellery. He's an accountant. Asked if I had a boyfriend. That's when I pointed at you."

"Charming," Danny said. "That's one advantage the apps have over bars—you can block sender."

"He might have a job for me. He needs work done in his basement."

"I'm sure he does," Danny said. We all laughed, even Michael.

"No, he was nice," Michael said. "You don't mind, do you?"

"No," I said. "Of course not."

6

THE NEXT MORNING, I awoke with a start. I'd had a strange dream in which I was masturbating and then, just as I came, remembered that I wasn't supposed to. Holy shit, I'd thought to myself in the dream, then ran to the pantry to see what, if anything, I could eat that would increase the quantity of my sperm. The pantry was empty.

I rolled over and checked the time: 7:35 a.m. Instead of going back to sleep, I decided to get up. I looked over at Michael, fast asleep; both of our cats were on the bedspread, curled up in balls at our feet.

Careful not to wake them, I got up out of bed and dressed in my running gear. I then went into the kitchen to put on the coffee. There, I came across the broken chunks of my mug, next to the sink. I sighed. What to do with the pieces? I gathered them up to throw them away, but there was no garbage bag in the bin. I looked under the sink to get a new one, but there weren't any. I took the shards and left them in a pile by the garbage, then headed out for my weekend run.

It was cool outside. The heat of the day before had been cut by rain overnight, but it was sunny out now, small puddles of water evaporating in the morning light. Not five minutes into my run, I felt my phone vibrate and stopped to check the message. It was Wendy. *Good morning,* she wrote. *Heading out for breakfast with friends. Will text once we're on the road. See you soon!!*

I thought about their drive as I ran through the neighbourhood, an egg on its way. And deep inside me, millions of sperm preparing for their own journey. At the end, a spark? A big bang in her belly?

Before returning home, I swung by the dépanneur and picked up a box of garbage bags in addition to the weekend newspaper. Michael was up when I got back. He'd been going through an Annie Lennox phase and was listening to *Diva*. I caught him singing along to "Little Bird," while stirring sugar into his coffee.

"Someone's in a good mood," I said.

"Just another day in paradise," Michael said.

"What's that supposed to mean?"

"Nothing. I'm not being sarcastic," he said, and came over to my side of the island to kiss me on the cheek. "I'm happy, that's all. We need garbage bags," he said, turning to drop the spoon in the sink. I placed the box down on the island. He smiled, amused. "We also need a million dollars." Michael turned to me with the mug's broken pieces. "Are you going to throw these out?"

"What else can we do with them?"

"Can I have them?"

"What for?"

"For drainage," he said. "I'm thinking of adding more plants to the garden."

We had a small balcony outside our kitchen that Michael

had adorned with large bushes of basil, dill and a multitude of pansies. It was hardly a garden, but it did add welcome greenery to our view. "Sure," I said. I poured myself a glass of orange juice from the fridge and went outside to read the paper.

Our back balcony overlooked an alleyway where kids were already playing at this time of the morning. In the sky, I noticed a distant plane coming in for landing. I hadn't realized, when I bought the place, that the building was in the flight path for the Pierre Elliott Trudeau International Airport. In the end though, it wasn't so bad. You didn't hear much when you were inside, and it was only noticeable at certain times of day.

"Air Canada," Michael said, joining me outside.

I looked up. All I could see was a grey blurred body. "You can tell that from here?

"You can't see the leaf on the tail?"

"No, I can't. I guess my eyes are getting old. I should get them checked."

"One came in so low the other day; I swear I could see right through the windows."

"Well, now you're showing off."

I began to sort through the newspaper. Michael examined the basil, pinching the tops so they could grow more. "Have you heard from Wendy and Eve?"

"They're out for breakfast. They said they'll let me know when they're on their way."

"How do you feel? Nervous?"

I put down the Business section, already done with it. "No, not nervous. Anxious, maybe. Can you believe it? For the first time in my life my sperm is going to be inside of a woman."

Michael laughed. "I hope they have GPS. They're going to get lost in there... By the way, you were talking in your sleep last night."

"Was I? What did I say?"

"It was hard to make out, but I think it was something like 'I'm sorry.' Feeling guilty?"

"That's weird," I said. I told Michael about my dream. "I mean, it's been years since I've had one, but could you imagine if it had been an actual wet dream?"

"Sounds like you *are* nervous," he said. "Speaking of nocturnal visits, I'm pretty sure we have ghosts."

"Ghosts?"

"The other night, I woke up around two and I was sure there was someone standing next to the bed. At first I thought it was you, but then I reached over and you were sleeping beside me. Then whatever it was I saw disappeared into the background. Turned into the heap of clothes on the dresser."

A chill passed through me. "Well, that's creepy," I said.

"Freaked me out too. I'm going to smudge the place again. Do we still have the sage?" Michael had picked up a bundle of white sage to burn and rid the apartment of evil spirits when we first moved in.

"I think it's in the drawer in the hallway," I said.

Michael went back in to clean up the kitchen while I stayed outside and read a few more sections, then took a shower. When I was done, I opened the bathroom door and the steam collided with the smoke from the sage. Michael was listening to *Medusa* now, singing along as he passed from room to room, waving the burning embers into the corners.

Another text had come in from Wendy, telling me to expect them around four. The plan was for them to swing by to pick up the donation then head off to their hotel for the first attempt. We'd try again the next day too, before they had to return home. That's it. Only two attempts on this trip, with no time for a dinner at our place. I was all set to go: washed and dressed, my dates for the weekend—the clear plastic cups with sealed orange caps—waiting on the nightstand.

Without anything much to do, I puttered around. I spent a few minutes perusing the titles on my bookshelves. I was hungry for something fun and light to read, so I picked a slim classic, a book I hadn't read in years, Ethan Mordden's *I've a Feeling We're Not in Kansas Anymore*, and went into the living room. Done with his chores, Michael was now in front of the TV, sketching, watching an episode of *The Mary Tyler Moore Show*.

"Isn't Lou hot?" he asked as I joined him. "Him and his little sausage fingers."

"You definitely have a type," I said. "God knows what you see in me."

Did Michael think I looked like Ed Asner? My face wasn't nearly as wide, nor did I have his ears, but I did have dark bushy eyebrows and a receding hairline. Not that Michael cared. Michael had always found balding men attractive; men like Bruce Willis and Christopher Meloni and that man who had hit on him at the bar. I, however, wasn't keen on seeing my hair go. I had taken to styling it to hide my encroaching baldness and spent a significant amount on a special shampoo to encourage growth. Michael would tease me any time he saw me fuss with my hair in the mirror. He'd say something like he'd be more concerned if I was losing the hair on my legs or my back.

As he watched TV, Michael sketched. For the past two months, he'd been working on a series of anthropomorphic images of Malone. In Michael's drawings, Malone stood up straight and was as tall as we were, but he had his usual pattern of black and white fur running down his body. The one Michael was currently working on had Malone on the terrace of the Black Eagle bar, enjoying a summer beer with friends—two humans with happy faces, pulling bottles up to their mouths. There was another cat with them as well, and I could tell from his reddish colour that it was Sutherland. The two cats chatted with their friends, paws gripping the railings of the terrace, shirts off and hanging from their back pockets. Michael had drawn us too, sitting at our own table in deep conversation.

"Your drawings are really good," I said.

"Thanks."

"You've created this whole world for our cats. It's like they're our friends."

Michael considered it. "I think of it more like Malone if he were me. Like if he were an alley cat, hanging out with the boys."

"You should do something with this."

"Like what?"

"I don't know. Turn them into a comic book?"

"No, I don't think so. I wouldn't know how to come up with a story."

"There's already a story. But if not that, maybe you could sell them? Like at Expozine, that arts and crafts fair they have in the fall? I'm sure you could sell prints of your work there."

"Nah, this is for me."

I admired Michael for his talent, but I wished he would try to make a buck from it. He needed to bring in more money. I knew what was in the envelope from the federal government he'd yet to open. It wasn't the first such letter to arrive. Michael owed $5,000 in back taxes, and the government wanted him to pay it all within a year. And if Michael wasn't able to pay, they would send a debt collector to seize his assets. Not that he had any, besides his car. I had no clue how he was going to pay it all back in time.

Around 3:30 p.m. I got a text message from Wendy that said they were close and should arrive within twenty minutes. Michael and I hopped onto the bed and fooled around while we waited. I kept looking at the clock, and as we neared the ten-minute mark I got nervous. I had to make sure that I finished first, in the cup and away from Michael, and also make sure that Michael's fluids stayed away from mine.

"I think it would be better if you didn't come," I said, and he agreed.

Then the second text arrived, saying they were off the highway. I shifted position, took out the container and removed the protective seal. Two minutes later the third text rolled in, telling me they were outside. Michael kissed me to help me get close, and when I was ready I pulled away and came inside the plastic cup.

93

It didn't look like it would be enough. It was white, thick, warm. I supposed its viscosity could be considered "normal," but it looked strange running down the walls of the container. I had thought that making this donation was going to feel like a medical procedure, like having blood drawn, so it felt strange to be hit with a wave of pleasure while negotiating the narrow opening of the cup.

I sealed the container and threw on sweatpants and a T-shirt and brought it out in a paper bag to them in the car. "That was quick," Wendy said.

"I can't stay out here too long," I said. "It's weird. Good luck."

I hugged them both in the car and they drove away. Back inside, I helped Michael get off. We spent the rest of the afternoon on the couch, watching *The Mary Tyler Moore Show* and eating pizza, our legs intertwined.

The next morning, we met up with Wendy and Eve at Café Minnelli.

"It was strange, seeing it. Having it inside of me," Wendy said. She couldn't stop laughing. "Let's say that I became very intimate with your fluids."

"It wouldn't stay in," Eve said. "It all kept running down her leg and we'd have to scoop it back in."

I couldn't help but wince and laugh at all of the grossness. "Lessons for next time."

Michael swung by our table and refilled our water glasses. He may not have been working, but he was still a dutiful employee, running around to clear tables and jumping behind the counter to help when the line got long. The place now offered a simple breakfast. There were only two items on the menu, but they now also sold a slew of fresh pastries that Michael kept bringing us.

"So, no visit to Eve's parents on this trip?" I asked.

"No," said Wendy. "It's in-and-out this time." She was still laughing. "I could've stayed longer, but Eve has to be back for an important meeting tomorrow. We also don't want our parents to know too much about how we're doing this."

"No?"

"You know me, Paul," Wendy said. "I prefer to keep my parents in the dark. Eve's parents are fine, but mine are way too pushy, asking too many questions. Do you know that when I told them we had asked you to be our donor, my mother wanted to send you money? She didn't think it was right that we weren't reimbursing you for your donation. They have so many questions and want to poke their noses into everything. I want this to be about us."

"And your folks?" I asked Eve. "How do they feel?"

Many years ago, after we first met, Eve had told me the story of how hard her family took it when she came out, and I remembered, when she and Wendy first started dating, how awkward it had been for all of them. Time, though, had mellowed her parents, and then Wendy and Eve's marriage three years back further legitimized their union.

"They're excited," Eve answered. "But you know my mom and dad. I don't think they want to know too much about how this will happen—the nuts and bolts of how we're doing things—but they're happy for us. Excited to be grandparents."

"They're excited because it means they can stop thinking

about us having sex," Wendy said to Eve, before turning to me. "Nothing gets people thinking less about your sex life than when you tell them you're about to have kids."

Eve chided her partner. "Oh, come on. They've come a long way. I never thought I'd see my parents at my wedding or get excited about us having a child. Did Wendy tell you they want the baby to be baptized?"

"Really?" I said, surprised. "And what do *you* think of that?" I asked Wendy.

"I was against it, at first," she said. "But then I thought, what's the big deal? I'm not religious. Sprinkling the baby with holy water isn't going to hurt anyone. And if it makes Eve's parents create a better bond with the child, then I'm all for it."

"But we're not doing it at their church," Eve said. "There's no way I'm going back to that place."

"You should talk to Danny," I said. "He's pretty involved at his church—the Unitarian one in NDG?"

"Do Unitarians do baptisms?" Eve asked.

I didn't know. "They must have some kind of ceremony for babies."

"I keep forgetting that Danny is religious," Wendy said. "It's bizarre when a friend believes in god."

"Come on," Eve said.

"Well, you know what I mean. Religion. It's problematic. It's oppressive and fanatical. It's hard to believe that someone as smart as Danny believes we were created in seven days by a supreme being."

"I don't think that's what Danny believes," I said to Wendy. "You shouldn't make assumptions; you should talk to him about it. Spirituality is important for some. God knows he needed to turn to something when his parents died in that horrible fire."

Wendy winced, a pained look on her face. "I forgot about that. Well, I feel shitty now."

Eve changed the subject. "What about you, Paul? Have you told your dad?"

"No," I admitted. "I also want to keep this for us for now, until we have news to share." I reached over into our basket of pastries and took out another croissant. "I wonder if it worked," I said, biting into it. "Imagine if it did on the first try?"

After breakfast, the four of us walked back to our place so we could give Wendy and Eve a quick tour of our home and I could produce another sample.

"Do you want to insert it here?" I asked. "Michael and I could go out."

"No, we'll pull into an alley and inseminate in the backseat, then drive back," Wendy said. "I'll hoist my legs on the dash."

"Just what I'll want our child to know," Eve said. "That they were conceived in an alley."

When they were ready to leave, Michael walked them outside while I stayed behind. I entered the office and turned on the computer, but while it warmed up I felt awkward being able to hear the three of them outside, below the window, talking. I couldn't do it this way, with their voices clear in the background, so I left the office and walked into our bedroom. There, I took out a collection of dog-eared magazines from a box under the bed. I hadn't looked at them in years, but I remembered the images. The pages were worn and creased and falling out of their bindings. These men, who had got me off for years when I was young, were stuck in the same ridiculous poses, the same moments of frozen ecstasy. I still had the *Numbers* my sister had given me. I picked it up and flipped through the pages, settling on a familiar image of a bearded guy in the woods.

Later that day, I got a text from Wendy saying they had got home and thanking me for being so generous. Wendy said that she didn't think it had worked though, because she had taken her temperature and still hadn't ovulated. But then on Monday, I got another text from her telling me that she had. *Hopefully it worked!* I wrote back.

That evening over dinner, Michael and I talked about how odd the weekend was. It was hard to put into words. It's like you can take the sex out of the process, and break it up into pieces, but it's still making a baby. It still involved intimate acts that involved all four of us. I'd thought the weekend would have been celebratory, like a party, but it wasn't. I guess that's because there was something serious about what we were doing. It was like we had all robbed a bank and buried the money and now were going our separate ways until it was time to unearth the loot.

But then, two weeks later, I received a call from Wendy. She got her period. It was a strange period, she said. Not much blood. She wondered if it had been some kind of miscarriage. She gave me the dates for the next try and asked if I'd be willing to come to Toronto.

7

THE NEXT MONTH, I travelled to Toronto. It was difficult for Wendy and Eve to get the same days off, so when we first made plans they asked if I'd be willing to come to them a few times for the attempts. I told them it wouldn't be a problem. My company had an office on Bay Street, so I could always pop in and work from there. However, Wendy's cycle had once again linked up with the weekend, and I found myself on an early Saturday morning flight to Toronto.

I had told my friends that I was going to take the train, but before I knew it Wendy's mother had bought me a plane ticket. The flight from Montreal was a short one, but it was bumpy, the corridor between the two cities an agitated seesaw. It's the take-offs that I hate the most, those first few minutes as the aircraft gains altitude, when I wonder if everything in the cockpit is okay and I wait for the flight attendants to rise from their seats and begin to move through the cabin. I often think of my mother in these moments and marvel how she took to the skies day after day to do her job. Was she aware how the mere performance of her duties could calm a passenger like me down?

Soon, but not soon enough, our plane began its descent towards the city. After we disembarked, I headed towards the ferry terminal with my overnight bag and powered up my phone. The device came alive with shakes and beeps, as emails and messages rolled in. There were five texts from Danny:

- *Good morning!*

- *Hey! You up yet?*

- *Can you call me? You won't believe what happened last night.*

- *You must be busy. Call me when you have a sec.*

- *I forgot, you're on your way to Toronto! Call me when you get this.*

I boarded the ferry, got a spot by the window to watch the vessel traverse the short distance to downtown from the city's island airport, and put in my earpiece to call Danny. The phone rang once before he picked up, his voice loud and excited. "Finally!"

"Everything okay?"

"Yes, everything's great. Wonderful! I'm sorry, I know you're on an important mission to spread your seed, but I have to tell you about last night. You have a minute?"

The ferry doors closed and the motor started up. "Sure," I said. "What's up?"

"… I'm getting married!"

"What!? How? When?"

"Details! I don't know when. The groom doesn't even know—we just met! But I can see it, Paul, the suits, the dresses, the groomsmen, the flowers. His name is Vince and he's a Scorpio. I met him last night at soccer."

The month before, Danny had taken my advice and joined Les Renards, an informal queer soccer team that was mostly a game of pick-up for whoever showed up at Villeray

Park on Monday nights. Michael and I went with him to his first game and watched from the sidelines as the sun set and the field lights came on. For most of the game, we sat there stunned. Danny was good. Really good. Apparently, he had played the sport all throughout high school. Danny credited the neighbourhood bullies for teaching him how to run fast at a young age.

"Well, that was quick," I said, as the city inched closer. "I thought it would take at least a few matches before you fell in love."

"Last night was only my second game," he said. "I had to take some time off after that first one. I was so out of shape. I couldn't get out of bed the next morning. I thought I had sleep paralysis. Anyway, there were twice as many players last night as the time before, and there was this one guy who played defence. He was big and beefy, with short blonde hair and a small gap between his two front teeth. He kept smiling at me throughout the game. Well, you know me, I can't tell when someone is flirting. I thought that maybe I had something on my face, or he was making fun of me, but no. After the game, a bunch of us went out for beers, and we hit it off. He invited me home."

"Oh my god." I drew out the exclamation. "Who won?"

"Who won? Who cares who won! I won! Several times."

"He sounds hot."

"I'm sending you a picture from his Facebook page."

Several seconds later, my phone buzzed with the image.

"Handsome," I said. "He even looks like a soccer player."

"He does, doesn't he? He's taller than I am, around five foot ten. And strong too. He has these incredible legs. Thick, like yours. He's French-Canadian, but completely bilingual, my age, and teaches math at a high school on the South Shore. He's sweet and genuine and great in bed. I'm so sore again today. I don't know if it was the game or the sex, but I'm going to need to take an Epsom salt bath."

"That's amazing, Danny!"

"I realized I was in love when he laughed at one of my jokes. Paul, it was so much fun! At first, all we did was make out, long and slow, but then it got wild. Maybe it was all that cardio that served as foreplay, but when we were alone together I could feel the blood rushing through my veins, my heart pumping fast and loud." Danny sighed, thinking about it. "And his body is to die for. He has this huge penis too—like when a whale comes out of the water, you know how it breaches? It looks like that. Majestic and awe-inspiring. I kept looking for fins."

I laughed into my headset. "Watch out for barnacles."

"When we were done, we both fell asleep, and then we woke up and went at it again. I kept thinking that I should leave. I mean, that's what happens right? As soon as you're done, you go. But we stayed in his bed, talking and kissing and laughing! Oh, did we laugh! A couple of times I was worried his roommate was going to come in and tell us to shut the fuck up. Then, when I left, he asked for my number."

"That's wonderful," I said. "I'm happy for you, Danny Boy."

"I'm tired this morning, but I don't care. I'm on cloud nine. The crazy thing is I didn't think he would go for me. He's super-hot. Any of the boys in the game would have had him and all he wanted to do was play ball with me. But you know, even if this doesn't lead anywhere, last night is going to be something that I cherish for the rest of my life."

"Don't overthink this," I said, recognizing a pattern in my friend. "He obviously likes you. But don't start planning your wedding just yet. Enjoy this time!"

There was a deep thunk as the ferry connected to the terminal on the other side of the water. People picked up their bags. "Listen Danny, we'll talk about this more once I'm back home," I said, jockeying into position. "I gotta run."

"Take care," Danny said. "Get one past the goalie!"

A half hour later, my taxi pulled up to Wendy and Eve's house on a quiet tree-lined street in Toronto's Cabbagetown neighbourhood. The girls had heard the car pull up and greeted me in unison. "Hello," they shouted from the doorstep, grabbing my carry-on and hugging me as they pulled me inside. I hardly had time to take off my shoes before Wendy asked if I had one in me before we left for lunch.

"Uh, sure," I said, still getting my bearings.

Wendy had had her mother book me on a morning flight, as they were eager to try right away. Apparently, most lesbians have boys. It has something to do with inseminating on the day of ovulation. I had learned, in my research, that Y-chromosome sperm are faster than x-chromosome sperm. They are the first to get to the fallopian tubes. Wendy and Eve were hoping for a girl, so they figured if we tried before Wendy's egg appeared, all the male sperm would be dead, allowing the female sperm to arrive in time to fertilize the egg. Ingenious, I thought, imagining some kind of brutal car race. A *Mad Max* film in utero.

The girls ushered me to their guest room and Eve handed over another orange-capped container. I closed the door behind me and walked into the adjoining bathroom to wash my face and hands. I was envious that Wendy and Eve had a guest room with its own bathroom. It had been a few years since they'd moved in, but I still couldn't get over the opulence of the place, especially given their jobs. In fact, their whole house seemed unlikely for a couple sharing a high school teacher's and set designer's salaries, but I knew that the two had received a hefty down payment from Wendy's parents once they got married. Their Toronto home was unlike my small Montreal apartment, with its couch that Michael's mother would be sleeping on that night. The timing of my trip had proved perfect. Michael only had to wait forty-five minutes after dropping me off at the airport to pick up his mother. They would have two full days together before I returned home on Sunday night.

I didn't waste much time. I got down to business and produced a sample, sheepishly coming out of the bedroom with the cup. I didn't want to see Wendy or Eve looking at its contents, so I left the container on the hallway table. "I'm going to leave this here," I yelled, running back into the bedroom. "Take your time and let me know when you're ready."

"You're the best," Wendy called out. I heard the floorboards squeak, then the closing of Wendy and Eve's bedroom door.

Fifteen minutes later, there was a knock.

"Come in," I said from where I sat on the bed, leafing through an old issue of *Time* magazine I'd found on the nightstand. "That's it?"

"That's it." Wendy walked in and sat on the bed, hoisting her feet up on to the headboard. "We're going to head out in five minutes, if that's okay with you."

"Don't you have to keep lying down with your legs in the air?"

"I'll keep this up until we leave," she said. "We have a bit of a drive to the restaurant and there's usually traffic. I'll hoist my legs in the car too."

"Who'll be there again?"

Wendy listed her friends on her fingers: "Laura and Stefanie. Claudia and Sam. Jen and Nisha."

Eve walked into the room with her shoes in her hands. "Everyone got babysitters so they could meet you. That never happens."

"You make me sound like a circus animal."

"They're curious," Wendy said, patting my foot. "None of them used known donors."

"Be warned," Eve said. "They're going to have questions."

When we left their home, I sat in the back of their Subaru while Eve got behind the wheel and Wendy tried to get comfortable with her feet on the dash. It was strange to think that a part of me was inside of her, my DNA heading to its own meeting with Wendy's.

Soon we merged onto the Gardiner Expressway and headed to our destination, an Indian restaurant in the West End. The place was packed when we arrived, filled with families and oval plates of sweet and colourful food. All of Wendy and Eve's lesbian mom friends were waiting for us, sitting at a long table near the back of the room. They stood and I was introduced to everyone.

There were three empty seats at the end of the table, so we sat down and ordered. I made an effort to speak to each person, but mostly I chatted with Jen and Nisha, who sat across from me—academics who taught at the University of Toronto. I learned that Nisha's parents owned the restaurant, and that the two had a ten-year-old son named Hunter.

"He's so handsome," I said, after they showed me a photo the three of them taken last Christmas. "Where's he today?"

"At his friend Michael's house," Jen said.

"That's my partner's name!"

"The two get into so much mischief when they're together. Whenever we go out, Hunter's always pushing us out the door, yelling 'Bye!' and then hopping onto his bike to Michael's to swim."

"See, that's what I want," Wendy said to Eve. "None of this helicopter parenting bullshit. Just letting kids be kids. When I was young, there were days when I would take off after breakfast and my mom wouldn't see me until dinner."

"You grew up in Guelph," I said. "Not the most dangerous city in Canada."

"Still, parents are too protective these days," she said. "We don't allow kids to be themselves any more. We make them afraid of everything."

I thought back to my own childhood, biking around the streets of Pointe-Claire with my friends. I never once felt unsafe or scared. "But it's not the same world any more," I said. "It's much more dangerous."

"No, it's not," Wendy said, leaning in. "I read a story the other day that said it's safer for kids today. Most have phones, there are cameras on every street corner, it's easier to get

106

word out if one goes missing—and today's kids are smarter too, less gullible than we were." Wendy looked at Eve again. "Our kid's going to be a dynamo. And we're going to teach her krav maga and kung fu, just in case."

Eve smiled and shook her head. "Yes, my love, she's going to be a black belt by the time she's five."

The food arrived, and we all dove in. Jen and Nisha asked me a litany of questions as we ate. Where were you born? Do you have any brothers or sisters? What do you do for a living? What's your partner Michael like? I kept expecting them to ask what I thought everyone wanted to know: What did I think about what we were doing? How did I feel about children? What relationship did I hope to have with the child? But those questions never came. Instead, we meandered into a hodgepodge of topics, each more random than the next: long-distance running, urban beekeeping, Southern Italian cooking, the novels of Sarah Waters.

The meal was delicious but fast, and soon the plates were being cleared and Wendy and Eve's friends were getting out their cell phones to check in with babysitters. Nisha and Jen got up to head to the kitchen to thank Nisha's parents for lunch, then Laura and Stefanie, who had been sitting at the far end of the table, came to take their places. We lamented not getting enough time to chat, and Laura said she thought it was great what I was doing for our friends. "We're happy that Wendy and Eve might have a child to play with ours someday," Stefanie said. She then asked me about my family and what they thought of what we were doing. I felt bad admitting that I hadn't told my father yet, and I didn't feel like explaining my sister's situation.

We drove back to Wendy and Eve's home and tried again that afternoon. One of the women at lunch had mentioned to Wendy that having an orgasm before an attempt can increase the chances of sperm retention, so the next morning when we tried a third time I decided to give the two privacy in case they wanted to add that step to the procedure.

I went for a run, heading west, not sure where I was going. After about twenty minutes, I found myself in Queen's Park near the University of Toronto's Saint George Campus. The day was growing hot, and I spotted a few sunbathers around the park. I began to lose steam, so I cut the run short and stopped to drink water and catch my breath. I decided to walk back to Wendy and Eve's. On the way, I popped into Glad Day bookshop on Yonge Street.

I had finished *I've a Feeling We're Not in Kansas Anymore* and had passed the book on to Michael. "Is it any good?" he had asked, one night in bed, as I read its final pages. I told him its premise: "It's funny and light. About a group of gay friends living in Manhattan in the late seventies. I think you might like it." Michael never read books, so I was surprised to see him rip through it, laughing out loud at the witty and interconnected dramas. He was almost done and had asked if I had the second book in the series. I had looked for my copy of *Buddies* but couldn't find it anywhere. Thankfully, there was one at Glad Day, in the used section, the golden Stonewall Inn Editions cover an exact replica of the one I had misplaced. The book smelled musty and its pages were dry and yellowed. Inside, I noticed an inscription. "To Gary," it said. "Merry Christmas, 1991! I can only hope that the characters in this wonderful book will make you laugh, cry, think, remember and love—like they made me… Love Greg."

I bought the book and left, then went to a small park nearby to read a few pages. At some point, I called to check in on Michael and his mother. Michael was about to take her out to meet Gus and afterwards the three of them had plans to go to the lookout on Mount Royal, then have a late lunch in the Old Port. "Sounds like you've got a full day ahead of you," I said. "Say hi to everyone."

After the call, I got up and headed back to Cabbagetown. Walking along Wellesley Street, I ran into an old friend. "JF?"

"Paul!"

We hugged hello. "What are you doing here?" I asked. I hadn't seen JF in over a year.

"I live here now," he said, and gestured towards a bunch of buildings. "I got a job at Radio-Canada as a national arts reporter."

"That's wonderful!" I said. "I had no idea. And Simon? What's he doing?"

JF's face scrunched up. "Simon's in Montreal. We broke up."

I stood deflated; my left hand over my mouth. "Oh no," I said, then reached out to touch his elbow. "I'm sorry to hear that."

I had once envied JF and Simon's relationship. They were two well-dressed men with impeccable taste who threw the best parties. Simon was a gallerist, around my age, and JF a journalist, eight years older. Standing on the street before him now, I noticed more grey in his beard, and there were additional lines in his face too—but it all made JF more attractive, the weight of time anointing his brow and jaw with natural beauty. I'd had such a crush on him back in the day. JF and I would flirt whenever we ran into each other in the Village or at parties, but he met Simon before anything had the chance to happen between us. I remember a conversation we had soon after they first hooked up, a shine in JF's eyes as he spoke of his new love, and feeling a pang of regret that I'd never asked him out. I was sad to hear their relationship had ended. "Are you okay?"

"I'm fine," he said. "It hadn't been working out. The last couple of years we were more friends than lovers, and then the stress of buying a place pushed us over the edge. It was tough at the beginning—separating ten years of possessions, figuring out who would get the dogs. But I think we're going to be okay. Hopefully, we'll be good friends one day." JF then changed the subject: he wanted to know where I was working now, how was Michael, did I still see Danny and what was I doing in town?

"I'm here to make a baby," I said, feeling an odd sense of pride. We had said we would only tell our close friends, but it felt safe to share this information with JF. He didn't know Wendy and Eve, and besides, it seemed like they had already told their friends.

"Really?" JF asked, once I had explained the situation. "Are you going to be involved? Will you be the kid's dad?" JF told me he was interested because he had been put up for adoption as a baby. "I never knew my mom or my dad," he said. "I'll never know them, so I'm fascinated about why people do this. It's great that your friends are using someone they know. It'll allow their kid to grow up knowing where she or he came from. I wish I'd had that. It would've saved me a lot of grief."

JF looked at the time and said that he was sorry, but that he had an appointment to run to. He smiled and said he wished we had more time to talk. "Me too," I said. "I might be coming back to Toronto more often, depending on how long this takes. Maybe the next time I'm in town we can go for drinks?"

"I'd like that." JF punched his number into my phone.

That evening, I flew back to Montreal. It was Sunday night and it felt like the whole weekend had never happened. As I climbed the stairs to our home I started to bark, but I didn't hear any barks come back. I opened the door to find Michael at the kitchen table with his mom, painting her nails a light blue. "Hello, Paul," she said, a big grin on her face. "I'd get up to give you a kiss, but my hands are busy."

"Nice colour," I said, and kissed Michael on the head. "Hello, buddy."

"Hi, buddy." Michael was intent on his job, his eyes focused on the tips of his mother's nails. "It's periwinkle."

"No barks?" I asked.

"You know barks are only for workdays."

"Well, this weekend felt like work."

"How was the flight?" Michael asked.

"Not as bad as the one there, but I'm sure it still shaved a year off my life. Hello, Ellen," I said, and kissed Michael's mother on both cheeks, her hands still with her son.

"Welcome home," she said. "Was it a success?"

I shot Michael a look.

"I had to tell her," he said, caught. "We were running out of things to talk about."

"I'm happy for the both of you," she said. "Your friends chose a great guy to father their child. Your own dad must be thrilled."

I was annoyed that Michael had told his mother, especially since I hadn't told my father yet, but I was too charmed by Ellen's excitement to care; this woman thought of Malone and Sutherland as grandchildren.

"So, how did it go?" Michael asked.

"Fine," I said, and told them about the trip: the attempts and the lunch with the lesbian motherhood. "It's a waiting game now. I guess we'll know in the next two weeks."

"I can't believe how modern this all is," Ellen began, blowing the nails on her left hand. "Your life is so *fabulous*."

Michael looked to his mother. "Please don't say fabulous, Ellen."

I headed into the kitchen to get water. It bothered me that Michael called his mother by her first name. I couldn't help thinking of it as a sign of disrespect, but despite my objections I knew Michael had his reasons. When I first called him on it, Michael explained that it was a way for him to attempt to have an adult relationship with his mom, so he wouldn't be made to feel like a kid in her presence. I knew that Michael had a very different experience with his folks than I did with mine. When your parents help you through rehab, it changes things.

"And how are you, Ellen?" I asked, pouring myself a glass of water and sitting with them. This was the second time I was meeting Michael's mother, having first met her when she came to check up on her son during the first three months of our relationship. Still, she and I had communicated over the years—through Christmas and birthday cards, text messages and phone calls. She looked much the same as she had the last time: short and stout, with bright white hair and light brown freckles scattered across her cheeks and forehead.

"I'm fine," she said. "I've been reading a lot. I've started taking yoga and I took an Italian cooking course. I appreciate you letting me stay here for a couple of days."

"We wouldn't have it any other way. I hope the couch is comfortable," I said. "I'm sorry we don't have a guest room."

"Oh no, please. The couch is *divine*," she said, as if our living room was a suite at the Ritz-Carlton. "I love your place. It's such a wise investment, property. Michael took me on a tour of your neighbourhood today and you're close to all these great-looking shops and restaurants."

"Did Michael take you to Minnelli?"

"He did." She looked back at her son, proud. "Such a cute place. You guys must have so much fun living here." Ellen looked around the room. "You know, if I was thirty years younger, I'd want to live in a place like this."

"But you *can* live in a place like this," Michael pleaded. I was sure they had talked all weekend about her future, now that she had left Michael's father. "You could get a one-bedroom place like this somewhere within walking distance to a main transit line and a grocery store."

"Are you thinking of moving to Montreal?" I asked.

"No," Michael answered for her. "She's thinking of going back to my dad."

Michael's mom interjected. "No, I didn't say I was going

back to your father. I'm exploring my options." Ellen looked to me. "I don't know what to do, Paul. It's a battle between my heart and my head. I want to be on my own, but I also feel for Michael's father. He keeps calling me and sending me messages, apologizing for his temper. He says he's going to see someone about it, work on himself, but I don't know." She looked at the flip phone beside her. "I need my space now."

"How is this going to be different from any other time?" Michael said, putting the applicator back in its bottle. "Don't touch anything," he ordered. "I still have to put on a topcoat." Michael stood up and went to the fridge to refill his water glass. "He does this every time. Takes advantage of you and treats you like dirt until you do something about it and leave him. Then he realizes he can't do anything on his own and turns on the charm so you'll come running back."

Ellen opened her mouth to say something but didn't. Instead, she sighed into her palm.

"I wish you had moved out with me when I was eighteen," Michael said. "You were so close to doing it. Remember, I was even looking at places with two bedrooms. Had you come with me, you wouldn't be in the situation you're in now."

There was nothing for his mother to say; she sighed again and looked exasperated. Thankfully, Malone chose the moment to jump onto the chair that Michael had vacated. "How are the boys?" I asked, scratching behind Malone's ears.

"Good," Michael said. "But Malone bit me last night." Michael showed me the two red dots on the back of his hand. It looked swollen.

"That doesn't look good. What happened?"

"It's fine. It was my fault." Michael shooed the cat off the chair and sat back down to finish his mother's nails. "He

114

was on the bed and it was dark and I didn't see him. He's been gnawing on his paws again too."

I grabbed Malone and lifted him up to check his front paws. The fur around them was shorn to the skin, making it look like he had been freed after months in shackles. "Strange."

"Why do you think that is?" Ellen asked.

"I don't know," Michael said. "Some sort of PTSD? You know he was abandoned, right? With no claws in a barn one winter. Who does that to a cat? He had to fight for food and defend himself against the other barn cats. When we first got him, he was all scratched up and his face was red and puffy. But look at you now, buddy," Michael said, addressing Malone in my arms. "Who's a happy cat?"

I put the cat down on another chair and petted him. "Maybe I should get a cat," Ellen said. "His fur is so soft and clean, and he's always grooming himself."

"It's because he's happy," Michael said. "Happy cats take care of themselves."

I looked at my watch. It was only 9:30 p.m., but I was tired from the travel and work would come fast the next morning. "I'm going to take a shower and unwind. You feel like watching TV?"

"Oh no, I'll read and go to bed," Ellen said. "Unless of course you want to stay up. I feel bad for taking over your living room."

"No, it's fine," I said. "We often watch stuff in bed on our laptop. Michael, you staying up?"

"I'm going to have a joint while you take your shower. I'll meet you in bed." He put the finishing touches on his mother's nails. "There," he said.

"Thank you, Michael. They're beautiful."

Michael tightened the cap on the bottle and kissed me on his way to the office. Malone followed him out of the room.

Ellen stayed sitting at the table, looking at her nails, while I moved over to get a towel from the hall closet. "It's such a beautiful place, Paul," she said again, looking at the walls of our kitchen. "Michael is lucky to have found you."

I blushed. "Oh, I'm the lucky one."

Ellen looked down the hall to make sure Michael wasn't around. "How is he doing?" she asked. "Really?"

"He's fine," I said. "Concerned about you, of course. He wants you to be happy."

"Oh, I know. He's my knight in shining armour. Besides that."

"He's good. Work is slow, but it'll pick up. It's perfect that he landed the gig at the coffee shop. Michael's been drawing again too, which is great. He's so talented."

"I saw a notice about his taxes," she said. "I didn't tell him I saw it, of course. I know I shouldn't have snooped, but I couldn't help it when I saw it on the table. I'm his mother. I can't help but worry."

"Don't," I said. "Michael will be fine. He's trying to stick to a budget, paying down what he owes. It might take him a while to pay off everything, but he'll do it."

"I wish I could help, but I don't even know what I'm going to do." She looked at her nails, then up at me. "I know you help him out too, Paul, and we're grateful for that. I guess I'm surprised he even did his taxes. He avoided them for so many years."

"Well, I didn't give him much of a choice."

"The fact that you got him to do anything about it is a miracle. Paul, I don't say this enough, but I'm glad that Michael has you in his life. I know he hasn't had it easy, what with his hearing loss and the troubles he had at school—not to mention the drugs and the conflict with his brothers and father. His brothers really used him as a punching bag growing up—I kick myself for not knowing what was going on. But I'm happy he's been able to put much of that behind him, and that he's in a stable relationship now with someone who loves him and looks out for him, especially when I'm so far away."

I had never heard Ellen talk like this before, had hardly heard Michael talk about his past either.

"I think I knew he would have a hard life," she continued. "I don't know why we chose the name Michael, but I suppose it fits. Michael, like the archangel who wrestles the devil. I'm happy he has you, Paul. Whatever happens between me and his dad, I'm grateful that he has you in his life."

I was speechless. I didn't know what to say, so I thanked her and said goodnight, kissing her on the top of her head while she sat at the table waiting for her nails to dry.

I took my shower and got into bed, putting the Ethan Mordden book I had purchased on Michael's pillow. As I did that, I noticed there were additional knickknacks on his nightstand: a large Bart Simpson figurine and a ratty looking stuffed animal.

"You found it," Michael said when he saw the book, coming into the bedroom with the laptop. "I can't believe I enjoy reading now. I could never concentrate on books as a kid, but I can actually relate to these stories."

"We don't have to watch anything," I said, yawning. "You can read. I'm just going to fall asleep anyway." Michael put the computer aside. "Where did those things come from?" I asked, gesturing toward his side of the bed.

Michael looked over at his nightstand as he stripped down to his briefs. "My mom brought them. That's my dog Charlie. I've had him since I was four."

I reached over and picked up the dog. It was brown and white and seemed to be missing its nose. I noticed he had been stitched back together in multiple places, and he felt half-empty too, as if most of his stuffing was missing. I put him back on his nightstand. "So, how were the last two days with your mom?"

"Fine," he said, getting into bed with the book. "We got on each other's nerves a few times, but we didn't kill each other. I'm just afraid she'll go back to my dad."

I wasn't sure if it was the right time, but I asked my question anyway. "Is your dad's temper really that bad?"

Michael shrugged. "I spent my youth getting yelled at for doing everything wrong. Not being good in school, not hearing properly, being such a disappointment at sports. And I wasn't the only one who got it—my brothers got it, my mother got it most. None of us were good enough for him. It's like he wanted us to be another family."

"Was he physical?"

Michael closed the book. "He never hit me," he said, rather calm. "Never hit my brothers. He did hit my mom once, but he said it was an accident and never did it again. Still, he didn't need to hit us. It was verbal abuse, emotional abuse. Telling us that we were worthless and wouldn't amount to anything. I can't count the times my mom tried to hide her crying from me. But no, my dad didn't hit me, that was my brothers' job."

"Your brothers? You never want to talk about them."

Michael was annoyed now. He shook his head for a moment then opened the book back up. "They were bullies. Each one of them."

"Just to you, or at school too? Did—"

"—Listen Paul, can we not talk about this now? Not right before bed. I mean, if you want a guided tour of my trauma, I'm sure we can arrange for something tomorrow. I have a tour group coming in around ten."

This didn't sound like Michael. It sounded like Danny. "I'm sorry, I thought—"

"—No, it's fine," he said, shifting his pillow and fiddling with the book. "I just…" He softened. "I try not to think about that time, that part of my life. I mean, look at me now. I've met a great guy and we have a nice life together. We've got two wonderful cats—by the way, those toys in the hall are gifts from my mother, not me—I also work for myself and have a part-time job. I'm learning all this new stuff at Minnelli. Did I tell you they want me to help with kitchen prep? They're creating a lunch menu and need extra hands. Sure, I could be working more. Sure, I could have less debt. But I feel like I'm in control. When you're able to get away from all the negativity that's dragged you down your whole life, you realize you can't go back. And that's what I want for her. She's never had it. She almost did. But if she goes back to him, she'll never leave. In fact, if they get back together, I don't want to have anything to do with them ever again. They

119

can have their own twisted relationship. I don't want to be dragged down with it."

He opened the book and disappeared into its pages.

8

MICHAEL AND I KEPT A CALENDAR on our fridge. We rarely consulted it, appreciating it more for its vintage beefcake shots of men in classical poses. On the first of the month, I flipped the page from July to August. There, under a stunning black and white photo of a buff and smiling naked man leaning against a tree, his bush full and dark, I noticed that Michael had circled the sixth with the words "Paul's big day" in black marker.

Originally, the plan had been for me to host a dinner party on my birthday, but after I had told Charles and Danny about my idea that night in the bar, Charles had called and said no, I would not host my own birthday dinner. Instead, we'd do it at his loft and he'd be the one to have it catered. He also offered to make it one of his *souper des femmes*, so everyone would be invited to come in drag or a dress or any costume that undermined gender. I was touched.

The day before, I came home from work to find Michael sitting in front of the stove, the light in the oven on. "What are you doing?" I asked.

"Baking cookies."

"What kind?"

"Your favourite. Chocolate chip."

I kissed him on the head and left the kitchen to change out of my work clothes. When I returned, Michael was in the same spot, silent, watching the treats rise like a dog at the door waiting for its master. When the cookies were ready, he took them out and cooled them on the counter. He put a few aside and placed them in a plastic container, separating each one by a square of wax paper. "Who are those for?" I asked.

"The neighbours." Michael put on his sailor hat and kissed me as he zipped out the door to visit Jean and Alison, who lived downstairs. I snuck a cookie and went into the living room with a bunch of takeout flyers to order us dinner, but as I was about to dial, the phone rang in my hand. I looked at the call display and saw it was my father.

"Hello! Happy birthday, Son!" he said, after I answered.

"Thanks, Dad. It's not until tomorrow, you know."

"I know, I know," he said, and I could hear the joy in his voice. "I wanted to be the first to call. You were born three minutes after midnight, but I figured you'd be in bed by then."

"You'd have figured right."

"I can't believe you're turning forty."

"I can't either," I said. "I still remember the party we threw for your fortieth at the Legion." My mind saw blue and white streamers strung across bowling trophies, cases of Molson Ex and Labatt 50 behind the bar. "I must've been what? Fourteen? And Kate sixteen? I can't imagine what it's like turning forty with two teenagers in tow. How'd you do it?"

"Lots of beer," he said. "And of course there was your mother, god love her."

"How you doing, Dad? How's Debbie?"

"She's good. Off biking with her friends today."

I pictured Debbie in a helmet and dark sunglasses with a fluorescent cycling jersey and a plastic water bottle. "Didn't feel like joining them?"

"Not today. I'm coming down with a cold, so I'm watching daytime TV. Lots of talk shows and people arguing with each other. Everyone has an opinion these days. I'm tired of people's opinions."

"And you're not even on Facebook."

My dad laughed. "I wouldn't be caught dead on that thing. Debbie is on it enough for the both of us. I figure, if something important ever happens, she'll let me know… So, what are you going to do on the big day?" he asked.

"Just dinner at a friend's," I said, debating telling him that we'd be in drag.

"Sounds nice. So, when are you and Michael going to come visit?"

"I don't know, Dad. It's hard for me to get away."

"You'd love Kelowna. Debbie and I could show you around. And it would be great for you to get to know Patrick and Sue better. I wish you and Kate had come out to Sue's wedding. You could've met that whole side of the family."

Debbie's daughter, Sue, had got married the year before to a roofer named Neil, but neither I nor Kate had attended the wedding. I suppose we could've, but neither of us wanted to travel all that way. Plus, it had been Gay Pride in Montreal, and I didn't want to miss it. My dad might have considered Debbie's relations to be "that side of the family," but the idea was ridiculous to me. They weren't a part of *our* family, so we didn't need to be there. "I know," I said, "I'm sorry I missed it."

"It would be nice if you could come visit sometime—

your sister's been twice now. Anyways," he said, wrapping things up as our calls never did last more than several minutes. "Tomorrow will be a big day for you and I wanted to call and wish you a happy birthday before things got too hectic. You know, your mother would've been very proud of what you've accomplished."

I froze for a second, a flash of heat in my body. "Thanks, Dad."

"Love you, Son. Talk soon."

I hung up the phone and composed myself. My dad had got soft with age. He was sixty-seven now and more expressive than I ever remember him being. I don't think he had ever said, "I love you," to me growing up, but it's how he ended his calls with me for the past few years. I did feel bad for not visiting, but I only got so much time off from work. Kelowna might be nice, but it wasn't a bustling metropolis like New York City, nor did it have Provincetown's very gay, sandy beaches. The flight to Kelowna would be long too. I looked it up one afternoon and learned that it would take seven and a half hours to get there from Montreal. That's a lot of time in the air. There were no direct flights, too, which meant I'd have to experience twice as many landings and take-offs.

"Who was that?" Michael said, standing in the doorway to our living room.

"My dad."

"Calling to wish you a happy birthday? Did you tell him?"

"No." There still was nothing to tell. I had recently heard from Wendy, and our second attempt hadn't worked either. "We should really visit him and Debbie sometime. Or I should, at least."

"Sure." Michael wasn't listening. His attention was down the hallway.

"What's the matter?"

"It's Malone. Can you help me?"

I followed Michael into the dining room to find Malone scooting across the floor on his butt. "You have a hanger there, buddy?" Michael asked, and moved behind the cat to get a better look. "Looks like he's got some cat grass stuck in there. You ready?"

I made a sound of disgust, but I knew what I had to do. I went to the kitchen to get a piece of paper towel. Michael lifted the cat and rested him against his shoulder with one hand supporting his backside. Malone made an uncomfortable groan and I saw it: a rigid turd that was attached to his bottom via a dry piece of grass. This wasn't the first time it had happened. We had bought Malone cat grass to help with his digestion, planting it in a small pot on the balcony off the kitchen, but on occasion the grass would pass through him and get caught on the way out. Sometimes, when he had trouble going, Malone would come to see us and meow in a different way, like he was in pain. Michael would follow the cat to where we kept the litter and coach him. "Come on," I'd hear him say. "You can do it." The cat would miraculously poop with Michael there to coax him. I tried to snatch the hanger with the piece of paper towel. Malone meowed as I pulled out the turd, but the grass was still lodged in his butt. I ended up tossing the paper towel aside and grabbed at it with my hands. It slid out easy. "Gross," I said, and shivered. I threw the blade in the trash and turned to wash my hands in the sink. Over the splash of water, I could hear Michael whispering to the cat, telling him he was sorry if it hurt and that everything would be okay.

The next day, Malone and Sutherland let us sleep in. Michael awoke first and rolled over to kiss me. "Happy birthday, buddy!" We took a few minutes to fool around before hitting the floor. I put on the coffee and went for a run. When I got home, I found that Michael had made breakfast. We ate omelettes in front of the TV. After we cleaned up, he jumped me again and we had sex on the kitchen floor.

Later that day, the two of us went over to Charles's early to help him set up and select our outfits for the evening. Charles answered the door in a bright red ball gown with matching heels and a yellow flower in his hair. There were screams and laughs and much hysteria as we bustled into his loft with our bags and put them down to examine his handiwork.

"Wow, did you make this?" Michael touched the stitching.

"I did!" Charles sang, a smile on his face. He twirled for us. "God, I miss creating for queens. The production has me designing mafia suits and cocktail dresses. At least film pays well. I would never have been able to afford this place had I kept working for drink tickets."

We went over to the dressing area where Charles had a chilled bottle of Prosecco waiting. He popped the cork and poured Michael and me flutes so we could sift through his wardrobe in style. I felt like a bride, sitting on Charles's leather armchair while Michael took out dress after dress. "This is the one," he finally exclaimed.

"Purple?" I asked, finishing my glass and standing up. It had been a while since I'd had a drink, and the booze went down fast. Thankfully, I had permission from Wendy and Eve to indulge on my birthday.

"Of course, purple," Michael said, holding it against me. "You're a winter."

"Do you think I'll fit into this?" The dress looked small and flimsy, like a thin strip of elastic material. I took off my shirt and pants, while Michael dove back in, and stepped into the dress in my underwear and socks. "How is this even a piece of clothing?" I said, but as I pulled on the item it took shape and stretched to accommodate my body. I moved towards the mirror. I was bursting out, the chunky mix of muscle and fat at my chest transformed into cleavage. I turned to face Michael. "What do you think?"

Michael pulled his head out of the closet and had a good laugh. "Oh, my stars!" he sang, and came out to start fussing with me. He arranged the line at my chest then pulled the length further down my thighs. "You look fantastic."

"Well, hello beautiful," Charles said, entering the room to refill our glasses.

"Which event did you make this for?" I asked.

"Who remembers," he said, topping me up. "One of the World Balls for Unity, maybe. I can't believe how good you look," he said, examining me from the side. "You sure you're forty?"

"No!" Michael was now back in the closet and freaking out over a bright orange frock he'd found. The dress was made of textured polyester and looked like it was from the sixties or seventies, with short sleeves, bronze buttons on one shoulder and large lapels. "I could do Mary Tyler Moore with this. If only you had a flip wig."

"I do have one," Charles said, stepping into the fray. "Move aside." Michael stood there, vibrating with excitement as Charles pulled down a brown wig and handed it to him. "Oh my god," he said, gasping. He got into his outfit and the two of us shared the mirror and laughed.

I decided not to wear make-up or a wig, just the purple dress with a gold necklace and a pair of black heels. It wasn't much of an illusion anyways, with my beard, and the hair on my arms, legs, chest and shoulders could not be hidden. "It's funny," I said to Michael as we preened in the mirror. "All these years and I still get a thrill from playing in the closet."

Soon after, guests began to arrive. Kate was the first to show. She had dressed like a man, in a suit jacket, tie and pencil moustache. She also had her hair tied up in a bun, which she kept hidden under a top hat. "*Guten Abend*, Michael said in greeting as he welcomed her in. Danny and Vince arrived a few minutes later, in matching black gowns and wigs. "Liza two times," Danny said, leaving a light trace of lipstick on my cheek as we kissed hello. Vince seemed joined at his hip. "Bonjour, bonjour," he said, kissing me too. "Merci pour l'invitation." This was the second time I was meeting Vince, Danny having invited us over for drinks the week before. It was too soon to say, but I felt that anyone game enough to look this ridiculous in front of his new lover's friends was a keeper.

Gus arrived an hour later. His drag was messy—a bright green Halloween wig, Daisy Duke cut-offs and a Metallica crop top. He was soon followed by Kevin, who arrived just as we sat down to dinner. When we had first planned the guest list, Charles asked if he could invite Kevin. Thrilled at the prospect of finally meeting someone he was dating, I had said yes, although I didn't think he would come (none of them ever did). As he walked towards the table, I was surprised to find that Kevin was shorter than I had imagined, and a tad older than he looked in the photos we'd seen. He wore expensive-looking leather pants and a tailored black shirt, yet his face was still that of a young man, smooth and round and unblemished.

"Finally!" Charles got up to greet him, and Kevin offered his cheek up for a kiss. "I was beginning to worry. Let's get you frocked."

"No," Kevin laughed, almost embarrassed at the idea. "I'm okay like this. Thanks!"

Charles popped open another bottle of Prosecco and we sat back down to eat. The meal was stellar, the conversation loud and boisterous. I had forgotten how fun dinner parties could be with alcohol. Kate had just been to Japan for work and had stories to share about the food she had eaten and the places she visited. Michael played DJ, running back and forth to Charles's stereo to tend to the soundtrack. Gus was quiet, rarely left Michael's side, and spoke mostly to Kevin, who spent much of the time texting on his phone.

Vince, on the other hand, gladly participated and held his own, asking questions, speaking in French with Michael, sharing opinions and jumping into conversations with Charles and Kate in English. I caught Danny glowing at times underneath his pancake make-up, proud of his new man's energy and intelligence. In this way, Vince reminded me of Michael. How I never had to worry about him at a dinner party. I'd had so many boyfriends over the years who I had to coddle and check in with, and who wanted to leave early.

With Michael, he was in a conversation as soon as we entered the door and I never once had to worry about where he was, or if he was having fun.

Halfway through the meal, I began to feel a headache from the booze, so I stopped Charles from filling up my glass and switched to water. Once dinner was done, after I'd blown out the candles and the chocolate cake was served, I got up from the table and headed to the kitchen at the far end of the room to make tea.

Kate followed me, a gift in tow. "Here," she said, and handed over a square box.

"Now? You don't want to wait until later?" I was already opening the package.

"It's a rare whisky," she said, as I lifted out the bottle. The writing on it was in Japanese. "I didn't want to give it to you in front of everyone, the way this room is drinking. It's expensive, and you can't get it in Canada, so save it for a special occasion."

"I will!" I said, and gave her a hug and kiss.

"Listen, I've got to get going," she said. "It's winding down—or up, I can't tell—but I figured I would let you boys have some girl time. I get the impression that everyone is holding back because there's a gentleman in the room."

"The way you're dressed, I'm surprised they're not hitting on you."

Kate chuckled. "Also, I have to leave first thing tomorrow and I want to spend some time with Ben."

"Okay," I said, reluctantly. I didn't mind that Kate wanted to leave the party (even I was ready to go), but I hated that she was leaving to see Ben. "How are things with Christian?" I asked.

"The same," she said. "He's refused all attempts to talk and doesn't want to go to couples' therapy. He's more than happy to come home and sit on the couch, drink and watch TV. If I knew that married life was going to be like this, I never would've bothered."

"Where does he think you're staying? My place?"

She shrugged. "A hotel, I guess." Kate had long abandoned her top hat and wore her hair down, her pencil moustache faded. "I don't think I mentioned it. Honestly, he couldn't care less."

There was a loud break of laughter from the far end of the room, which caused us to turn our heads towards the dining table and its shimmering candles. Danny was holding court while Gus smoked a cigarette by the window with Michael beside him.

"Listen," Kate said. "I know it would have been too much to bring him tonight, but I'd like you to meet him sometime."

My chin went down and my eyes forward. "Ben? Why?"

"What do you mean, why?"

"Well, why would I meet him?" I took out two sachets of tea from Charles's cupboards. "He's not your boyfriend. It's not like you're going to have a relationship with him. Kate, you're married!"

My sister folded her arms. "Well, I'd like him to meet someone in my life. I've told him so much about you, and you're the only person I can introduce him to. I like him. I think you'd like him too."

I stood there, frowning in my dress. I could see how it would all play out. Christian being stubborn, refusing to change but not realizing what was at stake. I felt sorry for him because he was a nice guy and I knew he loved my sister.

But I also understood how Kate felt. What can you do with a partner who no longer hears what you have to say? Who no longer pulls you close at night?

I opened my mouth to say something, but stopped. Kate looked so small and determined standing there, deflated in her oversized suit jacket. How could I say no to my older sister? "Okay, let me think about it," I said.

"Thanks, Paul."

"Come here," I said, pulling her into an embrace. "I just want the best for you, you know."

"I know. I love you."

"I love you too." I patted her on the back. "Get out of here. It's just a room full of queens anyway."

"You rang?" Danny had appeared in the kitchen, his glass empty. "Sorry, am I interrupting?"

"No, I'm taking off. Good to see you tonight, Danny." Kate gave him a hug. "Vince seems great. Don't take each other for granted, okay?" She picked up her hat from the couch and went back to the table at the far end of the room to say goodnight to the others.

"What was that about?" Danny asked.

"I'll tell you later."

The kettle began to boil and I moved to pour the tea while Danny continued his search among the empty bottles on the counter. "There's got to be another here somewhere."

"So Liza, how are things with Whale Breach?"

Danny chuckled. "I can't believe I told you that. Aha!" Danny found one last bottle of red and pulled it out of a nest of empties. He yanked the twist top open and poured himself a deep glass. "Things are good, but I'm awfully tired."

"Tired?"

He took a sip. "We're seeing a lot of each other, and I find I'm getting up most mornings at six. It's when his penis gets up. We spent our first weekend together last week."

"How was it?"

"Good, I think. A lot of checking in and reassurance: *How are you doing? What's the matter? Are you okay? Is anything wrong?* At one point he went out to get groceries and I stayed behind and cleaned his apartment. I washed his dishes, scrubbed his fixtures, folded his laundry. I was like, *What am I doing? Am I nesting?* If I were a bird, I would have been out gathering twigs and sticks to bring back home."

With my tea in hand, and Danny cradling the open bottle, we rejoined the others at the table.

"Thanks for dinner, Charles," Danny said, turning to our host. "Everything was delicious. I'm glad it wasn't a potluck. Potlucks are such bullshit. If you invite me to your place for dinner, I'm not cooking!"

The music stopped, and Michael got up to put on something new. "Any requests?"

"Play something expensive," Danny yelled out.

It took Michael a moment to find something. "I don't know if this is expensive," he said, pressing play, "but when they came to town I couldn't afford to go." It was the unmistakeable opening of Pet Shop Boys' "Being Boring," its fanciful synths in a slow dance with guitar quips and bass steps.

It had an immediate effect on Danny. "Faggotry at its finest."

Michael swished back to the table, his wig lost somewhere in the loft. "Okay, present time!" he said and handed me a square package wrapped in grey paper with a large blue bow. There was no card, but written on the paper, in black marker, it said: *Happy 40th to my man! Love, Michael.*

I tore it open. It was one of Michael's drawings, but not one I had seen. This one was framed and in full colour. In it, Malone, Sutherland, Michael and I were all at the beach in Provincetown, nude, on a blanket by the water. The image was more cartoonish than sexy. Our bare bottoms faced up, while Malone and Sutherland sat back, heads tilted skyward, enjoying the sun. We looked like Looney Tunes characters— neutered, friendly—our faces bright and mouths open. In the distance was the Pilgrim Monument beyond the dunes, and at our feet a picnic basket and a tube of sunscreen. Michael had also placed a copy of Mordden's *Buddies* on the blanket next to me. It couldn't have been more perfect.

"I love it, Michael," I said, caught by emotion. "It's wonderful. Thank you."

"Let me see!" Everyone clamoured for it and passed it around, while I kissed Michael. Danny, Vince and Charles all made the necessary hoopla, happily reminded by the illustration that we'd all be in Provincetown in three weeks' time.

Charles's present had been the party and the catering costs, but he still had something for me to unwrap—a stylish green cashmere sweater and two colourful ties that must have set him back. "You can also keep the dress!"

"You're going to hate what I got you," Danny said, as he handed over a flat box wrapped in dark blue paper. I didn't understand. Danny had already told me what he was giving me—a year's subscription for two to the 2011/2012 season at the Centaur Theatre. Inside was a black vintage T-shirt with a silver and red decal in the centre with the words "Super Dad" on it. Everyone laughed. "I didn't get it because, you know… I got it because you're entering your daddy years."

"Your best years!" Michael said behind me, his hands on my shoulders.

"I love it," I said, and got up to kiss my friend.

"How goes the baby-making?" Vince asked, as I sat back down.

"It's going. We've tried twice so far and it hasn't worked. Third time's at the end of next week, and hopefully it's the charm. But it's normal, I suppose, for it to not work right away. I mean, what do I know about it, really?"

"Well, it's not like your sperm has had much practice," Danny said.

"I think what you're doing is great," Vince said, taking off his wig and placing it on the table next to the half-eaten cake. "To think, you might have a child by your next birthday. Do you wonder what they will be like? What he or she will look like?"

"Not really. I'm trying not to."

"What will he or she call you?" Kevin asked.

"Uncle Paul."

"Really?" Vince asked, surprised. "Not Dad? Isn't that what you'll be?"

"Well no, not really. The kid will have my DNA and everything. They'll know where they came from, but I won't be the *dad.*"

"Yes, you will," Vince said, unconvinced. "You're not going to be a *parent*, but you will be a father. We all have a father and mother."

"Wendy and Eve are sensitive about calling Paul the father," Danny explained.

"Well, that's too bad."

"Is it?" I said, unsure where this was coming from. "I don't feel any need to claim the term. They won't be my child. I'm just the sperm donor. I provided the genetic material to help Wendy and Eve start their family. Who cares what I'll be called?"

Vince dipped his fork back into the cake. "My dad's a complete deadbeat," he said, licking a thumb. "He's not in my life. I know him, I see him every few years or so, but I wasn't raised by him. He's not a stranger, but he's never been a parent. Never supported me or taught me anything. But he's still *my dad*! No matter what your friends *want*, you'll still be this kid's dad."

I didn't want to argue with Danny's new boyfriend, but I was also beginning to feel like my own father—tired of people's opinions. "Biologically, I will be the child's *father*. And the child will know that. But it's problematic for me to use that word. It represents a type of relationship I won't have with the child. I don't even know yet what relationship we will have."

"Let's say it's a girl," Kevin said, speaking up for what felt like the first time that night. "What will you call her?"

I hadn't thought of that. "I don't know. Whatever her name is, I guess."

"But she'll be your *daughter*," said Vince.

I had to laugh. "No, she won't."

"I understand, Paul, where Wendy and Eve are coming from," Danny interjected, finishing his glass and reaching for the bottle. "But I must agree with Vince. Wendy and Eve may not *want* you to use the words "dad" or "daughter," but that's what you'll be to each other. And who are you kidding? This kid will want to call you dad. You're not going to deny the kid the opportunity to have a father, are you?"

"Who said I would deny the kid anything?"

"It would be tragic for her to not have a father," Danny said, his make-up shiny in the candlelight. "I think you'd be great at it too. There are so many fucked-up kids out there. It's imperative that a child know their father."

"What!? Do you hear what you're saying?" I said, astonished. "That's the excuse homophobes have been using for decades to delegitimize queer families—that a child *needs* a mother and father to be raised correctly."

Danny sighed. "I didn't mean it like that," he said, apologetic upon hearing the tone in my voice. "I simply meant that this child could benefit from having a kind and caring man like you in their life." He reached over the table and held my hand. "We just want the best for you, Paul. We want to make sure you're thinking of yourself too."

Vince jumped back in. "But don't you think, when she comes out—and looks like your mother, let's say—you might feel different. You might *want* to be her dad."

I hadn't thought that the kid might look like my mother.

Gus, much like Kevin, had remained quiet for most of the evening, but suddenly he spoke up. "Just because you might want to have kids doesn't mean everyone feels that way," he said to Danny. "Not everyone thinks of family the same way. I'd be a horrible father." He smiled to himself, amused. "Thankfully, there's no danger of that. If men could get pregnant, I'd have fathered thousands by now."

Danny scoffed. "Oh yes, we all know about you and your boatload of boyfriends," he said. "I've met you on, what, three occasions now and you're always alluding to these *orgies* you get invited to. You've got to ride every cock like it's the Kentucky Derby. Receive more pearl necklaces than the stock boys at Tiffany's. There's nothing wrong with a little tradition, you know. You'll learn that as soon as you get older and become bored with all the nights out clubbing and cruising for sex. It's 2011. It's okay for gay men to want to get married and raise a family."

There was surprise on Gus's face as he crossed his thin arms against the Metallica skull on his T-shirt. "Honestly, I don't know why anyone wants to get married and have kids. The best thing about being queer is not doing what society expects of us, not buying into the lie of the white picket fence. It might be 2011, but gay men are too respectable these days. It was better when everything was underground. I think I was born in the wrong era. What I wouldn't give to have lived during the seventies."

"Well, you'd be dead by now," Danny said, the stain of wine in his voice.

"Danny!" I said.

"Well he would, the way he sleeps around." He turned back to address Gus. "I know what *you* think—that love is a weakness. You're bored by the thought that two men might want to be monogamous and spend their lives together and raise a family. You think life is one big Saturday night. That I'm a prude or a simpleton because I want to build a life with one person, and not be part of someone's harem."

Gus lit a cigarette at the table. "Listen, *you* can have

whatever kind of relationship *you* want. But it's dangerous to believe in forever love. There's no such thing."

"Sounds to me like you've never been in love."

"Do you mind smoking that near the window?" Charles asked Gus. "Only joints at the table."

Gus got up and walked over to the open window with his cigarette. "I've been in love plenty of times," he said, "but I believe you can love more than one person, that you can have many loves throughout your lifetime." He turned to the rest of us. "How many of your parents are still together?"

"Mine are together," Kevin said. He was the only one who answered.

"And you, Danny?"

"My parents are dead, Gus. And had they not both died together on the same tragic night, I'm sure they would still be married today."

I suddenly wished for more wine.

"All I'm saying is that you can't expect to get everything you need from one person," Gus said, glancing at Vince. He turned and looked at me. "And you're not going to be saved by having a *father* either."

Exhausted by the conversation, everyone was ready to go fifteen minutes later. I looked at the time, it was a quarter to midnight. Normally, after these *souper des femmes*, Charles, Danny and I would blast music, down a couple of shots and walk to a nearby Village bar in our dresses. But tonight Charles called a taxi for Danny, who was beginning to fade, and I helped Vince, who seemed quiet, to collect their things. Kevin said he was going out to a club I had never heard of, and Gus spoke of a date he had arranged with a couple on the apps. After everyone had left, I stayed behind to help Charles clean while Michael dozed on the couch.

"Do you think it'll be okay?" I asked. "With Gus coming to Provincetown?"

"I think so," Charles said. "Danny was so drunk; he won't remember most of it. And Gus doesn't seem like someone who lets people get under his skin. The house is big enough for everyone."

"Do you think Kevin would want to come?"

Charles started throwing cutlery into the sink. "No. To be honest, I think he came tonight to check you all out. See what it might be like to be around us for a week."

"Yikes. Well, I'm sorry about that." Charles started to wash the dishes, and I grabbed a towel to help dry. "You upset he went out?"

"Nah. He doesn't belong to me, he belongs to the city. I'll probably get a text from him in an hour, asking if I'm up and if he can come over. Then tomorrow, he'll be up and on his merry way. We'll see each other on set on Monday but won't talk. And then, like clockwork, I'll get a message a couple days later asking if we can get together over the weekend."

"I hate to say it, Charles, but I don't know what you see in him," I said, drying a salad bowl. "Sure, he's cute, but I thought actors were supposed to be wells of emotion."

"There's a deep side to him."

"Well, none of that came across."

"Listen, *you* don't have to see anything in him," Charles said, amused at my concern. "I'm the one who does. And I'll see it in him again too—every inch of him, in my bed, maybe even later tonight."

"That good, huh?"

"I hope he does come to Provincetown, then you'll see him in his bathing suit—his smooth chest, the curve of his leg muscles as they head to his ankles, the bones in his feet. I don't know why we lose all this beauty as we get older."

"Come on," I said. "We might not be the spring chickens we once were, but I still believe in original beauty. I see it in you, I see it in Danny. To hell with age. It's kindness that's beautiful, it's humour that's hot. When someone stands up for you, makes you laugh. Does Kevin do all that for you?"

Charles scrubbed the bottom of a plate that much harder. I took it as a sign to move on.

"I worry about Danny," I said. "Do you think he drinks too much?"

"If he does, we all do."

"It feels like it's *more* all of a sudden. I don't know, maybe I'm just seeing it now that I've cut back."

"Do you think your sister had fun?" Charles asked. "She left early. Usually, she closes the place."

I hesitated to tell Charles about what Kate was going through. She had asked me to keep it private, but I needed to talk to someone about it. So I told him everything—about her problems with her husband, how she met Ben, our own words at the party, and the added complexity of her inability to have children. "I feel like she's being selfish. She says she can't help it, that it's primal. I understand the need to push back against her husband, but I'd rather she leave Christian and reconnect with who she is, rather than jump into something else with another guy."

Charles stopped what he was doing and turned to face

me. "Don't you remember what it was like, Paul? The pull of desire inside you?"

I stopped, afraid of what he had to say. "Yes. It's far away, but I remember."

"I turned my back on my family—my own mother and sisters—when they refused to accept who I was. Do you think a houseful of Black Christians from Baltimore wanted a gay son or brother back in those AIDS days? I sacrificed everything to come to Canada in the depths of winter to find what I knew I needed. Just be there for her, the way she was for you."

I picked up another dish and started drying. "I know you're right. It's just so... lusty. It's like my sister's a gay man—coming out to tell me who she is and how it's all tied up with identity and desire."

Charles sighed. "Gus is right. We have become too respectable. I also miss the time when everyone didn't like us. Do you remember those days? We were so angry, so entitled. Everyone was dying around us, and we didn't know if there'd be a tomorrow. So we fought back. We took lovers. We made every moment count. And now? We have everything." He motioned over to the kitchen counter. "Those pills keep me alive. Gays can get married and join the military. Corporations beg for our money. And night after night we sit at a banquet with our friends, trading barbs and making each other laugh, when all I want to do is sneak out of my parents' house again to make out in a park with some guy I just met." Charles gave up on the dishes for a moment and sat down to light another joint. "I miss the days when kissing a lover on the Metro, or holding his hand, was a political act. I miss getting looked at in the street for wearing the dress that you're wearing right now and getting called a fag from out of the window of a passing car. I was never more sure of who I was when that was happening."

"Be careful what you wish you. It's still like that in many places in the world, I assure you." I took over for Charles at the sink. "I think we're very lucky," I said. "When I came out, there were two things I figured I would never get to do: get married and have children. Now we can do both."

The air felt still for a moment and Charles's breath caught on the smoke. "You're not telling me you're getting married now, are you?"

"It would be nice to have a party."

"Are you serious?"

"It's not important to me or Michael," I said, not wanting to toy with him further. "But if it was important to him, I'd do it. I have to admit that sometimes when I look at him, I think, why not? I love him so much. We're family. Why not make this grand gesture and throw a lavish party to let everyone know how much we love each other?"

"You've changed." Charles laughed.

"Have I?"

"Your job, your home life, your relationship. You're not the same angry kid I remember."

"Sometimes I worry that I've changed too much. I can be such a nag to Michael sometimes. *I'm not going to say anything*, I say to myself, but then I do. I wish I could relax more. I wish I wasn't so anxious."

On the counter, Charles's phone lit up with a notification. He picked it up and smiled. "See, what did I tell you?" He took a moment to reply to Kevin, then took one last drag from his joint before snuffing out the ember in an ashtray on the counter.

"Do you miss Alan?" I asked.

A silence passed before Charles answered. "Of course I miss Alan."

"Do you think of him as often as I do?"

"Yes."

"I've been thinking about him a lot lately. I guess it has to do with turning forty. We'd be celebrating his fiftieth this year, can you imagine? He'd be here tonight, sitting at the table in one of the dresses from your closet."

"Do you remember your first *souper des femmes*?" Charles asked. "You looked like a young Cyndi Lauper, with your wild orange wig and jean jacket. You were so drunk that you threw up in the bathroom and we had to put you to bed on the coats in my room."

I laughed. "I don't know if I want to remember that."

"Alan went in every fifteen minutes to check on you, and when the party was over, he picked you up and carried you home. You were out cold, like Michael is now."

I looked over to where Michael slept, splayed out on Charles's couch in his orange gown. He looked peaceful, his breath rising and falling. "You know," I said, careful not to wake him, "Alan would've loved Michael."

9

ALAN AND I MET in the spring of 1994. I had come out to myself (and my sister) in September of the previous year. At that time, my mother had been dead six months. Gone with her was any semblance of a normal life, so it was becoming increasingly difficult for me to look into the mirror and ignore what I saw. My sexuality was happy to keep my sadness company.

"Cool." That's what my sister said when I called her up to tell her in her dorm room at Trent. "Janet's older brother is gay," she added, referring to the bassist in her band.

By then I was twenty-two and in university, taking the train downtown to Concordia and hanging around the Village when I didn't have class. I was pursuing a degree in journalism, which I had begun to doubt was for me. I never wanted to get the scoop or chase the story; all I wanted to do was research in the bars along Sainte Catherine Street East.

"Can you be a professional homosexual?" I asked Kate one day. "Could someone do that for a living?" The people publishing *Fugues*, the gay monthly I discovered coming out of a bar one night, seemed to have made a career of it. At home, I read the magazine cover to cover behind my bedroom door, my dad downstairs watching TV.

Whenever I was home, I avoided my father. I couldn't stand the look of grief, the loneliness on his face when he tried to engage me: *Hi Son, how was your day? What time will you be home for dinner?* His pain reminded me of my own. With Kate away at school, our big house was now home to only my father and me. It was hard to be there, alone with him, in that dark cavernous space with all of its complicated memories. I began to go out at night, even if I had nowhere to be. I just needed to get out of the house.

On some occasions, I'd stay out until the bars closed and take the night bus home; other times, I'd pack a book in my knapsack and wait at a coffee shop for the morning trains to start up. The next night I'd be back at the bars, chatting up the few people I recognized from going out as much as I did. These young men seemed nice enough, but I would hardly call them friends. They were like classmates, associates, pretty faces who would humour me and my silly jokes. One of them was a Psychology student named David. He grabbed me one night, as I was about to leave the bar, and kissed me by the coat check. He invited me home with him.

When we got back to his place in NDG, I found out he lived with his parents and younger sister. He led me downstairs to his bedroom in the basement where we had quiet, anxious sex in the dark. "You can't be here when my folks wake up," he said, before I had even caught my breath. He turned on the lights so I could get dressed, then ran me up the stairs and out the door. It was my first time. It was clumsy, over so quickly.

Over the next month, I continued to see David. The subsequent hook-ups were not much better than the initial encounter, still dull and tepid. He'd invite me over when no one was home or arrange for us to use one of his friends' apartments. One afternoon, while his parents were out shopping, he said he wanted me to fuck him. I'd never done that before. I didn't know what to do. David got on top of me and slid down my cock. I panicked inside him. "But I'm not wearing a condom," I said.

Afterwards, David insisted that what we had done was safe. "Relax," he said, when I still seemed bothered. "You've never been with anyone—and the top can't catch anything, so you have nothing to worry about."

The whole thing made me feel ashamed and unsure. But it didn't stop me the next time we got together, or the time after that.

One day, while reading the April edition of *Fugues*, I noticed a call for volunteers for the city's Gay Pride celebration in August. Even if it wasn't a paid position, helping to produce Montreal's Pride parade would put me closer to my goal of being a professional homosexual. I took note of the date and time of the meeting, and asked David if he would come with me.

The organization's offices were on the second floor of an office building on Saint Laurent. The room was half full when we arrived, about twenty-five people standing around metal folding chairs that had been arranged in rows. I hung out at the back with David and watched the room fill up as we waited for the meeting to start.

"It's all older men and lesbians," he said, disappointed.

I found the mix interesting. I only ever saw boys my age in the bars I went to, but here there were *men*. Handsome men, like the older one with the shaved head at the front of the room who led the meeting.

"Bonjour tout le monde, I'm Alan," he said, alternating between French and English. "Thank you all for coming out to learn about this year's march and what you can do to make it a success."

He started off with the backstory for those of us who didn't know—about how the parade began in response to a police raid on an after-hours party called Sex Garage. Montreal police had taunted the partygoers as they broke up the event, leading to multiple arrests and beatings. "I still have the scar," he said, rolling up the sleeve of his blue plaid shirt to show us the gash on his forearm. "So you see, the police aren't our friends. We're going to need help with security on the day. And we're going to need your help in getting word out too—making calls to make sure we reach as many people as possible."

Alan listed all the jobs that were available.

"You sure you want to do this?" David asked, once the meeting was over. "Sounds like a lot of responsibility to me. I'd rather be partying." David picked up his coat. We had plans to get to the bar before cover charge. "You ready to go?"

"You go ahead," I said. "I'll catch up with you later."

I waited until Alan was alone then went up to introduce myself. "Crazy about your arm," I said.

Alan smiled, and lifted it again to show me. "Twelve stitches," he said, running his finger along the smooth line of flesh. "Looks worse than it feels."

"I'd like to help out," I said. "I don't think I'd be good with parade security, but I can help with other things. I know computers and I'm a pretty good writer."

"How old are you?" he asked.

I told him. "I live in Pointe-Claire with my dad, but I go

to Concordia—so I can come by after class or on weekends, or on Fridays when I don't have school."

Alan searched for a pen and wrote down his phone number on a piece of paper. "Why don't you come by the office on Saturday?" he suggested. "You can help me with the press list."

That Saturday morning, I got up early and said good-bye to my dad as I headed out the door. "Be back late," I shouted, and ran to catch the train into town. When I got to the office, Alan was there, in a plain army-green T-shirt, tufts of dark hair at his triceps as he sat at a desk in front of an old Apple computer smoking a joint.

"Do you think you could help us build a media list?" he asked. He led me to a pile of local and national newspapers and magazines on a folding table nearby. My job was to go through them and locate any stories about gay rights in Canada and around the world then clip them out and put them into a binder.

"Do you know Excel?" he asked. I nodded. He led me to another square computer and showed me where he wanted me to enter the names and contact info of any journalists I came across that might be sympathetic to our cause.

That day, I spent two hours reading, clipping and recording names. I came back the following two weekends to new piles and did the same. Mostly, Alan and I kept busy at opposite ends of the room, me reading with my head down while he made phone calls to city officials and gay-owned businesses. Often, random people would buzz the office and come up off the street to chat with him and share a joint. I used to wonder if my dad could smell it on me when I got home, if I got any contact high from being in that room for hours.

Before long, I found myself at the office two or three times a week, stopping by after class or skipping school altogether. Alan asked me to help with writing press releases, booking ads and pulling together the content for the program. I learned about how he had grown up in Ottawa and moved to Montreal at nineteen. "You'd have thought I couldn't have disappointed my parents more by being gay," he said one afternoon. "Imagine telling them that I was quitting university to become an activist."

After the first month, Alan trusted me enough to give me a set of keys to the office. Sometimes I'd crash there, sleeping on the love seat after heading out to the bars. Alan started to see a pattern in finding me on the tiny couch on Friday mornings, and he'd show up with an extra croissant. "You know, you're welcome to crash at my place," he said one morning. "I have an extra bedroom, and I live in the Village. You won't have to come all the way up here and throw out your back on this shitty couch."

Alan lived on Plessis Street, half a block south from the bars in the Village. I took him up on his offer. Once. Twice. Three times. Soon, my Thursday night ritual began with stopping by his place for a drink, dropping off my knapsack in his spare room and taking a quick shower before heading out to the bars. Alan would sometimes have a friend over (it was here where I first met Charles), but most of the time it would be just him and me. Alan would take out two Black Label beers from his fridge and we'd sit at the bar in his kitchen and drink and talk and listen to music. Alan played classical music at the office, but at home he'd play Pet Shop Boys. Their album *Very* had come out the previous year, and he was obsessed with it.

Alan didn't have an extra key to his place, so he'd leave his back door open on the nights I stayed over, the yellow light on his balcony beckoning me as I stumbled through his backyard to a comfortable bed. He was always asleep when I returned, but he made sure to keep the lamp on in the spare room, two towels on the bed, and several packages of rubbers and lube on the nightstand.

I knew I had his permission to bring someone over, and as much as the thought thrilled me, there was never anyone I wanted to bring back. I had recently stopped sleeping with David, as he'd become entangled with another guy we knew from the bars. Sometimes, though, David would still try to hook up with me. One night, when he found out I had a place to sleep, he tried to get me to take him there. "No," I said. "It's not that kind of place."

He continued to insist. I slipped out when he went to the washroom and went back to Alan's. I caught him in the kitchen on my way in, a sleepy look on his face, fridge door open, pouring a glass of milk.

"How was your night?" he asked.

"Frustrating," I said, feeling the beer. "I don't get gay guys. I thought it would be different after coming out. Dating never made sense when it was girls I felt pressured to sleep with. But then, after I realized I was gay, I thought that it would all click into place. That I'd feel more at home in my skin. But I don't. If anything, I feel skinned alive."

"How long have you been out now?" Alan asked. "A year?"

"Since September."

He smiled. "Don't worry. You're getting your sea legs."

151

"How long was it before you met someone you could trust?" I asked.

Alan shrugged. In his tired face I could tell it was too late for such contemplation. "I don't know," he said, and yawned. "It can take time. You're starting all over again. On your first day of high school, how do you know who's going to talk behind your back, who'd be happy to go with you to the prom? The great ones stand out from the rest over time. When you meet that person, you'll know. Just listen to your gut."

The next morning, my dad intercepted me on the way into the house. "Paul, why are you never home any more?" he asked, standing in the kitchen doorway. He wasn't angry, but I could tell he was bothered. "Where do you stay when you go out at night?"

"I've been staying at a friend's place," I said. "He lives downtown, and it makes more sense for me to stay there if I plan on being out late."

"Are you sleeping with him?"

"Dad!"

"Well, are you?"

I couldn't speak.

"You're going to tell me to mind my own business, aren't you? But why would you say that if it weren't true?"

"What does it matter?"

"So, you are."

"No, I'm not!" I said.

"Paul, just do me a favour, will you? Just be careful out there."

"Dad!" I was flustered. Was this it? My coming out moment? "I'm *not* having this conversation with you."

Over the next week, I tried harder to avoid my father. I thought about moving out, but how could I do that when I was in school and made no money?

The following Thursday night, I showed up at Alan's place earlier than usual. We were two weeks away from Pride, and it seemed like much of the office had been moved to his house, papers strewn everywhere, an ashtray filled with expired joints next to his computer. Alan was busy, but he found time to put on *Very* and sit down with me to have a beer before I went out.

Alan yawned. He had been working on the procession order for the parade and could no longer focus. "I think I should call it a night. It's too hot and my brain is fried."

It was the end of July and the days had been sweltering. Thankfully, the beer was cold and refreshing. Sitting there, drops of condensation running down the neck of my bottle, I no longer wanted to go to the bar. I realized that part of what I loved most about these nights were our talks in his kitchen. I took my time with my drink. When my beer was empty, I looked at the time. It was shortly before ten. If I wanted to make it to the bar before cover, I'd need to leave soon. Or I could stay. Could I? But what would I say? *Hey Alan, can I stay here with you instead? Want to watch a movie?*

I brushed my teeth and changed my shirt. Alan was starting *Very* up for a second time when I waved goodbye and left through his back door. I headed out to the alley, then up to Sainte Catherine Street where I made a right and darted into Sky Club, making it in time to beat the cover charge. I bought a beer, sat down on one of the windowsills near the pool tables, and waited for the place to fill up.

I recognized a few familiar faces, young men who, like me, came out every week without fail. In the distance, I saw the man that David was now dating with two of his well-dressed friends, visibly excited for their Thursday night. Normally, I would go up and say hi, make small talk before moving on, but I didn't feel like it. I didn't want to be here any more. The DJ began to play a remix of one of the tracks from *Very*. I took it as a sign.

I left my beer on the windowsill and headed back to Alan's place through the alley. He was in the kitchen as I entered, halfway through another beer.

"Back so soon?" he said. "Forget something?"

I threw myself at him. I grabbed at him with my mouth, all over his face, his neck, my arms pulling up his shirt.

Alan laughed as he kissed me back. "Easy, easy," he said. "What's the rush?"

I slowed down and let his kisses lead the way. Soon, his passion overtook mine.

It felt great being touched by Alan, his hands pulling my face, my body, close to his. This is the stuff, I thought to myself. This is the electricity I'd been waiting for. I loved the bitterness of his tongue, the warmth of his breath and the smell of his sweat. I reached for his shorts, and he pulled away.

"Follow me," he said. He led me into his bedroom. I reached to switch the light off, but he grabbed my hand. "No," he said. "Leave it on."

Alan sat me on his bed and went down on his knees. He popped open my button fly and pulled down my shorts. Time slipped away as I disappeared in his mouth, my head rolled back, my body losing its shape in a profound blaze of roaring pleasure. When it was over, I came harder than I had ever done with David, falling back onto Alan's sheets in a giddy exhaustion. "Wow," I said, almost laughing. "Can we do that again?"

Alan was breathing hard too. He lay down on the bed, next to me. "Any time," he said.

I reached over to take off his shorts. "No, I'm okay," he said, waving me off. "I've been wanting that to happen for a long time."

"Me too," I said.

Alan sat up. He looked at me and smiled, but the smile turned serious as his breath slowed and returned to normal. He put his hand on my leg and looked down at the bedspread. "Paul," he said. "If this is going to happen again, there is one thing you need to know. I'm HIV-positive."

I hadn't met anyone HIV-positive before. I sat there, still. "Sure," I said, trying to be nonchalant. "That's okay."

"What we did was safe," he said, "and I take my partner's safety very seriously, but I need you to know now. In case anything happens between us again."

I could tell he was nervous. It was the first time I had seen him this way, this man who I felt had all the answers, who spoke with such confidence when talking to businessmen, politicians and the police. It made no sense to me that anything could scare him. I sat up and turned to him. I placed my hand on his sober smooth face and extracted a smile from it as I moved up to rub the prickly hairs on his scalp then pulled him towards me to kiss him squarely on the mouth.

We both went into the office the next day, but kept what had happened to ourselves. It thrilled me to sit there on the other side of the room, memories of the night before flooding back with each glimpse of him. That night, I went back to his place instead of going home. We had sex everywhere—in bed, in the shower, in the kitchen. Pet Shop Boys playing every time: *Very, Please, Behaviour*. Alan's body was softer than mine; still he was fit with strong arms and legs, and a dimple on his stomach right underneath the spot where his jeans would button up. I loved this dent on his body; like the scar on his forearm, they were beautiful imperfections that made him that much more real to me. The signs of a life well lived.

The next week was the beginning of Pride, and I packed up five days' worth of clothes and left a note for my dad, telling him I'd be staying at a friend's. Alan and I spent the days in the office, working hard, and the nights in the bars, celebrating. One of the places he took me was this basement bar in the centre of the city called Le Mystique, where George tended bar and where Charles was a regular. I had no idea there were gay bars downtown, and when I went down the stairs with him that first time it felt like we had walked through a time warp to the seventies: the decor, the patrons, the music. At the end of another fun night, we stumbled home, beer on our breath, to make love in his apartment.

"I want you to fuck me," I said.

"What? I don't know, Paul. I mean, have you ever..."

"No," I said, quite drunk. "But I want you to be my first."

"Well, that's nice," he said, distracted while we kissed. "But maybe not tonight, okay? What's the rush?" We continued to fumble around in his room in the dark. I couldn't get enough of him, of the night we had just had, of this life that I had only recently realized was worth living. In all the bustle and excitement, I reached, took his cock and rubbed it towards my backside. He threw me off the bed and turned on the light. "What the fuck do you think you're doing?"

"What?" I said. "I'm sorry, I just got into it and I..."

"No!" He was angry with me now. "You can't do this, Paul! Jesus, Christ. You shouldn't be doing this."

I felt sad, scared for a moment. I was worried I had changed things between us. "I'm sorry, Alan. I just want to be close to you."

He got up from where he had been sitting, a pillow in his hands. "I don't think I can do this tonight. It's better if you stay in the spare room."

I felt like crying. "But Alan, no. I'm sorry. Can't I just..."

"Not tonight," he said. "We can talk about it tomorrow."

Dejected, I went into his spare room and sat on the side of the bed. I felt dizzy, my ears ringing from the bar. I got up to get water and heard the sound of the bathroom door closing and the run of the shower. I tried to open the door, to get in with him, but Alan had locked it. I turned around, and headed to bed. Almost immediately, I fell asleep.

The next morning, I awoke with a bad headache. I found Alan in the kitchen, reading the daily newspaper and drinking a cup of coffee. "Want some?" he asked.

I shook my head. "About last night," I said, sitting down. "I'm sorry. I don't know what I was thinking. I was drunk."

"Paul, you've got to be careful," he said, and put down the paper. "You're going to meet men who will fall for you, and you will fall for them. You're going to think that they can't hurt you, but they can. I don't want to be the reason you get sick."

Finally, we arrived at the day of the parade. I could see the joy on Alan's face as the procession got ready to leave, my own happiness reflected in the mirrored sunglasses he wore. I was dressed up too. Alan let me raid his closet. I found a rainbow coloured feather boa that I draped proudly around my shoulders. It was surreal walking the route with thousands of other queers, as spectators cheered us along from the sidelines. My face hurt from how much I smiled.

As the day came to an end, I ran back to the office to send out the final press release, and when I was done I rejoined Alan at the Pride stage in the park near the Village. After the last performer had gone home, I found him enjoying a joint in the backstage area with Charles. "Go," Alan said, after I asked him if there was anything else I could do. "Go out. Have fun. Flirt. Meet a cute boy. Wish him a Happy Pride and ask him to dance."

I gave Alan a big hug and a kiss. I took my feather boa and left to hit the bars. I wasn't drunk, but I did feel euphoric and invincible. There were still hundreds of people out celebrating along Sainte Catherine Street, hopping from party to party as midnight drew near. I decided to go to my favourite haunt, Sky Club, and treat myself to a beer, maybe dance a little before fatigue sent me back to Alan's.

On my way to the bar, I passed the park at the corner of Panet Street. There, I came across the AIDS vigil. About a dozen people were still there, determined to keep the flickering candles company until they melted down to their ends. I stopped and, for a moment, was transfixed by the shimmering light. I sat down on the ground and immersed myself in the glowing faces of the men and women around me, as they looked inside the flames for flickers of their lost friends and lovers.

I thought of my mother. I realized that for the first time in months I had forgotten my sadness. I felt happy with Alan in my life. I didn't say the words out loud, but I did say them in my head. *Mom*, I said. *I really miss you. Things haven't been the same since you left.* Tearing up, I wiped my eyes with the back of my hands. *I wish you could be here for this. I wish you could experience this exciting and terrifying time with me. It's not the same without you. I wish things didn't have to be so different now. But I think I've found what I've been missing. I think I'm going to be all right.*

10

AT THE END OF AUGUST, we packed our bags and headed south to Provincetown. It was a long drive, about nine hours with traffic and stops, but Michael loved every moment, shifting Baby's gears and hugging the road as we sped along the highways. A sense of euphoria hit as we neared the tip of the Cape, passing through North Truro to spot the tall sceptre of the Pilgrim Monument in the distance.

"This is it! We're here!" Michael gushed out the open window as we approached. "Oh, how I missed you P-Town."

Michael drove down the narrow roads to Pearl Street and our house, a 1920s arts-and-crafts bungalow sandwiched between two other cedar shake homes. We pulled into the small gravel driveway and once the ignition was off, he jumped up and out and ran around the house to the backyard while Gus and I stretched our legs.

"It's here," Michael called out from around the corner. "I can't believe it's still here."

I walked over to find Michael leaning over the garden's water spigot, fingering a gaudy hoop earring he had left across the spout the previous year. "I forgot you left that there," I said.

Somehow it felt that nothing had changed since we were here last, that the entire town had thrown dust covers over everything until our return. The back door to the house was unlocked and we let ourselves in. The place looked as I remembered; flawless, clean and ready for a week of seaside adventures. It had everything we could want: a large kitchen, a dining room, three bedrooms, an alcove with a pull-out, a common room, a deep soaker tub and stand-alone shower, and a full outdoor patio set and BBQ.

I poured myself a glass of water and walked back out onto the patio to take a moment before unpacking the car. I sat at the patio table underneath an elm tree and listened to the sound of the wind shaking through leaves, the chirps of birds and the hum of insects, the horns from the sea and the soft passing of a car on the road. I could hear the boys laughing in the house, Michael climbing the stairs and running through rooms, showing Gus where everything was.

It was Alan who had first brought me to Provincetown. Years later, when I was single, I came back with Danny. Last year, I decided to bring Michael, so I got Danny and Charles on board and rented this house. Before that trip Michael had never heard of Provincetown. I don't think he understood what he was in for as we packed for our vacation, but once we got out of the car and walked down Commercial Street, I saw on his face that he now understood that something so magical and charming was only a day's drive away.

Within fifteen minutes, I heard the other car pull onto the gravel. Charles was the first to appear with his pillow, followed by Vince and then Danny carrying a box of booze. Danny wasted no time getting installed. Instead of unpacking, he made cocktails. "Munichs, the drink of the summer," he said, handing them out. "It's Martha's recipe: gin, Prosecco, Campari and juice."

I made a toast as we gathered in the backyard. "I want to thank you all for making this happen," I said, raising my glass. "I love you all." Everyone raised their glasses and we all took sips from our drinks. "Jesus, Danny. You're going to have to go easy on the next batch. I don't want my stomach lining to *completely* erode on the first day."

"What should we do first?" Charles asked.

"Tea dance!" Michael yelled.

I shrugged. "We could pick up our bikes tomorrow."

Michael was already in short shorts, a tank top, and his sailor cap, spinning on the back patio to the music he had plugged into the house stereo. Within minutes everyone was ready to go. Together, the six of us walked down Commercial Street towards the West End. It was near dinnertime, and the street was filled with people strolling, biking, talking, buntings of rainbow flags billowing above our heads. I heard a bell from behind and moved out of the way to let a stream of shirtless men on bikes pass.

"Hello, sailor," one of them yelled out, causing Michael to beam ear to ear.

We arrived at the Boatslip, a poolside bar with a glassed-in dance floor and a large outdoor deck that overlooked the bay. The place was in full swing, a clamour of men's voices rumbling over retreating waves and Top 40 remixes. There was so much handsomeness—men in shorts with their shirts off, some in dresses, costumes or heels—I didn't know where to look. It was like a *souper des femmes* at sea.

"We're going to get drinks," Michael shouted, grabbing Gus. "Everyone want punch?"

I offered Michael money, but he waved me away. Turning

towards the water, I felt an immense sense of calm as I took in the smell of the salty air and watched the small boats rock in the distance. I felt lighter, ten years younger. Beside me, Danny and Vince were kissing and taking pictures of the harbour and each other.

"I can't believe we're here," Charles said, and lifted me from behind in a great big bear hug.

Michael and Gus returned soon after, each negotiating the crowd with three plastic cups between their hands. We took our drinks and toasted again, and once more I was hit with a jolt of booze as I took my first sip. I hadn't drunk this much this fast in a long time, but this was my holiday, I reasoned. I deserved time off from sobriety. Plus, Wendy and Eve had just come to town and we had tried the week after my birthday. If it didn't work this time, then it would be a few more weeks before another attempt. I figured that should give my sperm enough time to recover from any bender.

The DJ began to play a track by Whitney Houston and, before I knew it, Michael, Gus and Vince were all jumping onto the dance floor, leaving Danny, Charles and me behind. I took another sip and became sentimental, overcome with love for my friends. "Come on, you two," I said, grabbing Danny's hand. The three of us then ran off to join Vince, Gus, Michael and the throngs of other men lost in celebration.

Despite the cocktails, I felt fine the next morning. Not being able to sleep past my usual wake-up time, I got up and went for a run. I ran up Pearl to Brewster, then along Old Colony Way to Cemetery Road, around the city's small graveyard and back. We hadn't thought to bring coffee with us, so I picked up a bag from a nearby shop before coming home. When I returned, Danny and Vince were awake and outside, Vince doing stretches on a yoga mat while Danny thumbed through a *New Yorker*. "Why do you bring your *New Yorker*s on holiday?" I asked. "You never read them."

"I want to look smart at the beach, don't I?" he said, closing the magazine and chucking it aside. "I intend to read them, but there's too many words for a vacation." Danny spotted the bag of ground coffee beans in my hand. "Oh, thank god," he said, and jumped up to take it from me.

I showered while Danny made the house a pot of coffee. After both he and Vince had finished their cups, and the other boys began to show their groggy faces, I asked if the two of them would take me to the Stop & Shop to pick up provisions for breakfast. The three of us drove the five minutes to the grocery store in Danny's car. The aisles were full of straight families pushing full shopping carts with kids hanging off them and gangs of gay men picking up steaks and salads and bread and snacks. We had brought down real maple syrup with us, so I thought I'd make pancakes. I grabbed strawberries and bananas, placed them in our cart, then took off to find the flour and eggs, leaving Danny and Vince to hem and haw over what to make for dinner.

I soon found the dry ingredients so I headed off to the refrigerated section, and there, by the eggs, I saw the perfect man; he was tall, broad, with short dark hair and excellent posture. He was young, I could tell, but that youth was masked by his size and moustache. He was alone, studying a pint of yogurt, reading the list of nutrients on the side of the container. He was dressed simply; in close-fitting brown chino shorts and a tight black T-shirt, and out of the bottom of his shorts shot two thick legs covered in a thin layer of hair.

When I walked towards the shelf, he looked up, did a double take, and smiled, before setting the yogurt back down.

"Excuse me," I said, and reached for a nearby pack of free-range eggs.

"No problem," he said, smiling again as he took a step back.

He picked up another tub of yogurt. I got a better look at his hands as he handled the plastic container and felt a rush of jealousy. I wanted him to handle me too. I wanted him to use those full hands of his to push me down on to the linoleum floor and push his tongue into my mouth. I got hard standing there. This man was hot. Throw-your-whole-fucking-life-away-for-it hot.

"There you are," Danny said, interrupting. I turned with the carton of eggs blocking my erection to find my friend behind me, with Vince pushing the cart. "We're thinking of making paella tonight. You eat scallops, right?"

Before I answered, I turned back to face the fridge, but the young man had moved on.

When we got back to the house with our groceries, Michael was in the backyard, getting a buzz cut from Charles.

"What do you think?" he asked.

I rubbed the smooth top of his head. He looked adorable and I felt envious of his hair's density. "It's like I've got a whole new boyfriend," I teased, getting a few clipped hairs on my lips as I kissed him.

After I made breakfast for everyone, we ate. We had plans to pick up our bikes then head off to Herring Cove Beach for the day, but it took forever for the six of us to get ready, pack lunches and leave the house. It was almost one before we were on our way, the day sunny, hot and clear. We parked our bikes by the side of the road and walked through the dunes towards the shore. There, we found a spot on the sand among the dozens of men tanning themselves in the heat, snippets of their voices and music carried in the wind.

We set up our towels and umbrellas, then pulled off our shorts and shirts to reveal the swim trunks we had layered underneath. I watched Gus step out of the same denim cut-offs he had worn to my birthday dinner. His body looked smaller than I thought it would be from his online profile, and was filled with about a half dozen tattoos, most of which I could barely make out. He was already quite tan. As for Vince, I was shocked by how in shape he was, how chiselled and furry his chest and legs were, how big the tribal tattoo was on his back, and how large his cock seemed in his small blue and yellow Speedo. We all took quick looks as Vince pretended to ignore us, taking his place on the towel next to Danny.

"I wonder if we're going to see any whales on this trip," Charles said, gazing into the distance. I couldn't help but laugh, but then Danny shot me a look and I shut up.

We slathered our bodies with sunscreen and took our spots under the umbrellas. Michael had moved on from Ethan Mordden to the first *Tales of the City* book. He read my old dog-eared paperback while on his stomach. I closed my eyes and snoozed, listening to the sounds of the waves rolling in.

After about a half an hour, I sat up. I was hungry, so I opened up my beach bag to retrieve one of the prepared sandwiches we brought. "Anyone else?" I asked, and both Danny and Charles nodded.

"I think I'm going to go exploring." Vince said, as I doled out our lunches. "Anyone want to come?"

"I will," said Michael.

"Me too," said Gus.

"Have fun!" Danny called after them, looking into his sandwich. "Bring back some salmon!"

The three of them headed south along the shoreline, and when they were out of hearing range, I spoke up. "Danny, you weren't kidding about Vince. He's a brick shithouse."

"I know," he said, as we all watched Vince's chunky bottom move away from us. "Sometimes I'm afraid I'm going to break something. Thank god I have Blue Cross."

"I can't seem to get a signal out here," Charles said, lifting his phone to the sky.

"Will you put that thing away!" Danny barked. "You have a whole line of men right here," he motioned to the left of us. "What do you need that for?"

"You better keep it out of the sun, or it's going to get fried," I said. "I wonder, is sunlight bad for sperm?"

"I'm sure yours are fine," said Danny. "But hopefully, you're going to toss that batch before the day is over."

I looked over at Charles, who seemed distracted, a frown on his squinting face. "Charles, you okay?"

"Me?" he said, shaking off whatever he was feeling. "I'm fine."

"You upset that Kevin didn't come?"

He shrugged, trying not to look disappointed. "It would've been nice. I think he would have liked it here. I mean, look at today."

"I'm sure you'll find someone else on this trip to distract yourself with," Danny said. "And you won't need to use your data to do so. Did you see all those hot guys at tea dance yesterday? It's like shooting calamari in a barrel."

"How about you, Danny?" I asked. "Having fun? Is Vince happy?"

"He's gobsmacked. Can't get over the house, the shops and bars along Commercial. Nothing like someone's first time in P-Town."

"And how's it been with you and Gus?" I asked. "Is it awkward?"

"I've sparred with greater men than Gus. We'll just have to agree to disagree. Sure, I wouldn't want to have his life—or his godawful tattoos—but I'm not going to get in the way of him living his truth. He could fuck a shark for all I care."

About thirty minutes later, Michael came back alone from the dunes behind us. "Where are the others?" I asked. Danny was curious too.

"Right behind me. Gus is cruising some guy, and Vince had to take a leak."

"With that hose, it might take a while," Charles teased.

"Want to go for a swim?" I asked Michael. The two of us walked to the shore. The water felt cold, as we waded in to our knees. Not wanting to delay the inevitable, I dove into an incoming wave and came up feeling exhilarated, the taste of salt on my lips. "Come on," I said, as Michael took his time. "It's better if you get it over with." I splashed some water at him and he howled. "Oh, you fucker," he said, splashing back, but I was already wet. I went over to him and I grabbed him as he yelped and laughed, and brought him close. He looked cute with his shaved head. "See," I said, pulling him into the water with me. I took his legs and hooked them on top of my hips. "Much better."

"You're mean to me," he said, smiling. I kissed him in the waves, the water at our shoulders. "Salty kisses," Michael said, coming back for more. And there, with our bodies close, floating and light, I felt more in love with him than ever, as if nothing else in the world would ever matter more than the two of us, right here, right now, under the sun and submerged in the invigorating waters of this beach. I took out Michael's cock and played with it as I kissed him. It grew in my hand, and I jerked him off in the waves—looking into his eyes, kissing him deeply. I couldn't help it, but at one point I thought of the man in the grocery store; I thought of Vince too, but more about his own large cock pushing against the taut nylon of his swimsuit. And soon, Michael came in my hand, holding me tight, eyes closed to the sun, gasping in the swell.

Afterwards, we returned to the shore and rejoined our friends. Gus and Vince were back now, Gus lying on his stomach and Vince resting his head on Danny's belly. "Where's Charles?" I asked.

"He wanted to head back. He said he'll meet us at tea dance later."

"What time is it?" I asked.

"Ten to three."

I looked at Michael, and he nodded. "I think we're going to head too," I said.

Danny looked perplexed. "But we've only been here an hour." I knew what he was thinking. He dreaded Vince and him being left alone with Gus.

"Well, we got to the beach late, and I'm starting to feel the sun," I said. "I think I want to lie down before this evening. Don't worry, we still have many more days of beach."

"Did you sleep?" Michael asked me as I came out of our bedroom later that afternoon.

I nodded, a little zonked and sore. "Is it possible that I have heatstroke? We weren't out for long."

"You're dehydrated. Drink some water." He poured me a glass from the fridge.

In the thirty minutes it took for the boys to get ready for tea dance, I sat outside in a shaded Adirondack chair, flipping through a magazine as the sun dipped further towards the horizon and the day cooled down. I had two drinks in front of me that I took turns sipping from: a tall glass of cold water, and some bitter red concoction that Danny had made.

"So, what do you think?" Charles asked, coming out to show off his new kaftan, a large black hand-fan fluttering at his neck. "Too much?"

"Not for Mrs. Roper."

Charles laughed and thwacked his fan in my direction. "That's something else we should get Michael to watch. *Three's Company*!"

"But really, you look fantastic," I said. "Everyone's going to want to be your friend tonight."

Michael came out next, wearing black cut-off jeans and army boots, a pair of worn brown leather suspenders over a naked chest, and a plastic bear mask as a hat. He made a playful growl.

"Don't you look ferocious! Come on, let's go."

Gus joined us, and we said goodbye to Danny and Vince who stayed behind to prepare dinner. The four of us headed off on our bikes, Charles's kaftan bundled up in the basket at the front of his beach cruiser.

The party at the Boatslip was as raucous as the day before, the drinks as strong, the men as hot. People were in love with what Charles and Michael were wearing, and many asked to take their photos, which the two were happy to accommodate. We met a sweet couple from Austin, Texas, who were celebrating twenty years together, and Gus found a bearded young man to make out with on the dance floor. I measured our time in drinks: three rum punches. As seven o'clock neared, and the party wound down, I sucked at the remaining liquid from the bottom of my plastic cup and told Michael and Charles we should head home for dinner.

"Where's Gus?" Charles asked.

Michael went off to look for his friend, but came back without him as Donna Summer's "Last Dance" ended. "I don't know where he is. I guess he left."

"Do we wait for him?" Vince asked, when the three of us returned to the house.

"Nah," Michael said, mixing himself another drink. "Who knows if he'll even come home tonight."

Vince and Danny put the finishing touches to the meal, as Charles and I set up the table outside. We opened two bottles of wine and ate the boys' delicious paella. After dinner, Michael put on some happy tunes and Danny mixed us drinks. I didn't think I could fit any more inside me, but somehow each sugary cocktail was like a demented run at a slip and slide: fast and easy.

Night settled in, and the five us sat back on the patio's chairs and looked at the sky—black and serene and full of stars. Danny, Charles, Vince and I continued to chat and laugh, while Michael flitted in and out of the house, replenishing his drink and dancing on the patio. Soon I heard voices inside, and from where I sat I spied Gus in the kitchen, fixing drinks for himself and his bearded friend. Michael heard the noise too and got up to join them. Over the music I could hear introductions being made, deep laughs, the cracking of ice.

"Well, look who's back," Danny muttered, sipping his Munich.

The three of them soon came outside and Gus made introductions. The bearded boy's name was Carl and he was from Pittsburgh, staying with friends in the West End. He was around Gus's age with a ring through his septum and a neck tattoo. He took a spot next to me and rolled a joint on his lap while he spoke to Gus and Michael, who sat on the patio steps. I became caught between the two conversations, the three young men talking about bars and boys and music and pot, and on my right Danny and Charles arguing about musicals and soundtracks and which version of *Gypsy* was better.

At some point, the three on my left popped up and Michael turned to us. "Carl's going to take us to a party called Church in this basement bar on Commercial. Anyone want to come?"

Danny yawned. "That paella pooped me out," he said. "I think I'm going to stay behind and have an early night."

"Who's *pampa* now?" I teased, and Danny turned to me with his mouth open, feigning insult.

"I'll stay behind too and help you clean up," Vince said.

We'd already done the dishes, and there wasn't much left to clean, but I figured the two of them wanted the house to themselves.

"Charles?" I asked.

"I might have a date later," he said, scrolling through the apps. "Some guy who saw me at tea wants to try on my kaftan. Although, I might have to bail. I've had one too many Munichs."

I felt the same. I was drunk and in a good mood, but above all I was full. I looked over at Michael. He too had been drinking since we had returned from the beach. It was 10:30 p.m. "How about you?" I asked. "You feeling all right?"

Michael threw his head back. "Who me? I'm on holiday!"

I thought about letting him go with Gus and his new friend, of it just being the three of them. But then, I knew I'd worry and have trouble sleeping and find myself waiting for him to return. "Do you want me to come?" I asked. "Or would you rather it be just the three of you?"

"No, you can come." Michael said, and got up to head back to the kitchen. I heard him open and close the fridge door. More crushing of ice.

I went to join him. "What are you making?"

"Rum and coke."

I considered it. "Sure, I'll come," I said. "Make me one?"

Michael mixed our drinks and then headed to our room to change. I followed and watched him pull on a fresh T-shirt from a pile of clothes on the floor, working his arms back through his hanging suspenders and lifting them to his shoulders. "Don't forget your bear hat," I said.

The four of us said goodbye to our housemates, then hopped on our bikes and headed over to Commercial Street. Church was small and packed; the music soulful and celebratory. Within minutes, Michael had bought himself another drink and was heading to the dance floor. Immediately, he sweated up a storm—a drunk baby bear lost to the beat. The energy in the room was palpable, joy on people's faces as they lost themselves in music. I debated getting another drink, but I already felt half past gone; so instead, I stood to the side of the dance floor and watched as the jubilant crowd moved together. Soon the rhythm caught me too, and before I knew it I was joining them, dancing to some nineties house track from my youth.

One song turned into two, and then three and four. I closed my eyes while I danced, flashes of vibrant colour blasting through the thin membrane of my eyelids as I cocooned inside an elusive bliss, shoulder to shoulder with strangers in the tight dark space. At some point I looked up and searched for Michael, looking for his bear hat among the bobbing heads in the room, but I had lost him. There was no sign of Gus or Carl either.

I left the dance floor and went to check the bar area, then the dark couches in the corner where people sat and talked and made out. I went around to the bathroom and peered inside. I watched a man in a dress pee at a urinal, a stack of crinoline hiked up around his hips. "Not what I want to be doing right now," he said to those alongside of him, and all of them chuckled. None were Michael.

174

I left the bathroom and went back to the dance floor. Still not there. Perhaps they had gone outside for a joint? I went to look, but ran into Michael as he rushed back into the bar, the bear hat in his hands. "I have to go," he said. His face was pale and dotted with sweat. "I don't feel so good."

Immediately, I felt sober, blood rushing to my chest. I followed him outside and we headed over to our bikes. Michael couldn't walk straight. "What happened to you?" I asked, in a panic. "Did you take something?"

"I had too much to drink," he struggled to say. "I think I'm going to be sick."

Michael turned and threw up into the sand, his back towards me. It was a horrible sound, like he was being gutted, as if all the negative emotions he had felt in his life were fighting to leave his body. I took the bear hat from his hand and stood behind him and waited for him to finish. After several expulsions, Michael dropped to his knees. He coughed and retched and spat.

I felt everything in that moment—scared, sad, helpless, relieved he hadn't choked—but it was anger that prevailed. "Are you okay?" I half-shouted.

He didn't answer, just continued to breathe and spit.

I looked around, then back at the bar across the street, music blasting every time the door swung open. Where the hell were Gus and Carl? "Did they give you anything?" I asked, looking back at him on the ground. "Did you take anything?"

"What? No." Michael panted. "I'm sorry," he said, and spat again.

I waited for him to stop, for his breath to get lighter. "We need to get you home. We can leave our bikes here and get them tomorrow."

"We should bring them."

"No!" I shouted, done. "Leave them here!"

I started walking without him, but turned to see if he was following. "Come on," I said, getting impatient. "Let's go."

Michael followed me up to Bradford Street. Normally, it would take us ten minutes to walk back, but the way that Michael stumbled it would take much longer. I kept an eye out for taxis or pedicabs, but there weren't any on the street. Why the fuck would he do this to himself? I wondered, the music from the nightclub ringing in my ears. I walked ahead of him, and faster, so he would too, but several times I had to stop and turn around to wait for him to catch up. At one point, I heard a noise and turned to find that he had tripped and fallen into a bush by the side of the road. "Shit," I said, and rushed over to pull him up. "Are you okay?"

"I'm fine." He sounded sad.

"Jesus," I yelled back at him, stepping away. "You're such a mess!" I was mad—mad at him, mad at Gus, mad at Carl, mad at everyone. "You've got to be more careful, Michael! What would you have done had I not been here? Do you think you would've made it home by yourself?"

"I'm sorry," he grumbled again through closed lips.

My hands went up in the air. "Why do you do this to yourself, Michael? God! You need to take better care of yourself. I can't always be there to protect you."

Michael's face was white and full of sweat and exhaustion. He was crying. "I'm sorry I'm not perfect," he yelled back through tears. "I'm sorry I'm not the perfect boyfriend. Yes, I make mistakes. I don't need you lecturing me."

"It's not just this Michael," I said. "It's everything. It's your work. It's money. It's your taxes. How you treat your parents. You're not a kid any more. I can't always be there for you. I'm just… I can't," I said, exasperated. "I don't know if I can do this."

Michael went silent and then he cried. Just cried, as we walked the remaining blocks home.

I woke up with a dry mouth and a splitting headache. At first, I didn't remember anything, what we had done the night before, or how we had got home. But flashes began to come back, illuminated with the morning light.

I turned to find Michael awake beside me, his eyes open, staring at the ceiling.

"Hey, buddy," I said.

"Hey."

"I'm sorry about last night. I don't know what got into me. I guess I was pretty drunk too."

"You said what you said." Michael got up and left the bedroom. I heard him walk down the hallway and into the bathroom. The door closed shut.

I got up and went outside in my boxers, my hangover intense in the open air and sunlight. I turned around and went back into the house and poured myself a glass of water. It felt like pure life as I drank it down in gulps. I drained the glass and filled it up again, taking it and my phone outside to the patio table. Before I sat down, I noticed Michael's bear hat in the grass. I picked it up and hooked it onto the ear of one of the wrought-iron chairs, then sat down and checked my messages. There was one from Wendy:

Sigh. Didn't work. Sorry Paul. Maybe next time. Have a great time in P-Town.

Suddenly, I wanted to be back home. I wanted my cats, my apartment, my bed, my life.

Sorry to hear. I wrote back. *Don't worry, it'll happen. Hang in there.*

I put down the phone.

I tried to remember everything that I had said to Michael the night before, but it was hazy. Had I given him an ultimatum? We'd had such a wonderful day, our time in the water and at tea dance. Was this what I thought of him? Scratch the surface and there's the real me, angry at Michael for who he is? Whatever anger or disappointment I'd felt the night before was long gone now, and in its place was a feeling of shame and regret and self-loathing. Had I ruined things between us?

Danny came outside, his face twisted in the morning light. "Anyone get the number of the yacht that ran over me last night?"

"Same," I said.

"How was your night?"

"I don't want to talk about it," I said. "I don't think we're going to the beach today. I think we might stay in town."

I left Danny and walked to the bathroom. Through the door I heard rushing water. I knocked. "Can I come in?"

There was a pause. Then, "Sure."

I opened the door and walked in. Michael sat naked in the deep soaker tub, long face, water rising around him.

"Can I get in?"

He nodded.

I took off my boxer shorts and joined him in the tub. We sat there, quiet, looking at each other. There were no tears, but his eyes were round and sad. "I'm sorry, but I don't remember everything I said last night."

"Well I do. I remember everything, and I wish I didn't. Is that what you think of me? That I'm an irresponsible little kid?"

"No, well I… No, I don't. I just. I got angry. I was drunk. I said things I shouldn't have."

"You asked me if I was using again."

"Did I?"

"You asked if I'd taken anything. If Gus or Carl had given me something. Do you really think I would have done that?"

"I didn't know what was happening. I was confused."

"But if this is what you think of me… I'm not going to change, Paul. This is who I am."

"I know. I love who you are."

"But what if it's not enough? What if inside you're expecting—hoping—that I'll become someone else? My whole life I've had to deal with what other people expected of me, wanting me to be smarter or faster or the perfect son or the best in school. I'm none of those things. I'm never going to be those things. But if you're waiting for that, if you're waiting for me to be the person you *think* I should be, then you're going to be disappointed."

"You don't need to change," I said, massaging his foot under water. "I love you the way you are. I guess, I was scared. I looked around, I didn't know where you were. Gus wasn't with you, and you were wasted sick. I worry about you, Michael. I'm worried that you're going to get hurt some day."

"You don't have to worry about me all the time. I'm not a kid."

We stayed in the tub, sitting there, not saying a word. And when the water got cold, we drained the tub and got out. I poured us two glasses of water, and we went back to our room, where I closed the door. We slipped into bed and held each other and tried to go to sleep.

Two hours later, when I woke up, the house was empty. There was a note on the table from Danny saying that he, Charles and Vince had gone out to Race Point Beach for the day and that they'd be back around suppertime.

I went outside and picked up one of Danny's *New Yorkers*. I tried to read it for a bit, but Danny was right. There were too many words for a holiday. Minutes later, Michael joined me outside. "Are you hungry?" I asked, and he nodded. "Get dressed. We'll go grab something."

Michael was in a better mood by the time we left the house. He was still quiet, but he had put on his sailor cap and wore his short shorts and flip-flops. He was also sporting a pair of dark sunglasses and had grabbed a small rainbow parasol from his box of accessories to shield him from the sun.

We walked through town and ate some burgers and fries and felt human. After that, we went shopping; Michael bought a Christmas decoration for his mom (a lobster with a captain's hat) and I picked up a wooden salad bowl for our kitchen at home. By midday we were back in front of where we had left our bikes the night before. Silently, we unlocked our rides and rode them home. There, we took another nap, but woke up half an hour later, making love.

In the cool darkness of our closed bedroom, I could feel the sun in Michael's body, stored up from our trip. This heat was different from the one that churned within him as he slept back home, or the one that had poured off his face as we fought the night before. No, this heat was alive, glowing in the soft blush of his skin. And as I pulled him close and pressed into him, I could feel that energy transferring into me, wrapping me and comforting me in a warm invisible light.

Afterwards, we decided to make dinner for the boys and set to prepping a menu of steak, grilled vegetables and salad. Then, magically, when evening came and they had returned, everything was all right again. When I looked at Michael, I no longer saw his disappointment in me. Just his love.

On our last night in town, we had plans to attend another party that Carl had told us about called Fagbash. The theme for the party was High School Confidential and Michael was excited to go, having a number of items in his costume box that would fit the bill.

I sat outside with the boys as we waited for Michael to get ready. He soon came out in a bright blue wrestling singlet, a frown on his face. "Can I see you for a second?" he asked, then turned around and headed back into the house.

I got up and joined Michael in the bathroom. He was in front of the mirror, trying to draw triangles on his chest and arms with tubes of glow-in-the-dark greasepaint he had bought earlier in the day. "It's not coming out the way I want it to," he said. I looked at the shapes. They were thin and the colours didn't pop the way they did on the package. "Maybe we shouldn't go," he said, deflated, tossing the tube of red into the sink.

"What do you mean?"

"I thought Gus would be here, getting ready with me.

Instead, he's getting made-up with Carl and his friends." Michael looked dejected. "I feel like such an idiot. I've hardly seen him at all on this trip. Maybe I should change."

"Here, why don't you let me try?" I said, and took the tube from the sink. Michael's triangles were small in size and hollow. I had the idea to make them bigger and colour them in. I drew a red one on one arm, then a green one on the left side of his neck. Finally, I took out the blue and drew one on his breastplate just above the collar of his singlet.

Michael brightened up. "It looks better," he said.

"Do you have any other stuff? Something I could wear?"

He smiled. "Sure, take a look."

I went into the bedroom to Michael's tickle trunk, his chest for the land of make-believe. Inside, there was mesh and gauze and scissors and glue. There was the sailor hat and a pair of kneepads and a short skirt and a purse. I found a bunch of necklaces. One was silver with a string of squares hanging from it. I picked it up and put it on. I went back to Michael to show him. He said he liked it, but then he took me back into the room to go through the box. Michael pulled out a mesh football shirt and black shorts. "Here," he said. "Put these on." He took the foam kneepads and stuffed them in the shirt on top of my shoulders. Michael then put a glow-in-the-dark necklace around my neck.

We stepped back and looked in the mirror. Michael laughed, "It's like we're the slutty captains of the football and wrestling teams."

We left the house and walked to the club, Michael the cock of the walk, smiling to everyone we passed on the street. Dressed like this, I had an odd feeling. Like I had stepped into Michael's skin and could see the world the way he did, as a wondrous adult playground. We got to the party. I had no pockets, so, taking Michael's lead, I kept my identification and money in my sock. Downstairs, Michael's paint job and my necklace glowed bright in the dark. I don't know if it was because of our fight earlier in the week, but neither of us drank. Michael's wrestling singlet was popular. He got loads of attention as men passed him by, feeling the fabric. Even I got hungry looks I wasn't used to.

At some point I left Michael on the dance floor and went back to the bar to join our friends. Charles was having fun in his kaftan, swaying to the beat in the fabric with a drink in his hand. Danny and Vince, wanting to blend in, had removed their T-shirts and hooked them onto the backsides of their shorts. On the other side of the bar, I spied Gus and Carl, part of a cabal of five men dressed as cheerleaders.

Soon, Michael came up behind me to hug me, all sweaty. "Paul," he said, "I want to introduce you to someone." I turned around and there standing with Michael was the tall young man from the grocery store. He was all smiles and wore the same singlet as Michael, but in a larger size and in red. "This is Leo."

"Hello, Paul," Leo said, shaking my hand. I looked down across the stretch of spandex that revealed the outline that had hidden underneath his clothes the day I saw him. He looked like Superman, standing there—broad chest, a bulge at his crotch. "I remember you from the Stop & Shop."

My heart fluttered. "Nice to meet you, Leo, " I said, not sure what to add. "Where you from?"

"Provincetown," he said, cheerful. "I live here during the summer."

"Lucky you," I replied. "What do you do?"

"I'm a houseboy at Christopher's."

"Where do you live off season?" *God, what am I? A journalist?*

"New Orleans," he said, "But I might be moving to Atlanta next year... I like your football jersey," he said, and reached out, the large hand I had lusted over in the grocery store examining the material at my skin.

"Thanks," I said. "It's Michael's."

Leo let go of my shirt and put his other hand around Michael's waist.

"We're going to go dance," Michael said, touching my hip. "Why don't you join us?"

I looked at Michael, and at his larger twin, the two of them my high school fantasy. But I no longer felt as bold and as desirable as I had when we had first walked in. "Maybe later. You guys go. I'll catch up."

Michael gave me a big kiss on the mouth and headed off with Leo.

From behind, Charles came up to me. He had one word. "Honey..."

"I know. It's Michael's fun. I'll let him fly solo for a bit."

"You could fly too."

"Charles, I'm trying to get Wendy pregnant. I've made a commitment. Michael too. Nothing can happen."

"Well, that doesn't mean you still can't have a little fun."

I looked around. The place was full and raucous and celebratory with people living their best lives. I didn't know when we'd be back here next; it was our last night in town, and I'd be sorry to see this go.

I turned and made my way to the bar where I ordered myself a shot of whisky, then set off to find Michael and Leo. I found them on the dance floor, moving to the music, thigh to thigh in their singlets. I waited for a moment and watched as they kissed, Michael grabbing at Leo through the fabric. My eyes went wide, but instead of jealousy I felt a thrill, a pulse throughout my entire body. I continued to watch, on the outskirts, then walked over, through the artificial smoke and shirtless bodies, to join them. Leo saw me and smiled. He reached out with one of his arms and pulled me between them, and the three of us danced together. I felt their smooth fabric all around me, the curves of their bodies, the shape of their erections. Leo grabbed my face and kissed me on the lips.

TWO

The Thing About Things

11

UPON RETURNING FROM Provincetown, I began my final leg of training. I had run the 10K the year before, after training for six months, and was so elated by the experience that I made a pact with myself to attempt a half-marathon. The date was coming up at the end of September. I had spent the last year preparing for this moment, following an online schedule that had me on track for a decent finish time for my age. Even though I had slipped on our holiday, the last three months had seen me steadily increasing my long runs each week, pushing my distance beyond my usual fitness run.

A week before the race, Wendy and Eve came to town for another round of tries. They arrived sooner in the day than expected, while I was still at work, and asked if I could slip away. It was their third wedding anniversary, and they thought it might be good luck to try and then go out for a romantic dinner. To think that Michael and I had only been together eight months when I invited him to be my plus one at their wedding. As I waited for Wendy's text, I remembered how happy he was at the reception, smiling and dancing with me, telling me that he had never met anyone like me and that I had saved him.

"Saved you?" I had laughed. "From what?"

Michael looked at me sternly, annoyed that I hadn't grasped the weight of what he had said. I had ruined the moment.

"No, I'm sorry," I pulled him back. "I was being silly. I don't think I did anything special. I just... I love you, Michael." It was the first time I had said those words to him.

My phone buzzed with Wendy's text. I gathered my stuff and went downstairs to wait for them by the curb. Moments later their Subaru pulled up and I got into the backseat.

"How come I had to fly, while you got to drive?"

"Are you kidding?" Wendy said. "My mother wouldn't pay for *our* flights."

We drove to their hotel downtown. After they checked in, the three of us took the elevator up to their room on the fourteenth floor. It was fancy, something of a honeymoon suite with a soaker tub that opened up to the bedroom. Wendy and Eve dropped off their bags and gave me the familiar plastic cup. "Sorry we don't have any reading materials for you," Wendy said, looking at the tourist publications on the room's desk. "Maybe there's a cute guy in one of these?"

I shrugged and took out my phone. "I got what I need right here."

They headed downstairs to the lobby and left me to do my business. It was strange to be left alone in their pristine suite to jerk off, but I was sure this hotel room had seen its fair share of ejaculations. I scrolled through Tumblr. It took me no time to find an image to get me off. I left the container on the nightstand and headed down to meet them in the lobby.

We tried again the next evening, and then again the following day. Eve came by to pick me up on my lunch hour. I had about forty-five minutes, so it was a quick visit. I had been up and down that hotel elevator so many times I began to feel like a hustler. Then, on the Saturday morning, just as they were about to leave, I got a text from Wendy: *Took an ov test this AM and it looks like I got my LH surge yesterday. This would be a good time to try. Got one more left in you?*

I was already in my running gear, headed out the door. The thought of having an orgasm before my long run was not appealing, but I wrote back telling them, *Of course! Come on over!*

I was outside when they arrived.

"Thank you," Eve said, handing me the container through the car window.

"No problem. Hope these buggers clock a better time than me."

The following Sunday was the race. Michael and I took the Metro to the Village where we met up with Danny and Vince, tall take-away cups attempting to pry open their sleepy faces.

"Did you remember to bandage your nipples?" Danny asked, fussing with my shirt.

Vince was confused. "Bandage your nipples?"

"To prevent chafing," Danny explained. "Bleeding. The last thing you want is to cross the finish line with stigmata running from your breasts."

We walked to the base of the Jacques Cartier Bridge where we met up with the hundreds of other participants, men and women in colourful nylon and bamboo gear, milling about sponsors' tables filled with swag, radio stations blasting music.

"How long should it take you?" Vince asked.

"Given my pace, I hope to make it in under two and a half hours. But honestly, I just want to finish the damn thing."

"God, I'd be bored," Danny said.

"What will you think about?" Michael asked.

I shrugged, suddenly nervous. "I've got some running hacks. Some mantras to repeat. They say you should attempt math problems to distract yourself from the pain."

"Oh, Vince is great at that." Danny said, turning. "Give him one to solve."

Vince opened his mouth, but I stopped him. "—No," I said. "Thanks. Not actual math problems, more like multiplication tables or comparing distances or volume. Like, how many of my apartments can fit inside a football field."

"I have one," Danny said. "How many times could you listen to Madonna's 'Express Yourself' in a single year?"

I shook my head. "Sounds like more of an existential question to me."

At some point, the three of them said their goodbyes and wished me luck; Michael kissed me, and then they left to go cheer me on from the sidelines.

I gathered with the crowd of other runners in my group, most of us silent, waiting for our moment to depart. Soon a shot was fired and we were off. We ran close at first, but thinned out as we ascended the bridge. The course took us up the Jacques Cartier towards Île Sainte-Hélène, then down to the green spaces of Jean Drapeau Park. I took it easy at the beginning, despite the adrenaline pumping through me. I had been warned, from the online guides I had read, to run slow the first half of the race. The tortoise and the hare, I had to remind myself, even though a part of me wanted to fuel the fire and take off.

We ran around the roads and paths of the small island, around the alien mega-structures of the La Ronde theme park and on to the circuit of the Gilles Villeneuve racetrack. It was forty-five minutes before I realized that Danny had implanted "Express Yourself" in my ear. Could be worse, I thought as I kept my pace, singing along under my breath.

The other mantra I had when I started to feel the pain was, "One step at a time, just one step at a time." There were plenty of other thoughts that kept me distracted too. Against the changing landscape and bobbing shoulders in front of me, I thought about Michael's taxes and our next mortgage payment, due the same day as the first credit card payment since our trip. I thought of work. I thought of my dad, asleep in his time zone, wondering what his morning would be like in Kelowna. A glimpse of another runner's strong legs led to a welcome thought of Leo, flashes of him in his wrestling singlet next to Michael on the dance floor. And I thought about Wendy and Eve too, and our hypothetical baby.

Although I had resisted it until now, I tried to picture the child as I ran. All I could make out, though, was a three-foot object with dark hair and no discernible facial features—a doll in a horror movie. That's odd, I thought. I knew there would be a time when I'd look back on a moment like this and think how strange it was to live in a world where I didn't know them, or what they looked like. It was like with Michael. Before he came along, I had no idea if I'd ever meet someone I wanted to share my life with, let alone what he'd be like. Before Michael, I had been single for seven years. Of course

I had dated and hooked up during that time, but nothing much had come from it. Sometimes it was the other person, sometimes it was me. But after those seven years, I was no longer sure if I wanted the trouble of having anyone else in my life. I had Sutherland. I had Danny and Charles. I had Kate. Everything was fine the way it was.

But then, when Michael arrived and slipped into my life, it was as if he were the last piece of a puzzle I had long given up on solving. He didn't mind the relentless waterfall that was my affection. He filled up that empty space perfectly, and then, when I reached across for him in the dark, I knew what to expect—his touch, his shape, his smell—and I held onto it tightly. It was there when I closed my eyes. *Saved me?* It felt like the other way around. That I was the one who owed Michael a debt of gratitude for what he had brought back into my life, for what his presence continued to allow. Would it also be like that with this child? I wondered.

Or not?

As we headed back towards the city, past Habitat 67 and into Old Montreal, I thought about Kate. She and Christian had once imagined the baby they'd have. At what point did she give up on the idea? Or did she ever? Did she think of their baby in a cosmic waiting room the way that I now think of the one that Wendy and Eve and I are trying to create? And are we destined for the same outcome? We had tried four times now, and each time everything was monitored and manipulated to increase our chances. What if Wendy isn't able to get pregnant? What would happen then? Would Eve try? Or would they give up on me and try another donor? Or what if it was me? At the beginning—before all of this started—if they had told me they were going with an anonymous donor, I don't think it would have bothered me. Sure, I would have been disappointed for a moment or two, but now, after all of these attempts, I felt invested. I wanted to be a part of this. I wanted it to work.

This thought lingered as I hit the halfway point. I thought that maybe if I finished the race within twenty minutes of my goal, then maybe it would work the next time. It was similar to the bargains I used to make around my mother: *If I do these things, she'll get to her destination safely*. The thought helped me push through the pain and discomfort. Suddenly, I had no choice. I knew, if I didn't finish the race on time, there'd be no baby. The baby was the prize at the end of the finish line.

I kept seeing people pass me and started to pick up my pace. "One step at a time, just one step at a time," I repeated. I knew I had people waiting for me at the end, and they were counting on me. *And then I never have to do this again*, I almost laughed. "Just one step at a time. One step at a time. *Come on, girl! Do you believe in love?*"

Near the end, I began to struggle. I was trotting for part of the run, even walking for a few minutes at a time. My legs began to feel heavy, my lungs burning. I realized I was crying, unexplained water running from my eyes. But I was close. So close.

As I turned from Berri Street onto Cherrier, I noticed there were more people cheering from the sidelines now. This was the exact same street the Pride parade used to take to get to La Fontaine Park back in the day and I became emboldened by the thought—that even though so many years had passed, there were still people willing to cheer me on. I noticed a young girl coming up on my right with a sign. "If it were easy, everyone would do it," it said. That got me to smile. She noticed the effect it had on my gait and gave me a holler, holding out her hand for a high five, which I was more than happy to provide.

Suddenly, I found that last burst of energy I needed and picked up my pace, running along La Fontaine Park towards the finish line. I felt euphoric, crossing the threshold, a burn throughout my body as my breath continued its chase. Volunteers were on hand to give us water. I checked my time: twelve minutes over my goal, but still within my twenty-minute bargain with the universe. I received a medal for my participation—a large circular recreation of the Jacques Cartier Bridge. Michael, Danny and Vince soon arrived and ran over to congratulate me. "One more thing off the bucket list," Danny said, patting me on the back. They had Gatorade and a chicken salad sandwich for me. I drank but couldn't eat. I felt nauseous, to be honest, as my lungs continued to contract and expand. My friends stayed with me, walking me around, getting me to stay active and stretch so I wouldn't freeze up.

Afterwards, we took the Metro back home. It felt strange riding on a subway car after having run across town. A pregnant woman got on at Laurier station and Michael stood up to give her his seat. I took it as a sign.

The next morning we woke up to knocking at the front door. I heard it, but didn't get up, refusing to believe that someone was at our door this early. We had never got around to fixing the door at the bottom of the stairs, so it blew open at times.

It's got to be a mistake, I thought, lying there. They'll go away if we leave them alone.

Michael got up and went to check who it was, while I fell back into my pillow. Several seconds later he rushed back into the room and began to put on his pants. "It's the police," he said, grabbing a shirt. "There's been an accident on the street involving my car."

He was out again before I had a chance to say anything. I jumped up, put on some clothes, and walked out into the hallway. Michael had left the door open, but thankfully, the cats weren't around. As I struggled to put on my shoes, I heard a noise. A scream from outside. I shoved my feet into my sneakers and closed the door behind me as I ran down the stairs. And there I found Michael, several houses down from us, on his knees on the sidewalk, crying and wailing.

His car had been ploughed into, its backside smashed. I almost didn't recognize it from behind—the trunk bent open, the left rear tire buried deep into the wheel well. On the pavement around us were shattered pieces of glass and plastic. The rear windshield had been destroyed, cubes of tempered glass scattered across the back seats like confetti.

I asked the cops in French what had happened, and they told us that someone driving an SUV had fallen asleep at the wheel and crashed into Michael's car, and then left the scene of the accident. They told us that a neighbour had called 911 and they had followed the trail of fluid to find the perpetrator. He was given an $800 ticket.

"C'est tout?!" Michael yelled.

"Il n'a pas été arrêté?" I asked, in shock. I wanted the man's name, but the police officer wouldn't give it to me.

There's no-fault insurance in Quebec, he reminded us, which meant Michael would be compensated by the Société de l'assurance automobile du Québec and not the person who did this. However, I knew that Michael wouldn't be able to replace this car with whatever money he got. The car may have been special to him, but to everyone else it was old. The replacement value would be nothing—a couple thousand maybe. For that price, Michael wouldn't be able to replace this car he had grown up in, smoked joints in and fooled around in, that was his means of escape when things got bad at home, that was as much his friend as Gus or Danny or Charles or me.

The cops gave us our paperwork, but Michael was a mess. It was horrible to see him like this. With each passing minute it was getting lighter and lighter out, and with it the damage becoming clearer and more brutal. When the cops left, we walked back inside. The cats were up and confused, milling about the door. Michael reached for a box of tissues on the cabinet in the hall to dab at his eyes and blow his nose. I watched him as he turned and walked into the office, sure he was going to roll himself a joint.

I looked at the clock. How could it only be 5:51 a.m.? It felt strange to be up and so awake this early. And why did my body hurt? I wondered, remembering only then that I'd run a half-marathon the day before. Aching, I went into our room and pulled up the sheets to make the bed. I then went into the kitchen to put on a pot of coffee. Filling up the carafe and staring into the sink, I thought of the words I had said to Michael when he had broken my mug: *It's no big deal. It's just a thing.*

It's just a thing.

"It's not just a thing," I said quietly into the sink. This careless driver had destroyed a piece of the person I love, a part he was proud of. What will this do to his self-esteem? I wondered. Michael would have to get a new car now, or find another solution to get to his jobs. He was doing so well, up until this point, working to get out of debt, trying to pay off his taxes and reimburse me for the trip. Michael had just bought a P-Town sticker that he had affixed to the back bumper. It was now crushed under the chassis of his car.

Michael emerged from the office moments later, joint in hand, and headed to the balcony off the kitchen to light up. He spoke aloud, to the universe, to himself. He said that he thought she'd have a fiery end, and that maybe it would've been his as well. "It's so anticlimactic," he said, tearing up in the rising smoke. "I should have spun the tires out on every corner, hold on to your asshole, to the horizon and back."

"What are you going to do?" I asked him.

He shrugged. "Call my insurance, when it opens. Call my mechanic. See if I can push her into the alley."

"Is it really that bad?" I asked. "Don't you think you can fix it?"

Michael flashed me a twisted smile and laughed. "No, there ain't no fixing that," he said, taking in another haul and exhaling. "She's dead. She's gone."

Several days later, I got a text from Wendy: *Arg! Got my period! I don't understand. We hit the nail on the head this time. Going to make an appointment with our MD.*

We spoke on the phone two days later. "Think you can

come to Toronto for the next round?" she asked. "Looks like it'll be during the second week of October, around Thanksgiving."

"Sure thing," I said, checking my calendar. "But I'm taking the train."

"I have a good feeling about next time," she said. "I've started taking acupuncture to help me along. Six needles for forty minutes, once or twice a week. I had my first appointment yesterday and left thinking, *I paid for all that?* But then I went on to have the most incredible, stress-free day. I was so calm that Eve didn't realize I had returned home for over an hour."

Michael could use acupuncture, I thought, hanging up. Losing the car had been hard on him. On the day it happened, he pushed Baby to a neighbour's parking spot in the back alley. He filled out all the paperwork for the insurance, had the car evaluated (it was a total loss), and sold her to a scrapyard.

Michael wanted one last day alone with her before they took her away, so I made myself scarce. On the day they were scheduled to pick her up, I left early for work. Michael got the call as I collected my things. I could hear him speaking to the person on the line: *Oui? Ok. Midi aujourd'hui.* After he hung up, he released a big sigh and then came over to kiss me goodbye.

"Are you going to be okay?"

"I will," he said. "Eventually."

"What will you do?"

"Spend time with her," he said. "Sit inside and roll on the roof. Look under the hood one last time. Remove her radio and stickers and the things that meant something to me."

I knew there'd be tears. Part of me wanted to take the day

off for moral support, but I knew I'd want to comfort him and that would just piss him off.

That evening when I got home from work, Michael was asleep. I could see his day all over our home—the 325i lettering from the car's trunk, and with it the chunk of stereo and plastic shards from the brake lights, an empty mickey of scotch and a tumbler glass on the kitchen table, Madonna's *True Blue* LP spinning at its end on the record player.

In the following days, Michael seemed to hate everything about life and work. Without a car, he now had to take public transit or taxis to his jobs, lugging his tools and equipment across the city. When he got home he was exhausted. His most recent client was a short and wiry man in his sixties who had hired him to paint five rooms in his house, as well as the basement. It was taking Michael longer than the man felt it should and he kept pressuring him to finish faster.

"Well, what does he expect?" Michael complained, one night after returning home, all sore and covered in paint. "He bought the cheapest stuff possible; it's going to take several coats to get the job done."

Michael said he wanted to quit, but I wouldn't let him. "No, you have to see this through. You don't want this to tarnish your reputation. And you need the money."

Michael relented, and later that day called me on a break to apologize for being so negative.

The following week, Michael packed for San Francisco. It was a last-minute trip. Gus was going to meet up with Carl there, but when he heard about what had happened he insisted that Michael join them and bought him a plane ticket. Gus and Carl had rented an apartment in the Castro, and the place had an extra bed. I could come if I wanted to, Gus had said. I thanked him but declined. The trip would overlap with my visit to Toronto.

As always, Michael waited until the last minute to pack. He wasn't thinking about what to wear and stuffed whatever was clean into his duffle bag.

"Don't forget to bring sweaters and jackets," I said. "It may be California, but the temperature in the Bay Area can change quickly in an afternoon."

Michael sifted through the closet. "Can I bring this?" he asked, pulling out an old leather jacket. "Of course," I said. I hadn't worn it in years. "But don't lose it. It was Alan's."

Michael put it on and gathered his bags by the door. He took a moment to say goodbye to the cats. "Do you mind calling me a cab?"

I dialled the number. "Did you remember your passport?"

"Shit," he said, and took off to find it. I heard him frantically looking around, pulling open drawers and throwing aside papers. Thankfully, there was no real crisis. He soon found it and emerged from the office red-faced and flushed.

"Have a great time," I said, and handed him his bag. The look on Michael's face was long and beat.

"Thanks, buddy. Sorry to leave you on Thanksgiving."

"I'll be with the girls. I'll be fine," I said. "Have an amazing time. Call me from the airport if you want."

The cab pulled up outside. I followed Michael down the stairs and watched him load his stuff into the trunk of the car. I gave him a big hug, Alan's jacket squeaking in the embrace. I kissed him goodbye and watched him get into the back seat. The taxi drove off.

I was also scheduled to leave town that day. I had a train ticket for the evening express to Toronto after work, and so I left the house that morning with my own luggage rolling behind me. I spent the day moderately anxious, looking at my watch, waiting for word that Michael's first flight had arrived safely in Denver and that he would make his connection to San Francisco. Thankfully, work kept me busy, and it was only in the quiet moments that I wondered where in the sky he was. I finally did get a text saying that he had made it to his first stop, and got another series of hearts and exclamations as he and Gus boarded their second flight and had to switch off their phones.

Around 4 p.m., I met up with Kate and Ben for an early dinner before my train. The two had been seeing each other for six months now, with Kate coming to town every few weeks. I still wasn't keen on meeting Ben, but I knew I had to for my sister's sake. And maybe I could get a read on the guy, I figured. Find out more about him so I could reason with her and understand this new language she had learned.

I'd chosen a restaurant in Chinatown we both liked; it was also close to the train station. I arrived first and played with my phone until they showed up. I stood to greet them, kissing my sister on the cheek and shaking Ben's warm hand. Ben was tall and attractive, with a clean-shaven face and a buzz cut. He wore a slim-fitting grey suit with a navy blue tie. He looked stylish yet corporate, much better dressed than Christian, but in his face I immediately saw similarities to Kate's husband.

"So Ben, have you been here before?" I asked as we sat down.

"No, never," he said, making room in front of him for the waiter who had brought us tea. "I don't know why, but I never think to come to Chinatown."

"Kate and I used to come here all the time after the clubs let out. There's nothing like a plate of greasy chow mein at three in the morning."

"So many good times," Kate echoed. "So many lost brain cells."

"Is there anything you don't eat?" I asked, grabbing the pencil and pad left by the waiter on the table. "We usually get a bunch of things and share them, if that's okay with you?" Ben nodded and I took to writing down our order, checking with Kate to make sure I had picked the right things.

"So, how was the marathon?" Kate asked, once I'd handed the selection to our waiter. "You must feel great, now that it's done."

"I do," I said. "But it was a half-marathon. Much harder than I thought."

"Are you going to keep running?" Ben asked.

"I hope to," I said. "Maybe not as long or as often, but I like the way it makes me feel. The way it clears my head."

"Ben runs too," Kate said, looking at him.

"But I've never done a half-marathon." He shook his head. "I run once or twice a week on the treadmill at the gym. Sometimes I get overloaded with work and stop for a week or two. It's hard to get back into it afterwards."

"It's the same for me," I said. "I have to run every second day, or it becomes too difficult."

The beers arrived, and Kate took a swig from her bottle. "Paul's on a roll," she said, looking again at Ben. "He turned forty, two months ago, and in the last year he's bought a place and run a half-marathon—all that and trying to get his friends pregnant too! If you're wondering, Paul is the over-achiever in the family."

"Kate mentioned that you're going to be a sperm donor," Ben said. "How's that going?"

"Uh, fine," I laughed. "Honestly, it's such a surreal experience, the whole process. Never a dull moment. It hasn't worked yet, but who knows, there's always this weekend." There was a buzz on the white plastic tablecloth as my phone received a text. It was from Michael. "Michael's landed in San Francisco," I relayed to our group, relieved. "He says hello."

"How's he doing? Any better?"

"He still feels like shit," I said, sending back a string of hearts by text. "Hopefully this trip will do him some good."

"What happened?" Ben asked, and I told him about the accident. Ben winced when I shared Baby's year and model. He then recounted his own story of the car he had at eighteen and how it died on him and his mother halfway to Florida. The car was old, he said, so he had no choice but to pay the tow-truck driver to haul it away to a scrapyard and continue their trip by bus. "I'll always remember the image of her being dragged away," he said. "Still gives me chills."

"It's too bad Michael isn't here," I said to Ben. "You have a lot in common."

Ben asked how Michael and I had met, and I told him the abbreviated version: met in a gay bar, together three and a half years. "That's great," he said.

The dishes arrived and our team of waiters dropped them on the table along with plates and cutlery for us to use to divvy them up.

"And Michael, what does he think about you having a kid with your friends?"

"He's indifferent. He's not the biggest fan of children, but he's supportive and happy for me. He's pretty easy-going. Doesn't seem bothered by the concessions we've had to make."

"Concessions?" Kate said, pulling noodles onto her plate. "Like what?"

"Well, you know... When they come to town it's intense—go, go, go. We also can't have sex for five days prior in order for them to use the good stuff. And the whole process, it's not sexy or romantic. It's rather clinical."

"Are you guys in an open relationship?"

Kate scolded her lover. "Ben!"

"What? Was that not polite to ask? Sorry. I figured, you're both guys—it's hard to go long periods without it." I noticed that Ben ate quickly, like he was worried someone would take his plate. "I have two friends at work who are gay and in open relationships," he said with his mouth full. "They're both allowed to fool around on the side, and it doesn't seem to affect their relationship."

"No, we're not open," I said. "You can't be if you're trying to get someone pregnant." But then I felt annoyed and backed into a corner by my answer. I didn't want this guy to pigeonhole Michael and me into any part of his limited worldview. "But that's not to say we'll always be monogamous," I added. "Who knows? There might be a day when we're open. I wouldn't feel threatened if Michael slept with someone else, if Michael made out with someone else. We love each other. We're great friends. I hope he'll be in my life for a long time, but do I expect to be the only other person he ever sleeps with? For him to be the only other person I sleep with? No, I don't."

Kate was surprised. "Really?"

"But then how would that work?" Ben asked. "I never understood it with my co-workers either. Wouldn't you get jealous?"

"I don't know, do you get jealous?" I asked him. "I mean, Kate's married."

"Paul—"

"Well, you are, Kate."

"Well, Kate's not sleeping with her husband any more," he said, looking at her. "She's only sleeping with me."

"And are you only sleeping with her?" I asked. I tried to temper my tone to not sound challenging. The last thing I wanted was a fight. "I mean, you only get to see each other, what, once or twice a month? Are you saying that you can't imagine going without sex, but that you're not sleeping with anyone other than my sister?"

I half-expected Kate to protest, but she didn't. She too was interested in Ben's answer.

Ben could've responded defensively, but he didn't. He was calm in his reply, looking at Kate with devotion. "I'm not sleeping with anyone else," he said. "I can't imagine sleeping with anybody else. I love your sister, Paul. I don't want to be with anyone but her."

Ben's answer caught both Kate and me off guard. I could see in my sister's face that she was speechless and didn't know what to do with that answer, so she smiled at Ben and grabbed his hand, quickly letting go before picking up the napkin in her lap.

The table went silent. I thought I'd change the subject and reached over to grab the plate of salt-and-pepper shrimp. "Hey, Ben, did Kate ever tell you about our tradition?" I asked. "It's called 'Toast to the Shrimp.'" I placed one on his plate, then one on my sister's. Finally, I took one for myself. "Every time you take one, everyone at the table takes one too. Then you toast in the middle, and savour it, because it's the most fucking delicious thing on the menu and you want to make sure everyone has the same amount. Cheers," I said, and lifted the shrimp with my chopsticks. We toasted them together like flutes of champagne.

For the rest of the dinner, we talked about mundane things—work, Ben's tattoos, the crime novel he was working on, where we grew up, what Kate was like as a child. It was oddly normal, but at the same time rather strange. Here we were, the three of us, out for dinner while Kate's husband sat unawares not three hours away. I did wish Michael were with us, and not just for the car talk. I knew he would've inserted himself easily into the conversation and taken some of the pressure off me by talking to Ben about cars or international banking or woodworking or any of the other subjects he felt informed enough to discuss.

After our meal, when the orange slices and fortune cookies came, Ben's cell phone rang. He looked at the number. "I'm sorry, I have to take this," he said, and got up to take the call outside.

"So?" Kate asked, reaching for her cookie.

"So?" I said, taking one too.

"Well, what do you think?"

"Now? You want me to tell you now?" I said, opening

mine. "I don't know, Kate. He's opinionated, but he seems fine enough. Doesn't seem like a serial killer or anything—"

Kate's mouth dropped open.

"What? Don't get me wrong. He's nice and smart, but don't you think this is weird? Us, here, tonight? Having dinner, while Christian is at home? It's not just sex any more Kate, he said that he *loves* you! Do you love him? Are you prepared to leave Christian for him?"

"I don't know. Maybe."

"Is that enough? It's been six months. Shouldn't you know by now?"

"Listen, I don't need you pressuring me," she said, putting aside her fortune cookie and taking out her wallet. We hadn't received the cheque yet, but she was ready to leave. "I was hoping you'd keep an open mind. I guess that was too much to ask."

"Tell me you're having safe sex with this guy."

"Why? What's the point?" she shrugged, getting out her credit card. "It's not like I'm going to get pregnant or anything."

"Pregnant is not the only thing you can get. How would you want to explain a case of chlamydia to Christian?"

"I can't believe you. Why do you care so much about Chris? It's all you can talk about. Can't you think about me for a minute? About what I want? Can't you be in my corner for once? Ben could be someone important in my life."

"I don't see how."

"Do you think I liked Michael at first? Do you think I thought he was the guy for you? No, I didn't see the appeal at the beginning. I thought he was using you, for your money, for your home. He was always so negative. But I didn't say anything. And I was wrong! I *love* Michael. But I had to learn to love him. I had to learn to hold my tongue, because you were happy and I trusted you, and that's all that mattered."

I was in shock. Kate hadn't liked Michael? I thought back to our nascent beginnings. The moment I introduced them, all the dinners and drinks we'd had together… But if that was the case, then this was different. "Well, if you ever thought I was doing something stupid, I wish you'd let me know."

"Oh, really?"

"Yes, really."

"Then I'd think harder about what you're doing with Wendy and Eve."

"What do you mean?"

"I think you're making a mistake, Paul. I don't think you know what you're doing. Giving away your child like that. I don't think you'll be able to let it go when it's time—I don't see how you can. This kid is going to be a big part of you, and your friends won't let you in. I mean, they won't let you be on the birth certificate. They don't want you to use the word 'dad.' But the kid will be your child, Paul, and a part of *our* family. Dad's grandkid. Haven't you thought about that? How I might feel?"

"I did ask you."

"How Dad might feel? You haven't told him yet because you know it's wrong. You know how he's going to react, and so you don't tell him."

"That's not why I haven't told him," I said. "And I don't think you know what you're talking about. I know how you can see it that way, but you forget: I never wanted to have kids. You did! I understand how tough it must be for you.

But do you expect me *not* to help Wendy and Eve out because it makes for an uncomfortable situation with you or Dad? No. It's not a reason not to do it. It's different, Kate. I'm not bringing a child into the world with my partner. I will not watch my partner become pregnant and grow a baby inside of him for nine months. I will not be there for all the tests and excitement. I won't witness the birth, pick the name, or bring the child home from the hospital. It's going to be different Kate, and I'm sorry if—"

Ben came back into the restaurant. "Sorry about that," he said, sitting down. "I needed to take that call." He reached for the last cookie on the table. "Did you open yours? What's it say?"

We stared at each other from across the table. Kate read hers: "Laugh long, loud and often."

I read mine. "The current year will bring you much happiness."

Ben cracked open his. "Huh. I didn't get a fortune."

After dinner, I walked to the station to catch my train. The days were getting shorter and the sky was already dark. Drying brown- and yellow-coloured leaves collected in pockets on the street, and I felt compelled to walk through them, kicking and crushing them underfoot. I was upset, but most of all I was surprised by what Kate had said about Michael. Why hadn't she liked him? Had my dad not liked him either?

I soon arrived at Central Station and queued up for my train. Once on board, I found my window seat and took out a book to read, but instead just stared out at the platform, caught up in my own thoughts as we pulled out of the terminal.

On paper, I understood how my relationship with Michael might not make sense to the average person. That Michael might appear lost. Even I, at the beginning, had reservations when he told me about his crystal meth addiction as a teen. How his trouble with bullies and focusing in school had led him to spend time with the wrong kinds of people for days on end. He'd travelled a hard road into addiction and back, with a lot of casualties along the way—from his education to his savings to his self-worth—but so what? So what if he has all these ghosts in his past? If people thought I should be with someone else, someone with a steady income and less baggage, then they didn't know Michael. They didn't see the joy he brings me or know the love we have for each other. So he's a bit lost, who cares? So there's a scar that runs down the middle of him where he still hurts. That's not a reason not to love someone.

I knew, when Michael and I started dating, that a part of him was broken. I saw the crack in the things he said. There was a flinch, a skip, a soreness, every time Michael talked of his life in Moncton, like it was all throwaway, the footnote to a story of no consequence. And there had been a sense of finality to the things he had said too, a moderate nihilism about the future—both his and of the world. We shouldn't eat fish because of what we're doing to the oceans, humans shouldn't live in Southern Florida because we're destroying the wetlands, what's the point of going to school when the education system needs to be dismantled, we're all a blight on this whole damn world anyway and someone should just drop the bomb and put us all out of our misery. He said these things like jokes, like they were the sad punchlines of the human condition and it was a fact that nothing would ever get better and that we were all biding our time before the end.

In those first few days of dating Michael, they were signs that things might be hard down the road. Maybe that was what Kate saw. Why was I in Christian's corner anyway? She and I used to be such good friends. I didn't need to act like her parent.

As for what Kate had said about me being a sperm donor, we'd need to talk about that too, in time. I realized it was naive of me to think that she wouldn't be upset, that there might not be a hidden bruise around my news.

12

It was almost midnight when my train pulled into Toronto. I quickly hailed a cab and travelled to Wendy and Eve's. We took a few minutes to catch up before Wendy handed me a cup and sent me to my room. I whipped out my phone and opened up Tumblr, producing a sample in no time. "It's here," I shouted, once again leaving it on the table in their hallway. "Goodnight." I ran back to my room to go to sleep.

The next morning, I slept in later than usual. When I got up, Wendy was in the kitchen making breakfast—pancakes and bacon. "Good morning," I said, and sat down to check my phone. I yawned and reached for a glass of orange juice. "Smells delicious."

"Sleep all right?" Wendy asked.

"Like a rock. I had the strangest dream," I said, trying to grasp its outline before it slipped away. "Michael and I were in Queen Elizabeth's spare bedroom, packing for an overnight flight back home from London. It was delayed and I kept checking the time on my phone as we placed stuffed animals into plastic bags and tried to pack a large clothing rack into our suitcase. Nothing would fit. And there was a TV on in the room, showing us the violent storms back home that were the cause of the delay. And then Justin Bieber came out to sing a high-energy love ballad while being carried across a stage by three huge men."

Wendy laughed, and poured another large dollop of batter into a pan. "God, I hope our kid gets your imagination."

I noticed we were alone. "Where's Eve?"

"She went to get batteries."

"Oh?" I asked, not understanding.

"They're for my vibrator. When we try this morning, I want to have an orgasm."

"Ah," I said. "Well, why should I be the only one?"

After Eve returned and we ate, I produced another sample and left them to the procedure in private. I should be staying at a hotel, I thought, leaving the house. It's such an intimate thing to be around for. I would have gone running to kill time but had neglected to pack my gear. So instead, I walked to get a tea and the newspaper, then went to sit in a park not too far from their place. I looked at the time. It was almost noon; about nine where Michael was. I figured it'd be safe to call.

"Hi, buddy," he answered.

"Hi, buddy. Having fun?"

"Oh yes," he said, and in his voice I recognized the drawl of fatigue and dehydration. "We struck the jackpot because the weather is supposed to be super nice for the next few days. So far it's been fun, went to three bars last night. Gus and I might get a tattoo tomorrow. I'm thinking of getting one to commemorate my car."

"Make sure it's a clean place," I said. "How's the apart-ment?"

"Amazing," he said. "It's so big. I wish you could've come! We're on Castro Street, right across from the theatre. We couldn't be more central."

It was a nice thought, discovering another city with him. "I miss you already," I said.

"I miss you too, buddy."

"Any boys hitting on you?"

"I don't know. Maybe. It's San Francisco."

"Well… If someone kisses you, you can kiss them back, okay?"

"What?" he laughed. "What are you saying?"

I wasn't sure. "I don't know. I want you to have fun. Meeting Leo was fun. I want you—if you have the opportunity to—to have fun too, you know. Just remember, we're still trying."

"I know." I heard him call out to someone in the apartment. "What? Okay… I got to go now. We're heading out for breakfast. Text you later!"

I hung up, got up, then walked around the neighbourhood before heading back to Wendy and Eve's. I had been gone an hour, so I figured I'd given them enough time, but when I got back, they were still in their room with the door shut. I went into mine and collapsed on the bed.

Bored, I took out my phone again and opened up the apps. I browsed the profiles in the area. There was *Luke, 27. Single. Looking for NSA, dates or relationships. Church/Wellesley. Loves cycling and jogging and camping.* There was *Amir, 42. In an open relationship* with a link to his boyfriend's profile, *Tony, 45.* And *Wayne, 36. Single. What are all these couples doing here?* his profile shouted. *Your open relationship is bullshit!*

I closed my phone, not sure what to do. Read? Maybe

I should go back out, I thought. Or maybe I should do that later tonight, after Wendy and Eve go to bed? Michael is out having fun, why shouldn't I? Then I remembered JF. I had his number in my phone. It was last minute, I knew, but I figured it didn't hurt to text him.

Hey JF. It's Paul. In TO for the next couple of days. Free for a drink?

JF texted back soon after: *Paul! Nice to hear from you. I'm free tonight if you are. Meet for a drink at Woody's 10 PM?*

Sure, I responded. *See you then!*

When I arrived, Woody's was full of large groups of men spiking their drinks with bursts of laughter. I did a quick tour to look for JF but didn't see him, so I went up to the bar to get myself a cocktail. Tired of ordering sparkling water, I asked the bartender if he could make me something non-alcoholic.

"You like grapefruit?" he asked, and I nodded. He made me something tart and fizzy.

JF arrived soon after. We hugged and held the embrace for a second longer. He looked good in his dark green khakis and dense navy sweater, more stylish than the hoodie and jeans combo that I was wearing. JF told me he had come from birthday cocktails for one of his co-workers and was two drinks ahead of me. "Can I get you something?" he asked, gesturing towards the bar. I thanked him, but pointed to my glass on the table, and he took off, returning a minute later with a pint. "It's so good to see you," he said, sitting down.

JF pulled up the sleeves on his sweater, exposing a silver watch and furry forearms. "Likewise," I said. I got a faint whiff of his cologne from across the table, subtle and earthy.

JF took a sip of his beer. "It's good to see a familiar face. I've been in Toronto almost a year now and hardly know anyone."

"Really? I thought you had friends here."

"They're mainly Simon's friends," he said. "But to be fair, most have been nice to me. There's one, Valerie, who's gone out of her way to invite me to things. I'm having Thanksgiving dinner at her place tomorrow, but I really don't know the others who'll be there. I didn't think it would be this difficult, but it's hard making new friends when you're older. Everyone already has their own gangs and traditions. There's not a lot of space for someone new, and those willing to make room often don't have much of it. I know I'm low on the priority list, so I'll take what I can get. But I have to say, I do miss having a group of friends I can call at a moment's notice to go for a drink after work. So, thanks. This is going to make my weekend."

I smiled. "Aw, shucks," I said, trying to be funny. "It's my pleasure. You know, I don't think the two of us ever went out for drinks together. I mean, I saw you in the Village all the time, and we'd catch up at the bar, or we'd talk at one of your fabulous parties, but I think this is the first time we've made an actual date."

"That's a shame," JF said. "I meant to. I always found you super interesting."

I blushed. "Really? Why's that?"

"I don't know. Please don't take this the wrong way, but I always thought that you were very nice."

"Nice?"

"You know what I mean. That'd you'd be a good friend

to have. You're kind to people. You were always volunteering, too. In those days, before I met Simon, I'd see you at these AIDS fundraisers and come up and talk to you. I admired you. You were involved in the community, you gave back. You cared about your friends and even those you didn't know. You made time for people. You're like this... connector. I always meant to ask you out, but I never did. I don't know why. I guess I figured, you worked for Pride, you must have had your pick of men."

All this made me blush even more, and I had trouble getting my mouth around the words I wanted to say. "Uh, I don't know about that," I said, embarrassed. "I was too timid to do anything. To tell anyone I found them attractive— present company included. I used to think that working for Pride, I would meet all these interesting men. And I did meet people—a lot of people—but I never did anything about it. Well, rarely, anyway. Gay Pride? It was more like Gay Prude."

JF laughed.

"Everyone thought I was hooking up, but I wasn't. I was too afraid to in those days."

"You weren't the only one," JF said.

"It's funny," I said, "Now that I'm in a relationship at forty, I wonder where my youth went. A part of me feels like I should have had more sex when I was younger. That, in a way, I missed out."

"You're still young. Life begins at forty."

That old adage had been thrown at me numerous times in the months leading up to my birthday, but there was something poignant about it being shared tonight. "Yes, it does," I said. "But to be honest, I'm happy with my life the way it is now. It's what I wanted growing up, what I hoped forty would be: stability, a home, a good job, someone to come home to. However, there was a point, in my youth, when I wondered if I should've acted more on my libido, thrown caution to the wind and had adventure after adventure. Taken more risks. But it just wasn't me. I wanted it to be me, I waited for it to be me, but it wasn't."

"There's nothing wrong with that," JF said. "Everyone is different."

"Sometimes I feel that it was stolen from me. That with everything happening to those around me it was impossible to let go. I don't know, am I crazy? Did you ever feel that way?"

"I think we all did," JF said. "I was scared shitless and made mistakes, but still," he began to smile, "I had fun in my twenties. I took risks. But yes, I'm sure everyone in our generation felt that way at some point."

"Not today's kids. They're fearless. I've been out since 1993? That's almost twenty years!" I realized. I gestured to the rest of the room. "Some of these men were babies then. So much has changed. I have a friend who is HIV-positive and in his fifties, and there's no end to the young men willing to sleep with him now, which wasn't always the case. But having come out in the nineties, that feeling is still there for me, this worry. Like a phantom limb. Some kind of lingering post-traumatic stress. It was always safe sex, safe sex, safe, safe, safe, be safe—drilled into my head to the point where I became worried about every new guy I slept with. After every encounter. Was it safe? Did anything happen? There was a time in my life when I wondered if I'd even make it to forty, because so many didn't." I stopped, realizing this was getting heavy.

"I remember Alan," JF said. "Alan was great."

"Yes, he was," I said. "If you want to give credit where credit is due, it was Alan who got me involved in the first place, got me to be this connector, this organizer." The role felt strange to assume. I had never thought of myself in that way, but JF was right. "I don't know where I'd be today if it wasn't for him."

I stopped again. For a quick moment, I thought that I might cry; but instead, I picked up my drink and brought it to my lips. The fizzy cocktail did its job, distracting my senses as I took a long sip.

"So, did you think that life at forty would also include a kid?" JF asked, lightening the mood.

I almost laughed. "Uh-uh. No way."

"How's that going?"

"It's okay. Slower than I thought," I said. I then told JF everything: the changes I had to make to my lifestyle, how each attempt was a little different from the next. "This morning they used a vibrator before trying," I said. "Did you know that having an orgasm can increase a woman's chance of getting pregnant by fifteen percent? I've learned more about a woman's body in the past four months than I did all throughout high school."

"You'll be an expert before you know it."

"What about you? Did you ever want kids?"

JF looked into his beer. "No," he said. "Simon and I did talk about it once. But if we were going to do it, I wanted to adopt... How about Michael? What does he think of what you're doing?"

"He's supportive, doesn't want kids of his own."

"How long have you been together now?"

"Three and a half years," I said. "It's going good. A little predictable, but good."

"The three-year itch," JF said.

"Is that a thing?"

"Well, it happens to couples at different times, but normally around the three-year mark, when you've been together for a while and start to feel antsy. You love each other and are still having sex, but you're also distracted by what else is out there. It's not that you want to *be* with someone else, it's just… there are shinier things."

"Well then, it's right on time," I smiled. "And if you can get past the three-year mark?"

"If you can get past the three-year mark, you can do anything. Sure, there are other tests, but you know you can get through them."

"What happened to you and Simon?" I asked. "You were together, what, seven years?"

"Just shy of eight," JF said.

"Then why'd you break up?"

JF sighed and leaned back in his chair. "I don't know, really. We just, wanted to be other people again. Or, be who we were before becoming a pair."

"Were you open?"

JF leaned back in and nodded. "The last three years. Then we started seeing someone together on a regular basis. This guy Marco. We met him online and had a fling. At the beginning it was so much fun and we got along great, so we kept seeing him. Simon and I would look forward to it—it

222

reenergized our sex life. But after about ten months, the two of them started pairing off, and I got pulled into work and was presented with this opportunity in Toronto. I saw it all happening. I guess I could have done something to stop it, but I didn't."

JF continued, "I think we were both in denial for a long time, even when we were at home and making plans to flip our place. We wanted it to work; we were partners, but it had been a while since we were a couple."

"I'm sorry to hear that," I said. "You were so good together." I struggled, thinking about what I wanted to say. "Role models, in a way."

"Yes, many people said that. It was a lot of pressure."

"I'm sorry," I said. "I don't know if you knew this, but I had a big crush on you before you met Simon." JF smiled. "And then when you met, I became envious. I thought you two had it all: great jobs, good looks, so many friends. You were smart and funny and ambitious. It was like you were the complete package."

"Don't get me wrong, those years were great," JF said. "And I still love Simon. He's family. Although we're no longer together, and it's hard to be friends right now, I'm sure we'll get through this. We're still in each other's lives. We own property together. Still have two dogs. Eventually, it won't feel as awkward or as bad. And one day, I'll meet someone too. Then maybe, we can all be friends. I mean isn't that the great thing about being gay? That often, our lovers can remain our friends. That our friends can be our lovers." He downed the rest of his beer. "Can I get you another drink?"

"Sure, but I'm not drinking alcohol," I told him. It felt

like an apology. "Wendy and Eve have asked me not to, so I'm going to be a good boy. But maybe another one of these grapefruit spritzes? Here, let me get it."

"No, it's on me," he said, standing up. "Next time I'm in Montreal, you can take me out."

I smiled as JF went to the bar. While he was gone, I took out my phone and sent a text to Michael. *Hi buddy! Hope you're having a good time. Love.*

Seconds later, the reply came. *Hi buddy!!! Things are great. I'm a little drunk... Getting ready to head out to a bear party in SOMA. Miss you so much. Love!!*

Have fun! I replied. *Be careful! Talk tomorrow.*

JF came back with our drinks, but this time, instead of sitting across from me at the table, he sat beside me so we could watch the room together. "Cheers," he said, and we clinked glasses. "So many people tonight," he remarked. "I mean, it's usually full, but tonight seems more so."

"Thanksgiving weekend, I suppose. People needing a break from their families."

"It's like that here at Christmas too."

"Is this your bar?" I asked.

"I come fairly often. The Eagle, too. Crews and Tango if I want to see a drag show. I live a block away. Have you heard of *Vaseline Tower*?" I shook my head. "You'd recognize it from the street. It's a tall round apartment complex filled with gay men that overlooks the Village. Like *La Cage aux Folles* on Papineau does. The elevators are as cruise-y as the baths during a full moon. Where you staying?"

"With Eve and Wendy," I said. "Not far from here, in Cabbagetown."

"Nice."

"It is," I said.

JF's cologne was that much more seductive on this side of the table. I could smell it on his sweater, his skin, his hair. We both took sips from our drinks and when we had put them down, JF's hand was on my leg. "I had a crush on you too," he confessed, looking ahead.

I felt an immediate rush through my body. "Really?"

He nodded. "I wish I had done something about it."

I put my hand on JF's leg. "You should've." I said.

JF leaned over and kissed me. It was a slow kiss, soft and cheerful, made with the patience and care of someone who knew what he was doing. It lasted less than a minute, but in that time I vanished in his lips, the background of the bar fading away as his scent, his taste, his breath, enveloped me.

We pulled back and smiled, squeezing each other's legs. I took a sip from my drink, and he his. We put down our glasses and kissed again, this time with a little more of the comfort and wonder and memories of youth.

Then we stopped. That was it. Two kisses.

When we finished, we both exhaled as if we'd been holding our breaths for a decade. We sat back, but I left my hand in his as we took a moment to sip our drinks and watch the room, the desire slowly ebbing from our bodies.

JF spoke first, clearing his throat. "So, why did you say yes?"

I looked at him puzzled.

"To your friends, when they asked," he said. "Why did you say yes?"

"To help them, of course."

JF turned to face me, and as a result we let go of each other's hands. "But it's got to be more than that. What do you hope to get out of this? What do you think your relationship with the kid will be like?"

It was hard to qualify a response, to look into the crystal ball when I've never been able to predict the future. "I don't know," I admitted. "There's no frame of reference for this. I've never been an uncle. It'll be as new to me as it will be to my friends and family." Still, I didn't want to give up on this thought, so I allowed myself to explore it. "But if I close my eyes, and I try to imagine a future with this kid in it, it looks like a kitchen table. You know, when you go to a friend's place and they have a teenager who comes out of their room at dinnertime and keeps everyone entertained with the things they're learning—telling you about something they read in class, or this new band they've discovered. But then, instead of going home and never seeing the kid again, you see them all the time. They know your name. They know your birthday. You give them things to read or listen to; you help them with their assignments and personal dramas. I think it's a connection with the next generation I want most. How do we have that, if we're not uncles? And Wendy and Eve are giving me that."

The next day, we tried a final time. It was the day before Thanksgiving and Wendy felt we had done as much as we could and that any additional tries would be useless. To celebrate, Wendy and Eve prepared a small feast, a roasted chicken with quinoa stuffing, and we sat at the table and wondered aloud if it had worked. "Wouldn't that be something?" Eve said. "If next Thanksgiving there's one more of us at the table?"

"Two more," I corrected. "You're forgetting Michael."

The next morning, the three of us woke early and had breakfast. Eve drove me to the station to catch the 11:30 a.m. train back to Montreal. It was dusk by the time we pulled in to the city. I grabbed a cab outside and headed home, window rolled down to let in the cool evening air. As we headed up Saint Denis, the sky a shifting shade of purple, I was hit with a wave of euphoria. I had only been gone the weekend, but I became overwhelmed with a feeling of love for my city and my life. When I got home, I opened the door and the cats came running. "Hey, boys," I said. "Did Uncle Danny treat you well?" They followed me into the bedroom and jumped up on to the bedspread, looking for attention. I lay down and joined them, taking out my cell phone to text Danny: *Thanks for taking care of the kids!*

There was a noise and both cats were startled, ears pricked up in alert. I sat up and looked around the room. "You heard that too?"

The place was quiet now. The only noise was the yellow-ing tree outside our window rustling in the wind. I noticed that our closet door was open, having been left that way by Michael as he had packed. I got up to close it and noticed the hanger that had held Alan's jacket askew. I set it straight then closed the door shut.

I looked at the time. I was hungry, alone on a night when people all over the country were gathering for a Thanksgiving meal with friends and family. And though I had no plans, my life felt full and blessed. I was thankful to have this crammed but charming home that I owned and shared with my partner and our cats. I was thankful to have great friends like Charles and Danny. I was thankful for Michael, that he was someone with a big heart who continued to challenge me and my way of thinking. I felt thankful for Wendy and Eve too, great friends who were giving me a gift by letting me be a part of their family. And then, my sister Kate. Even if this situation made things awkward between us, I was thankful that we had remained close all these years and not drifted apart like we had with our father. And although I wished my mom were here, I was also thankful my dad could find happiness after she had passed, even if it did take him to the other side of the country. And finally, I was happy for the other father figure in my life. For Alan. For his ghost. Because even if he didn't haunt the rooms of our home, I felt his presence. And I was thankful for all he had taught me.

13

Four days later, Michael returned from San Francisco.

"You bleached your hair," I noticed, as he walked through the door that evening. I took his bags and placed them on the floor so I could give him a hug and a kiss.

"Too much?" he asked, exhausted but happy to be home.

"You look younger," I said, pulling away to get a better look. "But I like it. I missed you, buddy."

"I missed you too."

Michael played with the cats at the kitchen table, while I made us dinner. "You have no idea how much I missed this," he said. "The smell of food cooking, the taste of veggies. I don't think we ate much while in San Francisco."

"Drank your dinner, did you?"

"Most nights. Otherwise it was late-night burgers on our way home from the bars, or greasy breakfasts the next morning."

"Sounds wild," I said, placing a chicken and rice plate in front of him. "Did you behave?"

Michael looked up with a delinquent grin. "Somewhat. I didn't get a tattoo or anything, but I did come back with a small burn." He lifted his left elbow to show me the pockmark. "The result of a drunken collision with one of Carl's cigarettes."

"That all?" I asked.

Michael wiped the corners of his mouth and smiled again. "… I did make out with someone." He was shy about it, almost couldn't look me in the eye. "An older man from St. Louis. We were dancing at this bar in SoMa, and he was flirting with me. He was *so handsome,*" he added as an excuse. "But to be honest, it made me feel weird and miss you even more. I started to get homesick by the end of the trip."

"That's okay," I said, not bothered. "You were allowed. I missed you too."

I then recounted to Michael the details of my own trip, the attempts with Wendy and my night out with JF; however even though Michael had told me about his kiss, I neglected to mention mine. I wasn't sure why.

Now that he was back, Michael displayed a newfound energy. He was in a better mood, making jokes, asking for more time in the bedroom. The sex we had on his first night back was frenzied and intense, the first quality time we had spent together since Provincetown; I was relieved that all it took to reignite our passion was a week apart (and, I suppose, kisses with other men). Soon, Michael was drawing again and hitting the gym every other afternoon. He took on several more painting contracts too, and began looking for a car whenever he had a free moment. His insurance had informed him that he'd be getting $1,400 for Baby, which wouldn't be enough for an adequate replacement. I offered Michael money, but he refused. He said I had already paid for most of our Provincetown trip and had loaned him money for San Francisco. Instead, he'd put his tail between his legs and ask his dad for help.

I watched from the kitchen as he paced the house with the phone in his hand, mustering up the courage to call his father. He settled in a chair by the window, near where Malone and Sutherland were curled up in the sun.

"Salut, Dad," he said in the dullest, gruffest voice I'd ever heard him speak in. "Ouen… Ouen." Michael spoke to his dad in Chiac. The harsh amalgamation of French and English was bewildering to me. "Chequ'un a crashé mon car last month," he said, almost apologetic. "So j'ai besoin un autre."

I got the gist of what was being said, recognizing words more than sentences. I wasn't sure when the two had last spoken, but Michael's tone was less strained than I had anticipated; it might not have been jovial like the calls in English with his mother, but it wasn't angry like the few times I had asked him about his dad. If anything, Michael sounded like a timid animal on the phone, a defensive porcupine face to face with a potential threat. I knew this must be humiliating for him, to ask for help.

"Head up, porcupine," I mumbled. "Head up."

Once the call was over, Michael let out an exasperated sigh.

"So?" I asked. "That didn't sound too bad."

Michael was incredulous. "He thinks I should get a minivan."

I had heard the word repeated on the call. "A minivan?"

"For my tools, I guess." He stood up. "To transport things. He has one in the shop and wants me to come get it, but I'm not fucking going back there. I'm not getting a minivan."

"Will he lend you the money for what you want?"

Michael shook his head. "I didn't ask. I thought that maybe he'd offer, but no, he hasn't changed. Fucking guy… He *might* offer me the money one day, but only after I jump through a bunch of hoops. Not until he holds it over my head a little longer. He just wants me to see him come to my rescue."

It seemed juvenile, this stalemate. I wish I could've understood it more. "But Michael, maybe if you impressed upon him that you—"

Michael interrupted me. "Nah, thanks Paul, but I don't want to talk about this with you. Not now." Michael put his phone down and nuzzled the heads of both our cats. "Who are my good boys?" he said, rousing them from their sleep. "Who loves you?" He turned and patted himself on the chest. "Well," he exhaled. "I need a joint." He took off to the front to roll one.

The following week, Michael turned twenty-nine. To celebrate, we went out to an Italian restaurant in the Plateau with Charles, Danny and Vince.

"To be twenty-nine again," Danny sighed.

Michael shook his head. "Honestly, I'll be happy to say goodbye to my twenties. I can't wait to be old."

For his gift, I got him drawing supplies—a quality sketching pad and a set of graphite pencils—as well as the remaining books in the *Tales of the City* series (now that he had read the first two). And Charles gave Michael another accessory from his closet, a string of pearls, which he wore proudly at the dinner table.

The next day, Michael found a car—a champagne-coloured 1995 Acura in decent condition. It wasn't the exact car he wanted, but it would do. With the insurance money and the little he was able to put aside, Michael still needed an extra $1,500 for the purchase. He reluctantly asked if I would be comfortable loaning it to him. That way he wouldn't have to involve his father.

"Sure," I said. I was a little concerned about our finances, but I didn't want to burden him with that news. "That's what lines of credit are for, right?"

"Thanks," he said, relieved. "Just add it to the pile I owe you."

The next day, Michael bought the car and picked me up at work.

"Not bad," I said, getting in. "What are you going to call her?"

Michael considered it. "Darlene. She's automatic, so you can drive her too."

Soon Michael was being offered jobs clear across town, where having a car made a world of difference. He also picked up more shifts at Minnelli, where the owners wanted him to help prepare a new lunch menu. "If this keeps up, I'll be able to pay you back in no time," he said.

Between searching for used cars and Michael's birthday celebrations, it was a busy few weeks, so I didn't think too much of it when I hadn't heard from Wendy and Eve. Then one Saturday morning, I got a text while I was home.

You around? Can we Skype?

I answered the video call. The two of them were sitting on chairs in front of their computer. I recognized their guest room in the background, the headboard under which I had recently slept, the red nightstand beside the bed with the same *Time* magazine I had flipped through. The framed picture over their bed was gone, however, and in its place was a draped sheet. "You redecorating?" I joked, after we had said our hellos. "What's that behind you?"

"Oh this?" Wendy and Eve both got up and pulled down the sheet to reveal a homemade banner with the words, *You ready to be an uncle?*

"What?!" I shouted. "Oh my god!"

"Oh my god!" my friends repeated in unison.

"Can you believe it?" Wendy said, as they both sat down. "We're in denial too! It's very soon."

"How long?"

"You count from the first day of your last period, so just over four weeks."

My hand went over my mouth. "Oh my god…"

"Wendy thought she was getting her period on Thursday," Eve said, "but then she took a test. We saw a line, but it was faint. Then we realized, *Why did we get a test with a line? We should've got one of those 'Yes or No' ones.* So we went back to the pharmacy and got one and did the test again, and it said Yes!"

"Four weeks!" said Wendy. "At this stage the embryo is the size of a poppy seed."

"Oh my god," I repeated a third time. "This is nuts… Congratulations!"

"Congratulations to you too!"

"When I didn't hear from you, I didn't think anything of it." I said. "I thought, maybe we'd got to the point where you didn't need to tell me every time it didn't work, and that I'd hear when it did. I can't believe you're pregnant!"

We laughed and squealed and shared our excitement, then before the call ended Wendy and Eve asked me not to tell too many people. "It's early and there's always the danger I might miscarry," Wendy said. I agreed and told them that I would only tell Michael and my sister. "You can tell your dad too," Wendy added.

I closed the computer window and found myself unable to move. I picked up my phone and called Michael. "Wow, I'm happy for you, buddy," he said, taking a moment from his job for the call. "I had no doubt your boys had game."

After he went back to work, I didn't know what else to do. "Wow," I kept repeating to myself. "Holy shit." I paced around the place. I could go for a jog, but I didn't feel like it. Since the half-marathon, I had got lazy about my runs. I looked at the time. Michael was still working for another five hours. I could do work, I figured, and opened up my email, but all I could think about was Wendy's uterus.

A poppy seed.

I opened my browser and searched for "four weeks pregnant" and sifted through the results. I read about the embryonic period and the fetal period. The embryos in the accompanying images all looked like translucent alien blobs, or the battered pieces of salt-and-pepper shrimp that Kate and I would toast to on our nights in Chinatown. What will this kid look like? I wondered.

I got up from my desk and left the room to retrieve a shoebox of old photographs I kept in the cupboard. Back before digital cameras, I would shoot at least four rolls of film every Pride, and a pile of these photos spilled out onto the kitchen table as I opened the box. Each year blended into the next as I sorted through the rainbow-coloured mess of crowds and floats. I looked for old pictures of Wendy and me, and soon came across a bunch taken when we'd travelled to New York City. In one of the photos, the two of us had our arms around each other, she in her "I Can't Even Think Straight" shirt, me in my "Nobody Knows I'm a Lesbian" one. I must have been almost half my age, I figured twenty-three or twenty-four, and much thinner. There were angles to my profile that were now hidden in my full face. There was no beard, no chunk, no sign of the bear I would become. Wendy, too, looked different. Back then, she had dyed her hair blue and wore it short and spiky. Looking at us together in the streets of New York, hanging off each other like the best friends we were, I felt as if I were staring at what could be our kids.

Feeling nostalgic, I kept on digging. I came across a few of Wendy with old girlfriends, each one odder than the next: Marie-Pierre, France, Angie. I also found a stack from when Wendy first met Eve, then a bunch from when the three of us lived together in the Village. Near the bottom of the box were some of Alan too. I'm not sure why, but I don't have many photographs of him, maybe a dozen. I hadn't seen these photos in years. In them, Alan looked younger than I remembered. These were taken during our time together— Alan in his early thirties, in jean shorts and a tank top, at the Pride parade or at protests. I'm beside him in some of them. I look thin and fragile, like you could break me in half. In one, taken at the *Ça Marche* AIDS walk, I'm wearing baggy jeans and a tight black shirt that seems to disappear into the hollow of my chest. In another, Alan and I are drinking beer in the Village, decked out in our Doc Martens and bomber jackets. And there is one I took of the two of us in our tent in Provincetown, camera stretched out at arm's length to catch us cuddling. But the angle is off. You can only see my chin and upper torso in the frame, but you get a direct shot of Alan's young face and bare chest, alive and alight and happy in the way I remember him being.

The photos were still out when Michael got home.

"Fine wine," he said.

"What?"

"You're a fine wine. Look at you. You're such a kid here," he said, pointing to a picture of me wearing a red baseball cap. "I wouldn't have looked at you twice."

I thought about that for a second. "You were thirteen when this picture was taken!"

Michael grabbed me by the belly. "You're much sexier with all this extra meat on you." He kissed me and proceeded to drag me into the bedroom. "Come on," he said. "Let's go make some more babies."

Two days later, I got an email from Wendy:

Boo!! it began. *I think it's fitting that today's Halloween because I'm spooked as hell about what we're doing. It's weird not to tell anyone... Especially at work, because I feel like it's such a big thing. I'm so tired lately, I almost fell asleep standing up in the streetcar this morning. Hehehe, so crazy that I'm forming life. Supposedly, the most important time is these next few weeks when every organ is created. No pressure right!!*

We've got a plan to eat healthy and Eve bought me all this organic produce. Last night she cooked up a heap of salmon, sweet potatoes and dark leafy greens. And I get to have the leftovers too! I'm so thankful for her. I keep having these "Shit, what did we do?" moments and Eve keeps looking at me like I'm mad. Crazy!!! Right??!

I felt the same way. Since learning that Wendy was pregnant, I kept having these *Oh shit!* moments too. After spending a large chunk of my Saturday reading articles online about prenatal growth and development, I went out shopping and found myself loitering in the kids' sections of clothing stores and bookshops, purchasing a soft white onesie with a moose on it and a children's book for adults I thought Wendy might like called *Go the Fuck to Sleep*.

That Halloween afternoon, on my lunch hour, I bought a bag of miniature chocolate bars at the nearby pharmacy. I had never done this before, but I thought it might be fun to give out candy to kids trick-or-treating. Since Michael had the day off, I texted him and asked if he could pick us up a pumpkin. He had it carved for when I got home, a happy orange monster with two triangle eyes and a jagged mouth. We ate quickly and set up a table outside with the lit jack-o'-lantern beckoning to the street. Michael wore his bear hat, and I dressed as a cowboy, and the two of us sat on our steps outside and waited for kids to come.

Unfortunately, none did.

"Maybe it's our street," Michael said, eating another mini Snickers. "Parents probably prefer more residential streets with fewer cars."

"Maybe," I said, blowing out the candle.

* * *

The following weekend, I got a frantic call from Danny. "Where's Michael? Is he there? Let me speak to him!"

"Danny, what is it?"

"That fucking friend of his is a fucking asshole! Did you know that he had sex with Vince while we were in P-Town?"

"What? Who, Gus? No, I didn't know that."

"Did Michael know?"

"No, I don't think so, Danny. He didn't say anything to me."

"I've been trying Michael's cell, but he won't pick up."

"He's at work."

"The nerve of that creep, right under my nose and on our holiday!"

"What happened?"

"Well, we had the talk, Vince and I. We've been together over three months now. I figured it's a good time to discuss how we're feeling and if we're going to be exclusive. You know—just us, right? But no. Apparently, this entire time he's been sleeping with other men. And when I pushed him, I asked if anything happened in Provincetown. He squirmed. Remember how Vince, Gus and Michael took off into the dunes that afternoon? Well, it happened there. And you know what? That was my fantasy! I would've loved to do that! Why didn't Vince ask *me* to go for a walk? Fucking Gus and his libido. I swear the next time I see him I'm going to cut off his balls and wear them as earrings."

"I'm sorry, Danny. What did you say?"

"I said a lot of things—you know, I didn't expect us to be exclusive at the beginning. I'm not naive, I know how things

239

work. That's why I wanted us to talk about it after three months. It was time. And I needed him to know that even if he's sleeping with other men, that I'm not. How could I? It's not like me." Danny stopped for a brief moment, sadness in his voice. "And I'm smitten, Paul. I can't think of anyone else. I wish he felt the same way."

"Who says he doesn't?" I said. Danny didn't respond. "So, what happened?"

"What do you mean, 'What happened?'" Danny took a deep breath. "I forgave him, of course." He sounded embarrassed, and toyed at being smart. "I mean, I'm a Christian. I'm supposed to forgive. But it's not easy. It still hurts! And it hurts that it was with that idiot Gus. I think that's the thing that bothers me most. He's had it in for me, that fucking weasel, ever since your birthday dinner. God, I want to punch him in the nuts!"

"Easy, Danny. What do you want me to do? Do you want me to come over? Do you want me to speak to him? Have Michael speak to him?"

"No," Danny said, the anger evaporating from his voice. "I just needed to vent. I thought he was the one, Paul. I really did."

"What do you mean, you *thought* he was the one? You said you forgave him."

"But it's not going to be the same. And it's not just because of Gus. There were other men too. This entire time."

"So why does that matter? He loves you, doesn't he?"

There was silence on the other end of the line as Danny thought about it. "I know," he said, his voice heavy. "It makes sense in my head, but not in my heart." I couldn't tell through the phone, but it sounded like Danny was crying. "It's like I was in a different relationship than the one I was in, you know? Like our time in Provincetown—it was the happiest I've been in years, and then to learn that the trip was something else entirely for the person I took it with. I should've known that it wasn't going to work. He's a Scorpio, and I can't keep up with someone who looks like that. Call me greedy, but I don't want to share."

"So, what then? Has he agreed to be exclusive?"

"He says he'll try. He said he didn't know it was important to me, but that's bullshit. He was at your birthday dinner. I probably scared him from talking about it. But he says that he doesn't think of sex the way I do. That sometimes it's fun to have an adventure, and I know he's right. I just… I feel so jealous and possessive. And I don't want to."

"You know, Danny Boy," I said, reaching for something, anything, that might be helpful, "Gus was right about one thing—you're not going to meet someone who will be everything for you. That's why we have friends. No one's perfect. You're just two imperfect people trying to support each other while living your own lives. I know Vince loves you. So he fooled around, who cares? He wants to be with you. Just listen to him and hear what he has to say. Yes, it was a mistake for him to sleep with Gus, and I'm sure he knows it. Don't throw away your happiness, Danny, out of jealousy. Don't let Gus ruin that for you too."

I seemed to have adequately talked Danny down from the ledge, and he sounded calm and reassured by the time we hung up. When Michael got home that afternoon, I asked if he knew if anything had happened between Gus and Vince.

He told me that he did. He hadn't seen it happen in the dunes—at some point they went their separate ways—but Gus had told Michael about it one night in San Francisco. Michael said he hadn't told me because he didn't want to give me the burden of the news, nor interfere with Danny and Vince's relationship. I understood that.

That night, I had a dream about Danny and Vince. They were sitting at my kitchen table, whispering to each other and staring at me. I couldn't tell if they were fighting. Kate was in the dream too and announced that she was two days pregnant. Before I knew it, her baby was in the room with us and I was carrying it around, putting it places—on top of shelves, in a clothes hamper, in front of the TV. At one point, she asked to have her baby back, but I couldn't find it. I looked for it everywhere, in the hamper, in the kitchen closet, in the oven and fridge; and then I found it, sitting on the floor behind the door to the bedroom. The baby had no face. I picked the child up and ran it over to Kate, but as soon as I passed it to her the baby dissolved in her hands and turned into a pile of dust on the floor.

I woke up startled, with an empty feeling. I hadn't seen Kate's reaction in the dream. I awoke before I could; but I felt the residual coldness lying there in the dark—this sadness, this desperation I had left her alone with. The curtain on our bedroom window wasn't sufficiently closed, so a sliver of light from the street lamp outside ran across the room. At the foot of the bed, I saw Sutherland. He sat with his body towards the door, but he was looking at me over his shoulder. After a moment, he looked away.

The dream was still with me when I woke the next morning. It was accompanied by a feeling of guilt. I had known Wendy was pregnant for over a week now and hadn't told Kate. In fact, we still hadn't spoken since our fight. But then shortly after noon, as I tried to figure out how to tell my sister, I received a text from her.

Hey, I'm in town, it said. *Can I come over?*

Of course, I replied. *Any time.*

I readied our home for her arrival, tidying up the kitchen and boiling the kettle. I assumed the visit would be like the other tête-à-têtes we'd had over the years after a big blowout: she'd come over, we'd expose our bruised feelings, fight some more, and then, after we had said all there was to say, there'd be a dramatic switch in our tone and both of us would apologize. This time, however, I would have important news to share.

Kate didn't look ready for round two when I opened the door that cold Sunday afternoon. Her face was deflated. "I told Chris," she said, wine bottle in hand. "It's over. He's moving out."

I took the bottle from her and pulled her into a big hug. "I'm sorry, Kate," I said, holding her tight. "What happened?"

"Nothing," she said, incredulous, placing her coat on the rack. "I mean he was surprised and angry; he yelled and said horrible things—like I had no morals or loyalty," the latter said in comical disbelief. "But what hurt most was that he didn't fight for me." She started to cry, and I hugged her again.

"Here, come inside," I said, and led her into the living room.

"He didn't fight for us," she continued, grabbing tissues from the coffee table as we sat down. She dried the corners of her eyes and sniffed. "It was like, all this time he'd been look-ing for a guilt-free way out and I gave it to him. I cheated and he took it as a reason to walk out the door." Kate said that their conversation had lasted only twenty minutes before he grabbed his duffel bag and filled it. "How can it be over that quick?"

"What are you going to do?" I asked. "Are you going to move back to Montreal?"

She shook her head. "It's too soon to say."

"Have you told Ben?"

"No, I haven't." She blew her nose. "He doesn't know I'm here; I'm staying at a hotel... It's funny, I wanted Ben, his touch, more than anything. But now—at least, right now—I feel grossed out by everything. Maybe we did go too far."

My sister looked tired, her face long and dazed. There was a bowl of leftover Halloween candy on the table in front of us, chock-full of miniature Mars, Coffee Crisp and Twix bars. She looked at it and sorted through the selection, picking out a Twix and opening its wrapper.

"I know what you need," I said. I got up and, putting away the bottle of wine she had brought, went to retrieve the Japanese whisky Kate had got me for my birthday.

"You haven't opened it yet?"

"Waiting for the right time." I set down two tumblers and twisted off the bottle's cap. I poured us each a dram. We took sips and tasted.

"It's good," she said, licking her lips, tears on her cheeks. "Goes good with the chocolate." She set the glass back down and sighed. "What am I going to do, Paul?"

I put my glass down. I didn't know what to say.

"Listen, I want to apologize." She straightened. "For what happened last month. And I'm sorry it took so long to call you. I just needed not to think for a while."

"There's no need to apologize," I said.

"No, you were looking out for me—I know. It was a lot for you to handle. I get it. You're my brother. You were being protective. I'm sorry to have dragged you into all this."

"Please. You're my sister. I should've been more understanding. I didn't want you to get hurt."

"I'm sorry what I said about Michael, too. Is he here?"

"No, he's at work," I said. "It's okay. I'm just relieved you like him now."

"God, Paul," she said, palm to forehead. "I feel like such an idiot."

I put down my drink. "You're not an idiot. I know it doesn't feel like it now, but remember—you didn't want this either. Try to think back to the headspace you were in before this happened. Christian wasn't being a good partner. You tried to get him to address your problems, and he wouldn't. Who blames you for wanting something different? You went for it! Not everyone does that. Some people are happy being miserable, but not you. I know it hurts now, but it won't always."

Kate grabbed my hand. "And I'm sorry about what I said to you about Wendy and Eve. It's none of my business. I suppose it hit too close to home. I couldn't do it, but it's a wonderful gift you're giving to them. But I, too, don't want you to get hurt."

The room went still. I became aware of where we were, on the couch in my living room, the remaining yellow leaves on the tree outside reflecting the sun onto the walls. There were many things I wanted to tell my sister. I wanted to tell her that I was sorry, that this was all unfair and that I would do anything for her, even take years off my own life, if it meant that she could have a child.

"Kate," I said. "Wendy's pregnant."

My sister smiled, tears gathering in her eyes. For a moment she didn't say anything. She almost laughed, then reached out to grab my hand. "I'm happy for you, Paul," she said, her hands cold as another tear streamed down her face. She sniffed. "I know you think I'm not, but I am."

14

EVERY YEAR, ON NOVEMBER 19, I bake a strawberry pie for my mother's birthday. It's a tradition I had started a year after she died, and I've kept it up ever since. It was her favourite dessert and, at the beginning, I would invite friends over to share it with me. Other times, I would sit in front of the TV and eat the whole thing. One year, I donated it to a bake sale at Danny's church. Another year, I brought it to a dinner party that Charles was hosting for an old friend. But since I'd met Michael, I've shared the pie with him, the two of us divvying it up after dinner, by candlelight. And though neither of us is religious, we'd say a prayer.

I had another tradition, too: As the pie cooled on the counter, I'd call my dad.

I sat down at the kitchen table with the phone, determined to finally share my good news with him. I mean, how could I not on my mother's birthday? Even though we only spoke once a month, and only for a few minutes each time, I would have never thought, growing up, that one day he and I would spend this much time together on the phone. When I was young, asking to be picked up after playing at a friend's house, or as a teenager, when I'd call in to see if I had any messages, I'd flinch if my dad answered. "Can you put Mom on?" I'd say. I never knew what to talk about with my dad. He was like a stranger who lived with us, but one who paid the bills and kept us fed. Not that my dad was withholding. He would often try to connect with me, suggesting we go into the backyard to play sports or go see a movie. I didn't want to, though. Inside, I could already feel myself pulling away, aware that my life would be very different from his and not knowing if he'd ever understand.

The phone rang once before he answered. "Hi, Dad," I said. "I baked Mom a pie."

My father let out a deep sigh. "She would have been sixty-seven today; old like me."

"You're not old," I said. "You're more active than most people your age."

"I think I can smell the pie," my dad said. "How does it look?"

I admired its golden crust. "Delicious. I added rhubarb this time. Want me to ship you some?" I joked.

"As tempting as that is, I'll have to pass. I'm not supposed to be eating sweets these days. The doctor says I'm prediabetic."

It was the first I had heard of this. "Well, that's not good."

"No, I don't like my doctor right now," he said. "But whatever. Debbie's got a subscription to *Bon Appétit*. I'll ogle the pictures." That made me laugh. "Have you spoken to your sister?"

"Yes," I said. "This morning."

"How is she?"

"She's fine," I said. "Today's tough because Christian is picking up his stuff. She wants to make sure he doesn't take anything that belongs to her."

"I'm happy she has you close," my dad said, a pang of regret in his voice. "Even if you do live in different cities. I know she feels the same. I hate being far away from the two of you. I'm going to call her later."

"And you?" I asked. "What's new? How's Debbie?"

"We're doing great." There was a smile in his voice. "Actually, I have news."

"Oh?" I said, wondering how it would compete with mine.

"I'm going to be a grandfather."

"What?" I said. I was confused, and not sure I had understood what I'd heard. "But… What?"

"Debbie's daughter. Sue. She and her husband are going to have a child. She's only about one month along. They told us yesterday—so please don't say anything to your sister yet; I'd like to tell her. But isn't that exciting? I'm going to be a grandfather! You and Michael are going to be uncles. Isn't that wonderful?"

"Uh huh," I said, immobile. "That's great, Dad. Wonderful."

"They've been trying for a while, but it finally worked. Debbie's excited. We're going to go shopping later for wool. She wants to start knitting blankets right away."

I didn't know what to say. All I could think of was Sue's happy face, a hand at her belly. "Well, that's great Dad. I'm happy for you—for them. But," I realized, "maybe don't tell Kate today. She's got enough going on with Christian getting his things."

"Maybe you're right. Your poor sister. I'll wait a day or two."

A month along. "Well," I said, needing to wrap up the call, "please congratulate Debbie for me. And Sue, and her husband..." I had to think of his name. "Neil! I'll send along a card or something. Congratulations, Dad. You'll make a great grandfather."

"Thanks, Son. Let's speak soon." And then he hung up.

I was preoccupied by the news for the rest of the day. I wanted to call and talk to Kate, but I needed to take my own advice and let her deal with Christian. Instead, I went for a long walk around the neighbourhood. I walked to Jarry Park and sat and watched the ducks. I then went to the Jean Talon Market and picked up steaks for dinner. Everywhere I went, I saw images of my dad and Debbie in my head, the two of them fawning over Sue and her baby, which for some reason I had no trouble envisioning—an alabaster child with blue eyes, wrapped in wool blankets and smelling like apple sauce.

When I got back, Michael was home, smoking a joint and closing up the garden on our back balcony. "I think we did a good job this year," he said. Everything had died or gone to sleep about a month ago, but he was right, our garden had been beautiful. "I saved seeds from the petunias."

"Need help?" I asked.

"No. Almost done," he said, a black trash bag in his hand, smoke coming out of his mouth in curls. I told him what my dad had told me. "Really?" He exhaled, the rush of grey a temporary beard beneath his chin. "How about that? Did you tell him?"

"No, I didn't tell him. I didn't know what to say after that."

Michael pinched out the end of his joint and left it in

250

a nearby ashtray. "Actually, can you help me with this?" He handed over the garbage bag so I could hold its mouth open while he grabbed at the dead twigs and plants and threw them into the plastic. "You're going to have to tell him soon. I think the stress is getting to you. You were talking in your sleep again last night."

"Really? What did I say?"

"Something like 'No, not today.'"

I wasn't listening. I was busy wondering if I told my father, would Debbie knit for Wendy too? "They told them after a month," I said. "*A month!* Wendy is only seven weeks along and I still haven't told anyone but you and Kate."

"Debbie's daughter is younger. Less chance of anything going wrong."

"Still," I said, shrugging. "I guess that means both kids will be born around the same time."

"Yeah," Michael said, thinking about it. "That's going to be weird."

I helped Michael clean up the rest of the balcony. We stacked the empty clay pots in a pile by the door and swept the leaves off the side of the railing. Afterwards, we struck up the barbecue, one of the last times we figured we'd use it this year, and cooked our dinner. Once we'd eaten, Michael and I shared the pie, the cats circling, waiting for Michael to drop a morsel or two onto the floor.

"Since when do they like sweets?"

"Since always." Michael crumpled up some crust in his hand and dropped it at his feet. The cats dove in.

"You spoil them," I said. "You worry about Malone's poops, and you give him stuff like that."

"What's that?" Michael asked Malone. "Daddy's no fun? I'm your favourite?"

We couldn't finish the pie, so I got out a piece of shrink-wrap to cover the remaining third. "What are you doing?" Michael asked. "Give me that. You shouldn't do it like that."

"Like what?"

"Like this. See?" Michael showed me my ineptitude at affixing plastic wrap to the pie plate. "It's not sealed shut. Air's going to get in and make it stale."

I stuck out my tongue in jest and let him put it away. I blew out the candles on the table and was about to head out to the front to watch TV when he stopped me. "Here, wait," he said, and pulled out a bunch of fifties.

"What's this for?" I asked, circling back to take it from him.

"For food, the mortgage, the car, for everything."

It was a welcome five hundred dollars. "You sure you don't want to put this towards your taxes?"

"I made my payment this month," he said. "I can keep it if you like."

"No, that's okay." I laughed and pocketed the money. "Just in time for us to turn on the heat. We're supposed to have a cold winter." I turned to head out of the kitchen, but he stopped me again. "What? What is it?"

Michael was impatient. "Can you sit down please?"

I did what I was told and sat down at the kitchen island. Michael opened one of the drawers below him and pulled out my old Freddie Mercury/Lady Diana coffee mug.

"What?!" I exclaimed, not sure what I was looking at. I reached over to take it from him. It wasn't perfect, but somehow it had been reassembled—bright pieces of gold holding the shards together, running through Freddie's face and Diana's arm, all around the cup. "How did you…"

"There's this guy I found in Vancouver. He uses a technique called *Kintsugi*. It's an ancient Japanese way of repairing broken things. They use liquid metals like gold or silver to fix broken pottery or ceramics. The idea is that an object's scars become a part of its history. Not something to hide, but celebrate. That makes the object special, and stronger."

I looked it over. It was incredible. A solid piece that was both the original gift from my sister and an apology from my partner. I was in awe. "Wow, Michael," I said, and started to tear up. "I can't… I mean… Thank you."

He smiled. "I had hoped to give it to you on your birthday, but it took him a while to work on it. I guess I could have kept it until Christmas, but I couldn't wait."

I put the mug down and got up to hug him tight. I whispered into his good ear. "Thanks, buddy. You're the best."

I continued to get regular updates from Wendy. They were always excited and came with many exclamation points. *I feel like I'm in The Princess and the Pea!!* she wrote one day in an email. *I know it's only the size of a blueberry, but I'm convinced I can feel it! I just can't get comfortable! Not that I'm having any trouble sleeping, I'm tired all the time. And boy, am I nauseous!! Eve keeps cooking me all this healthy food, but it's like I can't keep it down. All I want to eat these days is pasta!!!*

Another day, she called me over lunch and told me that her breasts were starting to hurt, and that she sometimes had to get up to pee five times in a night. It might have been an overshare, but I liked getting the news. It made me feel like I was part of it all and reminded me how close we had been when we'd lived together, when personal ailments like menstrual cramps, hangovers, and the odd case of crabs became end-of-the-world tragedies we'd experience together.

I assembled a package of creature comforts—things like teas and lotions and slippers and magazines—and mailed them off to her with a card thanking them again for including me in all of this. Wendy was touched when she got it, calling me up to tell me she was going to have to hide the chocolate and asking where in the world I had found a pair of L Word pyjamas.

That month, I didn't have time to do much more than work. November had kept both Michael and me busy: he winterized clients' homes, including ours; and I prepared to launch a new shoe line for an American sneaker company. The client was LA-based and super demanding, with emails coming in at all times of day. I found myself working into the evening to accommodate their time zone, dealing with numerous emergencies to make sure everything was ready for their Christmas campaign. In the end, it all went off without a hitch—the client was happy, my employer was happy. Then one afternoon, I was called into my boss's office to find out the company was giving me a raise.

"We just want to thank you, Paul, for always going above and beyond," my boss said. "I know this job can be demanding at times, and we come to you with all sorts of last-minute requests and changes. But our clients love working with you, and we appreciate you being so flexible and a team player. Congratulations, we're bumping you up a notch in salary."

I called Michael as soon as I was out. "I got it! I got a raise!" I yelled into the phone in one of the empty conference rooms.

"Yeah, you did," Michael said. "You worked so hard. I'm happy for you, buddy."

That night, we celebrated with a dinner out. Then, that weekend, we drove to IKEA to treat ourselves to a new bed frame. At the store, I once again found myself looking at things for children. Michael caught me in one of the display nurseries surrounded by three pink walls and stuffed animals, staring into a bassinet.

"What do you see in there?" he asked, peering in.

Although the store had gone to great lengths to decorate this make-believe room, it still felt empty. The crib had no sheets, no pillows. The pictures in the frames on the shelves held dull stock photos. I looked at him, and then around at all the faux furnishings.

"What life might look like," I said. "If we were fathers."

On the first Saturday in December, Michael and I attended Charles's annual preseason holiday party. "I think I'm going to wear my pearls," Michael said as we got ready, putting them over a black turtleneck. He had recently shaved his head, so his hair was back to its original dark colour.

I was looking through my closet. "I need to go shopping," I said. "I don't fit in anything any more."

It had been almost two months since I had gone out for a run, and in that time I had put on weight. This meant doing the sit-down test with my dress shirts before leaving home to see if my belly busted against the clasps. I put one on and sat down, and the skin and hair on my stomach was visible through figure eights. "I guess I can give this one away," I said, taking it off and searching for another.

"Isn't that the purpose of ties? To cover the split down the middle?"

"I'm not wearing a tie to Charles's party." I pulled out a black button-up from the back of the closet. "I suppose I could just stand all night."

Charles had been throwing this same party for more than a decade. The event always fell within the week of Alan's birthday; it was a holiday fundraiser, with all the money going to a local AIDS organization. At the beginning it had been a sombre affair, but it soon evolved into an epic party that was the highlight of the social season. I had yet to miss one. Over the years I had attended with Wendy and Eve, and also with the men I dated. And when I was single, I would come hoping to meet someone new. Many of the men who attended Charles's parties were people I never saw anywhere. It was a who's who of eligible bachelors—smart professionals in tailored suits and expensive eyeware, colourful activists with sharp tongues and raucous personalities, shy artists who circled the room but who would pounce on you when taken home. It was here where I first flirted with JF, where in the laundry room I made out with a doctor visiting from Bolivia, where I hooked up with a candidate from the Parti Québécois who kept correcting my pronunciation of the word *queue*. Michael came dressed as Mrs. Claus one year and gave out Timbits. And once I drunkenly sang "Baby it's Cold Outside" as a duet with Danny, the two of us playing the room for laughs with Danny in a fake-fur coat pulled from Charles's closet.

As this year would've been Alan's fiftieth, Charles went all out. He ordered a six-tiered rainbow birthday cake and hired a burlesque troupe to perform. And he served a special drink for the occasion—a Puerto Rican–style eggnog called a Coquito that was a delicious mix of coconut milk, condensed milk and lots of rum.

"I thought you weren't supposed to drink," Danny said, clocking me as I reached for my third cocktail.

"Oh, bah humbug," I replied. No longer needing to cut back, I indulged myself. I was also feeling good, having received my first pay cheque since my raise and having Skyped with Wendy that morning. "Nine weeks," she'd said. "Should be the size of a kidney bean around now." I wanted to share this news with my friends, but it was still too soon. "Where's Vince?" I asked, and took another sip from my sweet drink.

"Having cocktails with friends. He's supposed to come later."

"Did you see that Gus is here?"

"Yes," Danny seethed. "I don't know why Charles insisted on inviting him. But as long as he stays on his side of the room, I won't set him on fire."

"A Christmas miracle."

Charles zipped by, filling up glasses with eggnog. "Careful," I said, pulling mine away. "These go down too easy."

"Speaking of which, Charles, why did you invite Gus?" Danny was annoyed. "Or is this supposed to be a murder mystery party?"

"I think we'll know who did it," I said.

"Be nice," Charles said to Danny. "Where's your Christmas spirit?"

Danny chugged back the rest of his Coquito. "At the bottom of this glass." He thrust his empty drink towards Charles. "Alms for the poor?"

"I see you invited Kevin too." I looked at the far end of the room where Charles's ex-lover sat speaking to Gus by the Christmas tree. "Didn't think he would come."

Kevin had all but disappeared from Charles's life. Once the film wrapped, and the two of them no longer worked on the same set together, Kevin stopped texting. Charles told us that Kevin had recently been cast as a regular on a popular new French sitcom and was sleeping with the director.

"I didn't invite him," Charles said, filling up Danny's glass. "He must have come with someone else. Honestly, I don't know about a quarter of the people here."

"A sign of a good party," I said.

"Well, that's bad form," Danny said. "Shall I ask him to leave? Maybe see if Gus can escort him home?"

"It's a fundraiser, so the more the merrier." Charles put down the pitcher of eggnog and took a sip from his glass. "Besides, I've moved on. Did I tell you about the three guys I hooked up with this week?" He smiled. "The first was a repeat from last year who wanted to swing by on his way to class. The second was someone I met at the gym. And the third was this soon-to-be-married guy looking for one last lay before tying the knot—although, I think we'll be seeing each other again. I tell you, Christmas came early this year."

"Now, there's a holiday classic," Danny said. "This week, Charles was visited by three twinks: the twink of Christmas Past, the twink of Christmas Present and the twink of Christmas Future. By the end you're running through the streets, kissing everybody."

I laughed, feeling a warm sense of love for my kind, drunk and hilarious friends. "Guys," I started, then turned to pull Charles and Danny into the laundry room. "Come with me for a second."

"Where are you taking us?" Danny asked. "Isn't this where you made out with Doctor Bolivia?"

"Wendy's pregnant," I blurted.

"What?!"

"Wendy's pregnant!" I repeated, a grin from ear to ear. "We're having a baby!"

"Oh my…" Danny grabbed me by the shoulder. "That's incredible!"

"That's amazing! I'm happy for you, Paul," Charles said. "Congratulations!"

"It's early though, about nine weeks, so please don't say anything. Not until we make it public."

"When's she due?"

"July."

"A Cancer," Danny observed. "At least their house will be clean."

There was a second fridge in Charles's laundry room and he opened it to pull out a chilled bottle of bubbly. "I was saving this for New Year's, but this is a much better use." He popped it open and caught the spill in the drum of the open washing machine. "I don't have any glasses in here, so we'll have to drink out of the bottle."

"Not something I'm unfamiliar with," Danny said.

Michael walked into the laundry room, clutching his pearls. "My heavens," he said, attempting a southern accent. "What's going on in here?"

"I told them," I said. "I had to!" Again, I felt like I had at Thanksgiving. My life is good, I thought, laughing in this laundry room with my closest friends. Real good. Look how far I'd come from being that lonely kid in the suburbs.

"Can you believe it?" Danny said. "You're going to be a dad!"

"I know," I said, and then repeated. "I'm going to be a dad!"

The next morning, I woke up with a hangover. I was alone in bed, not sure how I had got home. Through the closed door of our bedroom, I could hear Michael in the distance—the muffled sounds of him singing along to music.

I stood up, put on a pair of sweatpants and a shirt, and opened the door. Our apartment was full of light and sound, which was jarring. I found Michael in the kitchen, pouring ingredients into a mixer. "Sorry. Did I wake you?"

"No," I said, looking at the time on the wall. "I can't believe I slept until noon."

"You were wasted last night," he laughed.

"I hardly remember a thing."

"Do you remember flirting with the cab driver?"

"Not really."

"You had this big conversation about homosexuality and the holidays. I don't know where it all came from, or even what you said. It didn't make much sense."

I felt embarrassed. "It was all that Puerto Rican eggnog. What are you making?"

"Pancakes."

"Thank god! I'm starving." I looked across the kitchen

island and then to the dresser in the hall. "Have you seen my phone?"

"You asked me to plug it in when we got home. It's on your desk."

I went into the office and sat down at my computer. I turned over my phone and noticed a series of text messages from Wendy, sent about an hour ago: *Hey Paul. Wasn't feeling well last night, cramping and spotting. Got an emergency appointment at the clinic this morning. Doctor wasn't there, but I saw someone and he didn't hear a heartbeat. Trying to process. Will have ultrasound on Tuesday. Waiting game now, which sucks. Will call later and explain.*

When I hadn't heard from either of them that afternoon, I called their house. Eve answered. "Wendy's not up to talking right now," she said. "We're managing expectations. Trying to be realistic."

I wanted to be positive. "But doesn't this happen all the time?" I asked. "Maybe the heartbeat is just really faint?"

"I don't know, Paul. We've heard it loud and clear before. The look on the doctor's face also seemed worried. And Wendy says she can tell, she can feel it. Something's wrong."

I told Eve that it was early and not to lose hope. But then I hung up and went to lie down in my bed, consumed by a bad feeling.

Two days passed without a word. I wanted to call, but I also wanted to give them space. Then, on the morning of their ultrasound, I texted Wendy: *Thinking of you. If you feel like it later, give me a call. Love.*

Within five minutes, I got a response from Wendy: *Worst day ever. We'll get through this, but it's awful. We're closer to making decisions on how to proceed. How to miscarry, if it comes to that. Will be in touch. Love.*

And then, later that day as I left work, I received another message: *Will talk later when up to it. Baby is gone. Procedure is Friday am. Love you and will try again soon.*

I took the Metro home in a daze. Was this my fault? I wondered, walking the three cold blocks to our home. Had I ruined everything by telling my friends? I knew that wasn't the way the universe works, but I did feel some guilt and disappointment for allowing myself to think this could be possible.

As I opened the door at the bottom of our stairs, I had the reflex to bark, but didn't. Once inside, I heard Michael in the kitchen, playing music and running water. Our home was warm and all the lights were on.

Michael came out to greet me. "Hi, buddy! Is that you?"

"You're wearing an apron," I said.

"I'm making pasta. What's wrong?"

"It's gone. The baby."

Michael's face fell and he pulled me close. "I'm sorry, buddy," he said, and I stood there in his arms, frozen.

We were quiet for the rest of the night. I had brought work home, but couldn't concentrate. Instead, I got out some blankets and Michael and I sat on the couch and watched home renovation shows. I didn't cry. I just felt blue. More than anything, I felt sad for Wendy and Eve, particularly Wendy, not knowing how she would handle the night and days to come.

I didn't hear from the girls for a while. It felt strange to no longer get regular updates, and I often wondered what was going through their heads. I figured they just needed time to rest, mourn and make new plans once they were ready. As for me, I tried not to think too much about the loss. I had to tell Charles and Danny, of course, who both offered to come over. "No, it's okay," I had said, not sure what we would even talk about. Kate showed up at my door the day after I told her, with a bottle of wine and copies of *Hello*, *Tatler*, *Majesty* and *Royal Life*. We sat in my living room and flipped through the magazines, getting tipsy and ordering pizza. "You sure you don't want to talk about it?" she asked before leaving.

I shrugged. "I really don't know what to say."

A few weeks later I finally received an email from Wendy, letting me know that they would be in town for Christmas. She asked if we could go for dinner, just the two of us.

We met at the same restaurant where this all began, at a table by the window. Wendy seemed in good spirits, despite everything; eager to have a bottle of wine after abstaining for six months. She had lost weight it seemed; her face thinner, or older, than I remembered. She told me that she felt different—not the way she did when she first found out she had miscarried. She told me she had wanted to see it, and they showed it to her.

"What did it look like?" I asked.

"Like nothing," she said. "Like jelly. Bloody jelly. I'm not sure what I expected it to look like."

"How do you feel?"

"Like I never want to go through that again," Wendy said, almost angry. "Next time, I'm not going to approach pregnancy in the same way. I'm going to try not to think about it as much, not think of it as anything more than what it is—a developing embryo. Not until we're in the clear, that's for sure. That was way too hard." She told me that she had received condolences from my friends. From Michael, from Charles, from Kate, from Danny. "Danny said he lit a candle for us, which oddly moved me. Made me duck into a church around the corner from our place to light my own candle, something I never thought I'd do in a million years. A lot of people—some of our Toronto friends and co-workers—asked us how you were. I thought it was nice of them. How are you feeling?"

I didn't know what I was allowed to feel. "Sad," I said. "Disappointed. I told myself I wasn't going to get all caught up in everything, but I did. It was hard not to think about what was happening and wonder, you know? I even bought a few things—a book and a cute onesie. I've put them away. It's too hard to look at them now."

Wendy sighed. "I haven't been able to go into our guest room yet. We were turning it into a nursery. Eve was painting it this yellow finch colour, but we've decided to stop for now. I'm tired of fucking yellow. I think about it every time I see it."

"Did you have to tell many people?" I asked. "I mean, your parents knew, right?"

"Our parents knew, yes. And actually, we ended up telling quite a few of our friends—all the people you met at lunch, plus others. That was horrible, having to call them all. But the worst was my dad. He cried on the phone." Wendy wiped the corner of her eye with her sleeve. "I was trying to keep it all together, but once he cried, I cried."

"I'm glad that I never got around to telling my dad," I confessed. "I didn't tell you this, but my dad's going to be a grandfather."

"What? Kate's pregnant?"

"No, not Kate. Sue. Debbie's daughter. I was about to tell him about us when he told me. After that, I couldn't."

"Well, I can understand that," Wendy said. "That's got to be weird."

"It *is* weird," I said, happy for the acknowledgement. "Like, I never even considered it before, but of course Sue was going to have a baby! Why wouldn't she? It's just so strange. It's like, my dad has this different life now, all the way on the other side of the country. He has another wife, who has children of her own—do you know that Debbie's kids go over to their place for dinner every Sunday? I feel like they must know my father better than I do. They all live in the same town—Debbie's family, brothers, sisters, nieces, nephews—all in Kelowna. I don't even know how many of them there are. My dad's not on Facebook, but Debbie is, and sometimes I see him in the pictures Debbie posts and wonder who all these other people are he's surrounded by. Who are they to him?"

"Have you visited him yet?" Wendy asked.

"No."

"Why not?"

"I don't know," I said. "Maybe I don't want to face it. Maybe I don't want proof that they are this perfect family. I mean, I don't doubt that my dad loves us, but it's like we tried it and it didn't work: his wife died, his daughter can't have kids and he has a gay son. It's like we're a failed family, like he got a second shot at that life he wanted."

Wendy wasn't having any of this. "Well, that's stupid. You're not a 'failed' family. I know your dad, Paul. There's nothing he wouldn't do for you. Debbie's kids are not replacements for you and Kate."

"I know," I said. "It's just been a while since it felt like we're a *real* family. I mean, I can count the number of times the three of us have been together in the same room in the last five years on one hand."

"Well, change that," Wendy said. "No one's stopping you from having a relationship with your father."

After the meal, we paid and got ready to leave. I called Michael as Wendy checked her messages.

"Hey, Wendy," I said, with Michael still on the other end of the line. "You feel like a night cap? Michael's at this karaoke bar nearby with friends singing Christmas carols."

"Um, yes," Wendy said, rising from her seat. "I don't have to be up early."

"All right," I said into the phone. "We'll join you. See you soon, buddy."

As we put on our coats, Wendy asked, "Why do you call each other that?"

"Call each other what?"

"Buddy. You guys call each other buddy all the time."

"No we don't!"

"Yes, you do," Wendy laughed. "You know that."

For some reason, I blushed. "I don't know. A term of endearment, I suppose. Most of the time, I don't even realize I'm doing it. But honestly, it fits. He's my buddy. I'm his. We even call our cats buddy, sometimes. And dogs too, if I pass one on the street. Anything that's cute, really."

"Eve would kill me if I used our nicknames on animals."

"What do you call each other?"

Wendy smiled. "It's not very creative, but she calls me 'my love.'"

I suddenly remembered. "Oh, yeah. What do you call her?"

Wendy chuckled. "Biscuit."

That one was new. I couldn't help but laugh.

The karaoke bar was three blocks away, and we were there in minutes. Gus was on stage, singing Wham's "Last Christmas," as we walked inside. We found Michael, with two other friends, at a table nearby. Michael looked happy and drunk, a string of silver garland around his shoulders. "Hi, buddy!" he shouted when he saw me. "Look at me. I'm Judy Garland!" We laughed and took our seats at the table with them.

I ordered us drinks, and as Wendy grabbed the list of songs, Michael sidled up next to her and gave her a hug. "I'm sorry, Wendy," I overheard him say, his glassy eyes twinkling in the bar's festive lights. "But if I can say, there is some good news here. This means you *can* get pregnant. It just wasn't the time. Your baby's still out there. She's just waiting for the right time."

Wendy nodded, wiping back tears.

15

On New Year's Eve, the city was hit by a snowstorm. Michael and I were supposed to go to a party with Danny. Instead of going out, we decided to stay in and order food.

"Come on," Danny pleaded on the phone when I told him. "The guy throwing the party is friends with Justin Trudeau! And it's at this mansion on the Boulevard in Westmount! You've got to come—if only to see the place."

"Sorry, Danny Boy," I replied, looking out at a heavy sheet of blowing snow obscuring the street lamp across the street. "There's no way I'm leaving home." I told him to have fun, drink responsibly, and tell me all about it the next day.

After hanging up, I called our favourite Indian restaurant to place our order, then joined Michael in the living room. He had cranked up the thermostat and lit candles, so the room was warm and bright; a noticeable change from the rest of our home. "It's like the tropics in here," I said, closing the door. "The restaurant said it might take ninety minutes, given the weather. If you're starving, you might want to snack on something."

Michael was sprawled across the couch, his hand deep in Malone's underbelly. "That's okay. I got all I need right here." Malone was enjoying the rub and purring away. "If I get hungry, I can feast on some kitty tummy. Right buddy? Who's a good cat?"

The cats stayed with us in the warm living room for the rest of the night, Sutherland licking his lips as I passed the butter chicken to Michael. We went to bed half an hour before the countdown.

The next day we woke up to five feet of snow. Michael went to dig out the car, while I made us breakfast. He was gone maybe thirty minutes before I heard his boots stomp back up the stairs. The door swung open and slammed shut. "Fuck, fuck, fuck," Michael spat out, pulling off his hat and mitts. "Fucking piece of shit—the fucking car won't start."

"What? What's wrong?" I said.

Michael flipped off his boots and tore off his coat and dove into the blankets on the couch in the living room. "What happened?" I asked.

Michael's face was red and wet from the cold. "She won't start. I tried a bunch of times. It won't turn over. I think the battery's dead."

I sat down next to him. "Did you leave the lights on?"

Michael looked at me as if I were stupid. "Of course not. But I've tried everything. I'm going to leave it and hope it works in an hour."

Michael had been having car problems with Darlene over the past month. She had been slow to start and sometimes, when I was in the car with him, I'd look to Michael to see him praying under his breath and thankful every time the ignition caught. "Maybe it's just cold out," I said.

Michael sat there, deflated in the same warm blankets

269

we had cuddled in the night before. I didn't feel like enabling his anxiety, so I got up and returned to the kitchen where I continued to cook us breakfast. The meal was ready in ten minutes and, once the table was set, we ate in silence. It wasn't the way I had hoped to start the New Year, but I didn't feel like bullying him into a good mood. An hour later he went out to try again, only to return frustrated. "Have you seen my phone?" he shouted.

"What?"

"My phone. Have you seen it?"

"Do you want me to call it?"

"Yes, please. I have to call my dad."

I picked up my phone and called Michael's number. We both heard a vibration and Michael turned to find it on the couch among the pillows. He put on his boots and went outside with his phone.

He came back in twenty minutes later. "So?" I asked.

He looked at me blankly, his shoulders covered in snow. "So?"

"So, did you get it to work?"

He shrugged and all the snow came off, falling onto the mat by the door. "What do you think?"

"I don't know what to think," I said. "I'm not the expert. What did your father say?"

"He thinks it's the starter, but it can't be that. Maybe it's the battery."

"Why don't you call your mechanic?"

He was annoyed with me now. "Don't you think I tried that? It's New Year's Day! They're closed." Michael spent the rest of the afternoon in nervous anticipation, watching

YouTube videos in the office and smoking joints. The next day, he went to Canadian Tire and used the last of the Christmas money he had received from his mom to buy a new battery. That too didn't work. Michael was panicked when he came back in. "I have to move the car! I have to move the car! The signs are up. They're cleaning our side of the street tomorrow."

"Call your mechanic first thing in the morning. Have her towed."

"I don't have the money, Paul. I spent the last of it on that fucking battery."

"So, put the tow on my credit card," I almost yelled. "Let's do this and fix it so it's no longer such a stress, okay?"

Michael mumbled under his breath as he took his phone into the other room to leave another message. He heard back from his mechanic early the following morning and he got up to wait outside for them to send a tow truck. I stayed indoors and did laundry, making us lunches for the following day. At some point, I heard a noise and looked out the window. There, I saw Michael standing in the snowbank, his jacket hood thrown over his head and his hands in his pockets as he watched the truck hoist Darlene. Once she was up, Michael disappeared into the truck's cabin and off they went.

He returned without the car an hour later. I heard the Christmas bells on our door jingle as it opened and closed. "So?" I asked him.

"It looks like it's the starter," he said. "They think it's shot. Going to be $400 to fix. Well, if it's cash anyway. Otherwise, it'll be more." Michael took out a handkerchief from his back pocket to wipe his nose. "Just my fucking luck…"

"What do you want to do?"

He threw his hands up in the air. "I don't fucking know. She's a fucking piece of shit. I never should have bought her. I should have got that stupid minivan. Of course, he fucking told me so." Michael took off his boots and threw his coat onto the floor.

"But—"

"I can't talk about this now," he said, and walked past me into the office.

I had been reading before Michael got home, so I returned to my place on the couch with my book. I had hoped to have one last peaceful day of vacation before returning to work, but now I found myself caught up in Michael's stress. I couldn't focus, so I closed my book and turned on the TV.

At one point, I heard the door to the office open and Michael walk to the kitchen. After a moment or two, music began to play, then I heard the clamour of dishes and bowls being taken out of cupboards. I turned off the TV and got up to join him. Michael wore his apron, and there was a collection of silver mixing bowls on the counter in front of him. "What are you doing?" I asked.

"Baking. I need an outlet."

I could tell he was still angry, the way he shut the kitchen drawer and pulled the eggs from the fridge. "Whatcha going to make? Your cookies? I love your cookies."

Michael stopped. He let go of the measuring cup in his hand and placed his palms on the counter. "I'm sorry," he said, head down, and then repeated, shaking his head this time. "I'm sorry..."

"That's okay. It's shitty."

"It's just. I wish I handled stress differently, you know?"

"I know."

"I wish I didn't have my father in my head *all the fucking time*." There was tension in his face as he moved the package of flour from one side of the kitchen island to the other. "Even when he's not there, he's there. I don't want to be like him, Paul. I don't want to react to things the way he does. This disappointment over every little thing I do."

I took a moment. I needed to say something, but I wanted to be careful. "Michael, I know how you must feel," I said, "but you need to remember that you are *not* your father. You are *not* in Moncton any more. You're here. With me. And we don't treat each other like that. I don't treat you like that."

"I know," he said, and grabbed his head. "I know."

Later that week, I met up with Danny at the theatre. So far, we had seen three of the plays in the season he had got me for my birthday. We lined up along with the others to get our seats, tickets in hand. "It's all older women," Danny whispered, disappointed. "Don't gay men go to the theatre any more?"

"Remember the time we went to see that play at the Fringe?" I asked. "We paid fifteen bucks to see a six-foot-tall man with a seven-inch dick stand naked in the middle of the stage for an hour and yell poetry by Jean Genet? Every show was sold out."

Danny shook his head. "Gays are so predictable. Put 'full frontal' on the poster and we'll give it a Tony."

"There's one," I pointed out. A young man with a pride necklace and a tribal tattoo on his arm was about ten people ahead of us. We watched as an usher took his ticket and tore it, returning half to him. He disappeared into the theatre.

"Who the hell is giving this generation all these horrendous tattoos?" Danny said. "I mean, is it a university major now or something?"

"Doesn't Vince have a tribal tattoo?" I asked.

"Yes, and I can't stand it. Only strippers should have tribal tattoos."

"There's something we haven't done in a long time," I said, handing over my ticket. "Maybe we can go to the *ballet* tonight after the theatre?"

Danny made a disgusted noise and handed over his own ticket. "I don't know. I'm sick of the male body right now. I'm more of a homo-sectional these days. I just want to spend time with my couch. But if you wanted to go see women strippers, I might be down for that." Ticket stubs in hand, we headed into the room. "Have you ever been to a female strip club?" Danny asked. "It's like going on safari. The women are like gazelles, graceful and powerful. And they know how to dance and leap and snap, not like the shuffling Neanderthals they employ in the Village."

We found our seats, midway down the aisle.

"Are you okay, Danny?" I asked, once we had settled. "You seem tense."

He rubbed at his brow. "I think Vince and I are breaking up."

"What? Why?"

"I don't know. The way things are now… Christmas was no fun. It's like something has changed between us."

"Like what?"

"We had this huge fight the other night. We went out to this club his friends go to. They know the DJ, blah blah

blah. And I started to feel resentful. He knew everyone, and I wondered how many of them he had slept with. What was *that* look and *that* laugh about? And then I turned into a complete monster. Drinks were sixteen dollars, but I kept knocking them back. I accused him of not being truthful, and it was like I had killed his buzz. I pushed him, got him to admit that he'd prefer we be open. Sure, he says he loves me, but he wants other experiences too, with people who are *not* me. Well, merry fuckin' Christmas! You know, he wouldn't even come with me to Christmas Eve mass. I told him it was important to me. But no, he's 'not religious.' Yet we had to go out with his old university roommate and their friends to some stupid after-hours to watch them worship this horrendous DJ from Ibiza. You're lucky you haven't had to meet Vince's friends yet. They're these evil circuit queens. I call them the Death Star, because they're this inescapable black hole of entitlement. Travelling to Ibiza and Burning Man, fucking everything that moves. I'm exhausted just thinking about them. We argued. I said I couldn't accept it. And he made a low blow, said my insecurity was a turn-off and that it wasn't a boyfriend I wanted but a drinking buddy. I mean, the nerve. Sure, I like to drink, but I'm not a drunk or anything."

"You do drink a lot, Danny."

"Not more than any of you."

I shifted in my seat, rolling the evening's program in my hands. "So, where did you leave things?"

"Nowhere." Danny rested his chin in his hand on the armrest next to him. "We haven't talked since—that was two days ago. I don't care right now, to be honest."

The room filled up, people were laughing. I looked at my watch. The play would start soon. "Danny, would you rather go some place and talk?"

"And miss the play? Are you kidding?"

"Why is monogamy so important to you?"

"I don't know, Paul." Danny gripped his own program tight. "I can understand that a couple might want to open their relationship after five or six years. When the sex isn't as exciting as it once was. But now? At the beginning? You don't start a relationship like that. And I think our sex life is great! You should see me, Paul. I'm excited every time Vince and I have sex. It's like we're playing soccer and the coach is calling me in off the bench and I can't wait to get on the field. It saddens me to think that I'm not enough for him, when he is more than enough for me."

"What about a threesome? That's adventurous, and you'd get to be a part of it."

"No, I know myself. I'm far too jealous to let that happen. Plus, I don't think it's what he wants either. He wants to be able to have an adventure whenever it presents itself. To follow the rabbit down the hole, so to speak. It can't be planned. It just, is…" he sighed.

"You know, I've never had a threesome."

"Really?" Danny sounded surprised. "Not even with Alan?"

I looked at him like he was crazy.

"I did," he said. "Once. A couple I met at the Stud years ago. But it was awkward. One liked me more, and the other seemed to resent me."

"I hear it can go that way."

"I could tell after it was over that they were going to have a fight," he said. "I couldn't get out of there fast enough. I never understood men in relationships looking for a third. When I was on the apps, I would get frustrated. There were couples there, like you and Michael. Handsome, funny and interesting, looking for someone to play with. It would bug me to no end. It's like, 'We've found each other and love each other, and we're going to let you into our lives, but only just a little bit. We'll give you the sex, but withhold all the fun parts—the love and the history—and then you can go home by yourself and leave things like strawberry picking or day trips to the Townships or dinner parties to us.' It would drive me crazy. Why anyone would play with losing what they had found, I don't get. I just want what my parents had. I want someone to grow older with. I'd even want kids too, with the right guy. Why are gay men so afraid that someone might want us and only us?"

"Look over there." I pointed five rows down to two men in their mid-seventies on the aisle. They were dressed proper: one in an ascot, the other a tie. "There's a pair of gay theatre-goers. Think they're a couple?"

"They've probably been together forty years," Danny said. "One of the first gay men either of them met. They've seen it all, I bet. Bar raids and the back of cop cars, explaining away their roommates to their mothers, losing friends to AIDS, hook-ups in tearooms, Judy Garland, genital warts and hemorrhoids, so many bottles of wine, infidelity, half a dozen cats."

"Do you think they stay together for the cats?"

He laughed. "Maybe."

"The sex?"

"Definitely not."

"So, if sex isn't as important, then why do you care? If Vince gives you all the other things, why is it important if he wants to have a casual encounter with someone else?"

"I don't know, Paul. I guess that's the question. Anyway," he said, banishing the thought and unrolling his program, "what are we seeing again?"

After the play, Danny wanted to go home. "We'll save the *safari* for another time," he said.

The door was unlocked when I got back to our place, and Michael's wet boots were on the mat near the door.

"Hi, buddy," I called out.

"Hi, buddy," I heard from the living room.

I took off my boots and coat and went to find Michael on the couch licking a joint closed. His face looked tired, long and dazed. "How was work?" I asked, sitting next to him.

"Can we switch?" I was on the side of his bad ear, so we changed spots. "I'm zonked," he said, collapsing back into the cushions. "I painted ceilings today, up and down on the ladder. My back is killing me."

"Want a back rub?" I asked.

His face lit up. "Maybe later," he said, twirling the joint in his hand. "After I smoke?" A large yawn erupted from Michael's mouth and he shook it off. "I'm so happy to have Darlene working again. I couldn't imagine having to lug all that equipment across town today."

Of course I'd given Michael the money to pay for his car's repair. The day we learned it was the starter, I transferred him cash from my credit line and Michael called his mechanic. It would be a tight month, but that would be okay. At least Darlene was back, sandwiched in the same parking spot across the street. Michael dove into his pocket and gave me a fifty. "Here," he said. "I know it's not much, but I have more work coming. I should be able to pay you back for everything soon."

"That's okay," I said. In addition to being tired, Michael looked pensive. "You all right?"

Michael yawned again. "I'm exhausted," he said. "Physically, emotionally. I want to know if I'm ever going to get out of this debt. If I'm ever going to be able to help you out in some way."

"You help me out."

He wiped his eyes with the back of his hand. "I know," he said. "But sometimes, I feel like such a drain and it drives me mad."

"You're making progress," I said. "It might not feel like it at times. But each step is a step, then you look back and you're somewhere else. You think I ran a half-marathon just like that? It took me weeks to be able to run half a block."

"I know," he said and exhaled. "I remember being in Moncton and saying to myself, 'I'm moving to Montreal.' I didn't think I'd get to do that. I just told myself that to survive, to get me to the next day. And now I'm here. I have my own business. I'm working as a prep cook in a restaurant. I have friends, this home, the cats, you. I know that I have it good. I know. It's just, sometimes I don't feel like I'm doing enough."

"Do I pressure you?"

"No, you don't pressure me," he said. "Well, maybe you

do, but in a good way. I'm the one who's too hard on myself." A tear dislodged from his eye and ran down his face. "You're so fucking good to me."

I reached out to comfort and hug him, but I felt how tense he was inside, how unwilling he was to relax. Michael sniffled and wiped his eyes with his shirtsleeve. "You give me everything," he said as we let go. "I just have to do something with it."

The following week was our fourth anniversary, and that morning over breakfast I gave Michael a gift—a pair of bright red Adidas running shoes that I had bought way before the car had broken down. Michael had wrapped up something for me too: a nice new leather wallet to replace my frayed canvas one. "I love it," I said, filling it up with all of my identification and a photo-booth snapshot of the two of us I always kept with me. We spent much of the day at home, doing our own thing in separate parts of the house, coming together for lunch or to fool around in the bedroom.

That evening, the two of us prepared for our night out. We had decided to go dancing to celebrate our anniversary, even though it was twenty-seven below outside. The plan was to attempt a Provincetown night in our city to see if we could summon up any of that magical heat to warm our cold bones.

"Want a drink?" Michael asked as we got ready. I nodded and he left the room to put on music and fix us a couple of Manhattans. When he returned, I was in the midst of trying on a bunch of shirts, none of which I could decide on.

"I think I'm too old for clever tees," I said, looking

at myself in a mirror in a black athletic T-shirt that said, "Queens 69."

Michael handed over my drink. "Well, you're only as old as you feel. But this one is threadbare. Maybe it's time to retire it."

Malone and Sutherland sat on the bed and watched with puzzled expressions as I pulled the shirt off my body. "Why not try something sexy," Michael said. "Like a tank top."

"I'll be too cold."

"I'm going to wear one." Michael opened his dresser and pulled out a red and black tank top. "Don't worry," he said. "I'll also wear a sweater."

I took out the "Super Dad" T-shirt from my dresser and put it on. It was much snugger than it had been in the summertime. "What do you think?" I asked. "Too much?"

"No, you look great," Michael said, putting down his drink.

"You sure it's not too tight?"

He grabbed me by the belly. "Nope. It accentuates your assets." He kissed me, then patted me on the bottom. "Now let's finish our drinks and get out of here."

We took the Metro to Papineau station. It was so cold outside that my eyelashes and the hair under my nose had frozen on the short walk to the Stud, but they thawed out in the heat of the bar as we handed over our coats and sweaters at the coat check.

I bought us each a shot and a beer. "This should warm us up," I said, and we downed the whisky. Michael and I took our drinks and headed upstairs to the eighties room where a crowd was dancing. We immediately joined them, revelling in the classics sung by women in gay bars the world over: "I'm Every Woman," "Venus," "Girls Just Want To Have Fun." I thought, if I closed my eyes, this could be Provincetown: the music, the sweat, the temperature of the bodies moving next to us. Last summer felt far away, but there was tonight. And we had just made the first deposit on the house for a week in August.

After a few songs and two empty bottles, Michael and I took a break and went to the bar to order another round. "So, what do you think of me going to P-Town early to work for a couple months this spring?" he asked while we waited for our drinks.

"To do what? Bartend?"

"Leo has connections and I thought I could line up some handyman jobs and a place to stay before the season begins. If I could, I'd stay all summer and join you and the boys when you come in August."

"Well, that's an idea," I said, not sure what to think. "You still talk to Leo?"

"Sometimes," Michael said. "I see him online and we chat."

I was a little jealous. "What I wouldn't give for a whole summer in P-Town."

"You wouldn't mind?"

I scoffed. "Mind? Why would I mind?"

Of course I'd mind. In the four years we'd been together, the longest we'd ever been apart had been the two weeks my company had sent me to Calgary to work with a client. But I knew this was only a pipe dream for Michael and probably wouldn't happen. It would require that he plan and orchestrate his stay, which I didn't see him doing.

"When would you go?" I asked.

"Leo says people need help to get their properties ready at the end of April. Summer season starts Memorial Day."

I nodded as our drinks came. We downed the shots and with it the conversation, returning to the dance floor. I couldn't remember the last time I had danced this much. Maybe our city isn't so bad in the depths of winter, I thought.

Around one in the morning, Michael said he was going outside to smoke a joint. "I'll wait for you here," I said, taking a spot on a stool at the bar.

There was much for me to look at while I waited for Michael's return. The TV in the corner played a porno that had a doctor examining a hunky guy in a hospital bed. Beside me, a man became frustrated with a video poker machine. And at the far end of the bar, two drunk men made out like it was the last night on Earth. Then suddenly, across the bar, I noticed a young man staring at me.

I smiled (a reflex) and he got up from where he sat, tall and lean, and walked over.

"Bonjour, Super Dad," he said. I had forgotten I was wearing the T-shirt.

"Bonjour," I replied.

We spoke in French. "Are you really a dad?" he asked. The man had curly blond hair, his pupils dilated.

"Not at the moment," I replied. "But I am trying to get a good friend pregnant."

He laughed, although I wasn't sure why. "How about getting me pregnant?" He reached down to my crotch and grabbed at it with his hand. I didn't know how to react, but he pulled away before I could do anything. "Disappointing," he observed. "Maybe this is more your speed." He grabbed my hand and thrust it to his pants. I had no choice but to feel his hard-on. Who walks around the bar with an erection? I wondered, and sat there, stunned. "I live three blocks from here," he said. "Care to join me?"

I pulled my hand away. "Non," I said, turned off but still wanting to be polite. "Mais merci."

He scoffed and rolled his eyes. "You shouldn't false-advertise," he said, switching to English. "Some 'Super Dad' you are. You smell like garlic anyway." And with that, he took off.

When Michael returned, I was ready to leave.

"What's wrong?"

I told him what had happened.

"What a fucking jerk! Where is he?"

"Oh, who knows," I said, sick of everyone. "Do I smell like garlic?"

Michael took a whiff. "No. But if you do, I do."

I felt gross, sitting at the bar in a T-shirt that was too small for me. "Can we go?"

Michael's beer was full and he looked at it. "If you want," he said. "But," he stopped, "it's our anniversary. We were having so much fun. Do you really want to let this guy ruin our night?"

Michael was right. Up until then we had been having fun. The music was great, the drinks were cheap, and we had laughed and danced and talked. It felt like the first quality time we'd had together outside of the house for months. "Okay," I said. "Maybe one more drink."

We finished our beers, but bought more, once again

pairing them with shots of whisky. Then we went back to dance. After a few songs, I decided to sit one out. I told Michael where I'd be and left him to go and get a bottle of water at the bar.

"I like your shirt."

The voice came from behind as I paid for my drink. I turned to find a tall redheaded fellow with a big smile standing next to me. "Thanks," I said, smiling myself. "A gift from a friend on my fortieth."

"What? You can't be forty," he said with a sufficient amount of polite surprise that communicated two things— one, that he found me attractive; and two, that he wanted me to know he found me attractive.

"I can assure you I am forty," I said, trying to sound clever. "Want me to prove it?" I took out my brand-new wallet and handed over my driver's licence.

"Cute picture," he said, again with charm. "But I don't see your birthday."

Oh, he must be American. "Canadian driver's licences put the birthday here," I said, and showed him the number. "It might come in handy if you work as a bartender one day."

"I could never bartend, I'm horrible with measurements. I'm Eric," he said, returning my licence. "And over there is Gary." I looked over my shoulder to see another handsome man walk towards us from the washroom. He was a bit shorter than Eric, with bushy eyebrows and trim facial hair.

I introduced myself and asked where they were from.

"New York City," Eric said. "We drove up today to celebrate our anniversary. Didn't realize it would be this cold."

"Two years," Gary said.

"Get out!" I shouted. "It's our anniversary too." I gestured over to Michael who noticed I had pointed in his direction. "Four years."

"Tonight?"

"Well, it's after midnight now, so yesterday. But yes, I'd still call it tonight since we're out celebrating."

"This calls for a toast," Eric said. "Can we get you guys something?"

"Sure," I said. "Whisky?"

Michael had now joined us, all smiles.

"Michael, this is Eric and Gary," I said. "It's their anniversary tonight."

"No way!" Michael shook both men's hands and then Eric passed out the shots, which we drank. We learned that Eric was a social worker, and that Gary was in law school. Both men were in their twenties—twenty-seven and twenty-five, respectively. I would have assumed Eric was in his mid-thirties, given his height.

"What are you going to do while you're here?" I asked, and they told us their plans. It was the things most people do during their first time in Montreal: have a bagel, eat smoked meat, go to the top of Mount Royal, visit the Old Port. They wanted to hit as many Village bars as they could too, and they wanted to go to a sauna. "We've never been to one," Gary said.

"Have you been?" Eric asked.

"No," Michael responded.

"Once. When I was young," I said. "They're not all that."

"You should come with us." Eric placed his meaty hand on my shoulder. I felt a charge go through my body, the energy in his right palm seeping into my chest. "Could I ask you a favour?" he said, before I could respond to his suggestion. "Could the two of you kiss each other in front of us?"

The request could have been creepy, but Eric seemed good-natured and happy, not drunken and overbearing in the way the guy from earlier in the night had been. I looked at Michael and shrugged. He was already leaning in.

We kissed softly, slowly, aware of our audience. "You guys are hot," Eric said, as we stopped. He moved in closer, his arm on my back.

I suddenly needed this to keep going. "Let me buy us another round," I said, and turned to get the bartender's attention. I bought us more whisky, and again we shot them back. The four of us proceeded to get drunk as the night progressed. We talked, laughed and flirted, the balm to soothe the burn from earlier. Although forward and direct, Eric and Gary were also kind and polite. They were curious about our life in Montreal and had questions for us: Where did we grow up? How did we meet? What advice did we have for them after four years together?

"Honesty," I said.

"And holidays," Michael added.

At one point, Eric asked if I had hair on my shoulders and I pulled up my right sleeve to show him. "Sexy," he said, brushing it with his hand. "Are you Italian? I love Italian men."

Soon, the bar announced last call, and I got up to go to the bathroom. I walked into the empty washroom and took a spot at one of the urinals, staring at the top of the shiny valve as I emptied my bladder. Within seconds, Eric was next to me.

"Hello," he said at his own urinal, looking down.

"Hello," I responded and froze. I could no longer go.

"So, are Montreal men cut or uncut?"

I chuckled. "You'll find both here."

"And you?" he asked.

"Uncut," I said.

"I've never seen an uncut dick before."

I hesitated, but then pulled back from the urinal and showed it to him. Eric leaned over and placed his large hand into the cold basin. My dick grew in his soft, wide hand. "Wow," he said, marvelling at it. "It's so smooth. And your balls are huge," he added, cupping them from underneath. I laughed, and with that he stepped towards me and kissed me, his hand still around my cock.

There was a sudden noise, so we pulled away and faced the wall again. Someone had come in and was using the urinal at the far end of the room. I still had to pee, but wouldn't be able to with this erection. I looked to Eric who stood there, pretending to go, his face caught in a playful smile. I knew what would happen once this other person left. I'd find it hard not to push back into Eric and let my own hand squirrel down to his belt. Then what?

I finished up and buttoned my jeans. I headed back out, Eric trailing behind.

"I think we should head home," Michael said, as we returned.

"Really?" I said. I knew it was time.

"So soon?" Eric asked. "I thought you might want to end the night with us."

"I'm sorry, guys," Michael said. "But not tonight. Thanks

for making this anniversary so memorable, though. I'm sure you'll have a great time without us."

"Ah," Eric said. "All right. I understand. But let me give you my number." Eric put it into Michael's phone. "We're here until Monday."

The next morning I awoke to a P-Town-size hangover.

"Can you believe last night?" I said to Michael, chugging cold water from the fridge. "I felt so close to doing something I would have regretted. Imagine having to tell Wendy and Eve?"

"Tell them what?" he said, getting out bowls from the kitchen cabinets to make breakfast. "Aren't you stopping trying until they're ready?"

"Yes, but I'm not going to take all the tests again. We're not allowed to do anything until this works."

He opened the fridge and retrieved a carton of eggs. "Fine by me."

"But I don't know. I wanted Eric bad, Michael. I feel like if I were any drunker, I would have dropped to my knees right there in the bar."

Michael smiled. "You wouldn't have done that. And I wouldn't have let it happen."

I thought again about how outrageous it had all been, Eric and I alone in the bathroom. "It was fun though."

"Yes, it was."

"I didn't tell you this," I said, sitting down at our kitchen table, consumed with fatigue. "But I made out with JF in Toronto. We kissed the night we went to Woody's. It was just a kiss. Well, two. I don't know why I didn't tell you."

"That's okay," Michael said. "I don't expect you to tell me everything."

I spent the rest of the day in a haze, rehydrating and watching TV. At times, I found myself thinking back to the night before, the songs being played on the dance floor, the drinking and flirting, the kiss in the bathroom. This would have been Danny's worst nightmare, but I had found it all fun and exciting. Was that what our life as a couple would be like next year? Once Wendy and Eve had what they needed from me and my sperm was mine again, to do with as I pleased.

16

ONCE THEIR DIVORCE became official, Kate and Christian sold their house.

"Where will you live?" I asked her.

"I've decided to move to Montreal for a while," she said.

I screamed into the phone, which made her laugh.

"At least until I figure out what to do next," she continued. "I'm going to go live with Ben for the time being."

This news surprised me. I had thought the end of Kate's marriage had also meant the end of her affair; but no, she continued to see Ben. I knew it was a lonely time for her, and I suppose the love and attention she continued to receive from Ben was a welcome distraction. She asked if Michael and I might help her move.

"Of course," I said. "Just tell me when."

And so, a few weeks later, on a bright Saturday morning in the middle of February, Michael and I rented a fourteen-foot cube truck and drove it to Ottawa. "It's like driving a rolling toaster," Michael said as we hit the road.

Ben was already at her house when we arrived, taping up boxes and stacking them by the door. He looked different than the last time I saw him—younger in his weekend wear, his tattoos exposed on the muscled arms he swung around the room. I shook his hand and thanked him for his help, realizing as I spoke how condescending it must have sounded. When I introduced him to Michael, the two leaned in and vigorously shook hands.

Kate's home wasn't huge, but it seemed cavernous and empty. It wasn't going to take long to pack up everything. I found her in the kitchen, kneeling in front of the fridge. "Do you want some mustard?" she asked, when she saw me. "For some stupid reason we have a ton of mustard." She was chucking the plastic bottles into a box at her side. "Honey mustard, Dijon mustard, sriracha mustard, yellow mustard. Why the fuck did we have so many kinds of goddamn mustard?"

"Where is everything?" I asked, looking around. "Did you give stuff away?"

Kate stood up. "A few things," she said. "But most of our furniture was Chris's from before we met." She gestured towards the sparse room off the kitchen and grinned. "Doesn't this remind you of my first apartment? Nothing but a futon and an end table in the bedroom."

It took only an hour to load everything into the truck. Michael and Ben were eager to impress each other with how much they could carry. When it came time to say goodbye to the place, Kate didn't look back. She put on her coat and grabbed her keys. "Come on," she said, heading for the door. "Let's get out of here."

We drove back to Montreal, a length or two behind my sister and Ben.

"He seems nice," Michael said as we bounced along in the truck. "A little macho, but friendly."

I smiled. "He wasn't the only one acting macho," I said. "It was like the two of you were football players at spring training."

Michael laughed. "You're mixing sports, that's baseball."

"Whatever."

"But yes," he said. "A reflex from living in Moncton, I suppose. Every time I met a straight guy, I felt the need to appear to not be a fag." His hands were on the wheel, but he was able to shrug.

"But Ben's not like that," I said. "He has gay co-workers. Kate says he's even slept with a guy before."

"Really? I wish I'd met more open-minded guys like that when I was growing up," Michael said. "He's pretty hot. I mean, did you see those arms?"

I was not going to picture Ben having sex with my sister. "Yes, I did, but stop now."

"Are you warming up to him yet?"

I sighed. "I suppose. I mean, I guess it's official now. They're going to be living together. Even my dad knows about him, although I don't think Kate told him she was see-ing Ben *before* Christian left. But I might as well treat him like any other guy she'd be dating." I thought again about Kate giving Michael a chance, even though she wasn't sure she liked him at the start. "I mean, I'd expect the same from her, wouldn't I?"

We soon arrived in Montreal, where Michael followed Kate's car to the storage centre. There, we unloaded two-thirds of her belongings into a midsize locker then left to take the rest to Ben's. His apartment was a tiny one-bedroom. I wasn't sure if all of Kate's remaining boxes would fit, but we found corners to stack them all in.

Once we were done, we turned to say our goodbyes. "You're leaving?" Kate asked, panic on her face. "Why don't you stay for dinner? Ben's a great cook."

Michael was already at the elevator. "Thanks, Kate," I said, "but some other time? We have to return the truck, and I've got plans with Danny."

My sister looked overwhelmed standing in the doorway, her eyes wide with what she'd done. "It's okay," I whispered, as Ben rearranged the boxes at the far end of the room. "You're going to be okay."

Michael and I dropped off the truck then went home. I spent the rest of the afternoon killing time around the house until Danny and I were to meet, but then, two hours before our date, he called. "I'm sorry, Paul," he said, "I'm going to have to cancel."

I was disappointed. I had been looking forward to seeing him. "But why?"

"It's over," he said. "We broke up."

I gasped. "Oh Danny, I'm sorry. What happened?"

"Nothing happened, that's the problem! Just more of the same, over and over. Anyway…"

"You don't want to get together? To talk?"

"No, the last thing I want to do now is talk," he said, exasperated. "So this means Vince won't be coming with us to Provincetown this summer." He was suddenly all business. "I'm going to refund him what he paid, but I don't want any money back from you. I'm going to assume the cost if we can't find anyone to replace him—but please, please, whatever you do, do not invite Gus. If you do, you might as well invite someone else too because I won't be coming."

"Danny, are you sure you're going to be okay?" I asked.

"I'm going to be wonderful, Paul," he said. "Just watch me. *Wonderful!*"

My plans thwarted, I stayed in with Michael. We ordered food and ate wordlessly in front of the TV. After we cleaned up, Michael noticed he had missed a call. He dialled in to his voicemail.

"What the actual fuck?" he said, listening to the message.

"What?" I asked, putting away a final dish. "What is it?"

Michael didn't answer me. He just hung up and walked into the next room to make a call. After a few seconds, someone answered. "I don't understand," I overheard him say to whoever it was on the line. "Why are you doing this? You said you weren't going back."

His mother.

"But it's not going to be different," he pleaded with her. "You said it yourself, when you were here. Don't you remember? Don't you remember everything you said to me? Where did all of that go?" A pause. "What? What did he do to get you back this time? He charm you or something?"

I walked away from the kitchen and headed to the front to give him privacy. He must have been on the phone for twenty minutes before he reappeared, his expression blank, his cheeks red. I asked him what happened and he told me. "Apparently, he's been so sweet to her since Christmas," he said with disdain. "Writing love notes, sending her flowers and gifts. She said she found herself powerless in the face of all that kindness and remorse."

"That doesn't sound like your dad. I mean, it is kind of cute, isn't it?"

Michael was not impressed. "No, it's not cute, Paul. He does this all the time! She leaves him, then he makes this grand gesture to get her back. And she always goes back to him! And he knows it. It never changes anything. Soon, he'll start acting the same way again and yelling all the time, taking her for granted—and she'll be upset and depressed and here on our couch, you'll see." Michael was deflated. "She was doing so well. She was on her own for ten months! That's the longest it's ever been."

The next day, Michael's father tried to call him a couple of times but he wouldn't answer. He'd just look at the call display, which he had programmed to register his dad's number as "Do not pick-up," and throw aside his phone. I tried to reason with him. "Maybe it'll be different this time," I said. "Maybe your dad wants to apologize, to start over again—with you too. Can't you be optimistic?"

"No, I can't." Michael sounded as angry with me as he was with his dad. "I won't be dragged back into it. So, can you please stop acting like my mother? He was horrible to us—to me, my brothers—the cause of all the stress and pain in my family for years. You don't know what it's like to have a father who would yell at you all the time, who showed your own brothers how to mistreat you, how to mistreat each other. He may be sorry, but I can't just *forget* all of that."

I approached Michael where he sat at the kitchen table. "You're holding on to your anger," I said, reaching out to massage his neck. "You should let it go."

Michael shook me off. "You know, I don't think I want to talk about this with you anymore," he said. "I'm done." He took off to the office to be alone.

* * *

The following week, Wendy came to town. The miscarriage was behind her now—well, as behind her as it could be. She had got her period again and was eager to start over. This time, however, she would have to do the insertions alone, as Eve had to remain behind to work. It had snowed in the days leading up to her trip, so instead of driving she took the train. I met her at the station and the two of us took a cab to her hotel.

"I don't know why you didn't want to stay at our place," I said, as we checked out her suite at the Saint James. "I mean, this is gorgeous, but it must have set you back." The room had a masculine look, with dark wood-panelled walls, leather chairs and heavy majestic drapes. "You could have had our bed," I said.

"Have you seen this bathroom?" was Wendy's answer. The walls were all marble, the tub a deep soaker. "Eve wanted to spoil me since she couldn't come, and I'm going to pamper myself. And honestly, I do need privacy for this. Thanks, though."

"So just tonight and tomorrow then?" I asked. "No more?"

"I think twice will be enough." She sat on the bed to feel it out. "Honestly, I'm worried I jumped the gun again on this one. I took my temperature this morning and I'm still not ovulating. My cycle might be out of whack."

I stood in the room, not sure what to do next. "Oh, here," she said finally, and went into her bag to retrieve the container. "I'm going to get a couple chocolate bars downstairs. Want something?" I shook my head, and Wendy walked to the door. "It feels wrong to do this without Eve," she said, then left, leaving me to do my job.

The next evening, we tried again. I went over to the Saint James after work and kept Wendy company afterwards. We ordered room service and sat on the bed, Wendy's legs elevated while we watched television.

At twenty to ten, I finally got up to leave. "Heading home?" she asked.

"Actually, I'm meeting the boys for drinks," I said. "Charles, Danny and I haven't seen each other in a month and there's this new gay bar that opened in Old Montreal we want to try out."

The words "gay bar" lit up her face.

"Want to join? It's only ten minutes away."

Wendy's mouth bunched up as she hemmed and hawed. "Let me change first," she said and propelled herself off the bed.

Minutes later, we were out the door, walking along the cold snowy sidewalks towards de la Commune Street and the Old Port. Outside the bar, we ran into Danny getting out of a cab. I hardly recognized him given the size of the winter jacket he wore. "Do you have your own fireplace in there?" I teased.

"I need it to store nuts," he said. "It's been a long winter."

We walked into the bar and found Michael already there, at a table with Charles. "Do you see the size of their drinks?" Danny gestured to a group of men by the dance floor as we sat down. "It's like they're drinking from crystal balls."

The music was lively, and Michael was enjoying it. "I'm going to go dance," he said, as if it were a crazy idea. He gave me a kiss and took off.

"Find out what they're drinking," Danny called after him.

"I don't know where he gets his energy," Wendy said.

"Well, there's still a two before that nine," I said.

"Yes, why is everyone so young here?" Danny asked, looking around. "How the hell am I supposed to meet anyone in this dating pool?"

"I told you," Charles said, his phone in his hand. "Get back online, create a profile."

Danny rolled his eyes. "I created one a week ago but deleted it the next day. Everyone on them is either partnered or looking for no strings attached. It's like an insane game of musical chairs where no one sits down once the music stops. No, I have to come up with novel ways of meeting people— like walking up to someone and saying, 'Hi, can you hold this for a second?' and then jumping into their arms."

Wendy cracked up. "Oh, I've missed you Danny."

Danny sighed. "Oh, Wendy. What I wouldn't give to be a lesbian. You're like those penguins that mate for life. I saw a documentary about them on the CBC the other day and almost threw my TV out the window."

"Stop it," I said to Danny. "You're going to be fine."

"Of course I'm going to be fine!" he said as if there weren't any question. "When you fall off a horse, you get back on it again. In fact, I bought myself a saddle and a nice pair of leather chaps the other day. It was just a setback. I've learned my lesson and I'm going to find another husband, by hook or by crook."

"No hooking!" Charles said.

Danny stood up from his seat. "Okay, it doesn't look like

this place has table service, so I'm going to get us a round of whatever is in those fishbowls. Wendy, can I get you something? Kombucha perhaps?"

"I'm not that much of a lesbian," she said. "See if they can make me a virgin one of those." After Danny left, Wendy turned to me. "I forgot about how much of a tornado Danny is."

"Well, it's winter now," I said. "He's more like a blizzard."

"What happened between him and that guy he was seeing?"

I told her the short version. She had to lean in to hear me. "God, it's so fucking loud in here," she said, once I was done.

"Good for the egg," Charles said. "All those vibrations might give the kid some rhythm, like Michael over there." We all looked at Michael, dancing alone with such happiness and purpose.

I smiled. "We're such different people, he and I," I said. It was a comforting thought. "He's so outgoing. Extroverted. He's like this radiating ball of energy, while I'm so serious all the time. I'm surprised he's not bored with me yet."

"Eve and I are opposites too," Wendy remarked, and although I had never thought of it before, it was true. "We came from different backgrounds. She grew up in the sub-urbs and was a straight-A student, while I went to an all-girls private school and almost flunked. She was the *good* daughter while I fought with my mother and snuck out at night to smoke cigarettes with boys in the park. She likes rock music, I like country. Somehow, we make it work."

"We're often attracted to our own shadows," Charles said, putting his phone down. "Not to those who are like us, but to those we'd like to be. They often end up being the most significant relationships because we learn from them. Like Danny and Vince. They had things in common, but they were polar opposites. Danny is too close to it now, but one day he'll see the value in what he's learned. Even you, Paul—you and Michael. He's your shadow." A notification lit up on Charles's phone and he picked it up. "I mean, how boring would it be to date someone who is exactly like you."

Just then, Danny returned with two large drinks. "This one's for you," he said to Wendy, giving her the virgin cocktail. He gave Charles the other one and took off only to return seconds later with one for him and me. "Don't forget to tip your waiter," he said, sitting down. "Now what were we talking about?"

"Our shadows," Wendy said.

"Groundhog Day was weeks ago," Danny said. "Is it true that if a gay man sees his stomach the first week of February, he has to do six more weeks of CrossFit?"

"What are these called?" Charles asked, bringing the globe to his lips.

"Black Holes. Some kind of rum-based drink."

"Sounds ominous."

Danny took a sip. "You could disappear in this."

I took a sip. It was strong. Wendy eyed me. "It's okay," she said, and patted her belly. "Knock yourself out. I've got what I wanted."

After about a half hour, enough for us to drink most of our cocktails, Wendy began to yawn. "Sorry fellas," she said, her own glass only half empty. "It's way too loud in here, and I'm trying to create life. I'm going to go back to the hotel to watch some bad TV in my bathrobe." She kissed me on the head and said her goodbyes.

We finished our drinks, and I bought us another round. Michael kept getting up to dance, smoke a joint outside, or talk to Gus who I noticed was now hanging out near the DJ booth. "That guy is going to follow me everywhere, isn't he?" Danny said, looking over at Gus as he and Michael chatted beside the turntables. "I'm going to be in the old folks home for queers, and he'll be the godawful DJ they hire to play the mid-morning tea dance. I'm going to have to wrestle the MDMA away from the drag queen nurses so I can overdose." Danny stood up.

"I'm not sure you can overdose on MDMA," I said. "Where are you going?"

"Whore tour," Danny said, taking another sip of courage. "Wish me luck."

Our table went quiet with Danny, Wendy and Michael gone. I sipped my cocktail, while Charles continued to scroll and text. "You're going to give yourself carpal tunnel of the thumb one day." I said. "What's so interesting?"

Charles put down the phone. "Setting up a date for later."

I looked at my watch. "Later? It's 11 p.m."

"I'm a night owl."

"I think the animal you mean is cougar. Who's the guy?" I asked.

Charles picked up his phone and found a picture to show me. The man was cute, but again, young—tight black curly hair, topless and skinny with a fuzzy treasure trail leading down to his jeans. "His name's Mark," he said, taking back his phone. "He's a design student at the National Theatre School. I met him at a gallery opening three weeks ago."

"Sounds on-brand," I said. "Is he *your* shadow?"

Charles smiled. "I wouldn't say that. We're too similar—creative, stubborn, horny. He's super talented, but tortured."

"Kinky?"

"A little *too* kinky for my tastes," he said. "He wants to role play, calls me 'Daddy,' which gets old fast. I don't know, I think I like him too much to sleep with him. He's smart, but he makes horrible decisions. He got into the NTS, which isn't easy, but he keeps phoning it in and falling behind. That's not going to end well."

"Were you like that when you were young?" I asked.

"Maybe a little," he smiled. "But I wasn't so irresponsible. I did the work."

I looked over at Michael, chatting with Gus. "Sometimes I wish I didn't have to be the responsible one," I said. "The one who chases after him to go to the dentist or pay his bills or take his shower in time for us to leave."

Charles put his phone back down. "But that's who you are, Paul. You need to be useful to people. It's in your nature. You're like the Littlest Hobo."

The thought made me laugh. "What!? Like the dog crime fighter?"

"He wasn't a crime fighter. He went from town to town, helping people, like a samurai. And Michael is your someone in need. He needs someone to look out for him, at least for now. That's you."

I still couldn't get over the comparison. "Okay, that might be true, but I don't *feel* helpful. Michael's had so

303

much bad luck: his hearing, his family, his car, his taxes. And I've always felt so goddamn lucky."

"I don't believe in luck," Charles said. "Luck is just being prepared when opportunity presents itself. The reason you've got to where you are in life—your home, your job, even your relationship—is not because you're lucky, but because you've worked hard to get to the place where you're ready to receive what the universe has to offer."

I wasn't convinced. "So, what would bad luck be then?"

Charles thought about it. "Not being prepared?"

Danny returned, and sat down hard in his chair. "All right then, I'm leaving."

"What? No," I said. "What happened on your whore tour?"

"I ran into Andre."

"Who's Andre?" Charles asked.

"You know. The twenty-four-year-old I dated last year. Well, he's not twenty-four any more." Danny downed the rest of his drink. "He's twenty-five now. Twenty-fucking-five!"

"Come on, Danny," I pleaded, and lifted my glass. "One more trip to the Black Hole."

Danny ignored me. "He looks good. I saw him near the bar, next to this other young pony, both of them tossing their manes about and grazing on the stares that everyone fed them. He took one look at me, turned and left." Danny stood up and put on his coat. "No, I'm done for the evening. Everyone here is too young anyway. I feel like a pedophile at a playground. I keep expecting someone to come up and ask me to leave."

And with that, Danny kissed us both goodbye and headed out the door.

Michael and I stumbled up the stairs to our home, mumbling barks and laughs in the darkness of our stairwell. The hallway's light was off, so it took us a few seconds to find the keyhole and open the door. Inside, the cats were waiting for us. I reached for the switch on the wall and turned on the lights, taking off my boots.

Walking into our home, I noticed that the place had been left a mess. Lit up, our apartment looked like a teenager's room. Michael hadn't made the bed. The door to the bedroom wardrobe was open and discarded outfits lay on the floor. In the kitchen, there was clutter on the island. Michael had forgotten to close the whisky bottle, and the shot glass he'd used had left a sticky ring on the surface. Next to the sink was a pile of dirty dishes: half-empty water glasses, stained coffee mugs he had shuttled from his desk in the office, his breakfast blender jar caked in milk and hemp seeds. And on the floor, next to the washing machine, the laundry pile untouched in its hamper.

"I thought you were home today."

"I was," Michael said.

Immediately, I felt the blood rise to my face. "So, what did you do all day?"

"It was my day off, so I spent it drawing."

I shook my head and closed my eyes. "So, you couldn't have done one load of laundry?" I asked. Any fun we'd had before coming home was now discarded with my boots at the door. "Couldn't have done your dishes at some point? What, do you expect me to do them? Even though I work *all the time*, it's my job to clean up the place when I get home too?"

"I didn't say that."

Suddenly, I had a headache. I could feel the evening's Black Holes pulling on my brain. "Come on," I said. "Look at this place. Tomorrow's Saturday. I'm going to wake up before you to this mess, and have to clean it up myself."

Michael headed to the sink and turned on the water. "No, it's fine," he said, and began to do the dishes. "I'll clean up."

Great, this is exactly what I didn't want—a fight. "No," I said. "I don't want you to do them now. I'll do them tomorrow. The time to do them was today!"

"No, I'm doing them."

This was making me angry. I could feel the adrenaline running through my body. "God, Michael," I said, turning to leave. "I wish you had the reflex to take care of our home more."

He stopped doing the dishes. "Don't act like that," he said, equally annoyed. "I do things around here. Who cleans the toilet and washes the floor? Who tends to the garden and waters the plants? Who takes care of the litter?"

"Fine, but is it so hard to pull up the covers of the bed? Can you not wash a dish after you use it?" I picked up a plastic cow figurine, a toy essentially, that was on the kitchen island. Another one of Michael's trinkets from Moncton. It felt like they were everywhere now—on his nightstand, in the pantry, on bookshelves, around the edge of the bathtub. "And these things. Do you have to leave them out? Can we not find a place for all of them? I'm sick of seeing these things around the house."

He pulled the plastic cow out of my hand. "Hey, this is my place too! I might not be able to pay you much to live here, but I *do* live here. So what if I leave a few things out?" He shook the figurine in his hand. "Do you even know why I do this? I didn't have the same *wonderful* upbringing as you, Paul. So I need to surround myself with happy reminders of my childhood, things that make me feel good about myself—because there aren't that many, you know? You've spent your whole life here! You have your friends, you can see your past in the streets. But I don't have any of that. These are the only things I have left from my youth that are mine."

Michael took the cow and headed to the front to the office. I was right behind.

As he entered the room, he placed the cow on the shelf above his desk and sat down. He got out his grinder to prepare a joint. I opened my mouth to say something, but stopped. "I... I'm sorry, Michael. I didn't realize that these things meant that much to you. I... I just, I don't do well with mess." I tried to laugh it off. "And there seems to be a lot of it these days."

Michael swivelled in his chair to face me. "In case you haven't noticed, I haven't been in the best mood lately. Do you know how much of a failure my mom going back to my dad is for me?"

"What? Why? Why is this a failure for you?"

"Because I couldn't get her to leave!" It was like he was pleading with me. "Do you know it was my mom—my mom, Paul—who got me off drugs? The one who actually did something and intervened? When my brother dropped dead from all the fucking heroin, meth and other junk he pumped into his body, she was the one who stood up and yelled and screamed and got me to quit. Who kept me at home and helped me navigate all the panic and anxiety and suicidal thoughts that wanted to destroy whatever was left. And I couldn't even do this for her. This one stupid thing! Get her to save herself, like she saved me. Why? Because she's a fucking martyr! Throwing herself on every lost cause—like me, and like my dad."

I stumbled with what to say. "But you're not a lost cause. You—"

"And it's not the only thing I'm failing at." He was emotional now, struggling to hold back tears. "I'm trying to pay the government what I owe, trying to pay you, trying to drum up work. And I didn't tell you this, but business at the coffee shop has been down since it's so *fucking freezing* outside. They have no work for me for the next few weeks. No work! So, sometimes it's hard for me to get motivated, okay?"

I felt like shit. There was nothing I could say.

Michael tried to roll his joint, but he was agitated. "Do you know how hard it is to be me some days?" He sniffed and wiped his left eye with his wrist. He gave up on rolling. "How hard it is for me to put on a smile and attack the day?"

"I'm sorry, Michael. I just... I had no idea."

"I'm sorry if I'm not as together as you'd like me to be." The tears came out now, falling down his face, and I knelt in front of where he sat, my hands at his knees. "But this is my life! My goddamn life, Paul! I have no choice."

He collapsed in my arms and let out a cry, as loud and as painful as the morning he had lost the car. "Don't you think I wish things were different?" he choked back into my shoulder. "Don't you think I feel guilty for leaving her there?" I just held him and listened, not letting go until his tears began to dissipate and he began to calm down. "I stayed as long as I could, but I had to go, I had to leave," he said, pulling away and wiping his face. "I wish she could find it within herself to leave too."

Soon after, I went to bed. I was completely sober now, but exhausted. I wanted Michael to come to bed with me, but he said he wasn't tired and that he'd stay up for a bit.

"Are you okay?" I asked him.

"I made it this far. I think I can make it a little more."

The next morning, when I woke up, I noticed that the dishes were done. My head was still foggy from the Black Holes. This was becoming a sad habit, I realized. Drinking occasionally, but to the point of hangover. I missed the days when morning meant a jog through the neighbourhood. I should go for a run, I thought, but then I looked outside and saw the fresh snow. I didn't want to leave, not even to get the newspaper. Instead, I put on the laundry and a pot of coffee then climbed back into bed with Michael.

He made a pleasant half-asleep groan as I pulled him from behind. Lying there, I thought of what Charles had said the night before, about me needing to be useful and Michael needing help. But for the first time in our relationship, I felt useless and scared. What if I wasn't able to truly help him?

THREE

Last Dance

17

It was another few weeks before I heard from Wendy. This time, however, I did wonder if something was up.

She called me at work and we made small talk, mostly about her folks and Eve's upcoming show. At some point I felt a text message vibrate through, but didn't look at it. Finally, I asked Wendy if she had any news.

She was vague. "Still waiting on stuff," she said. "Hey, check your phone. I sent you something."

I opened the screen and looked for her message. There was an image. At first, I didn't know what I was looking at. It seemed to be a bunch of sticks and wrappers. Was this a pregnancy test? "Wait, are you pregnant?"

"Yep!"

Looking closer, I noticed that it was five sticks, all positive. There was no doubt. "Holy cow!" I said. "That's crazy! And you thought it didn't work!"

"I know!"

"Those must have been some tenacious swimmers to have survived inside of you for that long. Olympians!"

"Maybe Charles was right," Wendy said. "Maybe the club's vibrations helped it along."

This time, I decided to wait before sharing the news. I told Michael, of course, and my sister, who was thrilled, but I decided I would only tell my friends once Wendy was further along, and not before I had told my father. Danny and Charles would sometimes ask for updates. I'd look down and say, "We're still trying." Soon they stopped asking. Maybe they could sense we were in limbo. Michael started referring to the situation as the "elephant in the womb."

It felt unreal. And at times, I forgot about what we had done. I was not going to allow myself to get excited, in case we lost this one too. Instead, I took Wendy and Eve's lead. I only wanted to get excited when they got excited, and Wendy was in as much denial as I was. At six weeks, she told me that one of her friends had taken her to look at maternity clothes, but it was all too much and she almost fainted in the dressing room. She said it was still too early for such plans and that she felt like a phoney, acting like an expectant mother when she didn't want to feel like one yet.

As we entered the last week of March, Michael seemed happier. We had spent most of the last two months indoors on the couch, cranking up the heat and running down to the street to move the car whenever the plough was scheduled to pass. Michael had finished the books in the *Tales* series and was now diving into other classics on my shelf, alternating his reading with hours spent on new illustrations in his sketchbook. I had hoped to start running again, but the cold temperatures and deep snowbanks continued to be a deterrent. Michael and I kept looking out the window, desperate for the first real signs of spring.

By the time the snowbanks were finally receding for

good a few weeks later, Michael began working evenings at Danny's. Danny had hired him to help with an "updo" as he called it. He wanted to paint his bedroom, bathroom and kitchen in vibrant new colours, and he wanted to turn his spare bedroom into a library and office. "No in-laws are going to come visit me now. Not until I find a new husband, anyway." Michael had helped Danny pick out a leather club chair and a refurbished old teacher's desk that they had trouble getting through the door.

One evening that week, I came home from work with a frozen pizza, expecting to find an empty apartment, but the door was unlocked, and Michael's gym bag and shoes were in the hall. "Hello?" I called out.

"In here," Michael yelled.

I took off my coat and found Michael in the office, Skyping with a friend. "Oh, sorry," I said. "I didn't know you were on a call."

"Paul, look, it's Leo," he said.

I looked at the rectangle on the screen and made out the face of our summer friend. "Hello, Leo," I said.

Leo smiled and waved back. "Hello, Paul."

"Nice to see you again. Where are you?"

"Portland. I'm visiting a bunch of radical faeries I met at a gathering last year. I'm baking them a cake!" Leo had no shirt on, just bare skin behind a white apron.

"Be careful not to burn yourself," I said, aiming to be flirtatious but realizing it had come across rather motherly. I lifted the pizza box in my hand. "Well, I'm going to go make dinner. You take care, Leo." Then I turned to Michael and kissed him on the head before leaving the room.

Twenty minutes later, Michael joined me in the kitchen. "Hi, buddy."

"Hi, buddy." I was chopping carrots, a pasta sauce simmered on the stove.

"I thought you were heating up a pizza."

"I decided to make something else, since you're home. Weren't you supposed to be working at Danny's tonight?"

"No, he has a concert." Michael stirred the sauce in the pot with the wooden spoon on the counter. "You didn't bark."

"What?"

"Coming up the stairs. You didn't bark."

"Well, I didn't know you were home," I said, transferring the carrots to the salad bowl. "And come on, are we really going to do that forever?"

He shrugged. "Smells good. Can I help?"

I looked around. "Want to wash lettuce?"

Michael opened the fridge and got out the bag of greens and proceeded to wash the leaves.

"So, how often do the two of you talk?"

"Leo and me? Not often," he said. Michael's back was to me; mine to his. "Maybe four or five times since last summer."

"How's he doing?"

"Good. A bit nomadic. Doesn't seem to have a fixed address, but he's twenty-five so who cares, right?"

I moved from cutting carrots to celery. "What do you talk about?"

"I don't know," Michael said. I heard the drips of water as he examined each leaf for specks of dirt. "Things. Provincetown. I told him I wasn't going to come down to work for the preseason."

"You sure?"

"Yes." Michael didn't sound convinced. "I mean, I haven't set anything up. And it looks like Leo's not going to be there until late May anyway, so I don't know where I'd stay or who to talk to about finding jobs. I should have looked into this months ago."

Like I thought. "Did you give him our dates?"

"Yes. He should be there."

Michael put the last piece of lettuce in the salad spinner and spun the leaves dry. He brought them over to the island, next to me, and tore up the lettuce into pieces and tossed them into the salad bowl.

"Do you guys fool around?" I asked, intent on green onions now. "On Skype?"

There was a pause before he answered. "Sometimes," he said.

"What do you do?"

"I don't know. We've jerked off together." I felt a flush of heat in my face and chest. "A couple of times. You mad?"

"Mad?" I wasn't sure what the feeling was. "No, I'm not mad," I said. If anything, I was curious. Nothing had been able to happen between the three of us last summer.

I finished up the salad, dousing it in olive oil and red wine vinegar. I served us two heaping plates of pasta, and we went into the living room to eat in front of the television.

That weekend, Michael and I went to my sister and Ben's for dinner. We had yet to be invited over since Kate had moved in, and I saw why as we walked through the door.

"Ignore the mess," Kate said, a little exasperated, perhaps reading my surprise at how little had been unpacked. I could tell, however, that they had cleaned up, as the overflow was neat and orderly; a red tablecloth covered a stack of brown moving boxes, and I could see that the couch had been pulled away from the wall to hide even more boxes behind it.

Kate took our coats and disappeared into the bedroom, while Ben approached us, in a festive apron, and shook our hands. "Welcome, welcome," he repeated.

"Thank you for having us," I said. "We baked cookies." And I gestured over to Michael who handed them over.

"Beware of the bottom row," Michael said. "They have an extra ingredient."

Ben understood and chuckled. "Can I get you a glass of wine? A beer?" he said, heading back to the corner of the room that was his kitchen.

"We brought wine, but I'll start with a beer," I said, as Kate returned.

"Sit, please," she said, and gestured over to the green couch by the immaculately set kitchen table. Kate went to the fridge to retrieve beers for Michael and me.

"Nice place," I felt compelled to say. In all, it must have been six hundred square feet, one bedroom at the back, one bathroom, the rest an open-air living space filled with the cluttered agglomeration of two full lives. "Gotta be a bit tight for the two of you, but it looks comfortable."

Kate glared at me. "Can't move soon enough," she said.

"But we're managing," Ben said, as he chopped.

"Can I help?" Michael was up, standing next to Ben in the kitchen.

"Sure. Do you want to cut those onions?" He called out to Kate, who had taken Michael's space beside me. "Hun? Do

318

you want to get out the decanter? Maybe get that red they brought breathing before dinner?"

Kate looked confused, but pushed herself up off the couch to head towards the cupboard. "I don't think it's in here," she said.

"It should be. In the back, by the martini glasses."

"We packed those away," she said. "Remember? To make room for my blender."

Ben looked flustered. "I don't remember doing that. Why did you pack the bar?"

I could see the annoyance in Kate's movements, the jolts with which she moved her arms and head. "Because I didn't think we needed to have a complete bar set at the ready," she said. "I mean, how often are we going to entertain in a space like this?"

"Do you remember what box you put everything in?"

"No," she sang. "I don't."

Ben scratched his nose with the side of his arm as his hands continued to be busy. He huffed. "Maybe it's in one of the boxes in the bedroom?"

"You want me to look for it?"

"Guys," I said, "it's no big deal. I'm sure it'll be just fine without the decanter."

I looked at the clock. This was going to be a long night.

Kate came back to the couch with her drink and sat next to me, her head on my shoulder. I kissed her on the forehead.

"So, congratulations," Ben said. "I hear your friend is pregnant."

Kate lifted her head and turned to face me, smiling. Of course I didn't expect her to keep the news from Ben.

"Thanks," I said. "We're excited."

"How far is she along?" he asked.

"Nine weeks," I said. It was exactly this time that Wendy had lost the first one, and I felt nervous talking about it, worried again to jinx anything; but I didn't want to remain a prisoner to such thoughts. "Not out of the woods yet, but Wendy is feeling pretty good about everything, sleeping a lot."

"That's a good sign," Ben said. "When my sister was pregnant she slept through an actual tornado."

"Where does your sister live?" Michael asked.

"Leamington," Ben said. "Oh, wait a minute. Can you watch this pot for a second?" he asked Michael, wiping his hands on his apron. "I have something for you guys."

Ben took off, while I looked at Kate. She sat there and shrugged, pretending not to know where he was going. Ben came back in the room, a wobbling baby mobile in his hands.

"Didn't have time to wrap it," he said.

"Oh my god," I said. The mobile was large and it tinkled as I took it from him. "This is gorgeous. Did you make it?"

"Yes, he did," Kate answered while he beamed. "Took him only two weeks."

The mobile's hanger was made of smooth natural wood, and its colourful central pieces were in felt. There was a cactus, a cloud, a rainbow, a bear.

Michael came to admire it, also spellbound, as Ben returned to the stove. "You made it here? In this apartment?"

"I have an atelier I work in, but I only needed the lathe to make the frame."

"Thank you, Ben," I said, looking again at Kate. "This is so thoughtful. The girls are going to love it."

Michael joined me on the couch with his drink and the two of us kept our hosts company as they readied our meal, a dash of tension simmering under every moved pot in their tight kitchen. Around half past six we sat down to eat. The plates were our mother's, a warren of small rabbits at the centre of each dish.

"Cute!" Michael exclaimed as we smothered the rabbits in gravy. It was a delicious meal, albeit a stressful one. Ben was worried he had overcooked the chicken, and Kate didn't do much to assuage his fears by dousing her plate with more gravy several times. Michael and I tried to diffuse any hostility we felt between them, looking at each other from across the table as we carefully navigated topics.

When dinner was over, Michael got up to clear the plates but Ben wouldn't let him. "What are you doing? Sit, please."

"Sorry," Michael said, sitting back down. "Habit from the coffee shop." I could tell that Michael wanted to leave and his attempt at clearing was not just him being polite, but also a desire to move things along.

Ben picked up the bottle on the table. "Here, have some more wine."

Michael was quick to place his hand over his glass. "No, thank you," he said. "I have to drive." I let Ben top me up.

"Spoke with Dad today," Kate said, as Ben filled her glass too.

"How is he?"

"Fine. You know him. Was headed out for a walk with Debbie. God, I hope I'm as active as he is when I'm his age. I told him you and Michael were coming for dinner. He said he wished he could be here too."

"You should invite him to visit sometime," Ben said. "I'd love to meet your dad."

Kate ignored the comment. "Have you decided on when you're going to tell him?"

"I don't know," I said. "Soon. I should tell him soon."

"He has no idea you're trying?" Ben asked.

"No, he doesn't."

"Why haven't you told him? Wouldn't he want to know?"

Maybe it was the red wine, or the mobile Ben had made us, looking at me from where it sat on the sofa, but I saw my answer in Ben's stemware. "I guess I'm afraid to tell him," I said. "I'm afraid of what he's going to say."

The next day, I found myself alone at home with nothing to do.

Michael was at Café Minnelli, in the middle of something important when I called. "Can I borrow the car?" I asked. "I'll be quick."

"Of course. I'm not using it," he said. "What for?"

"I want to go for a drive. Maybe get a few things at IKEA."

"Sure. Get me tea lights if you can." And with that, he had to go.

I grabbed our extra set of keys from the dresser in the hallway and went down to find Darlene, parked a block north from our building. It felt strange to sit in the driver's seat. I noticed things that I hadn't before, namely that Michael kept a bag of liquorice in the driver's side door and there was a small "Hang in There Kitty" sticker on the dashboard beside the headlight switch.

It took me a few blocks to get comfortable behind the

wheel. I rarely drove, and it had been decades since I had borrowed my father's car with any regularity. I took the car up to Highway 40, then drove west for about twenty kilometres. Once off the highway, I turned down the familiar streets, lengths I had walked hundreds of times to grab trains or buses, trajectories I took to school or to the park or to visit friends on the weekends. Soon, I found myself on Empress Street, and then, at the end of the block, I came to Hastings. And there it was, at the corner. My old house.

I parked the car across the street. It looked the same, from the two-tone brown shingles on the roof to the dark red fence around the back. The lot looked smaller than it did in my memory. It also didn't look like anyone was home. There were no cars in the driveway, no lights or movement in the windows.

I got out of the car and closed the door, leaning against Darlene's frame as I observed the building. I looked towards the windows where Kate's room had been. I remembered looking out of her window as a kid, at the sky and the street lamp on the corner. (It too had not changed.) There was something about the view from her window that I had loved. Sometimes, I'd sneak into her room after suppertime—if she was out with friends or flipping through TV channels in the basement—and watch the sun set. In the retreating colours, I would wonder about my future, about the friends who would someday be mine. I pictured us gathering as the day drew to a close and imagined the adventures we might have together, when our lives only began as night fell.

I walked around the corner to the side of the house, towards the back to where my room had been. There I saw

323

my old corner windows, smaller than Kate's and looking out onto the backyard and the trees behind it. We had a swimming pool back then. I could still hear the sound of its filter, lulling me to sleep on hot summer nights. The pool was gone now. Through the slats, I saw that it had been replaced by a large shed and a two-tiered patio deck, each covered in melting snow.

I looked back up at the top floor windows. How small my room must have been, that warm space that had cradled me while I slept—or didn't sleep, as I lay awake at night, thinking that I might be gay. It was there that I had cried myself to sleep when I realized it wasn't a phase, but it was also where the shame had lifted, where I came to terms with my sexuality and learned that all was not lost. This room, where I would get ready in front of the full-length mirror, where I retreated after an argument, where I wrote the eulogy for my mother, where I changed into a black suit on the day of her funeral, and where I lay in the darkness and stared at the walls after she was gone.

"Est-ce que je peux vous aider?" A man had come out of the house's side door.

With the tone in his voice, it didn't sound like he wanted to help. I laughed and apologized. "I'm sorry," I said in French. "I don't mean to pry. I used to live here when I was a kid." I pointed to my room at the corner.

The man's demeanour changed, and he smiled. He was around my age, with a paunch and thinning hair like me. But somehow, he seemed older and made me think of my dad when I was a teenager—a middle-aged man with a wife and kids, proud of his home, coming out to talk to a neighbour

"When did you live here?" he asked.

"Almost twenty years ago. You've taken good care of it." I said. "It's the same colour, but it looks like you've repainted. The driveway's nicer and you've got a bunch more bushes at the front."

"My wife likes to garden."

So does my partner, I wanted to say. "Sorry, I don't want to disturb you. I was just in the neighbourhood and feeling nostalgic. I was curious to see how it looked."

The man hesitated for a second, but then said, "Would you like to come in and have a look?"

The offer caught me off guard. It was awfully generous. I thought about it for a minute, about entering all of the rooms and the memories that might evoke. "C'est gentil, mais non merci," I said. "I think I'd like to keep my memories the way they are."

Back in the car, I called my dad.

"Hi, Dad. You'll never guess where I am. I'm sitting in front of the old house."

"What? What are you doing there?" he asked.

"Feeling nostalgic… Listen Dad, I have news."

"Oh?"

"I'm going to have a kid. With Wendy and Eve. The two of them wanted to start a family and asked me if I'd be their sperm donor. I said yes. Wendy's pregnant now and going to have a baby."

"Oh… really?"

"Yes, really. She's about nine weeks along."

"Well, I'll be…" It was complete and utter shock.

"I'm sorry I didn't tell you earlier. We wanted to keep it

to ourselves at the beginning, in case it didn't work—Wendy miscarried last December, and it was horrible. But I felt bad that I didn't tell you then. We weren't sure it would work this time, but it did... I guess you didn't expect to hear this from me."

"Uh no, I didn't. Wow. That's... I... Congratulations, I guess. I... Does your sister know?"

"Yes, Kate knows."

"Are... Are you going to raise the child?"

"No. It'll be Wendy and Eve's child. They're the parents. But they will know where they came from, who I am and who you are. I just won't be the kid's father—not in the traditional way. They won't call me 'Dad' or have our last name. I won't be on the birth certificate. But you and Debbie will be grandparents, if you want—Eve and Wendy want you to be. Kate will be an aunt. Michael and I will be uncles. They want all kinds of love for their child, which I think is great. What do you think?"

There was a pause, and then I heard my dad exhale (or was it a huff?). "Honestly, I don't know what to think, Paul. This is... such a shock, in a way. But as long as you're happy, I guess... Does Michael know?"

What a silly question. "Of course, Michael knows. He's happy for me too—for us! We're all looking forward to this. You know, being gay I never thought I'd ever have a kid. But now, I feel excited at the possibility of it."

"Well, then, I'm happy for you, Paul... Grandparents, huh? Wow. I. I don't know what else to say."

I was at a loss too. "I think that's understandable," I said. "There's no guidebook. I know it's not the same as with Sue.

I'm sure it's a lot and confusing. I just wanted to let you know before it became too long. We can talk about it another time, okay? Take care and speak soon."

I hung up and felt a slight tremor in my hand. The car was cold. I turned on the ignition, then the heat.

I'd forgotten how awkward it used to be with him. How opinionated he once was about everything I did—who I hung out with, what I spent my money on, where I wanted to go to school. It was long ago, but it used to drive me crazy. Over time, it dissipated. Then after my mother died, nothing seemed worth arguing about. He hardly batted an eye when I finally came out—I mean, he wasn't thrilled with the news, but by then any illusion of what our futures would be like as a family had shattered. Life was too short. But now, hearing that tone in his voice again, I felt like a kid.

It had been almost twenty years since I came out. I thought back to that time in the nineties. How much chaos there was in those days. Alan, my work with Pride. I was so active then, so angry. I felt like a domesticated animal now. All that rage was in the past, and the world was a different place. Then what was this strange disappointment I hadn't felt in almost two decades? I was doing the most traditional thing one could expect, I was having a child. But once again I felt different.

"HE'S GOT ANOTHER HANGER. Can you help?"

I put my book down and came running. Michael was with Malone, watching as the cat skidded his butt along the floor of the hallway. "But I just washed it!" Michael groaned. He picked up Malone and with that came an uncomfortable meow-moan. Not bothering to reach for a tissue, I grabbed at the turd with my hand. Malone meowed again and I removed the chunk and threw it in the toilet off the hallway before turning to wash my hands in the bathroom sink. "Should we change his food again?"

"No," Michael said. We watched the cat, momentarily inconvenienced but now oblivious, walk off to the next room. "He'll be fine."

I headed back to the balcony off the kitchen, my book and my Queen mug of tea waiting. Michael followed behind and soon began fussing with the pots in our small garden. "These are coming in nicely," he said about the bulbs we had planted. "I'd like to get more today. Maybe do the front balcony as well."

"It's Mother's Day," I said. "The market's going to be packed. Are you going to call your mom?"

Michael had taken out a bag of earth and was adding

scoopfuls to the annuals. "I haven't decided."

"What's to decide? She'll be heartbroken if you don't."

"Well, I might be miserable if I do." Michael was forceful with his pots. "What?" he said to my silence. "Every time I speak with her, I get angry. I don't feel like ruining my day."

I heard a noise and looked up. Another large plane coming in with hundreds of bodies hurtling towards the ground. "Well, what do you feel like doing today?"

Michael shrugged. "I think I might go to Danny's. He's changed his mind on the 'updo' and has all this extra work for me now. Didn't say what exactly. He's so fickle. I mean, he changed his mind about the paint colour three times."

I closed my book. "Maybe I'll join you," I said. I hadn't seen Danny in a while. "I could keep him company while you work—or I could help—then we can all have dinner together."

I texted Danny my plan and he thought it was a great idea: *Come over any time*, he wrote back. *Don't bring anything! I have a brand-new bottle of Aperol and have been dying to break out the BBQ.*

Later that morning, I called Wendy and Eve to wish them a happy Mother's Day. It was Wendy who answered, as Eve was out getting groceries. "Thanks for the blankets you sent," she said. "They're so soft and colourful."

Earlier that week, I had mailed off a collection of swaddle blankets made from bamboo fibre and muslin. I might not know how to knit, I thought, but that doesn't mean the baby can't be comfortable. "You're welcome," I said. "I saw them and thought of you. You'll be able to wrap up the kid like a burrito."

"Still can't get over the mobile Kate's boyfriend made." Earlier in the month I had also sent them Ben's gift. I suppose I could've waited to give it to them in person, but I was too excited not to. "Think we can get him to make a crib to match?"

Despite the playfulness of her comment, Wendy sounded tired and bored. Not the same vibrant person on our regular calls. "So, how are things?"

"Things are good," Wendy said. "But I'm a bit distracted. We had a scare a few days ago. I noticed a bit of blood in the morning when I went to the bathroom. But then we saw the doctor and everything looked fine. They're not sure what caused the bleeding."

We had just passed the three-month mark, but maybe it had been wrong to assume the pregnancy was out of danger. "That must have been stressful," I said. "Do you trust your doctor?"

"God, yes. I don't know what I would do without that woman. But listen, Paul, I want to apologize."

"Apologize? For what?"

"If I've been sounding weird lately."

I tried to think of what she meant. "I don't think you've been sounding weird."

"I don't want to talk about it too much, because it's something I have to work through myself. But I've been having a hard time with what we're doing. I know it's the hormones, but the feelings are there and it sucks sometimes."

I was confused. "I don't understand. Do you regret asking me?"

"No, no," she said, "it's nothing like that. It has nothing

330

to do with you. I'm having a hard time with other people. Like my hairdresser the other day. We were talking about my pregnancy and he asked me point-blank, 'What does the father do?' I almost fell out of my chair. He knows I'm a lesbian. I had to ask him to repeat the question and was worried that I was going to lose it on him. It's all playing with my head—not being able to have Eve's baby, having to involve someone else to make our family. I've read that it's common to have these feelings, but I don't want to talk to you too much about them because I want to protect our friendship. I know that you don't want to be a father to our child, but somehow everyone is making me crazy to think that you might."

I felt a tad defensive. I had gone out of my way to make sure Wendy and Eve never felt I was taking up space. Were the blankets too much? Ben's mobile? I opened my mouth to say something, but stopped. Instead, I said, "Well, no worries. I understand how strange everything must be for you. It's got to be tough doing things this way. But remember, Wendy, we *are* doing something that's different. It's not 'normal.'"

"I know," she said. "I know."

Later that day, Michael packed his tools into the car and we drove over to Danny's place. Danny greeted us at the door in a tizzy, books and vinyl all over his kitchen table. "We're going to move the turntable over here, back into the living room," he told Michael. "And we're going to take the desk out and put it in the dining room for now."

"You're not getting rid of it, are you?" Michael asked. "It was so hard to get in here."

"And it's beautiful," I offered, admiring its colour.

"Well, it's yours if you want it," Danny said. I looked to Michael, but he shook his head no. "I've got someone to agree to come get it on Wednesday, but if you want it you're going to have to take it before Vince moves in next week."

"Wait," I said. "Vince is moving in? Danny, you buried the lede."

"We got back together," Danny said, his face alight. Before I could say anything, he interrupted. "We ran into each other about ten days ago in the Village. We decided to go for coffee, then coffee turned into a movie, and then a movie turned into dinner. Before we knew it we were back at my place making the beast with two backs to the new Beach House. We've been inseparable ever since."

I was slack-jawed. "I don't believe it."

"Well, it's a perfectly fine album to have sex to."

"That's not what I meant."

"Well, what do you want me to say, Paul?" Danny said, flustered by my reaction. He looked guilty, his hand in the cookie jar. It was clear to me that he wanted to smooth this over, pretend that the last few months—and all he had said to me during them—hadn't happened. "The time apart has made us both realize how much we love and care for each other. How we don't want to be apart again. I know I don't."

"So, he's going to move in here? Right away?"

Danny turned and walked into the once spare bedroom, now office, soon to be spare bedroom again. "Isn't it wonderful?" I noticed he had already taken down his pictures, leaving chipped holes in the walls Michael had recently painted. "He's keeping his furnished apartment to rent out online, but he'll live with me full-time—well, most of the week anyway. And we'll use this room to house both of our things and turn it back into a second bedroom for when his family visits. His cousin is already talking about coming this summer."

Michael asked, "If he's renting out his apartment, then why doesn't his cousin just stay at his old place?"

Danny rolled his eyes. "Because you know how much I love to entertain," he said. "I want a spare room anyway, for guests and such. Who knows, we might even need to turn it into a nursery one day."

"Take it easy, Danny," I almost laughed. "You just got back together."

Danny grabbed me by both hands. "I'm not letting go this time, Paul. God, I missed him. Those three months apart were torture. It felt so long, it might as well have been a decade in solitary."

Danny let go and turned to face Michael. Again, I was speechless.

"Michael, I'm afraid we're going to have to repaint," he said. "I'm finding it way too dark in here now. And we made all those holes putting up the pictures. The new bed we're getting is going to have a headboard and that will mess with the artwork."

Danny's picture frames were in a pile on his desk. I walked over and sorted through them. There was one of a slim teenage Danny wearing a soccer uniform on the field. There was one of him and me, taken on our first trip to Provincetown together, our goofy faces squinting on a bright sandy beach. And there was one of a young couple dressed up and sitting for a portrait. "Are these your parents?" I asked. "I don't think I've seen this one before."

Danny took it from my hands and admired it. "It was taken in Detroit on their honeymoon. Why anyone would drive from Toronto to Detroit on their honeymoon is beyond me. Still, it's one of my favourite shots of them," he said, smiling. "Wasn't my mother a looker?"

Danny and I moved to the kitchen to prepare dinner, while Michael began his work. "Will Vince be joining us?" I asked, still in disbelief.

"I think so." Again, more surprise. "He wanted to go to the gym today and was supposed to meet up with an old friend for coffee. God, I can't tell you how good it feels to have him back in my life. To be able to reach out and call him. And see him. Not wonder what he's up to or who he's with, or if he's thinking about me or missing me. Sometimes you need time apart to put things into perspective."

"Well," I searched for the words, deciding to be supportive, "that's great Danny. I'm happy you're happy." I noticed there was a cluster of vegetables and two cutting boards on Danny's kitchen counter. "What can I help with?"

"Maybe prepare these for the grill? I'll start on the meat and marinade."

I grabbed a yellow pepper and a kitchen knife, and chopped it into chunks, the rhythmic snaps of each slice competing with the zips coming from the spare room as Michael removed screws from the wall with his power drill. "So Danny," I started, looking at him as he cut a round of beef into smaller cubes for skewers, "what about the stuff that caused your break-up in the first place? Were you able to come to an understanding?"

"No, not really," he said, intent on the meat. "We'll talk about it again, I'm sure. But I don't want to—not now, not just as we got back together. I don't want to bring this all up and find us fighting again just as we're falling back in love."

"But it will come up."

Danny tried to hide his annoyance. "So, it comes up…" He stopped cutting and put his knife down. He looked at me. "You know Paul, if Vince needs to have this to be with me then I will let him have it. It doesn't mean I want to know about it. Doesn't mean we're going to have one of those relationships where I'm packing him a lunch and kissing him as he heads out the door to his next date, saying, 'Be safe, wear a condom.' No. I'll live oblivious in my happy little world, with my man at my table and in my bed at night, with our friends over for BBQ and his family visiting in our spare bedroom. It may not be everything I want, but it's close enough."

"And are you sure you're going to be able to handle that?"

Danny put down his knife again, showing annoyance this time. "Hey, aren't you the one who told me how I needed to learn how to compromise? I'm compromising."

My cell phone rang. "I'm sorry, Danny," I said, fishing it out of my pocket. "I'm looking out for you is all." I looked at the call display. It was my father's wife. "That's odd," I said and answered. "Hello, Debbie. Is everything okay?"

The earliest flight we could get was the following morning. I met up with Kate at the airport. She looked as if she hadn't slept, bags under her eyes and her hair a mess. We didn't talk much, just waited to board then took the two flights in silence. Somehow, being in the air didn't bother me.

After we landed, we grabbed a cab and headed straight to the hospital. Kate had been to Kelowna before, so the landscape was not as alien to her as it was to me, the rolling mountain ranges and open sky making it feel like I was somewhere in central California. It was a short cab ride, about twenty minutes, and once we arrived we paid our fare and set off to find our father. I thought it might be difficult to navigate the hospital floor plan, but we found my dad's ward and room easily enough. He was asleep when we entered, Debbie knitting in a chair beside him. When she saw us, a big smile erupted on her face and she got up to give us both big hugs. "He's going to be okay," she whispered, keeping it together. "He's just very tired."

There were two visitor seats, so I let Kate sit in one as Debbie sat back down in hers. I stood, arms folded, and took in my father as he slept. He had lost weight since I had last seen him, but he still seemed fit, even with the tubes coming out of his nose. And although he had been with Debbie twelve years, it was shocking to see him lying there beside her instead of my mother, Debbie sitting at attention in a bright coloured scarf and with a big leather purse.

"So, what happened?" Kate asked.

We had heard the rushed story over the phone, but Debbie recounted it to us now in detail. "Well, we went out biking along Mission Creek with our friends Marsha and Ian, like we do most Saturdays. About ten minutes in, your dad needed to stop and catch his breath. I asked him if he needed water and then he fell over—thank goodness he had his helmet on, otherwise his head would've hit the pavement. Fortunately, there was an ambulance nearby. They were there within minutes."

My dad coughed, and shifted in bed. "Wha?" he kind of said, and began to wake up. "Gio," Debbie said, her arm on his. "Kate and Paul are here." My dad coughed again, and we approached so he could see us. A smile crawled onto his face and his eyes lit up. "Kate, Paul." He repeated our names like they were the happiest words in the English language. I teared up and turned to see that Kate was crying. I touched his leg at the bottom of the bed. "How are you doing, Dad?"

"I've been better," he said, and cleared his throat. "Water?" he asked, and Debbie reached for a cup, helping my dad take a sip.

"You had us scared there."

"I was scared too," he said, attempting to sit up. He looked over at Debbie. "But my angel was there, looking out for me."

There was a shine in Debbie's eyes as she looked at my father.

"Any word from the doctor?" Kate asked.

"Not yet," Debbie said. "The nurse says she should be by soon."

"I'm sorry it was this that got you out here," my dad said, and coughed again, repositioning himself to get comfortable. "I would have preferred to show you around, rather than have you in this hospital with me."

"Stop," I told my dad. "There'll be plenty of time for that."

Now that we had arrived and I could see my father's face, a part of me felt relieved. At least the heart attack wasn't severe, I thought, heading out into the hallway to find another chair. At least he still looked like himself.

We spent the rest of the next hour making small talk, the

four of us in the same room for the first time in years. A few times, my dad would close his eyes as if wanting to go off to sleep, but then he would open them and try to sit up, forcing himself to stay awake. At some point, I began to get hungry and asked Kate if she wanted to go look for something to eat. We took the elevator down to the ground floor and found the hospital cafeteria, a small room called the Royal Bistro that smelled of burnt coffee. I ordered a ham sandwich, figuring it was a safe bet. As the volunteer behind the cash prepared my order, I stared blankly at the register.

When we returned to my dad's room, the doctor was there. "It will take another few days for your father to be stable," she repeated for our benefit. "But I can tell he is already doing much better." Turning to him, she added, "You're lucky the paramedics got to you when they did. Any longer along that trail and who knows how long it would've taken."

"No more biking," I said to my father. "At least, not for a while anyway."

We stayed with my dad while he ate his dinner, heading out afterwards to give him and Debbie privacy when he had to use the bathroom. As visiting hours drew to a close, we collected our things and kissed him goodnight, telling him we'd see him again in the morning.

In the elevator, I asked Kate if the hotel she had reserved was far.

"You're not staying at a hotel," Debbie said.

"Well, Debbie," Kate said. "We didn't want to impose."

"I won't hear of it," she said as the doors opened to the lobby. "We have many bedrooms. Your dad will be angry with me if I let you stay at a hotel."

We got into Debbie's car, and she drove us back to their place. Debbie seemed small behind the wheel of her large SUV, but she drove attentively and purposefully the entire way. It was getting dark out, the moon high in the sky. I hardly recognized the house as we pulled into the driveway. It seemed smaller than in the photos I had seen, a one-floor bungalow sandwiched between two duplexes. "How long have you lived here?" I asked.

Debbie turned off the ignition. "About thirty-five years." She opened the door and collected her purse and cell phone. "My husband and I bought it in 1977. My sister lived in it for a couple of years while I was in Montreal, but it's the same old place it's always been." We got out of the car with our bags and followed Debbie to the side door. She fished in her bag and pulled out another set of keys and opened the door. We followed her inside.

An overweight calico came running as Debbie flicked on the light switch. We were in her kitchen. "Hi, Frankie," she said, bending down to pet the cat, her purse in her hand. "Did you miss me?" Then, "Close the door behind you, will you? Frankie's not allowed outside." I reached over to pet Frankie, but he took one look at my hand and ran away. "He's skittish," she said, then handed me a tub of wet wipes, taking one for herself. "You're going to want to wash your hands."

I did what I was told and threw the wet napkin into the garbage by the door. Debbie walked further into the house, turning on lights as she went. Although the house had looked small from the outside, the inside was spacious with tall ceilings and large windows. Debbie's lights, however, must have been low wattage because they didn't illuminate much, small yellow bursts brightening up the crowded corners of her dark kitchen. I noticed a big living room with two couches off the hall, and to my right a set of stairs that led to the basement. "Are you hungry?" Debbie asked. Kate and I looked at each other and shook our heads. "Well, there's chicken salad in the fridge if you want. I'd stay up with you, but I'm too tired. It's been a bear of a day."

"That's okay," I said, and looked once more at Kate. "We're both zonked too."

Debbie opened a closet door and gave us both fresh towels, then led us through the hallway to the bedrooms. "Kate, you can have Sue's old room like last time; and Paul, you can take Patrick's at the end of the hall. The bathroom is here on the left. See you in the morning."

We said our goodnights and I gave Kate a quick hug and then rolled my suitcase to the end of the hall, plush towel in hand. Inside the room, I felt for the switch on the wall and turned it on, closing the door behind me. I got the sense that Patrick's room had not changed much since he had last lived here. The room was that of a young man's, posters of the Kelowna Rockets hockey team and Red Hot Chili Peppers above a single bed pushed against the wall. On his shelves, I spied old high school agendas from the nineties and textbooks from his time in university. Above his desk was a shelf of binders. I took one down and leafed through it; it was filled with rows of baseball cards, each one in its own plastic pocket.

I sat on the bed and turned on the table lamp. It too gave off a mild amber glow. I took out my phone to look at the time and saw that I had a text message from Michael. *Thinking of you*, it said. *Call me before you go to sleep.* I looked at the time. It was after 9 p.m., but then I remembered the time change. I took a chance Michael was up and called him, lying down on Patrick's bedspread.

"Hey, buddy."

"Hi, buddy. Did I wake you?"

"No," Michael said. "Just hanging in bed with the cats. How's your dad?"

I yawned. "Fine from the looks of it. Hooked up to a bunch of machines, but the doctor says he'll recover. They're going to keep him for a few more days. I'll stay until he's back home."

"He must be happy to see you."

"He is," I said. "It's good to be here. Good to be with Kate too. How you doing?"

"Can't complain. Went back to Danny's today, got work done. I'm going to miss you tonight," he added. "Bed feels awfully big."

"You'll never guess where I'm sleeping," I said. "Patrick's old bedroom."

"Really? What's it like?"

"Like a straight teenager's," I said, and looked around the room at its overstuffed features. "It's like a shrine to him. I mean, they could've turned this room into an office, or a spare room, once he moved out, but it has all these things from his youth. Posters. A catcher's mitt. I'm looking at the ceiling now and I think I can see those glow-in-the-dark stars and planets. I'm sure they're going to light up the moment I turn off the lights." I yawned again, the fatigue settling in as my body realized it was horizontal. "Listen buddy, I'm exhausted. It's been a long day. I think I'm going to go to bed."

"All right," Michael said, yawning in tandem. "Good-night. Pleasant dreams."

"Goodnight," I said, and switched off the light. The ceiling glowed. "Love you."

When I woke the next morning, I wasn't sure where I was. I had slept through the night, weighed down by Patrick's heavy blankets and dense pillows, but came around with the morning light as it spilled through the room's thin curtains. I tried to go back to sleep, my arm thrown across my eyes as I lay on my back, but I soon found myself staring once more at the walls of the room.

Through the closed door, I could hear the beginnings of the day, the running of water in the kitchen, the opening and closing of cabinet doors, the soft murmurs of my sister and Debbie in conversation. I checked the time, 6:10 a.m. Getting up, I reached for my jeans and pulled them over my underwear. I grabbed my shirt from the day before and smelled it to make sure it was fine before putting it on. I walked out barefoot into the kitchen; the room smelled of coffee and fried bacon.

"Good morning," I said.

"Good morning." Debbie was at the stove, cooking. "How do you like your eggs?"

I yawned and sat down at the kitchen table. "Whichever way you're making them."

"There's coffee," Debbie said, nodding toward the machine.

"Thanks, but I don't drink coffee."

"Have some juice, then."

Kate was in the pantry, looking for something. "I can't find the sugar."

"On the second shelf. In the red container."

I looked past my sister to see a row of sugary breakfast cereals on the top shelf. "Are those cereals my dad's?" I asked, zeroing in on them.

"He's like a kid with those things. Froot Loops, Cocoa Puffs, Frosted Flakes."

"He shouldn't be having sugar cereal," I said, getting up. "Not when he's prediabetic."

"You think your father listens to me?" Debbie said, as I passed behind her. "I've told him he shouldn't eat that junk."

I waited for my sister to come out of the pantry before I went in. I grabbed the five boxes I found and took them to the garbage by the door. "By all means, throw them out," Debbie said, happy to see them emptied into the trashcan. "Better you than me."

We ate our breakfast, and Kate and I took showers. We got dressed and drove back to the hospital. My dad was awake when we arrived. There seemed to be less equipment attached to him and more colour to his face. He was sitting up in bed, all smiles, and joking with one of the nurses. "That laugh," Debbie said. "I recognize that laugh."

"How are you feeling today, Dad?"

"Much better than yesterday, kitten." My father leaned over to receive a kiss from Kate. There was a third chair today, so we all sat down. Debbie handed over a bunch of newspapers and magazines to my father. He opened up the *Globe and Mail*. The first thing he took out was the crossword puzzle, and we all tried to help him with it. "Shakespearean king," my father said out loud. "Lear," he answered before any

343

of us had a chance to guess, and wrote it onto the newsprint.

"You're supposed to tell us how many letters," I said.

"Senate's counterpart, five letters," he said.

"House," Kate answered.

We got the easy clues quickly and struggled with the harder ones for longer than it was fun. After lunch, Patrick came to visit—rugged and handsome—with his equally attractive girlfriend, Denise. I stood to greet them, shook his hand, and with an odd sense of intimacy revealed that I'd slept in his old bed the night before. His sister, Sue, arrived within the hour, by herself and seven months pregnant. "Neil sends his regrets," she spoke of her husband. "He had to work."

Once Sue sat down, the conversation turned to her pregnancy, her latest cravings, how her feet had started to swell and how itchy her skin had become. She kept touching her belly, drawing attention to the soon-to-be newest member of the family. Her baby bump seemed small for seven months. At one point, Sue used the word "he" to describe the baby.

"He?" I asked. "So, it's a boy?"

"Yes," Sue said, her hand once again dropping to her midsection. "Little Ethan."

"That's wonderful," I said. "Congratulations!"

"It's a great name too. Ethan," Kate said, trying it out.

"It was Neil's father's name," Sue said.

We were a noisy crowd now. Eight in one room, if you counted the man in the other bed behind his own curtain. I waited for Sue (or Patrick, or my dad) to ask about Wendy and Eve and their pregnancy. Didn't anyone want to know how Wendy was doing? Maybe Sue might have advice for her, being further along. I considered saying something but felt mute and immobile standing there. A part of me wanted to see how long this could go on before it came up, but then, as Sue got up to leave with Patrick and Denise, I realized that maybe they didn't know. Maybe my dad hadn't told them.

That evening, we went back to the house and I made the three of us dinner. Debbie sat at the kitchen table knitting while Kate enjoyed a glass of red wine, alternating between answering work emails and checking for flights back home. "I think I'm going to stay an extra few days," I said. "If that's okay with you, Debbie. I'd like to wait at least until he's home."

"Up to you," she said, creating a tight stitch. "But please don't stay on my account. I know you have work to do. Your father and I will be fine."

Looking at the two of them, busy at the kitchen table, I realized that Kate and I had never spent any real time alone with our dad's wife. It felt strange to think of her as that— our stepmother. Surprisingly, she hadn't said anything off-putting so far, which, to be honest, I was afraid she would. And it didn't feel uncomfortable having to make small talk during these shapeless hours between visits. Standing at the stove, frying onions, I wondered if this was what life was like for my dad here in this house. One dutifully making dinner, while the other sat quietly at the kitchen table. I also had a similar flash later that night as I sat in what I presumed to be my father's recliner and watched television. The living room was as crowded as Patrick's room and, like the rest of the house, didn't feel like my father—not in the colours of the walls, the style of the furniture or the shape of the knick-knacks. All I recognized were the size of his feet in the pair of slippers by his chair and a row of hardback mystery novels on a bookshelf, some of which I remembered from our old home in Pointe-Claire.

The following day, we went back to the hospital. My dad seemed joyful, sitting in bed like he might have done when we were kids and we'd bring him breakfast on Father's Day. "The doctor came by this morning and told me she thinks I can go home tomorrow."

"That's great," I said.

"Wonderful news," Debbie said.

Kate came to the side of the bed and half-sat on it. "I wish I could be here for that, but I have to head back tomorrow morning. There's an important sales conference in Toronto I can't miss."

"I understand," my dad said, grabbing her hand. He looked at me. "You too, Son. I know you both lead busy lives, and Michael must be missing you. It has been great to see you both. Hopefully, you'll come back again soon so we can show you around."

"Why don't you two go visit downtown?" Debbie said, before I could respond. "I'd hate for you to look back on Kelowna and only think of the hospital. Here, take my keys." She was already handing them to Kate.

"You've got to be bored," my dad said. "Go for a couple of hours. Before your sister has to leave."

I looked to Kate; the two of us shrugged then got up to give our dad a quick hug before heading to the elevators.

We got into Debbie's SUV and drove to the city centre, using the maps on Kate's phone as a guide. Downtown was

346

five minutes away. We parked the car on what looked like a busy street and walked along the strip, ducking into any shops that caught our eye. I ended up buying Michael a book about BMW cars I thought he might like and then, in another store, I picked up another baby gift for Wendy and Eve. It was a soft white plastic teether in the shape of a giraffe named Sophie. Sophie was French, it appeared from the Eiffel Tower in the background on the box.

At some point we got hungry and began to check the menus of the restaurants along our path. We ended up on Abbott Street in front of a place called the West Coast Grill and Oyster Bar and decided to try it. Our waiter came and we ordered two club sandwiches and two iced teas. While we waited for our food, I took out my bag and removed Sophie, taking a picture of the toy and sending it to Michael.

"It's adorable," Kate said, looking the box over. "They're going to love it."

"I hope so. Wendy tells me they've decided not to spoil the kid with toys, and they don't want things that are too gendered. But I think this is okay, no? I don't think Sophie the giraffe is going to impose any gender roles on their baby."

"It might make the kid curious about Paris." She handed it back. "Who knew there were French giraffes?"

A text message came in from Michael: *Cute!* it read.

"Kate, did Dad tell you that Sue and Neil are having a boy?"

She nodded. "About a week ago. I called him with a question about my taxes."

"He didn't tell me," I said. "And I don't think Dad told them either."

"Told them what?"

"About Wendy and Eve. About me being their donor. Or if he did, they didn't say anything. I kept waiting for someone to mention it. Waiting for Patrick or Sue or Debbie to ask how things were going, but none of them did."

"Of course, he told them," she said. "Why wouldn't he have?"

I shrugged. "Maybe they're homophobic. You saw how many churches this town has."

"Patrick and Sue aren't homophobic," Kate said, as if I were crazy. "But if it makes you feel any better, they didn't mention Ben either. Dad never brings him up."

I felt guilty that I, too, hadn't asked about Ben in a while. "How is Ben?"

"He's okay," she said. "He wanted to come out here with me, but I said no. I think that would've been too much." She stopped talking while our waiter set down our iced teas.

"Have you found a place yet?"

"No," she said. "I've stopped looking."

"What? Why? I thought you wanted a bigger place."

"I do. It's just… I don't think I want Ben to move out with me. I don't know if I'm going to stay in Montreal much longer."

I was crushed. I loved having my sister close. "But, where would you go?"

"Toronto," she said. "I can do my job anywhere. And I have friends there. It's time for a change and Toronto's got a lot going for it."

"It does, but… What about Ben? I thought, you know…'

"Come on," Kate said. "You never saw us together long-term. Also, I feel like I'm falling into the same domestic

348

pattern again, just with someone else. I catch myself being quietly upset, or leaving things unsaid. I think I need to take some time and figure myself out before committing to someone else again."

I shrugged. "I didn't want to say anything about that night we came for dinner, but it was awkward." Still, I felt sorry for the guy. "It's too bad, I've actually grown to like him." That got her to laugh, and I laughed too. "I know, I know," I said. "But he's a decent guy. He's handsome, talented, caring. He's got a good job, an okay sense of humour."

She continued to be amused. "I don't freaking believe you," she said, sipping her drink. "You hated him. I didn't want to hear it, and you were right."

"I didn't hate him."

"Yes, you did."

"Well, he's grown on me. But I can see how after Chris, settling down with Ben could end up feeling like more of the same."

"Thanks, brother," she said.

"Oh my god," I said, thinking about it. "He's going to be devastated."

"He'll be fine," she said. "We all will… What about you? How's Wendy?"

I didn't feel like getting into everything that Wendy had recently told me, about how she was internalizing her feelings about what we were doing. I knew it might breathe some life back into any doubt Kate kept hidden from me. "Things are good," I said. "The baby's growing nicely—god, that makes it sound like a houseplant. To be honest, it still feels unreal, theoretical. Maybe it wouldn't if I saw them more regularly."

The waiter came by with our dishes.

"So, what do you think of the house? It's weird staying in Dad's home, isn't it?" Kate asked, adding ketchup to her fries. "Especially with Debbie there."

"I'm glad you said that." I grabbed a square of my sandwich. "I keep having these flashes of what it was like for Patrick and Sue to grow up in such a normal house."

"I don't know how normal it was," Kate said. "I mean, they do have Debbie for a mother."

"Be nice," I said. "Debbie's been nothing but great since we got here. What's crazy to think about, though—when I look at Patrick's old stuff and how the house is decorated— is that Dad lives there too! It's weird. It's like we're in an alternate universe. Does Dad ever feel like a stranger to you?"

Kate thought about it. "I don't know if he feels like a stranger," she said. "But it does feel like he's got a whole other life, a different life than the one we know."

"Sometimes I don't recognize him. I wonder if he feels that way about us."

Kate didn't respond, just took another bite of her sandwich and looked at the television above us, which was playing a tennis match. "Sometimes, I wonder if there's an alternate universe version of me out there," she said. "One of me as a mother. I wonder what that would've been like, what kind of mother I would have been."

"I think you'd have been a great mother," I said.

"How do you know that?"

I thought about it. "You babysat me once."

"That doesn't count. We were kids," she said. "I never had to take care of someone else's child as a teenager or an adult."

350

Kate played around with her fries. "I wonder if I would have been a tough mom. Or would I have been a pushover? Or if I had a daughter, would we have fought all the time? If she was like me, would I have celebrated that? Or would I have tried to rein her in, knowing what I know now?"

"You weren't that much trouble."

"Oh yes I was. Remember the time Mom and Dad had to come get me after Annie's party? I wasn't at Annie's place. I was at the police station."

"What?"

Kate laughed while she chewed. "I never told you this, but Annie and I got picked up for drinking in the park. Mom didn't want me to tell you, so I didn't."

"I can't believe you've kept that from me all these years."

"I know if I had a daughter, she'd be just like me."

"And if you had a son?"

Kate thought for a second. "He'd probably be like you. I hate to admit it, but I'd go easier on a son. Turn him into a complete momma's boy. What about you?" Kate asked. "Have you ever thought about what kind of dad you'd be?"

"Kate," I grumbled. "I told you, I'm not going to be a dad."

"Not this situation. If you were to have kids of your own."

"I don't know," I said. It was like trying to imagine what Wendy and Eve's child would be like, a form without a face. A Paul I didn't recognize. "In this situation, is Michael in the picture?"

"Yes, sure, why wouldn't he be in the picture?"

"Well, if Michael were in the picture—and remember we're being hypothetical here—if Michael and I had kids, I think *he'd* be the better parent. Maybe not if we had kids at the beginning of our relationship. But now, definitely. He'd be the tough one, making sure the homework was done and the chores were completed, teaching them how to work with their hands, sending them to bed without dessert if they misbehaved. I'd be the pushover, sneaking pie to them upstairs afterwards."

"You have a second floor in this hypothetical situation?"

I smiled. "And a garage. I'd be the one letting them stay up late at night and eat too much Halloween candy."

"And if Michael wasn't in the picture?"

I thought about that for a moment. "I don't know what kind of father I would be then," I said. "I don't know who that person is."

After we ate, Kate and I walked back to the car and returned to the hospital; then, at the end of the afternoon, we said our goodbyes and Kate gave our dad a tearful hug and kiss, as she would be heading home in the morning.

The next day, we all got up early and Debbie and I dropped Kate off at the airport before heading to the hospital to pick up my dad. The tubes had all been removed and he was eager to leave, dressed up in the clothes Debbie had brought him the day before. All of his personal items were collected in a bag on the stand next to the bed. "I have to wait for the duty nurse to discharge me." He sounded anxious. "I also have to sign some papers. Apparently, I can't leave on my own. They have to wheel me out the door."

"I think that's the law," I said.

"Have you seen the nurse?" Debbie asked.

"No, not yet."

"Well, this is ridiculous." And with that, Debbie left the room.

I sat down in one of the chairs. My dad seemed nervous, flustered. "It's okay, Dad," I said. "We'll be out of here soon."

My dad caught himself and smiled. He got up from where he was sitting on the side of the bed and came over to sit in the chair beside me. "Thanks for coming, Son," he said and patted my knee. "I know she won't say anything, but I'm sure Debbie was happy to have you at the house. Made it feel less empty. In any event, it made me relax knowing you were there with her."

"It was my pleasure, Dad," I said. "You're not going to be happy, but I threw out your cereal."

He smiled through his teeth, embarrassed. "I do have to start eating better."

"That's some house, though. It's nice. But I have to say it doesn't seem like you. Don't take this the wrong way. I suppose I had a vision of your life here with Debbie, and the reality is much different. It's like an alternate version of what life was like for us, with Mom, in Montreal. I guess, that's why sometimes it's still a shock to see Debbie."

My dad raised his eyebrows and looked down at the floor. "I wish you guys would give her a chance. We've been together for twelve years, you know? She loves you, and she's great to me. To Patrick and Sue. She sure raised those kids right."

I listened for the hallway. "Dad," I said. "Did you tell Patrick and Sue about Wendy?"

"What about Wendy?"

"About what we're doing?"

"Yes, I told them."

I hadn't expected that answer. "Oh, it's just… neither of them mentioned anything to me."

"Well, there's a lot going on at the moment," he said. "With my heart attack and Sue's own pregnancy."

I got up and walked over to the window. I needed to stand up for this. I needed to be not so close. "You haven't said anything either," I said. "I don't think you've said a word since I told you over a month ago."

"Well, I don't always know what to say, Paul. It's a lot to take in. I mean… I think, if it's what you want to do with your life, I'm not going to stop you."

"But you don't approve."

My dad opened his mouth, as if to say something, and looked at the ceiling. "I don't know, Son. It's not what I would have chosen for you. Maybe it would be different if this was going to be your child, but it's not. You're giving over your rights to Wendy and Eve. The kid won't have our last name and you're not going to be the father, but you want us to be grandparents?"

"If you wanted—"

"How can we be grandparents if you're not the father? This is just, too much right now… I don't know, Paul. I've let you do what you want with your life. I made the decision years ago to not interfere, because I wanted you to be happy. But I worry you're going to regret this. That this is going to come back and bite you in the ass."

"I'm not going to get hurt, Dad."

I leaned back against the bottom rail of the window.

was hurt. For a moment, I looked outside and watched as a couple below took a newborn out of the front doors of the hospital to a car across the parking lot.

"You're going to fall in love with that kid," he said. "Fall in love with it the way I fell in love with you, and what will you do then?"

I didn't want to argue, but I felt the need to say something, anything, to defend my choice. "You know, this is a great opportunity, one that doesn't come around often for people like me. I need you to accept what I want to do with my life."

My father sighed and rubbed his hands across his legs. "Paul," he said. "It's not just a one-way street. If you want me to be more a part of your life, then you have to be more a part of mine."

"What's that supposed to mean?"

"It means you have to stop being so selfish." My dad wasn't angry, but he was speaking plainly. "I've asked you to come visit me for years—years—and you never have until now. I asked you to come to Sue and Neil's wedding, to try to get to know them better, but you didn't, you don't—and I never say a word. I know how you think of Debbie too. But I'm not asking you to think of her as your mother, only as my wife. Son… sometimes it feels like your friends are more of a priority to you than me, or our family."

"I… Well, my friends are family to me," I said. "That doesn't mean they're *more* important. But they are important."

"Still, I wish you would try harder sometimes… I was scared, you know," he said, a quiver in his voice that quickly disappeared. "I was scared I was never going to see you again. Scared that this might be how we leave things—you finally coming to Kelowna, but for a funeral. Finally getting to see what my life is like, but I'm no longer here."

The thought was chilling, and I saw what my father saw: me walking through the dark rooms of his house for the first time, meeting his friends and Debbie's extended family as we gathered in some church basement to say our goodbyes. "I'm sorry, Dad," I said. "I'm glad that didn't happen either. But I don't always feel like a part of *this* family, a part of your life here. I don't feel like I measure up."

My dad's vulnerability was gone. "Well, that's ridiculous," he said, almost upset.

"But it's true. Why don't you ask me how Wendy's doing? Why doesn't Debbie want to knit something for us too? I know the way I live my life is very different from yours. I know you don't think of Michael and me the same way you think of Sue and Patrick and their partners, or even Kate when she was with Chris. Sure, you think of Michael as my *friend*, but not my partner, not someone I'm building a life with."

My dad was annoyed now. "Now, that's not fair," he said. "Why would you say that? I adore Michael. I'm glad you have each other. But would I feel closer to him if you came to visit? Yes! I'd actually *get to see him* on a regular basis for chrissakes. But if you don't feel like I'm more a part of your life, Paul— that I'm not up to date on all the ins and outs of what's going on—well, that's on you."

"Me?"

"You pushed me out, Son. When your mother died, you just shut down. You went upstairs and closed the door to your room and never let me in again. I never knew why. Was

356

it something I did? I wondered. Did I say something wrong? I tried to stay connected to you, but I wanted to give you your space. I knew there was a lot going on inside of you. And so, I gave you time. I waited for that door to open back up, but it never did."

It was true. I had pushed my father away. I thought back to those days when I just wanted to be left alone, or run away somewhere deep in the city, reverse course on the path that had been laid out for me. But that was a long time ago. I had been a kid then.

I was about to say something, but my dad spoke first. "When your friend Alan died, I was there," he said, hands at his knees. "And even though I never met him, I knew he was important to you. I went to his funeral." Immediately, I was brought back to the reception at Charles's place, my worlds colliding as my dad stood in a corner and Kate introduced him to everyone I knew. "I couldn't believe how many people were there, all these strangers who seemed to know you so well, who would come up to you and hold you and cry and offer condolences that felt way more meaningful than the ones I could ever give you. How could my son have all these friends and I not know any of them? And this man you were mourning, too—who seemed to hold such an important and special place in your life—how come I never got to meet him? I envied him, you know. What I wouldn't have given to have had that kind of impact on your life."

My dad looked exhausted. He had been out of his bed only minutes, but the conversation had tired him. "Paul," he said. "I accept that your life is different. It doesn't mean I love you any less. But you have to accept that mine is different too. I couldn't wait for you to come back to me. I had to find happiness again and get on with my life. But that never meant I didn't want you to be a part of it."

I heard the swish of scrubs coming down the hallway, and the duty nurse came into the room, followed by Debbie. "Okay, Mister Marino," he said. "You are free to go. I just need you to sign some forms and then we can get you out of here."

I sat there in silence and watched as we took the next few minutes for my dad to sign the forms he was given and receive instructions about his medication. An orderly soon arrived with a wheelchair and my dad got in. "Now, don't accidentally bring me down to the morgue," he joked. Debbie and I collected his things and we headed down in the elevator, the moment between us long gone. The two of them waited by the door as I pulled around Debbie's car. When we got home, Frankie came out to see him. "Hello, Frankie," my dad said as the cat came running.

"There he is," I said. "I think he hid the entire time I was here."

Suddenly, it didn't seem strange to see my dad in this house, walking through the rooms like he had undoubtedly done hundreds of times before, knowing where everything was. Not five minutes home, he went to the closet in the hallway and took out a towel. "First thing I want is a nice hot shower," he said. He closed the door behind him and I heard the water start up.

I looked at the clock on the wall, then went into the pantry to find something to make us for lunch. I took out a can of pea soup and placed it on the counter, getting out a pot from the cabinet underneath. I took out a tomato from inside the fridge and got a loaf of bread from the hanging wire basket next to the stove.

"Paul," Debbie said. "You're going to have to go easy on your dad."

I looked at her puzzled.

"The doctor said he can't get worked up," she continued. "Can't get angry. I know you can feel impatient with him at times, I do too. But he's an old man now. Stuck in his ways. You're going to have to be easy with him from now on. We all are."

I sighed, and didn't say anything. Just began to open up the tin with a can opener.

"Paul, what are you doing?" Debbie asked.

"I'm making lunch."

"No, what are you doing here? Your dad's back home now. You should go home, too." She looked at me, pleadingly. "Go back to your life. To Michael. I can take care of your father now."

19

"ARE YOU GOING TO BE out late?" I asked Michael. He was getting dressed in front of the mirror. Jean shorts, black mesh top, white runners.

"I don't know. But I don't want you to worry."

"I won't."

"Liar," he said. "How do I look?"

"Handsome. What's the name of the party again?"

"Dress You Up!" Gus had invited Michael to a loft party in HOMA. I was also invited, but had declined. It sounded like fun—eighties fashions, drag queens, nothing but Madonna—but it also sounded exhausting and the last thing I wanted was to go all the way to HOMA for a loud party.

"Why are you heading out so early?"

"Gus is having people over beforehand. We're going to order pizza and paint our nails. What will you do tonight? Watch one of your sad movies?"

"Maybe," I said. Michael hated sad films, so it was rare that we watched any together. I had a collection of films on DVD and VHS from when I was younger that I would unearth every couple of years. Queer films like *Parting Glances* or *Jeffrey* or *Torch Song Trilogy*. Michael never wanted to watch them. They were too tragic, he said, and he didn't want to watch movies where people died. "I might do that. Make dinner. Watch a movie. Enjoy a bottle of wine. You sure you're going to come home tonight? You don't want to sleep at Gus's place?"

"No, I don't think so. I mean, if I'm going to go all the way back to his place then I might as well come home. Besides, he'll most probably be bringing someone else home."

"Okay," I said. "Have fun. Text if you're bored."

Michael grabbed his wallet, phone and keys and gave me a kiss. He gave Malone a quick pat on the butt as he headed out the door.

With Michael gone, I didn't know what to do. I thought about watching a movie, but before I knew it, I had sat down at my computer and begun looking up recipes. Then, pretty soon, I was surfing Tumblr with my dick in my hand. The whole session was over quickly with no one but me to arouse. Once I was done, I closed the browser, revealing the tilapia recipe I had just searched in a window behind it. I no longer felt like cooking, so I grabbed the phone and ordered dinner: number four for two with extra naan. This way, I figured, Michael could also have something to eat if he was hungry when he got in.

Outside the window, an ambulance shot down Saint Denis Street. In its wake, I realized how quiet our home was. I walked over to the bar in the kitchen and found a cheap bottle of Merlot. I uncorked it and poured myself a glass. I then went back to my computer to wait for my meal.

I decided to see if there were any old films I used to love on YouTube that I didn't have on DVD. I found the full version of *Love! Valour! Compassion!*, which I watched for ten minutes. Then I found eight-minute clips from *Trick* and

Beautiful Thing. By the time my meal came, I was one-third through the bottle and feeling nostalgic. I kept watching as I ate, the Internet presenting me with an endless list of things I might like in the right rail. I followed it all the way down the rabbit hole, landing on *Longtime Companion*.

I could only watch the beginning of the movie any more, but I loved how it opened with scenes of the characters starting their day to the tune of Blondie's "The Tide Is High": the drowsy couple waking up in their underwear and getting ready for work; Campbell Scott jogging along the shore before running bare-assed into the water and passing by his crush, Fuzzy, on the boardwalk; Fuzzy then taking his groceries and the newspaper up to the rooftop patio of his friends' home on Fire Island. The Fire Island scenes got me excited about our upcoming trip to Provincetown. It seemed that somehow my life wasn't that different from this slice of gay life. We've been doing this a long time, I thought, watching the men flirt and drink and dance outdoors at tea dance. When was this movie made, again?

I opened up another window and consulted the film's IMDb page: 1989. Four years before I came out, when I was eighteen and still in CEGEP. It was remarkable to think that all this was going on before I was out, before I had any real friends. And although it had been a dangerous time, and all the people in the movie would lose half of those they loved, I found myself wishing that I could have been there to fight alongside them. To have been at the real-life pivotal events I had only heard about—the Sex Garage arrests and the International AIDS Conference in Montreal.

But I had to shut the movie off around thirty minutes

in, when the first of the friends was about to die. Usually, I would watch these films from beginning to end and have a good cry, but I didn't want to cry tonight.

Tired, I decided to go to bed early. Brushing my teeth, I checked my phone for messages. There were none from Michael. He must be having a good time. *Goodnight,* I texted him as I got into bed. No response. I turned out the light and fell asleep. About an hour later, I woke up and checked again. No message. I tried to go back to sleep, but it was difficult. I floated in and out as the time on the nightstand moved forward in chunks.

At 3:40 a.m., I heard the downstairs door open and someone come up. The door to our home unlocked and opened, and I could hear one of the cats jumping down from the couch to run towards the door. "Shhh," I heard Michael say. I heard the creak of the floor as he peered into the room. I lay there with my eyes closed, not letting him know I was awake. He went into the bathroom. I could hear the shower rush on.

With Michael home, I could finally relax. Before nodding off, I had a thought. Had this been what it was like for my dad, when I was living at home and staying out late? Had he also lain awake at night, tossing and turning as the clock ticked forward, waiting for the moment he knew I was safely home?

The next morning, I got up and went for a run. I had made myself a promise on the flight home from Kelowna that I would start running again. It was a difficult run, and I couldn't finish, but then the following day I did a shorter one, which led to a longer one two days later. Within two weeks, I was back into it, running every second morning before work. Soon, my energy levels were up: I was eating better, spending more time in the bedroom with Michael. All I wanted to do after work was come home to him and our cats. Danny kept trying to get me to come watch him and Vince play soccer, now that the season had started, but I'd always find an excuse to say no. I just wanted to lie on the couch and read, nuzzled next to Michael while he drew.

Michael had begun to include a lion character in his sketches. In one, Malone and the lion were checking each other out in a bookstore. In another, the two were at a cottage, swimming in a lake. The lion had a thick mane, a prominent moustache, short shorts, and combat boots, just like Leo.

During the second week of June, I got a text from Wendy: IT'S A GIRL!

I had no idea this news was coming. I was at work and jumped into a private conference room to call her up. "We had an ultrasound today," Wendy said after she answered, excited. "And it's clearly a girl. We saw her organs—they're perfect—and she has a strong heart. We saw all four valves, big and open and pumping. I wish I had thought to take a video to show you, but I only took photos. Here, I'll send you some." Within seconds, in popped a series of images, all black and white, spooky medical scans of the child all balled up in a blob.

"She has your eyes," Danny joked, when I sent him the images. Kate was also ecstatic when I called. "A girl!" she almost screamed into the phone. "Oh my god, I'm going to have a niece!" It finally felt real.

I decided not to wait to tell my dad and phoned him right after.

"Congratulations, Son," he said. He sounded happy for me, as far as I could tell. "That's great news. Have they chosen a name?"

"No, they haven't," I said. Wendy and Eve still hadn't shared any names they were considering with me. "But I'll let you know as soon as they know," I told my father. "How's Sue?"

"She's fine," he said. "Entering her last month, so there's a lot of excitement. It's been an emotional time for her and Debbie. Still lots to do and plan. They had me over the other day to help Neil baby-proof the place. Apparently, he's useless when it comes to this. Debbie keeps cooking up a storm. She bought the two of them a deep freezer for their basement and is filling it with frozen meals that Neil can take out and heat up for them when it's time. But I really don't know why. Debbie will be over there all the time."

It was exciting to hear my father talk about their plans. I suddenly wished that Wendy and Eve lived in the same city as me. Toronto wasn't far, but it wasn't close either. You couldn't go for the day. How fun would it be, I thought, to be able to help Wendy and Eve in the same way. Cook for them, clean for them, spend time with the baby while they caught up on sleep.

A few days later, a letter arrived for Michael with no return address.

"Michael, you got mail here," I said, coming through the door.

He was in our room, getting ready for his afternoon shift. I handed the letter over. "It's from my dad," he said.

"How do you know?"

"I recognize the handwriting." Suddenly, Michael's face was a cloud of stress and disappointment. "I can't read this now. I've got to go to work." Michael left in a huff, forgetting his phone on the dresser.

The letter remained unopened on the table in the hallway for the next few days. Every time I came home, I saw it there, asking me to open it. Wasn't he curious about what it said? How could he let it sit there and not read it? A couple of days later a call came from his mom. "No, I haven't read it yet," I overheard him tell her. "I don't know when." Michael was silent for the rest of the night.

That Sunday was Father's Day, and I returned from a run that morning to find the letter open on the kitchen island, its contents visible. I picked it up and I read it.

Michael, the note said. *I'm writing to apologize. Your mom made me realize how tough I was on you, on all your brothers, over the years. I want you to know that I only wanted the best for you, to toughen you up because I figured you'd be in for a rough ride. The world is a very different place now than when I was a boy. Still, I'm sorry. I should've gone easier on you and your brothers, but my dad was tough on me too! I don't blame you if you're mad, or angry or fed up. And I'm sorry if I failed you. But please be nice to me for your mother's sake. I'm trying real hard with her. I'm trying to be a better man. I'm taking anger management classes and we go out on dates. She's much happier now, and I promise to not take advantage of her and to treat her well. But she'd be happier if you were also happy. If you could forgive me for being so hard. So please call her, Son. I do love you.*

I put down the letter and went to find Michael. He wa

in the office, in the T-shirt he had slept in and a pair of boxer shorts, watching an old episode of *Roseanne* on his computer. "I don't feel like working today," he said, as I walked in. "I called in sick." I climbed in and watched an episode with him. "I used to love this show," he said. "They were poor and fought all the time, but there was so much love and fun in that house. I wish I grew up in that house."

That evening, we went out for drinks with Danny and Vince. The bar was throwing its own "Father's Day" bash with video screens playing *Mamma Mia!* and the bartenders all topless except for open Windsor knot ties around their necks. George was behind the bar and Michael got silly, flirting with him big time. It was all "Dad" this and "Dad" that, and it was getting on my nerves.

"Why do you insist on calling him that?" I asked.

Michael stopped smiling. "Because if I call him my dad, it means that maybe I don't have the other one. Maybe if I can imagine someone like George as my father, then everything is all right with the world." Michael got up and went to burn off steam with a game of pool. Vince followed.

Danny hung back with me and we watched as our men racked up the balls and chose their cues. All I wanted was peace for Michael.

"Don't they look good?" Danny asked. "Playing billiards together? Who would have thought, this time last year, that the two of us would be here a year later, out on a date with our men—them playing a game, while we gab by the bar?"

It didn't seem that surprising to me, but I could understand how it could be for Danny. Before Vince, I don't think the two of us had ever dated someone at the same time.

"See that flash of skin?" Danny asked. Vince had just leaned over the pool table to take a shot, his shirt falling away to reveal a line of flesh at his midsection. "That's my favourite part on him. Well, one of my favourites. I swear I'd follow that line anywhere."

"I take it things are good between you two."

"Good? I'm thinking of proposing," Danny said.

"Proposing what?"

"Marriage, silly. I'm thinking I might do it when we're in Provincetown. You know, the sky, the sea, the sand. I'll take Vince off on a bike ride to Race Point and stop on one of those sandy hills among the trees. Or maybe take a walk along the shore late at night with all the boats rocking and the moon overhead. Don't you think it'll be romantic?"

"Yes, it sounds romantic, Danny. But it's soon, no? I mean, you guys have known each other, what, less than a year? And you just got back together after being apart for months. You've had skin tags longer."

"I'll burn them off before my wedding night," he said. "Next month will make it a year since we met, and even if we were apart for three months, I know we were in love with each other all that time. Life is too fucking short," he said, with a sober heaviness. "My parents were not that much older than me when they died. I don't see the point in waiting any longer for what I know I want."

In the distance, Vince made a noise and winced. He seemed to have scratched, sinking the eight ball in the corner pocket. I could read the magnanimous condolences on Michael's lips as he smiled and offered another game. "I love him, Paul," Danny said. "I want to be with him every day

And I'm getting older too. I don't want to be left alone in my forties."

"That's not a reason to marry someone."

"Isn't it? I have this well of love within me. I can't help it. It's there, and it's always been gushing. All of my life. A big oil spill that can't be capped. And it's never had anywhere to go. It's always been wasted, spilled upon the shore and no one has ever come to collect it."

"That's an odd metaphor."

"But then Vince came along. Vince lets me love him. He lets the pounding waves of my affection wash over him and he never makes me feel bad about it, the way many of the others did: *Whoa, slow down there, boy. What do you mean today was like a Mariah Carey song? You think you're falling in love with me?* I've waited for a man like him my entire life and I don't want to lose him."

"Well, then, I'm happy for you," I said. "I think it's wonderful you feel that way. I'm sorry, if I sound sceptical. I just want the best for you. I love Vince too. He's a great guy. I hope you two will have a wonderful life together."

"Well, he has to say yes first."

20

In August, we left for Provincetown. We packed up Darlene and drove her down, the four of us: Michael, Danny, Vince and me. Charles came in the car belonging to the new young man he was seeing, a history student named Harry who none of us had met. Harry was a late addition to the trip, Charles having texted me the week before to ask how much the rental would be if we split it six ways instead of five. Part of me wanted to discourage him from bringing along someone at the last minute who we didn't know, but the appeal of saving some money overrode my apprehension. Danny acted unfazed, but I could tell that he was distracted about this wild card, another young man to distract Vince.

Once we arrived at our rental, we unpacked the car and entered through the back of the house. Charles and Harry had already arrived and had claimed a room at the top of the stairs. The place looked the same, although I noticed changes in the backyard. The owner had restained the deck and had purchased new patio chairs. There was also a brand-new gas barbecue and the flower garden had been pruned back. "It's gone," I heard Michael say, checking for the earring on the water spigot he had left again the previous year. He sounded puzzled. "I can't believe it's gone."

Inside, Danny made mojitos while everyone got settled. Michael got out the stereo and placed it close to the back patio, connecting his phone to the jack. He had recently discovered Patsy Cline and put on one of her albums, grabbing me to slow dance with him on the deck. Danny recognized the opening to "Stop the World (And Let Me Off)," and clutched at his heart, feigning a mortal wound. "Oh, Michael," he swooned, delighted by the selection, "you sure know how to make your mother proud."

It was agreed we would have one quick drink, then pick up our bikes before hightailing it to the Boatslip for the last hour of tea. I freshened up, changing into a pair of jean shorts and my "Super Dad" shirt. Michael grabbed his sailor hat and pearls from his tickle trunk.

The trip down had been grey and rainy, but the tip of the Cape had been spared and we were treated to the beginnings of a clear sunset as we rode our bikes to the bar. Skipping the dance floor, Michael walked right up to the railing overlooking the bay. Staring at the horizon, he wiped tears from his face with his palm. "I didn't realize how much I missed this," he said. I put my hand on his shoulder.

Harry was slack-jawed, staring at the surrounding beauty. I was surprised at how different he was from the boys Charles usually dated. First, Harry was older than most, pushing thirty from what I understood; he was lanky too, with soft features, sandy-brown hair and a conservative dress of chino shorts and a polo shirt. He seemed more together than Mark, the NTS student that Charles had briefly dated, and grateful that he'd been asked along for the trip.

"Like the view?" I asked.

"It's spectacular," he said, mouth agape. "Like gay heaven."

I asked someone nearby if he could take our picture and handed him my phone. The six of us lined up against the railing and its rippling rainbow flags and beamed as the shot was taken. Retrieving my phone, I looked through the snaps and posted the best one on Facebook. *These beaches!* I wrote as a status update. *Brace yourselves, P-Town! We've arrived!* Danny and I walked to the bar to order cocktails, and it was here where the memory of all our previous trips hit me—the smell of the bar mat drenched in the spill of sweet well drinks. Danny and I ordered six punches and brought them back to our group. We toasted them by the water.

Soon after, Leo arrived, unmistakable as he walked through the crowd. He still showcased the solid arms and thick legs that I remembered, but there were subtle additions to his appearance: longer hair and a full-grown beard. I also noticed a new tattoo of a crown on his right hand as he grabbed Michael from behind and lifted him in a joyful squeal. The two hugged as Leo placed him down, grabbing at me with a free hand to pull me into the embrace.

Tea dance ended soon after, and Leo invited us all to his friend Nick's house for a barbecue. We walked our bikes up Pleasant Street to the cedar-shake home where we found a dozen men laughing and drinking and eating outdoors in Nick's backyard. We were quickly introduced to everyone and entered into a half-dozen conversations. I met a writer from the West Coast whose new book had just been reviewed by *The New York Times,* and an architect with a loud voice who had spent the last six months renovating a penthouse in Dallas. Danny had them all laughing right away, hijacking the conversation as the hostages howled in drunken glee next to me. In the corner of my eye, I watched as Michael and Leo caught up by the garden, joking and jostling with each other like puppies at the park.

Night fell, and soon we stumbled out into the street and hit up the Porchside Lounge at nearby Gifford House, crowded with smoking or drinking bodies hanging off the building's wraparound railing. Inside, at the piano, a slim bearded man led a room full of revellers in a sing-along to "Suddenly Seymour." Like a mother running for the bus with her child in tow, Danny dragged Vince into the room with him, singing at the top of his lungs; Charles and Harry close behind. Leo, Michael and I, however, held back on the porch, watching the action through the doorway. There was a quiet moment while we stood there, the three of us, alone for the first time since we had arrived.

"Want to get out of here?" Leo asked.

We headed back down the stairs. I looked over my shoulder to see if I could catch my friends, but I had already lost them to the night. Underneath the porch bar, we unlocked our bikes and rode them down Commercial. At MacMillan Pier, Leo took a hard right and we followed him, zipping over the promenade's wooden slats towards the end of the wharf. There we got off our bikes by the water and watched the night sky. It was clear out, the moon shimmering in tiny ripples on the bay. In the distance, a blinking red dot signalled the location of the Long Point Lighthouse. The three of us went quiet, listening to the sounds of the rocking boats, the muffled pop carried on the wind from the bars along Commercial. Leo sat beside me. He was close, his knee pressing into mine. I looked back at him, a playful smile on his young bearded face. Leo reached across my back to grab my shoulder and pull me towards him where I landed in a kiss, as deep and mesmerizing as the water below.

Back at the house, we fumbled into the bedroom. We pulled off our clothes in the dark to stand before each other naked, our bodies cut with triangles of light from the street lamps outside. Leo looked like a tower of flesh standing by the bed, wide and round and smooth and tall. Despite having a full beard, his body was mostly hairless except for a tight square of dark pubic hair and a thin layer on his legs.

I went down before him on my knees, as Michael moved to kiss him. Leo's cock swelled in my mouth and in it I was drowning, swallowing the sea. Coming up for air, I stood to kiss him; and both he and Michael fell backwards onto our bed, their mouths together, their legs kicking for dominance. Thirsty from the day, I drank from both of them, running my tongue along Leo's back, Michael's neck, tasting the salt on their bodies. My palms pushed against their muscles, set alight by their temperatures, each torso a stoked furnace threatening to ignite the sheets and burn down the room. For an hour we crashed hard against each other like the tides against the rocks, until we came, coiled and twisted, the splash running across our skin in rivers.

I awoke several hours later, sandwiched between them. An odd feeling, being spooned between two people. I then fell back asleep and was pulled into another tryst around five. The sheets were damp with sweat by the time we were done, bunched up in the corners of the bed and coming off the sides of the mattress. We collapsed back into bliss as light seeped into the room.

I woke up again around 7:30 a.m. Not being able to sleep, I grabbed a pair of shorts and a T-shirt from the floor, left Michael and Leo cuddled up in the thin sheets and went out to the kitchen. I put on a pot of coffee for the house and then looked for my sneakers. The town was already starting its day as I went for my run, people strapping beach umbrellas to bikes, delivery trucks dropping off supplies to restaurants. I hadn't got much sleep and should have felt tired, but instead I felt alive and awake as I jogged along Bradford. Thoughts of the night before sent a tingle up my spine, my blood vessels opening to remember the familiar rush of the night before. Had we done all that? Was that me in those memories?

Returning home, I poured myself a glass of water from the fridge and took it outside. "Someone got Vitamin D last night," Danny said, emerging from the kitchen. Vince was behind him, struggling to open his eyes to the daylight.

"You heard?"

"Honey, people in Truro heard. And they felt the vibrations all the way to Boston." Danny had his cell in his hand and raised it towards me. "Didn't you get the tsunami warning on your phone?"

"Sounds like a good time." Vince smiled. "How was it?"

I thought for a second. "Amazing. Like being crushed by a tidal wave."

"It's a good thing you didn't drown." Danny looked up at the sky and squinted. "Beach today?" he asked.

"Beach today," I said.

By the time we arrived at Herring Cove, it was shortly before noon. We parked our bikes by the side of the road and began the procession through the dunes. The tide was in. Leo, taking my beach bag and putting it atop his head as we waded through waters waist deep, was a gentleman in the sand. Eventually, we made it to the shore and found a free spot among the rows of men to throw down our towels and pitch our umbrellas. I pulled off my shirt and removed the cap from the sunscreen. Michael took the tube from me and did my back without me having to ask. Then he did Leo's back.

Leo pulled down his shorts and stepped out of them to put on his swimsuit. We stole glances, all of us, as Leo flashed his modest penis and untamed bush of black hair framed by solid hips. It went quiet for a moment as each of us struggled with our thoughts, the only sound the wind blowing through the sand. As Leo sat down on his towel, Harry finally said something. "Who's up for a swim?"

"I'll go," Vince said.

"Me too," Michael said and looked at me. I shook my head no. "Leo?" he asked. Leo got back up and so did Charles, and the four of them walked down to the water.

"I'm warning you," Danny said, once everyone was out of earshot. "If he so much as looks at Vince I'm going to fling a batch of lobster traps at him and drown him in the sand. Harry too."

"Come on," I said to Danny. "Vince wouldn't do that to you. Not after last year."

"It's amazing what men will do if they think they can get away with it."

"Don't start your holiday like this," I said. "Getting al

jealous when you don't have to. Harry is here with Charles, and he doesn't seem the kind. As for Leo, he's here for Michael—and me too, maybe. Have your own fun with your man, and don't worry so much about what everyone else is doing. Did you bring the ring?"

Danny sulked. "Yes, I brought the ring. But do me a favour, will you, Paul?"

"What is it?"

"Go easy on this threesome stuff. Vince hasn't said anything, but I know he's thinking about it. We're all thinking about it. I mean how can you not when it's happening in the next room? This is exactly the thing that appeals to him— adventurous sex—and I just… I don't want to fight about this with him on this trip, okay? I don't want to place any doubts in his head, not this weekend."

After a few hours at the beach, as the sun moved to-wards the water, we decided to head home to shower and change for tea dance. It was a twenty-minute walk back to the bikes, the sun deep in our skin. We rode along Bradford with the cars and, once home, emptied our beach bags of sand in the backyard.

"I'm going to shower," Michael said. I soon heard the spray of water behind the door. I took Michael's damp shorts off the chair in our bedroom and hung them outside with the towels.

Having been reminded of Patsy Cline, Danny put on another one of her albums. "Going to add Patsy to the sound-track of the summer," he said, making himself a cocktail. "Want one?" he asked.

I heard the bathroom door open again and turned

to see Leo walk in and close the door behind him. Danny caught sight of it too and gave me a look. I shrugged. "I'm good for now," I said, and went to join Leo and Michael.

The trip went by fast and we had perfect weather the entire time. The days were hot and sunny, the evenings cool and clear. We saw great shows, met interesting people, laughed, shopped, danced and ate. We swam and sunned ourselves, Leo beside us most of the time.

Harry proved to be nice, but shy. He and Charles stayed largely to themselves, opting for other activities: biking along Martha's Vineyard, whale watching, getting up at the crack of dawn to see the sun rise on High Head. These were all things I had never done, and had wanted to do, but the call of the drinks, the bar and Leo's body kept us busy. I had discovered a new side to myself in Provincetown, one of a carefree Paul who saw no delineation between my pleasure and that of my partners. In fact, I couldn't remember the last time I had felt so carefree. I felt liberated, unchained. The thought surprised me, and though Danny had asked me to cut back or tone it down, I didn't.

I mean, I did a little, but I didn't let it stop me. Each new encounter was a welcome joy—frenzied and intoxicating.

Danny and Vince seemed to be enjoying themselves too and if Danny continued to be bothered by the sex we had he didn't say anything. He did, however, seem stiff at times and distracted. I chalked that up to nerves, of being unsure of whether or not to pop the question. I asked him several times if he was all right and he said that he was, the last time adding, "Will you fucking please stop asking me if I'm okay. You're making me feel like an eighty-year-old at the airport.

378

When I asked Charles how his trip with Harry was going, he just said, "I think I'm in love."

"What? No! You? Already?"

"Didn't you fall in love with Michael right away?"

"Is he your shadow?" I asked.

"Maybe. He's different from the other ones. So different from Mark, who was trouble, or Kevin, who was aloof. Harry's kind and generous and smart. He's got his head screwed on right... These last few days have been the happiest of my life."

In ways, it felt like that for me too. There was something about this place, and these seven days each year, where it felt like I was living my best life. There were no real chores, no responsibilities. No cats to feed, work to file, phone calls or emails to return. Each morning, I would wake up and ask myself, "What do I want to do today?" and each night I would go to bed with two wonderful men—one my partner and the other our lover. And Charles was right. In the same way I knew I loved Michael right away, I felt that with Leo too.

One afternoon, after we had come home from the beach, Danny set to preparing a marinade for dinner while the rest of us got ready for tea. "We're out of garlic," Danny called from the kitchen, and Michael offered to go pick some up at the nearby market. I stayed behind and took a shower. Afterwards, as I was back in our bedroom, examining the red sun marks that had wrapped themselves around my neck and arms in the mirror, there was a knock at the door. Leo walked in and feigned surprise at catching me in the nude. He closed the door behind him and approached me, where I stood in front of the large circular vanity.

"All clean?" he asked.

I attempted to be funny. "I'm sure there's still sand somewhere."

Leo brushed the hair on my chin with his hand and smiled. "You have more grey this year." He kissed me, long and hard, then dropped to his knees in front of me, fully clothed. *Where's Michael?* I thought. *This can't happen without him.* But in a moment I was in Leo's mouth. All I could do was stand there and watch myself in the mirror, look at my older chunky body as it was worshipped by the reflection of this young man. And I loved him for it. I loved him for being this generous to Michael and me.

On the last day of our trip, I started to feel anxious for Danny. He hadn't proposed, or if he had, he hadn't said anything to me yet. It was now or never.

We had spent another gorgeous day at the beach, then hightailed it home to get ready for the last tea dance of our vacation. As everyone showered and dressed, Danny mixed extra strong cocktails. ("Munichs," he said, doling them out. "Memories of last year.") He must have had three before we left, late for the bar.

On our way to the Boatslip, we stopped outside a shop while Vince bought gum. Sitting on my bike, my hands stretched across the handlebars, I noticed two gay men approach, pushing a young girl in a stroller. These men looked identical, dressed in the same beige shorts and sandals, with the same haircut and manicure. They stopped in front of a nearby restaurant to check the menu, and I couldn't help but stare at their well-behaved child—all knees and sunglasses and wide-brimmed sunhat.

Our baby, that first baby, would have been a month and a half old by now. Originally, I had forgotten the due date, but I'd been reminded a few weeks ago when Sue's son was born. My dad had called with the news while I was out for a jog one day and left a message on my voicemail. "Ethan was born last night at a quarter to midnight," he had said. "But I suppose that means he was born today where you are. Both baby and mom are doing fine. Five pounds, four ounces; Sue hardly needed any epidural! Do me a favour, will you? When you get a chance, can you congratulate her? I know she'd love to hear from you."

I didn't call Sue, opting instead to leave a *Way to go! So happy for you!* message on her Facebook wall. I noticed that Kate had done the same. *Congratulations!* her message had said. *Welcome to the family, little Ethan!*

Since I had interacted with her profile, Facebook now showed me everything about Sue's life. I was presented with dozens of pictures—images from the hospital, photos of the baby sleeping at home—all of which I'm sure were different, but looked the same to me. My dad was even in a few, holding the little football in his arms.

Our lives are so different, I thought, as we got back onto our bikes and headed to the bar, weaving in and out of the circus on the street. I might be ten years older than Sue, but in many ways I felt younger with what I had chosen to do with my life. But still, there was no doubt I was forty-one. Michael would be turning thirty in October, entering that greatest of decades. And here we were, on a hedonistic holiday with our nearest and dearest: forging new bonds, making new friends, dressing up in ridiculous outfits, drinking way too much and soaking up too many UV rays—all while Sue sat nursing at home and changing diapers. She and her husband would spend the next two decades growing and nurturing their child, putting him before all else, while Michael and I did what? I wondered, as we walked onto the crowded deck of the Boatslip and my friends beelined to the bar. Travelled? Had more encounters with men like Leo?

I thought again about what my dad had said. Was I selfish? Why was I not more like the two men walking down the street with their child? Had the kid come their way from surrogacy, or adoption, or was she the result of a previous relationship with a woman? I'd had a good life—a great life, even. Why wouldn't I want to be a dad to some kid, to try and give him or her the world because in many ways that was what I felt had been given to me? To put someone else's well-being before my own, because honestly, what was the point of life if not to try and make it better for someone else?

Danny and Vince came back with drinks and handed them out. I looked over at Michael and Leo as they took their first sips. The two looked adorable, wearing matching bear hats that Michael had brought. "Hey, let me get one of the two of you," I said, and grouped them together so I could take a picture and remember this moment. Should I post it? I wondered, looking at it to make sure it had come out. Would people wonder who Leo was? What would Sue think? Or Debbie, who seemed to like everything I posted? Wendy and Eve? Would they expect me to edit my life for their daughter?

The DJ started to play Madonna's "Vogue," and Michael and Leo went running to the dance floor. Standing there, watching them go, listening to the music and the voices and taking in the sky and sea, I wondered what she might make of this, this girl whose name I didn't know. What would she know of me? When she was, say, fifteen, and knew more about the world than either of her moms was aware of, would she be my friend? Or would I be an embarrassment? Would she judge me? And who would be the important names in her life? Who would be her Danny, her Charles, her Wendy, her Michael?

As the party came to a close, "Last Dance," heralded the time to go home. I looked at my watch. It was five minutes to seven. The last song of the last tea dance of the last day of our trip. I went to join the boys and found them by the speaker. I danced with them for a bit, but then I saw Vince too, dancing with a man who wasn't Danny. They weren't affectionate, but their movements were flirtatious, each keeping an eye on the other as they twirled and sang along with the rest of the dance floor.

I turned around to try to find Danny, to distract him and make sure he was occupied for the last minutes of the party, but when I came back to our spot all I found was Harry and Charles, sharing the last few sips of a drink. "Have you seen Danny?" I asked.

"I think he went to dance," Harry said.

I turned around and headed back to the dance floor. The song was almost over and people were beginning to stream out of the bar and onto the street. I looked for Danny, but couldn't find him anywhere. Gone, also, were Michael and Leo; but I did see Vince having fun, singing along with the man in front of him who he was now holding by the waist.

The song ended, and people began to disperse to a

clamour of voices and the sucking down of drinks. Everyone had to leave, so we began to stream out onto Commercial Street where people stood waiting for their friends. Outside, as the sky turned purple, I found Charles and Harry talking to a drag queen busking for her show, and Michael and Leo posing for someone who wanted to take their picture. No sign of Danny.

Vince showed up, pulling on his shirt. I watched as the man he had been dancing with walked the other way, throwing a final look over his shoulder. "Have you seen Danny?" I asked him.

"No," Vince said.

"Maybe he went home?" Michael answered. "To start dinner? Should we meet him back there?"

Michael, Leo, Vince and I grabbed our bikes. Charles, still in conversation with the drag queen, said he'd stick around a few more minutes, then head back. We took off, gliding back through town, through people. At home, I found Danny in the kitchen making dinner, a big glass of liquor and ice by his chopping board. He was cutting onions; water was boiling, Patsy Cline was blaring.

I turned down the volume. "You okay?" I asked.

"Okay, yes I'm okay," he said, anything but. "I mean, I just dropped a couple of grand on this trip, several more on a ring for the man I love, only to find him making out on the dance floor with some other guy on the night I planned to propose."

Vince, Leo and Michael were still outside on the deck all talking to one another, unaware of what was simmering in here. I tried to keep my voice low. "Danny, he wasn't makin

384

out with the guy. They were just dancing. It's not that big of a deal, okay? We went over this." Danny had a large knife in his hand and was frantic with his mise en place. "Put the knife down," I ordered. "Come here." Then I grabbed him by the hand and took him into the living room.

"Hey, babe," Vince said, coming into the room. "Everything okay?"

"Is everything okay?" Danny turned, shouting. "Everything's great. I'm just making dinner for my friends here, on our last night in town. Was going to make steak and veggies, but I wonder now if I have enough. I mean, will your friend from the dance floor be joining us?"

Vince rolled his eyes.

"But maybe he doesn't eat meat," Danny went on. "Maybe he just feasts on all the souls of the tea dance—like some forgotten phantom of the dick dock who rises from the wooden planks to lure men into his arms and break up healthy relationships with his siren song, huh?"

Vince turned around. "J'en ai assez," he said, raising his hands. Vince rarely spoke French with us, but it came out now with his anger. "Tu es malade mental, et t'es jaloux sans raison. I'm sick of being with someone who's so possessive." And with that he left the room and walked up the stairs.

Danny went after him. "Vas-y! Va le rejoindre! Is he waiting for you by the docks? Is that where you planned to meet later tonight?" Danny took off after him, up the stairs.

"What's going on?" Charles said, coming through the door. I looked out the window. Harry was outside with Michael and Leo.

"A meltdown. I'm going to…"

"No," Charles grabbed me. "Let them hash it out. I know you want to protect him, but he has to deal with this himself."

There was a laugh outside as Harry said something funny. I looked at Michael blankly, then at Leo, and I felt tired. Tired of the whole weekend. Night was approaching and we had plans for it, but suddenly I wanted to be home. I wanted the week to be over.

21

I DIDN'T SEE ANYONE for a few weeks after that trip. It had been fun but exhausting, the memory of all that had happened fading with each new morning commute. Soon, real life took over and once again I was working late and spending my nights with Michael and the cats on our couch.

"Come cuddle," Michael would say once our dinner dishes were done.

September was treating us to an extended summer and the apartment was sweltering. "It's too hot to cuddle," I'd say, but join Michael anyway. I'd hold him from behind while we watched TV, our horizontal bodies sticky in the heat.

The week after we got back, I heard from Wendy. She had entered her third trimester and just received the flamboyant baby onesie I had mailed her. I had to have it when I saw it in the store on our last morning in Provincetown—bright blue with the central message, "I love my two moms."

The following week, I got a thank-you card from Sue. I had picked up a onesie for her that morning too, a last-minute grab on my way to the cash. It had the words "Love, Pride, Family" in rainbow colours that I felt were innocuous enough for a straight family in Kelowna to parade their child around town in. Those in the know would understand that little Ethan had a diverse family.

The next time I heard from Danny, he asked me to meet him at a church in Westmount. There were a dozen people outside when I arrived. Danny and I didn't say anything, just nodded hello. Once the doors opened, we followed everyone in.

"Where do you want to sit?" I asked.

"Near the back, in case I want to leave," he said. "I don't feel like participating."

We sat at a pew in the back row, further down from a young man in a hoodie with purple hair. "Why aren't we at your church?" I asked.

"Mine doesn't host AA meetings. But if they did, I wouldn't want anyone to see me."

I looked around. It was mid-afternoon, but the building was dark and cold. Any external light came in through stained glass pictures of Jesus and the saints and the Holy Family. A crowd congregated at the back near the coffee and pastries.

"When will it start?"

"Soon."

"How are you feeling?"

"Like garbage. You?"

"I'm okay. What do we do?"

"We sit here and listen. Some people will talk."

"And you sure you don't want to say anything?"

Danny didn't respond. He looked towards the pulpit and altar. "Well, it's not tickets to the theatre, but I'm sure you'll be entertained."

"It's good that you're doing this, Danny. It takes a big person to admit they've got a problem."

"After what happened with Vince, I think my problem was obvious to everyone."

"How many days has it been for you now?"

"Fifteen, but who's counting?"

"Well, that's an achievement."

Danny rolled his eyes. "Let's talk in a few months. I came this close to falling off the wagon yesterday. I have the best intentions, but then I hear Loleatta Holloway and all I want to do is to have a drink in a gay bar."

A few more people walked in and took seats. I looked at my watch.

"At least it's pretty in here," Danny said, looking at the ceiling. "I love these old churches. I love how the light pours in through the stained glass and how the votive candles warm everything up." He turned to face me. "Did I tell you I've decided to redecorate my apartment again? Now that Vince is gone. I hope Michael won't mind, but I'm going to hire someone who specializes in light. I have this memory of the light in the house where I grew up: the amber blush of the lamps in the living room, the bright halogens coming up from downstairs and illuminating the staircase. When I was a kid and my parents had parties, I'd sneak down and hide behind the record player and watch them as they laughed and ate and drank in front of the twinkling bar lights, listening to Nat King Cole. So sophisticated, I thought."

Danny was picturing it in his head, I could tell by the shine in his eyes. "I don't know how I'm going to replicate all that," he said, coming back, "but I'm going to try. I'm going to feel that way again: warm and safe and fed and loved."

A man entered and headed towards the front with a

bunch of papers in his hand; but then it looked as if he had forgotten something, as he felt the pockets of his shirt, and he took off back in the other direction. "They're so disorganized here," Danny sighed. "Always starting late. Some of us have laundry to do, you know."

I looked up to the intricate wood rafters that gave the structure its frame. "It is pretty," I said. "Such a beautiful building—peaceful." I looked around at the people present, at their tired, troubled faces. "I wonder if this is what rehab was like for Michael. I'd ask, but he never wants to talk about that time."

"What's there to talk about? It's not like it's a crowning achievement, having an addiction."

"Treating one is."

"How is he doing?"

"Good. Busy. He hasn't stopped working since we got back from Provincetown."

"Any fallout from the Leo affair?"

"What do you mean, fallout?"

"You know. Once you got back to the real world, was the experience as you remembered? God knows that week slapped me in the face when I got home."

"No, there was no fallout," I said. "But the trip does seem strange when I look back. I don't recognize myself in the memories. Sometimes, I wonder if Leo was real or if he was a mirage. But Michael tells me he wants to come visit, so he has to be real. I can't tell if that's a good idea or not."

"Well, you know what I think."

"Michael also says he wants to go work in Provincetown next spring and stay for the summer."

"He's said that before, hasn't he?"

"I wish we could both go, but I can't get that kind of time off. But Michael's his own boss; he could do it. He'd have to quit the coffee shop, but there's so much turnover at that place they'd take him back in the fall. I mean, how great would it be to live in P-Town for an entire season?"

"It would kill me. And it would kill your relationship."

"Come on."

"Admit it. You don't want him to go," Danny said. "You don't want him to go because you won't be able to protect him if you're not there. Don't tell me you're not worried that something might happen, that something might wreck and destroy him. Wreck and destroy you too."

Those were heavy words. "I'm not worried it will *wreck and destroy* us."

"Please," he said. "You're our worrier-in-chief."

He had me there. "Ok, maybe I'd worry about him *a little*," I said. "But I'll learn to deal. I don't want to stop him from being who he's meant to be. I don't want to get in his way. The last thing I want is for Michael to feel beholden to me."

"Why would he feel beholden to you?"

"Because I've taken him in, because I provide for him. I'd never want him to feel like he has to stay with me, that he owes me something… But I'd be lying, though, if I said I didn't think that place holds some kind of special power over him. I knew it was dangerous to bring him there that first time. I have these flashes of driving him to the end of the Cape and opening the door. Like releasing a rehabilitated animal back into the wild."

"That's incredibly sad," Danny said.

"But isn't that how it goes? You know you're in love with someone when you don't want to stand in the way of them becoming who they're meant to be."

"You're a better man than me," Danny said. We went quiet for a minute, the two of us still contemplating the room. "You know, Paul," he continued, "I'm not sure I believe in heaven, but I do believe in hell. And hell is loneliness. It's being left behind. Not having someone to care for and who cares for you deeply. Family means the world to me, and having my own family is something I've wanted my entire life. But sadly, I don't have one. Not really."

"But Danny…" I was about to say something but he reached out to grab my hand.

"Oh, I know what you're going to say, Paul. That I'm your family. I appreciate that. I feel the same. We're lucky to have great friends. But that's not what I'm talking about. I'm talking about what you have with Michael. What my mom and dad had when they were alive."

Danny stopped and cleared his throat. He turned in the pew to face me. "I wish you could've met my parents," he said, stars in his eyes. "You would have loved my mother. She was a great cook, taught me everything I know. I suspect she knew I'd turn out gay—bought me a copy of *The Collected Works of Oscar Wilde* on my sixteenth birthday. She was stylish too. Each year, for Christmas, I wanted to get her something to wear—a new dress or a skirt, a pair of earrings or a brooch. I never did because I didn't know whether or not she'd like it. I wish I had though. Because if I had, she would have worn it. And it would give me such great pleasure now, to think of my mom wearing something I had given her. My dad, he was funny. He's where I get my sense of humour from. He got me hooked on music by playing the vinyl records in his collection and teaching me about the struggles of jazz artists. We had a tradition on Saturdays where we'd both read the newspaper and discuss the stories."

"You were lucky to have them," I said. "Some people, like Charles, like Michael and Vince, had shitty families."

"I know I was lucky," he said. "Still, I didn't have them long enough."

There was commotion. The man with the papers was returning to the front, and the people at the back began to take their seats. "But I don't think I'm asking too much," Danny said, straightening up. "I just want someone to love me unconditionally, like my parents loved me. Someone who'll never leave my side, because we're in this together. Who at the end of the day is as much my best friend as my lover." Danny looked up at the ceiling and exhaled. "God, what I wouldn't give to be in that light again."

In the weeks before his thirtieth birthday, Michael began to prepare for the celebrations. "Why celebrate on just the day?" he reasoned, planning a whole festival of events in the days leading up. There would be a spa day, an evening out with Gus and a *souper des femmes* at Charles's where we'd finally get to see Harry out of his Polo shirt and in a plaid 1950s housewife dress.

The day before his birthday, I found him at his desk at home writing a cheque.

"What are you doing?" I asked.

He put the cheque into an envelope and licked it closed. "I'm done paying off my taxes."

"Really?"

He nodded. "Yep. That's the last $500." Michael had refused to keep me informed about his payments. The only thing I knew was that he had missed his original deadline, but had somehow negotiated an extension. "I'm officially in the black now," he said. "Well, I owe you for the car and for Provincetown and for everything else, but at least *this* won't be hanging over my head."

"That's great, buddy!" I said." Congratulations!"

Michael kissed me as he left to mail his letter.

On the night of his birthday, the two of us went out for dinner and I gave him my gift, a simple jet-black wristwatch with golden hour marks. "Charles helped me pick it out," I said. "Do you like it?"

There was a shine to his eyes. "Very much," he said, cradling it in his hand as if it were alive. He affixed it to his wrist. "It's beautiful."

"I figured you already have the pearls."

After dinner, I asked Michael if he wanted to go home. He shrugged. "What else could we do?"

We grabbed a taxi to the Village for a nightcap. George was tending the bar.

"It's my birthday," Michael shouted as we entered.

"Happy birthday, kid," George said, and brought us a round.

We weren't there long before we noticed a young man at the end of the bar. He was bearded and handsome, wearing a plain black T-shirt, baseball cap and winsome smile. He seemed amused by Michael's energy and came up to introduce himself.

"I'm Samuel," he said, shaking Michael's hand. "Did I overhear it's your birthday?"

"It is," Michael said, showing off the watch I had got him.

"Regal," he said. "Let me get you both a drink." Samuel called George over, who seemed to know him, and bought us a round of shots. The purchase got the three of us talking, but it was really Michael and Samuel who spoke. I mostly listened, turning my head every now and then to watch whatever music video was playing on the screen.

After a while, I got bored. I felt left out of the conversation, so I decided to buy us another round, and bought one for George too. We shot them back and before long Michael had his arm over this young man's shoulder; the man's hand around his waist.

At some point, Samuel got up to go to the washroom.

"Can we keep him?"

I laughed. "What?"

"For my birthday? Can we take him home? Could be fun."

I didn't know what to say. With Leo, at least we had the chance to get to know him before anything happened. Yes, this guy was attractive, but besides that?

Soon, Samuel returned, and Michael replaced his hand around his shoulders. I looked at the two of them, so young and handsome and full of life. Maybe I could do this for him. Maybe it would be fun. "Samuel," I said to him. "Michael and I are going to get out of here. Do you want to come with us?"

We hopped a cab back to our place; I sat in the front with

the driver and caught glimpses of the two of them in the back, fidgeting with each other's fingers. The cats were waiting in the darkness when we got home, but they soon got out of our way once they realized we weren't alone. "Want something to drink?" I asked Samuel, turning on the lights. "A beer?"

Samuel nodded and followed me into the kitchen, while Michael went off to use the washroom and put on music. He sat down on a stool while I took three beers out of the fridge and opened them. I handed one to Samuel but noticed he had trouble meeting me in the eye. Was he shy? I clinked bottles with him as we waited for Michael to return.

"You have cats," he said, breaking the silence. "What are their names?"

"Malone and Sutherland."

He laughed. "Those are strange names," he said, looking for them on the floor.

Michael returned to the kitchen. "They're character names. From one of Paul's favourite books."

Samuel took a swig from his beer and the three of us toasted. Michael moved behind Samuel and began to rub his shoulders. A grin appeared on our guest's face, his eyes eclipsed in bliss. After a moment, he turned to kiss Michael on the mouth. I watched from the other side of the kitchen island, holding my bottle. Samuel turned his body to face Michael, and Michael pulled up his shirt while Samuel stood. I noticed that Samuel had dozens of pimples on his back, the results of shaving or waxing. I put my beer down and helped Michael lift the shirt off, placing it in a ball on the counter.

Soon we were in our bedroom, the cats jumping off the bed and running into the hall. From the front, I noticed that

Samuel had clipped his chest hair, its remaining length all straight and dark. In the cab, I could tell that he wore cologne, but now, exposed on our bedspread, I could smell more of him, a pungent mix of lavender and lemon zest.

I moved to get him to stand up and unbuckle his belt and pushed his pants down to his knees. The rest of Samuel's body was like his chest; he had trimmed back his pubic hair to its base, which made his cock look like a carrot. I went down on him for a while, as Michael kissed him, the sting of his cologne in my nose. During all of this, Samuel didn't touch me. He could at least play with my hair, I thought. Put his hand on my shoulders. Anything. Some form of contact.

After a while my jaw got sore, so I stood up. I asked Samuel to get up for a second too, and pulled off the comforter so he could fall back onto the sheets. Michael and I removed our clothes, but there was something missing this time, I felt, looking at Michael as my jeans fell to the floor with a thud.

I moved back down to engage with Samuel as he and Michael continued to kiss. Samuel's body felt almost cold in my hands. Was he nervous? Inexperienced? I moved up to kiss him, and Samuel kissed back, but tepidly. Mostly, he kept still, just stroking himself, reaching out to touch Michael now and again.

I wasn't sure if he was lazy or just not into me, but it did seem that Samuel enjoyed Michael's touch. Almost abruptly, he turned away from me and went down on Michael. I stood back and watched for a second, like what was happening was in another dimension, but then Michael met my gaze and gave me a look as if to say, *What are you doing? Get in here.* And he pulled me into a collision with the two of them.

Not sure what to do anymore, I went down again on Samuel. I suddenly wanted this to be over. I knew that he preferred Michael, that I was the collateral that came with this prize. It made me angry, but it also made me want to prove him wrong about what he might've thought about me. I suddenly wanted to show him that older men know what they're doing, and started to be more forceful and take charge, but then halfway through, I realized that wasn't me and this was just another blowjob he was getting from someone, anyone, willing to take his cock in their mouth.

Soon I got my wish and it was over—Samuel coming at the same time as Michael. I stood up from where I had been kneeling, my legs sore. Michael reached for me, but I shook my head and started to get dressed. Samuel pushed himself off the bed. "That was hot," he said, grabbing tissues from the nightstand. He began to look for his underwear and pants.

"You don't have to take off right now," Michael said. "Stay if you like."

I shot Michael a dirty look.

"Thanks, but I should go," he said. I let Samuel get dressed and collect his things; while he covered up his body, the memory of it lingered in my mouth. He then kissed Michael goodbye and looked to see if I too was leaning in. I wasn't.

"Goodbye," I said, closing the door behind him.

"You okay?" Michael asked.

I nodded. "Yes, I'm fine."

"Why didn't you come?"

"I didn't feel like it." I kissed Michael. "Happy birthday," I said. "I'm going to take a shower."

I scrubbed hard with the bar of soap to get the smell o

Samuel off me, but it was still there when I got out, absorbed by the bed sheets that Michael now slept in. I tried to fall asleep next to him, but was too grossed out, so I got up and went into the living room to sleep on the couch.

The next morning, I was in the kitchen when Michael woke.

"What happened to you last night?" he asked, as he poured himself a cup of coffee. "I got up to pee in the middle of the night and you were on the couch."

"Sorry," I said, tired from a restless sleep. "I didn't want to smell that guy on our sheets."

"Why didn't you say something?"

"You were asleep."

"I could've got up. We could've changed them."

"Michael," I said. "I don't know if I can keep doing this."

"What do you mean?"

"Last night. It was humiliating to be honest."

"Humiliating?"

"The guy was more into you than he was into me. And that's fine. It's just, I don't know if I want to deal with that any more. I did that enough in my twenties. Sleeping with men who didn't want to sleep with me, who just wanted to get off. I thought all that was behind me and to be honest it's not something I want to repeat."

Michael came up behind me and kneaded my shoulders. "I'm sorry, buddy," he said, but I shook him off.

"It's not your fault. It's just, I know that things are changing between us. Or evolving. I know that it's unlikely we'll be monogamous now that we've opened this door. Our sex life is good, but it's not what it once was. I know you want Leo to

399

come visit, but I don't think I can live like we did on holiday. Not on a regular basis. I don't think I'm that person."

"We didn't have to do it," he said. "You could have said no."

"But you wanted to!" I said. "You're thirty! I remember what thirty was like. You're in the prime of your life. Hardly had any experience in Moncton. You can't be completely fulfilled by me. I saw the connection you had with Leo. I know you Skype when I'm not around. I'm not stupid." For some reason, that thought hurt. "So, maybe we're not meant to be together," I said, wanting him to feel the hurt I felt. "Maybe if you want to be with someone else so bad, then you shouldn't be with me."

Michael was angry, but I could also see tears in his eyes. "That's not fair. I love you, Paul. You know that. I care for Leo, but it's just fun with him. Just sex. If you wanted me to, I'd stop talking to him, if it hurt you too much. Is that what you want me to do? Stop talking to him?"

"No."

"I will, if it means that much. But I think of Leo as a brother, Paul. I've never had a *real* brother. Never had a *real* family."

"But *I'm your family.*"

"Leo and I are just friends. I don't have too many friends here, you know. You grew up here. You have all these close friendships. I feel close to Leo, but I'd never go. I'd never leave you for him."

"Still," I said, exhausted. "All this, it just makes me wonder if I'm enough. If there's not someone else out there better for you."

I had really hurt Michael this time. I could see it in his face as he stood there in front of me with the same petrified

400

look as when he had broken my mug. "But Paul," he said, choking on his tears. "You changed my life. Don't you realize what I mean when I say that?"

The tremor in his voice parked itself in my own throat. I shook my head.

"I moved here—here of all places—because I couldn't take it any more. Couldn't see a future for myself in Moncton. You know, when your teacher tells your class that one in ten of you will be gay and everyone turns to look at you and laugh? When those same kids put dog shit in your gym shoes, or drop an envelope full of razor blades in your locker? You'd think with three brothers I'd have had at least one of them stick up for me, or have my dad come to my rescue. But no, they were as rotten and mean as everyone else. And when that happens, you can't imagine a future for yourself. Can't imagine ever having people who care for you... But I stayed. I stayed for my mom. I stayed way longer than I should've."

I stood before him in shock. "How come you've never told me this?"

"I left—I left my own mom behind—because there had to be something better out there," he continued. "And for a minute, I thought I found it. I was proud of that small apartment I had at first, the one I was living in when we met. It was gross and cold and took me forever to clean, but still, even after living there a few months, it was an empty apartment. The weight of everything was in the room with me. They say your problems follow you wherever you go, and they followed me here too. I had no future in Montreal, just like in Moncton. In those first few months, I hardly spoke to anyone. I'd spend my days walking around downtown, sketching in food courts. I didn't know what I was doing or even how I would live. All I had was a couple thousand in the bank. Enough to get by for a short time, and I didn't know what I was going to do when it was gone." Michael sighed, and then sat down at the table beside me. "Paul," he said, struggling. "I never intended on making it this far."

"What do you mean?"

"I cashed in everything and moved out here to have a few great months."

"And then?"

"And then... that would be it." He wiped his eyes and sniffed. "No one would care if I was gone, in a city where I knew no one."

It was only then that I truly understood what he had meant, the full gravity of our last four years together. Then the tears came. I collapsed in a puddle at his feet and cried at his knees. I cried for everything bad that had ever happened to him. "I'm sorry," I said, choking back my own tears. "I'm sorry, I'm sorry, I'm sorry, I'm sorry," I released in succession, each utterance a desperate, grasping plea for some kind of absolution—for him, for me—for it felt that I too had failed him.

"Shhh," he whispered, stroking the hair on my head. He almost laughed, smiling through his tears. "But then you came along, out of nowhere. Just walked right up to me in the bar. It's amazing how people can do that for one another. Just walk right up and change someone's life forever. And that's what you did. You saved me."

I had stopped crying, and looked up at him, at that face that beautiful face I could never picture not being in m

402

life. He stroked my head again. "How could I leave?" he said. "It took me twenty-five years, but I finally found you. And you gave me something my parents couldn't, my brothers couldn't. You gave me the start I needed. The ability to be myself, when everyone wanted me to be someone else."

22

THE TEXT CAME IN while I was jogging. *She's on her way,* Eve's message said. *We're in labour!*

I tried to keep running, but my head was elsewhere. I cut my time short and ran home to tell Michael.

Later that day came another message from Eve. *Still in labour and going to get an epi. Was hoping to make it without one, but Wendy doesn't think she can take the pain. We're going to let her come when she wants, so hopefully sometime today! Will keep you posted! Love ya!! Promise to name her by tomorrow!*

"They still haven't decided on a name?" Danny asked as we gathered at Charles's place that night to celebrate.

I felt like passing out cigars but opted instead for chocolates. "They said they were going to print out all the names they're considering and put them up on the wall of the delivery room."

"Lesbians are so organized," Danny remarked.

We sat down at Charles's table and ate and toasted Wendy and Eve. I kept checking my phone for updates, but I only got messages from Kate asking if I had news. I too wanted desperately to know how things were going, and at one point almost phoned Eve, but I didn't want to pressure them. I'd hear eventually. When we still hadn't heard around midnight, Michael and I headed home and went to bed. Every few hours, I'd wake to check my phone. Nothing.

But then the next morning there was an email in my in-box.

> *Hi Paul and Michael! First off, we want to apologize for the lateness of this message. We had a long night, but mom and baby are doing well! Allow us to welcome to the family...*
> *Emily Martin-Wu*
> *Born: November 10, 2012 @ 11:49 p.m.*
> *6 pounds, 10.5 ounces*
> *Length: 49 cm*

There was an image attached. I clicked on the thumbnail and suddenly she was there; the face that, until that moment, I had not been able to picture.

I'd like to say that I recognized myself in her right away, but I didn't. She looked like most newborns: impossibly small, with scrunched-up features and dark hair swamping her forehead. But she was beautiful. How much would I have loved for my mom to see her. I marvelled at the delicacy of her features, returning to the photo throughout the day to see if I saw something new.

We Skyped a few days later when they returned from the hospital.

"My god, she's adorable," I said, as Wendy angled the camera on their laptop so I could see her sleeping in her bassinet, her eyes tightly closed. I took dozens of screen grabs as we talked, images to share with Michael, Kate, my dad and everyone else. Emily looked so small lying there… Emily. I loved the name. I loved saying it. Suddenly, I was happy that they had not shared with me all the names they had been considering, because this was the only one, the right one, and I knew it belonged to her when I heard it.

At some point she made a brief sound and her jaw dropped open in a yawn. Wendy put down the laptop so she could pick her up. "The last thing I want to do is drop this on her," she chuckled. Wendy hoisted the baby to the camera and Emily began to move around, more yawns erupting as her eyes adjusted to the light of the world. I marvelled at how confidently Wendy held her. "It's amazing how fast you learn," she said, "but I have been carrying her around already for nine months." Emily's features were miniscule: small hands, red feet, a dense dark head of hair, the perfect nose and mouth. "She's got your eyebrows," Wendy pointed out. "And look at those long lashes. Those are definitely gay-boy lashes."

"Was it painful?" I asked.

"Excruciating," Wendy said, still in disbelief. "The epidural only worked on one side. I kept yelling, 'Fuck me, oh fuck me,' during the contractions to the point where Eve began apologizing to everyone."

"Are you still in pain?"

"Yes," she said. "What's crazy is how bad my breasts hurt. Did you know that when you breastfeed, the womb begins to contract back to its normal size? It's fucking painful! No one ever tells you these kinds of things."

Over the next few days, I felt elated. I sent the screen grabs to Kate and my friends and my father. My dad was very happy for me. "Congratulations, Son," he said when I called. "She's a gorgeous little girl. You must be so proud."

I did feel proud. I hadn't done anything, but I still felt proud.

Danny called to wish us all well. Teasing, he said he wanted to know if he could use the term "Super Daughter" on my Facebook wall. "No," I said, and left it at that. I spent most of that week fielding calls from friends and even Wendy's and Eve's families. I even heard from Ben, which was a surprise. When he and my sister had finally broken up, just before she packed up her stuff and moved to Toronto, he had said that he hoped we could remain friends. I thought he was being polite, but Ben continued to stay in touch. We'd even gone running together.

Michael's mom tried to call him a bunch of times, but he wouldn't answer his phone. "Come on," I pleaded with him. "She just wants to congratulate you."

"Me? For what? What did I do?" was his answer, and when I indicated that wasn't enough said, "Look, I just need a break okay? It doesn't mean I'm never going to speak to her again."

Finally, she called me. "Paul, I'm so happy for you," she said with the same gusto and warmth I remembered from my kitchen table. "She's such a lucky girl to have two great uncles like you and Michael. I envy you, this time in your life... How is my son doing?"

"He's doing well, Ellen," I said. "He's paid off his taxes and is working like crazy. Really built a small business for himself over the last few years. There are some days we hardly see each other, like passing ships. But I'm super proud of him."

"I miss our calls. I miss getting news from him. I know he's still angry, and I understand that. But do me a favour, will you, Paul? Let me know from time to time how he's doing? Or if I call, answer? Just to let me know he's okay."

"He's okay, Ellen," I said, reluctant to make any promises that might aggravate Michael. "But yes, I'll let you know how he's doing. Just give him time. You know he loves you. He just needs to be on his own for a while."

A few weeks later, Michael and I drove the 401 to meet Emily. It was early December, but it was mild out and there was hardly any snow on the ground. We had plans to stay with Kate, but instead of driving directly to her house I asked Michael to take me to Wendy and Eve's first. I wanted to see her right away.

"Boys, meet Emily," Wendy said, greeting us at the door. The baby looked like a Muppet in Wendy's arms, her eyes and face animated by her mother's movements. "Here," she said, handing her over.

"No," I said, nervous, but Wendy placed her in my arms anyway.

It was sheer wonder, holding her. This living creature that was somehow a part of me. I couldn't believe how light she was. Heck, our cats weighed more. She was soft too, and slow, and smelled sweet like banana bread. She had a face that reminded me of an old man—all gums and yawns and wrinkles. I placed my index finger in her hand and she curled around it for a moment.

"Jesus, Wendy, what did we do?"

Wendy chuckled and mimed her head exploding.

"Too late for that now," Eve said.

Looking at Emily, I didn't understand how they could do it. How they were not scared every single moment of every single day that something bad would happen to this gentle thing they loved. How some unknown force might come out of the blue to take her away. Or what if I dropped her? What if I held her the wrong way? Or accidentally hurt her? But after a few seconds, those thoughts dissipated and I just stared at her in awe. I could now see the family resemblance. As she moved and smiled and sighed and gasped, I could see my mom, my dad, my sister and me. I saw Wendy too, and her mom and her dad. And I wondered what she saw when she looked at me with those big dark eyes. Was I as puzzling to her? Did she know who I was?

Wordlessly, I made a promise to her, my brown eyes locked with hers. *I promise to love and care for you and be there when you need me*, I tried to communicate. *I promise to never hurt you, to never turn my back on you, or betray your trust. I promise to always be your friend.*

Later that evening, Kate came over and we Skyped with Dad and Debbie.

"She looks just like you, Son," he said. I could hear the joy and enthusiasm in his voice, and knew it was genuine. "You looked exactly like her when you were a baby. Honestly, if we were to put a photo of the two of you side by side, I wouldn't be able to tell the difference."

Debbie was doting too, with all of her oohs and ahhs and oo-coos. And even though no one used the terms, it still felt like they were her grandparents. Maybe we'd get there some day.

"Debbie," Wendy said, angling to get into the screen,

"before I forget, I want to thank you for the blanket." Wendy lifted a small navy blue afghan onto her lap.

"It was my pleasure," Debbie said. "I know you didn't want typical girl colours, so I chose blue."

"Paul's favourite colour," Dad said.

I took the blanket from Wendy and admired it. "You made this, Debbie?" I asked.

She nodded.

"Thank you," I said, holding back my emotions. "I'm touched."

The next day, Michael and I went shopping and returned with groceries. While I cooked, Michael took Wendy and Eve's car to the garage to have its winter tires put on.

"This is a real treat," Wendy said, as I whipped up a big pot of pasta sauce on the stove for both that night's dinner and their freezer. "I can't remember the last time I had your spaghetti. It's like when we used to live together. Remember, every Thursday we'd watch *Will & Grace* and eat in front of the TV?"

"I remember your tater-tot casserole," I said.

"Oh god, it's been years. What I wouldn't give to have some of that right now."

"No," Eve said. "That's not on the approved list."

Wendy's arm was getting tired. "Here," she said, lifting her daughter to her wife. "Take her for a sec?" I watched the three of them interact, Emily passed off in what would undoubtedly be a years-long relay race between her two moms. It felt so natural to see them together, a family unit that I still couldn't believe I had a hand in making.

When we first started this whole thing, more than a year and a half ago, Wendy and Eve had expressed concern that I might feel different once their child was born. And I wondered if I did feel different, now that she was here. I tried to think back to that night in the restaurant, to the Paul who had not yet been through all this. I supposed my feelings had changed. Or rather, grown and evolved. There had been a whole swirling range of emotions that had been brought up around creating this child, from joy and happiness to fear and sorrow. But still, knowing that I would soon head home with Michael along the 401, it felt okay. I knew I would miss them. Miss her. But we had our own family waiting for us: Danny, Charles and our two cats. And I'd also be leaving a part of me behind. In the same way that we had lived together, partied together, mourned together, another part of me would now always be here with Wendy and Eve, even when I wasn't. And that made me happy.

"So Paul," Wendy said, coming over to where I stood at the stove. "Remember how Eve's family wants Emily to be baptized? We've agreed to do it. It's going to happen sometime in January, in Toronto. Eve found a gay-friendly church that she likes, and her parents have agreed to come for the ceremony. My folks will also come in from Guelph. I know you're not particularly religious, but we wondered if you'd come up too. Maybe bring Danny? I think he might like it."

"Yes, of course," I said. I didn't want to say, but I had hoped to be invited back again soon, to be able to watch her grow in her first year and be there for them too. "I'd love to."

"And we wondered if you'd be her godfather." Eve said, the baby on her knee.

My mouth opened in surprise, turning into a smile. I looked at Wendy and she too was beaming. My face gave away my answer and I turned to hug her and then Eve with Emily. It was just a name, but it was something. And I was happy to have it.

Before long, it was spring.

"Did you check his poops?" Michael asked me on the phone from Café Minelli.

"Yes, I've checked three times today. There are no poops. Well not from Malone, anyways. But really, how the heck am I supposed to know which cat's poop it is?"

"Well, that's not good. It's been four days now."

We took Malone to the vet that evening for a check-up. "He's constipated," the vet said, and gave us a laxative to administer orally.

"He's not going to like that," Michael said. We gave him the shot in his mouth when we got home and the cat almost spat out the liquid. When it was over, he jumped off the table and left the room to hide under the bed. "I don't know why the vet couldn't give him the first dose. What are you going to do if this happens again while I'm gone? Will you be able to do this yourself?"

"I have Danny on speed dial."

Charles came over a few days later with Harry to drop something off for Michael. I took the garment out of its bag and let it unfurl to the ground. "Oh my," I said. "You made him a kaftan?"

"Well, he's going to have to make an impression at the season's first tea dance," he said. "I've got a matching one so that when we arrive everyone'll know we're sisters."

Michael tried it on when he got home. "Oh my god, I just love it," he said. It was purple and blue, some large tropical bird repeated in the pattern from his wrists to his ankles.

"Charles says it's more durable than the one he wore last year," I said. "You can take it to the beach and throw it in the wash." Michael giggled and went off to find his phone to call up Charles and give his thanks.

Michael would be going to Provincetown in a few weeks. At least that was the plan. When it came to Michael, I knew that things could change at any moment, but this time he had made arrangements. Leo's friend Nick had agreed to rent him a room (Leo would be staying there too) and he had already lined up his first job: staining Nick's deck.

"And there'll be some gardening," Michael said. "Nick knows a woman who has her own team and is willing to give me a try. I think it could be fun. Working in people's ornamental gardens."

"And educational," I said. "Think of all the things you'll find in the bushes."

As the days progressed and we got closer to his departure, I noticed that Michael was anxious. On the day he planned to give his notice to the coffee shop, he seemed unsure. He paced around the apartment, pulling at his hair and making faces. "I mean I'm doing this, right?" he said to himself; and then to me, "Should I go? It wouldn't be irresponsible of me to go, would it?"

I was in the kitchen, drying dishes. "I can't tell you what to do. You have to make your own decision."

I could see what was going through his head. He wanted

413

to go, but didn't know if it made sense. He still owed me money, and although he would make some in Provincetown, it wouldn't be enough for him to stay until we arrived in August. Not with all the nights out and the food and drink and everything else that was going to force him into his pockets. But I knew that work was not the only reason for the trip.

Michael left the kitchen and went into our bedroom. I could hear him speaking and when I looked down the hall I saw him through the doorway, talking to Malone. Asking him if he should go.

I didn't want Michael to go. Not really. And it wasn't because I would be left behind, but because I knew I would worry about him. I would sit all summer with the thought that something bad might happen to him. That there might be an accident, or someone would spike his drink at a club, or that he'd fall down and get hurt and I wouldn't be there to help. That he'd get into trouble with the law for smoking a joint or working without a permit. That he'd be in a car accident. Or get sick. That he'd fall in love and never come back.

I got angry with myself and stopped drying the dishes. Stopped trying to get the kitchen so meticulously clean. If Michael left, I would have this entire place to myself. The entire place exactly as I wanted it. Would I be happy then?

I went into the bedroom to see Michael. He was sitting on the edge of the bed and petting Malone, who was licking his paw. I kissed him on the head and pulled him close. "Go," I said. "You can go... I think you should go."

Michael looked at me and, in response, squished up his face.

414

"Don't feel guilty. I'll be okay. Go, okay? Go…"

Three days before he was scheduled to leave, Michael took out his suitcase from the closet and left it on the floor of the living room. Malone quickly took to sitting on it.

"He's knows I'm leaving," Michael said. "He can tell something is up."

"He's just leaving his scent. Wants to make sure other cats know you're his."

"Have you thought about what you'll do while I'm gone?"

"I don't know," I said. "Work?" That thought didn't seem too appealing. "Go running. Hang out with Charles and Danny. Maybe have a drink with Ben. Take up a new hobby. Knitting could be fun."

"A blanket for your bucket list."

"I was thinking I might go to Toronto for a couple of weeks," I said. "Maybe take the cats out by train and stay at Kate's, work from there, visit the girls, see if I can help." I didn't want to impose, but I thought they liked it when I came down. I had visited three times since our trip in December, and each time I was surprised at how much Emily had grown. "It'll be nice to spend a chunk of time with Kate again too. To get to know all of her friends in Toronto. My dad is even thinking of coming down."

"Really?" Michael said. "Shouldn't I be there for that?"

Yes, I would have loved him to. But this was more important. "There'll be other times."

The evening before he was to leave, Michael finally packed his bag. Since he was going for such a long time, I thought he might have spent more time thinking about what to bring, but instead he just threw things into his suitcase—shorts and tank tops and a couple of items from his costume box. What he really needed to keep room for in his car were work tools and clothes, but not so much as to alert the border guard if stopped.

The next morning, Gus showed up at the door with a duffel bag. Gus was going to spend a week in Provincetown. I was relieved that this meant Michael wouldn't be travelling alone. It would be a long drive and I knew I'd be more at ease if he was with someone. I checked my watch. It was a quarter to noon. It takes under eight hours to drive from Montreal to Provincetown, and would take less time than that with Michael driving. I thought about my day and what I might do to take my mind off his trip. Maybe I'd go for an extra-long run or see Danny or go into the office or invite Charles and Harry for dinner.

"You're going to be getting in a little late. Will someone be there to greet you?"

"Leo's already at Nick's," Michael said, "They're going to have dinner waiting for me." Michael gathered his stuff and left it by the door.

"I'll be outside smoking," Gus said. "See you, Paul."

"Can you bring down a few of the bags by the door?" Michael asked Gus. He twirled around the apartment, making sure he had everything—money, wallet, sunglasses, passport. He gave Sutherland a nudge but picked up Malone and held him close.

After putting him down, Michael headed to the hallway and gathered the last two remaining bags. He then stood between the door and me and turned to face me. In his eyes underneath the dark shades of his sunglasses, I could see his uncertainty, his fear.

Gus called from the stairwell. "Come on, let's hit the road."

Everything was waiting for him downstairs.

"It's okay, buddy. Go."

We hugged. I tried not to let my stress bleed through to him.

In this moment, I wanted to tell him everything. I wanted to remind him that I loved him. That he meant the world to me, and that he should behave and be good and drive safe and be careful and look around and call me when he got there. But I didn't. I resisted and bit my lip because I didn't know what any of that would achieve except making him more anxious. Instead, I said the one thing that mattered. "I love you, Michael."

"I love you too, Paul." There was a break in his voice. I pulled away and he wiped his eyes under his sunglasses and picked up his bags.

And with that, he was gone.

I closed the door as he sped down the stairs. It was so bright in our home, the sun coming in through the windows. I heard the closing of car doors, the ignition, the squeal of the tires. And then our home was quiet.

I turned to head towards the kitchen, but stopped. There were still dishes in the sink, but I didn't have to do them right away. I could do them later and then they'd remain done for the rest of the summer. Instead, I went into the bedroom.

On the nightstand I noticed a new doodle that Michael had left me. It was of the house in Provincetown with Malone standing in front of it. "See you soon, buddy," it said. I looked over at the bed where Sutherland was asleep, Malone sitting next to him. I sat down and Malone looked up. I scratched him on his chin. It was going to be a long summer and Malone would miss Michael. But I would take good care of him until he got home.

ACKNOWLEDGEMENTS

Immense thanks go to Dimitri Nasrallah, Simon Dardick and the rest of the family at Véhicule Press. Dimitri, I am forever grateful for all you've done to help me shape, sharpen and bring the story to life. I am also indebted to my wonderful friends who read early drafts and provided open and honest feedback: France Désilets, Jennifer Warren, Peter Dubé, Ahmar Husain, Brian Peters, Tina Blakeney, Lukas Rowland, Brian O'Neill and Raphaël Valensi. Extra special thanks to Neil Smith, Vincent Fortier, Leslie Seidle, Pierre Roy, Anthony Johnson, Jordan Arseneault and Eric Wirth for their support. I also want to thank my mom and dad. I was fortunate to grow up in such a supportive and loving home that when it came time for me to move out, I really didn't want to go. Thanks also to my brother, Mike, and my sister-in-law, Hiromi, for their love and friendship. I'd also like to thank my chosen family (too numerous to name you know who you are). It took me a long time to find you but I know I can count on you for anything. Thanks also to Ashley, Jennifer, Millie and the one-on-the-way for making me an important part of your family. And lastly, thanks to my buddy Greg Chisholm for all the wonderful years of love and joy.

ESPLANADE
Books

THE FICTION IMPRINT AT VÉHICULE PRESS